CANOPY HARVEST

The Stellar Ark Series: Beginnings

WOODY HAYDAY

ALCHEMIST BOOKS

This Book Helps Plant Trees

A minimum of 10% of the revenue of this book will go towards the planting of trees.

Woody Hayday is the founding author of Plant a Book, a collective of authors who use a proportion of their book revenue to plant trees. See the Plant a Book page at the back of this paperback, or visit plantabook.com for more info.

Free Advanced Reader Copies

Subscribe to Woody Hayday's newsletter for early-access to the next book in the Stellar Ark series, and free advanced reader copies.

Subscribe Here:
http://woodyhayday.com/early-access

To my dad, for teaching me perseverance

"The soul of a man harms itself, first and foremost, when it becomes (as far as it can) a separate growth, a sort of tumour on the universe; because to resent anything that happens is to separate oneself in revolt from Nature, which holds in collective embrace the particular natures of all other things."

— Marcus Aurelius, *Meditations*

CHAPTER 1
The Dust

One final mission to end the campaign, one last violent, necessary act, then Bear would be free, and he'd fly up to that ring in space and show his brother that he was not five years dead. Redemption, in the eyes of his older brother, was the only reason to finish this.

He squatted in dust. Holding his breath, he pressed his back flat against a slanted metal beam that rose up to support the tide-breaker. The ocean roared and beat against the wall. It shook everything. A jet of water lunged from a hole overhead, hissing like an adder, before falling to spatter the dead earth.

Bear tugged the cloth down from his face. "We move in sixty."

He could see everything from his perch by the rim. The whole damned man-made valley. It was a mile-wide metal bathtub bolted to the crust, only this tub kept the water out. One big gap in the ocean, built to catch the power that resonated down from the ring.

Guards buzzed around just within sight. Dried-out soldiers patrolling dried-out ocean dirt. Men and women distracted by orders beamed in by satellite, he knew, orders from men that would never visit this place. Orders from their thieving government. The same government that was stealing power from Bear's home sector, despite the unification.

"You sure support's still up?" said Trent.

Bear looked up into the fog hanging overhead, billowing in over the wall and dipping into the canyon. "Sure enough."

"We're heading into sensor range, drones will be up, they'll be on our —"

"Calm it. Support is up. You read the dispatch." He looked at Trent, moved through memories of his boyish face. He still seemed too young for this. Trent had followed him through hell; this mission was nothing. And it was the last one. "You ready?"

Trent nodded, drew a breath, then said, "Yes."

On the next wave. Support better be up.

A whirring sound grew; the thump was coming. Bear dropped a hand to his side and picked up the flasher. With swollen fingers he interrogated it, rubbing the raised ID marks, then lowered his arm like he was loading a trebuchet. *Here it comes.* He pulled up his half-mask.

The wave surged at the wall, its rushing sound reflected onto Bear and Trent by the low-set clouds.

Then, impact.

His arm shot up. He shut his eyes. Two clicks sounded. He flicked the release pin from his finger, and froze.

The force of the pissed-off ocean rumbled down his spine, and as water sprayed from crevices in the concrete, his chaff grenade disintegrated with a pop.

"Go!" he shouted, launching himself into the air.

Trent was already gone, several strides ahead. He reached the next support and slid through the dust, slapping into the metal of the beam.

Bear churned out rough breaths and skidded into place beside Trent, ducking behind the support.

"You see it?" said Trent.

Bear coughed. "Yeah."

"Gun's right on us now. Ugly thing. If it wasn't for the chaff disrupting it, we'd be—"

Bear stopped him with a tap on the armour. "Two more."

"Last two. You got it in you, old man?"

Bear scowled. "Three minutes, kid." The pain in his chest fell away and he appreciated the smile they shared. They'd be fine; just another day. Just one last day in this last sprint.

Two more waves hit in quick succession. The impact knocked a cough out of him. *Not many more of these missions left in me anyway. Glad it's the last.*

His eyes followed the nearest spit of water as it spluttered down onto a patch of rough slope. Old coral. The sea wanted it back. A second spurt of seawater filled the dried cellular structure and flung a flower of droplets back up into the air.

"You can see the whole of Arkbridge now that we're nearly there," Trent said, gesturing towards the buildings at the bottom of the valley. "The resonator here is huge."

"Second biggest in the line. Shame they're abusing it. Knew we couldn't trust them, all that 'nations uniting' crap that came in with the Earth's Halo plans. Earth's still as grimy as ever, even if the public doesn't know it. Even if the truth is hidden in these sea-ditches. Anyway, won't be anything to see in a few minutes time," he replied. "We'll make sure of that."

"They'll be equipped though, right? Auto-boats and stuff, this one will be low casualty."

Bear nodded. *Well equipped. That's why we've got to*

take the whole lot out.

"We'll need to extract fast, especially as the water will only take—"

"I know, Trent. I saw the same mission broadcast." He was off form, but Bear knew why. "You'll get back to her soon enough." They both had people to get to.

Trent frowned. "How did you—"

"Check your kit. Wouldn't want to send you back to Jessica missing some important part." It was the last mission, then Trent would go back to her, he'd go back to his other, quiet life working in her prosthetics shop. And Bear would go find his brother, show him he was still here. Still kicking. Show his face and say sorry for it all, tell him he was right. Bear looked at the power resonator. They needed to get this done. "We run now, and then it's all action. We won't have long, next stop. You ready?"

"This is the drone section, isn't it? Support better be up."

"You're telling me. Sixty seconds," he said, bumping Trent's fist. Bear thought he could hear the security drones already. He looked up into the sky, pictured their own aerial support unit, miles up, watching. A break in the cloud formed. *A good omen.* "Next wave is go."

He pulled out chaff number twelve. "Another one for the gun," he said, and cocked his arm in preparation.

The wave rumbled at them, and Bear threw the grenade. Two clicks then a pop. The wave hit with a heavy crash, and he moved with it, letting it help him to his feet. He ran towards the next beam, all too aware of the fast-moving shapes in the near-distance. He had to make this. Trent had to make it too.

"Drones!" Trent shouted.

Of course there were flipping drones.

4

The ground was wet at the base of the next girder, the mud deep. Bear felt it as he slid into the steel, clambering to keep hidden from the gun and get out of the slurry.

Air fled Bear's lungs, rasping at his throat. More going out than coming in. Dark shapes swooped in around them, mobile blotches of disturbed light. Drones.

"Peace symbols," Bear shouted, throwing up crossed arms, and showing his scarred palms. Then he shouted lies. "We're unarmed. Refuge! Refuge!" Twelve, he counted, more than the brief said. No matter, support would make it zero. "Refuge!"

The fast-moving shapes slowed. Two of them dropped closer and began to buzz around the men, interrogating them with various sensors.

Trent coughed and one jumped back, its triple blades accelerating with the recoil.

"Weapon detected," sounded the nearest drone, "both armed, multiple weapons detected." All twelve began projecting red beams of light upwards. They joined in a coordinated wail, "Unidentified armed. Unidentified armed."

Bear lowered his arms to shelter his ears from the shrill screams. What was support doing up there? Sleeping on the job? The drones would subdue them if support didn't fire quicker than—

"Do not move. Do not move," one drone changed its squawking and flew at Bear.

I could snatch you, you little bugger.

Then the support lasers fired. Twelve hovering sirens cracked and muted, their lights cut out and the drones fell to the dust as a useless collection of broken parts.

"Thanks, support," said Bear. He reached into his knee pocket to retrieve his thirteenth chaff grenade. He turned his head to see Trent static, his eyes transfixed on the shattered remains of the drones. "Trent!" he shouted.

Trent swatted him away. "Don't worry, I'm fine."

"Good. Ready yourself."

They looked each other in the eye, bright smiles shining through Arkbridge mud.

"Let's fill this dead ditch with life," Bear said.

"I'm ready."

They could do this, the last push before home. Last push, then he was going to see his brother. He looked up to the Earth's Halo, the distant shadow of the structure where his brother now lived. *I'm coming. Just wait for the wave, that's my ticket out of here.*

"They're mobilising, look," Trent pointed to the lowland. "Think that's for us?"

"You staying ready? Keep on task," ordered Bear. They were coming, surely. Those drones were just spotters.

"I'm ready, Bear. You know I'm quick to it."

"Where's our damned wave?" Bear said, tapping the grenade in his palm.

"There's something behind the wall," said Trent. "It's louder than a wave."

"Just listen for the wave. We move, no matter what comes over that wall." But he couldn't deny the sound of heavy rotor blades chopping at the sea winds. "Fine. We wait no longer than one wave for whatever that is to pass."

He hoped to hell that wasn't a roaming defence ship. They were cat-meat if it was.

The thwopping of the blades built until Bear could hear nothing else. An unexpected wave hit and water squirted from the wall above them. Bear bounced against the concrete, his back catching the tail of the wave. Then the craft crested over the wall, dragging itself through

6

the fog and slicing at the sunlight. Four contained blades cornered a square rig. Large containers clung to its sides, and a circular coil of wire was roughly welded to its mid. *That's not from Arkbridge.* He squinted as he searched for an insignia. Whichever side that ship was from, it wasn't on the brief.

"Power—"

"Pirates," confirmed Bear. "I thought they'd given up this side of the line."

The pirate quadcopter dropped into the valley and quickly moved to position itself over the resonating power ring. Soldiers fired up at it, but the small arms fire and fizzing projectiles didn't seem to affect the craft as it hovered over the power resonator before darting off into the distance, tailed by a sea of airborne drones. "Strange the sentries didn't react, but no matter to us. We'll drown this place, then they can take all the electric they want. Next wave." Bear turned to Trent and nodded.

Trent acknowledged. Then said, "I'm starting to think none of the other nations can properly police their power feeds."

"Not our fight," Bear told him, and looked up to the Earth's Halo. "We're here to balance this mess, so that hopefully, up there, they can work out a way to give everyone power."

They missed the next wave, feeling the thud but not catching the sound. Bear watched dust bustling around the broken remains of the drones, collecting in groves of melted aluminium and plastic.

"You're going to find him, aren't you? And tell him why you left?" Trent asked.

"So many things to tell him. I'm tired of hiding. This campaign, Trent, it's been so long."

"You sure he's up there?"

"Yeah. And because of me, too. I have to tell him."

"Last little sprint," said Trent. "Then space!"

"Here it comes," he said. "Ready up."

Then the wave came. Charging water struck the concrete. Bear watched a lick of ocean fly over the top of the wall just as his grenade popped. He jumped up and pushed toward the sentry. An ugly stat-gun. Tall grey spike, dual rail-guns, three legs at its base. Gun barrels squarely facing them as they ran.

And it was a long run. Further than he had judged it, and for many strides Bear expected the barrels to spawn unearthly light and end him. Each boot that met dust left him feeling blessed, and the next, fearful. His chest pounded. He'd seen what these things could do, and he remembered all too clearly the smell of their destruction. After they fired, the smell was the only thing they left. But it did not fire. Desensitised by his chaff grenade, it stood motionless, glints of sun catching its hopelessly searching camera lens.

Cover. They made it to the base of the gun, moved beneath it. Bear leaned on a rusted leg, coughing blood into the dirt. He urged his body to calm down, tried to focus on Trent, who was squatted, pulling explosives from his bag. But Bear couldn't stop his eyes darting around. His throat seized shut. *No—not now heart. Sort it out. Let me breath, damn it. This is the last of it. Nearly there.* He coughed loudly and stood up straight, fighting down the bile in his throat.

He looked away. This place was all dust anyway. It needed water. The only things alive were the guards, and they were distracted by amateur power-pirates. His eyes could just make out the hordes of soldiers bunched up by the wall the quadcopter had fled over. Useless. Swatting at flies. Only two trucks moved away in another direction, they seemed to be moving toward them. Bear cleared his throat. "How we looking?" he said, and reached up to knock the machined metal underbelly of the sentry.

"Good. Kit's all here and checks out. Ready to deploy."

A humming sound. "The gun," said Bear, "that was it coming back online."

He froze as the barrels circled. Servos sounded above and his eyes followed the underside of the gun as it panned in all directions. In the distance he heard the troops, and submitted to the moment, forcing himself back into motion.

"Another grenade, explosives on the wall, dead centre, then we run," he said. "We make the next girder, attach, and then flip the switch." As he spoke Bear tapped the detonator in his breast pocket.

"Got it," replied Trent, who turned to the wall with the block of explosives in hand.

This was it. Blowing this key bit of tide-breaker concrete would wipe out the sentry gun. It'd flood the whole of Arkbridge and there was no way anyone could stop it. In minutes this place would be wiped off of the map. Bear hated what he had to do. He looked at Trent, told him, "No waiting for waves now, we go on three." *And we better be half-gone by four.*

He pulled another grenade from his side, double checked the tag. He watched the barrels above and waited for them to flip to the other direction. "'Nade out," he said as the double-chaff left his hand. "One. Two. Three!"

Pop. Like clockwork. Trent dropped into a deep underarm throw; the explosives pack flew up high onto the wall, and stuck.

"Move!"

As Bear ran, his heart hurt for the lack of warning. No time to look back, though he wanted to. There were only bad things behind, rail-guns, explosives, and two trucks of soon-to-be sailors.

Bear had a brother to find. He had to tell him all of this, the false nation-pact, the general's lies. He would show his brother he wasn't dead. He would tell him all this and be forgiven. He ran from death, towards home, and he felt it.

Trent approached the girder, hopped over it, and then dropped out of sight. Bear was behind, and as his heart burned through his Kevlar, illogicalities ran rampant through his mind. *Turn your head, check on the dangers. At least look to the sky and check on your brother. What kind of a—.* He silenced the thought with a grunt.

He was only metres from the girder when it struck. The force hit somewhere below his navel, spinning him in the air. The crunch sound came after, and then the pain blanketed his senses.

He flashed back into consciousness with his face in the dust, grains of sand stuck to his eyeball. Raspy. He tried to reach up to free himself from the scratching, but his body denied him, at first failing to respond, and then screaming torrid pain from his abdomen, until finally, he dissolved back into oblivion.

Darkness dwelled, and when he found his way back, all Bear was given was sound. The moving of boots, the whirring and the crash of a wave. He waited for his body to shake, but nothing came. Muffled emotional voices came from scattered sources. A dribble of pain turned into agony, and then he heard it. The familiar double click and pop of a chaff.

"Bear! Wake the hell up." It was Trent, his face above

him, but something was wrong. He was upside-down. "Bear! Stay conscious, I'll move you on three."

Bear dripped away into a dream, the suffering left, but at three, he was back to reality. His heart thumping in his ears. He gulped. His throat burned as though he'd been drinking lit petrol. Inconsistent thoughts. A childhood memory of lying in a field, back when fields were still green. A misplaced feeling of innocence. A wave hit, and its shaking dredged his lower back, stones dug in like claws. But still he felt so innocent. Crying, he watched a jet of water catch the sun.

Trent grabbed him around the armpits and began to move.

"What—"

His head fell, he tasted the iron of his blood and his own voice told him to look down. He did and wished he hadn't. His face crumpled into a spitty, teary mess. He convulsed, but felt Trent's grip on his torso block the response. *Leave me,* he tried to say, *let me die, for your own sake, leave me.* But Bear could not speak.

They came to a stop. As he lifted an eyelid he saw the worried face of a good friend. "Leave me to die," he moaned through a static jaw.

"You had the detonator. Where's the detonator?" Trent said, patting the pockets nested around Bear's elbows. "Where is it? I can't get us out till I blow the thing." He tried the chest pocket but missed the inner layer.

Bear watched but did not respond. His thoughts were with the pain, and Trent's words were indistinct, comprehension delayed.

"Inner…" he said, grimacing with the pulsing pain of his own heartbeat, which kicked him with every spasm, "…inner pocket."

But Trent was already gone.

His head rolled on his neck, his spine saving it from falling to the floor. Water trickled down his back, and he bounced on the spot as the tide echoed through him. Opening both eyes, Bear saw the extent of his situation.

He was as good as cut in half. He saw his blood deserting him, and he wished it gone. But still, a part of him urged action, an officer in his head. *Move. Get up,* the voice told him. *You can see you're done, at least do some good with the thing, seeing as you're somehow still conscious.* And so he tried. Bear moved what he could, tensing his midsection and trying his torso, most of his body replied with pounding misery. He paused, slipping into anguish. It couldn't end like this. He had to at least see Trent okay.

His hearing seemed to be shot now, but he could move his arm. He grappled with the tide-breaker support, denying the thought of death, corralling himself between painful movements. He spat blood and cried out as his injuries demanded attention. But he managed it. He lifted his eyes high enough to take in the whole of the scene.

Men stood in the distance, staring up at the explosive. The sentry had its barrels pointed at the wall. He saw dry dust speckled with puddles of seawater, he saw red trails, and saw Trent. He was face down in a puddle of blood and mud. A collection of gnarled lumps of tissue. Bear instantly knew; two full rail-gun shots, perhaps the troops fired too. The report would read that he went back for the detonator. That he'd done everything, but forgotten the switch. That he had been hit by two rail-gun rounds because of his own negligence.

Trent wasn't moving. And he didn't have the switch.

Trent, Jessica: I'm sorry. Once Bear was dead Jessica wouldn't even be told what had happened. The truth would be buried. The pain seemed to die down as he turned back around, but kicked him again as he let his body fall to the side. "It was my fault," he whispered. "I'm sorry."

Bear awoke again, unaware how long he'd been out. He shook one arm, fumbled for the switch in his breast pocket. The compact detonator had a small crack on the side but it looked cosmetic. He decided against lifting himself to watch, and from his side, in the dust and blood, he flipped open the catch and hit the switch.

Something boomed a memorable bang. But as the floor shook his vision, he remembered the waves railing against the wall. He pressed it again, five times he hit it. Nothing. He screamed and thrust the switch away.

The pain's bad, I'll check out soon. So that's it, it's come. He didn't get to him, his brother. He didn't get to tell him the truth. It was all a lie - the unification, his death. He didn't die back there. But he'd die here.

His eyes wet, he scanned the sky for the faint line of the Earth's Halo. The fog had passed, and amongst the balmy blue, he found the space-ring at the boundary of his vision, its slender shadow hovering in line with the support-girder. *You're up there, and you think I'm dead, brother, but I wasn't - I'm not. Forgive me for that.*

Bear smiled wide at the thought of his older brother. Seeing the ring up there, the ring where Willsith lived; it almost made up for all this loss. It was almost as though he could bridge the gap. He hoped to pass away, he wished it to come, to seal the moment. But no. His sight was blocked. Two drones appeared and hovered above him, barking commands, flashing and spinning around, blocking his view.

He threw an arm up to bat them out of the way. *Let me see,* he tried to tell them, *I need to tell him. I need to see him.*

And then Bear died.

CHAPTER 2

Drasil-G

"Forget it. Let's just up, and then shunt to the site."

"Okay boss."

Willsith stepped out of the airlock door and looked down on the Earth. He'd never get used to trusting mag-support.

He floated himself to the side to let Lin out. "Straight up, then shunt," he said through the comms.

"You already said," replied Lin.

With the twitch of a finger control, Willsith propelled his suit up the side of the Earth's Halo, mapping the speckled hull of Section 229 as he went. The old ring had taken a battering.

The two men flew up. Willsith feathered his suit controls, taking care to slow to watch the wisps of sunlight give way to an immense brightness as he crested. As his eyes adapted, the wildness of space crept in around the sun's glare, muting it. And to each side, the ring bounded off around the planet. Earth's Halo.

He was there to work, a brute's life. But he had other motives.

Lin turned his suit so as to catch Willsith's eye. "It's still something," he said, "isn't it."

"Best part of my day," replied Willsith automatically, and then went on to say, "if half those politicians White keeps on about, saw this, I think he's right; things would change."

"He's not realistic. But it is pretty."

Willsith reached the top of the ring and hovered. "It's more than pretty, Lin." It wasn't as simple as that. It was a big, raw truth. It was everything, and it was right there in your face. "Anyway, they don't pay us to stare at stars; let's shunt."

"Connected."

Willsith tapped the small flat surface on the chest of his suit, and then reached out to hit a floating plate of metal. "Me too. Farl, can you—"

But before he could fire out the order, Willsith and Lin where gliding around the ring, fast. Tethered magnetically to a metal plate that tugged him forward, his suit froze at its joints, forcing his arms to his sides. And all at once he was disassociated from his mechanical shell. Captive. He felt the force of their motion push down on him. The soles of his feet pressed into the spongey stink of his space-boots, and the metal of his mechanised gloves dug into the wells between his fingers. *Against the spin.* Tensing his shoulders he widened himself against the hard shell of the suit to distribute the slight pressure. "Thanks Farl, could've given me a second."

Farl, the communications officer, spoke through the comms system, "Was ready with the command."

Willsith battled the force. Blinking his eyes, he tried to focus on the fast moving ring surface in front of him. His muscles strained, and his eyes caught up. Bursts of light. Each flash amongst the blur was a repair weld reflecting the sun, he knew - he had welded half of them himself.

Thousands over this section alone. *It's been a long five years.*

"Where's the impact? How long's this ride?"

"All the way to section 230 boundary, I'm afraid. You've got another sixty seconds till slowdown."

"I love mag-shunting," said Lin over the comms. It was his last time. It was a shame to lose him.

Willsith squinted. "Can you at least give us a good view, please, Farl."

"Sure. What angle you want?"

Willsith's suit spun around in static pose, and ended up facing the dark side of Earth. Willsith felt the stop and opened his eyes wide. As wrecked as Earth looked he did miss—

His suit spun again, flipping him to face away from the Earth. Starry wilderness. The penetrating scale of the darkness of space enveloped him. "Farl—" But it was too late. Farl had spun them again, and this time Willsith stopped face to face with his security officer. He spotted Lin frowning through his visor, then saw the frown relax into a grin. Behind him the sun blared, and Willsith saw the light catch the edge of his friend's suit, the same light which fell below them and lit up the oceans of Earth. Quite a backdrop.

"Thirty seconds."

"Farl, stop spinning us. I just wanted more than a view of burnt carbon and weld patches. Can you not—"

"Sorry, Willsith, wasn't sure what view you wanted. From here we have 360 views from your suit-cam, so it's hard to pick," he chattered on. "But anyway, you reach slowdown in ten, so I'll return you to position."

"For hell's sake, Farl."

"Was only a spin."

"At least this blast was in the right direction," said Lin.

"Don't remind me about that shunt. You're coming out, next repair, Farl. We'll leave the controls to White."

Lin laughed.

Farl coughed over the comms, "Not funny."

Then they slowed, and Willsith's suit began to respond to his movements again. He floated inside his metal skin until the suit unlocked its joints with a click. The metal plate that had been pulling them around the ring sucked itself down onto the surface below, and he righted himself.

"Not been out this far in a while; let's see what we have." And while he spoke the words of the man who he should be, who they all thought he was, his mind worked on other ideas. Willsith scanned the stars, and from behind the visor of his space suit, he begged the universe for alternatives. Alternatives to the grinding work. Alternatives to his life.

"It's sun-side, two panels around," instructed Farl. "Repair-bots are waiting."

More instructions came through the wireless comms. Willsith tuned them out.

Lin floated off, his silver-suit mapping the contour as he descended. Glorious sunlight painted the lower half of the ring golden, and Willsith hung for a moment, transfixed by the light, remembering the science of the thing. The sun hits the ring, the radiation gets converted via the jacket-system, and then the power's resonated to Earth. All that process just to sling down a bit of energy, and when up there, all he wanted was raw sun on his skin and silence. That bright light. He chuckled at the thought of shedding suit and taking in the rays.

"You coming?" Lin asked over the comms.

"Just checking the scene," replied the actor inside

18

Willsith's head, as he thought of other things. "Just checking."

He dropped down after Lin and headed for the circling repair drones. As he floated he imagined the sun therapeutically bathing him and his body tingled with reverence. He was a part of this universe. A tiny part. But a part. And up here he could do his bit of good to make up for what happened down there.

"It's a lump of C-type, small hull impact," Lin said, and then unclipped the glorified crowbar from behind his left forearm. "The bugs are liking this one."

He watched the small drones circle the head-sized lump of rock that sat jammed into a recess it had made in the Earth's Halo. The rock was coal-coloured, with faults of green running through it, and the drones mapped it with blue lasers. He couldn't hear them, but his imagination filled the scene with clunky machine noises as they darted around. Clockwork bugs. "Flies round a turd," he said, "look at them." Their lasers finished a pass and they grouped into a collective, backing off from the rock and shining their beams in unison on a calculated spot. The ideal point for leveraged removal.

Inspecting his tool, Lin asked, "Shall I?"

Willsith thrust the metal of his boot at the target.

"Willsith! You know they'll minus you for that. Fifty credits, minimum. And a badge!"

But Willsith was too busy watching the rock cartwheel off. As it spun, its edges caught the sunlight, generating obscure shapes. His mind projected all manner of objects onto the irregular surface of the fleeing space-rubble. First he thought he saw the face of a general, sullen, and then the rock turned, looked like some sort of a seed, a grenade, then the curvature of a woman. Finally the shrapnel disappeared into the far distance, leaving him with nothing but amorphous ideas.

The drones got straight to work, spiralling around the hole where the rock had been, scanning for leftover fragments of rock. They fired lasers from the bottom of their small cone forms, fixed on the specks that were left. As they flew in helix formation their re-adjusting beams pulsed hypnotically.

"There's something about kicking rock Lin, I can't explain it."

"They'll make you explain it,—" Lin started, and Willsith thought that he looked at him with a kind of ambivalence, "—boss."

"It's like playing catch with the universe. Did you see it? They just spin off into the black," Willsith said. "I've kicked hundreds of rocks this year, and still I see different things in them as they go. And where do they go? I never expected to see space this way, but it's gotten under my skin." He stopped, pulling himself back from the void, and then looked at Lin. All at once he felt exposed, and he quickly retracted. "You're young, Lin," he told him. "There's no need to listen to the jabberings of an old man. Flick out those teeth and keep us the shiniest one as a sample. They'll want a sample."

"They need a sample," Lin affirmed, leaning in with his crowbar to free several wedged nuggets of rock, before rising to watch them drift up, picking a green-encrusted piece about the size of a walnut.

Willsith smiled and said, "There's their sample." He turned back to the stars. The routine wore thin, and more and more, Willsith found himself concerned with the wild, rather than the work. His eyes scanned space, the old light from a trillion collapsed stars, converging at his retinas to show him how they once were. It was his ritual to ask himself hard questions when he was out, and to let the vast wilderness suck answers from him. For Willsith, space had become a vacuum into which he could unpack himself. But work got in the way.

"Sample locked. Drones have this repair," said Lin. "Ready to return to 229 when you are."

I doubt I'll ever be ready, my young friend. But he said something in agreement, and then huffed goodbyes to his searching state and to the stars, and dipped his head back into employment. First a check on the bots. One drone hovered above as the other three rotated around. A miniature team. They tugged on metal edges, cutting and welding and re-forming the machined surface of the ring. "I used to enjoy the welding," he said into space, and turned to address Lin. "All right, let's go; we're not needed here."

They flew back up to the top of the ring, meeting face-to-face as they reached the metal plate. Lin nodded, and Willsith watched him through the glass of his visor.

"You all right, Lin?" he asked, sure that he was withholding something.

"Yeah, never mind."

Farl burst into comms, "Look toward 230," he said.

He turned and caught the flash of an Earth's Halo laser as it fired into space. Following its direction they saw a long arm of rock explode. Several lasers fired again, ripping out into the sky, subdividing each fragment with a smaller blast. They watched two more rounds of laser clean-up before the inbound material faded into a handful of samples. And dust.

"Not every day you catch a live one," said Willsith.

Lin's exhale bled through the comms. "I'll miss this part," he said, "but don't you get bored Willsith? Don't you want to train with others like you? Don't you miss it?"

"War?"

"Protection...security. Warfare?"

"War," said Willsith, "is not something to miss, Lin."

And though he disliked the roughness of movement his suit afforded him, Willsith lifted an articulated hand onto Lin's shoulder. "It's wild, the view from here," he said. *As good as stretches off into infinity. Can hardly see it by the time it reaches the edge of the Earth.* He pointed far into the distance, following the Earth's Halo as it burst from the planet's blue aura and swelled into the metal surface that hung beneath them, and then off around the other side of the Earth. "We're attached with only electro-magnetism," he said, "just a fragile little anchor of electricity, tying us to this big ring, which encircles the whole planet". The whole scene was open. To his right the Earth lay dark; pin-pricks of light twinkled through whipped-up cloud systems, and where visible, the grey earth looked sombre, cold. To the left, the sun, and the ring's amber glow. And the planet below too, shone. The seas looked deep and the muddy land looked almost alive. "It's fragile. It doesn't need our wars."

"It needs protecting," Lin said. "That's why we're here. That's why we shouldn't break orders. It makes me jumpy."

Willsith dropped his hand from the man's shoulder. "Lin, all I did was kick the r—"

"Look, some of 230 are out!"

Willsith filed the conversation for later analysis and looked to where Lin pointed. The half-lit shape of two suits moved about slowly, their outlines vague, like the dark rock that tumbled off somewhere into space.

"I haven't seen another team since September," said

22

Lin. "Let's sign them."

Signing was another way to break the rules. And though Willsith didn't give a rock's arse about the rules, from Lin, it was a hypocritical suggestion. Funny, the double standards the armed forces gave you. Don't kick rock, but do all manner of shit in the name of camaraderie. He was glad to be out of the forces.

"Give me your torch."

Lifting both torches overhead, he fired them up. They flickered into life, pulsing blue light, then settling into two flames that warped away from the gas valve. He brought the steel-handled torches toward one another and felt the pull of their flames combining. He knew the shape that flared up above his head, they called it the 'Drasil-G'. The tree of life. He watched the man-shaped flecks of light in the distance, awaiting their reply.

"They see us; they're firing," said Lin.

He saw them bring the two dots of blue together, and the symbol burnt through the distance between them, into his eyes and further still. As the blue jets of two spark-welders struck one another at right-angles, they repelled and intermingled their layers, producing a curious side-effect. Curled flames spewed from their intersection, drawing a flaming blue circle above them. This greeting was a crude form of the symbolic ash tree which held Earth amongst its branches in ancient myths. "Can't keep that symbol down," said Willsith, lowering the torches.

And his own words stuck with him. He looked at the torches and remembered a grim operation, the destruction of a Drasil-G group back when the symbol had still meant rebellion. He'd picked up two torches that day, and fired them just the same, but it had been a lure; he was working for the state. His job, then, was to smash the rebellion. "Here," he said, slapping the torch into Lin's hand.

"It's good to know there's a comradeship amongst sections, that we still sign to each other, even though there's miles between us."

"That sign is older than sections, Lin. Older than this ring."

"Drasil-G is about unity," Lin began; "we need all you sections to work together. The world needs this ring, and the ring needs—"

"Maintaining?" replied Willsith, turning to face him.

Lin replied with obvious caution, "I mean…yeah. Maintaining, and protecting."

"So we maintain, and you protect?"

Lin nodded.

"Listen Lin, you don't want to hear it, I know, but I can't avoid it. You know my history, you know I've been through shitting hell down there," he said, pointing to Earth. "I've been through the system. I've done many things that were given many words to dress up wrong actions. They all mean war. Aggression. 'Protection' ain't no different. You shouldn't—" Willsith saw in his friend's face something that he already knew. Lin didn't care. He was closed to alternatives. An assault on war was an assault on him. "—Never-mind."

Over the past five years in space Willsith had worked his psyche well outside of the spasm it had been in. The war machine. He harboured strong dissidence, but outwardly he was a battle-worn soldier, and it was in this conflicted state he held himself, cloaked. "You're right Lin. This needs maintaining. Comradeship includes everyone. That symbol, it means something, it's more than just a greeting between sections, but it's still good we show each other that we're unified in this work."

"Willsith, my career is there, in the control hubs. They pulled me up here for that, and even though you have the best intentions, it's a different world than the one you…fought on."

"It's the same up here as it was down there." He wouldn't believe that, but it was true. Maybe he hadn't seen enough misery, maybe he'd only seen dramatised murder; streamed violence. "No matter, you'll be back on your way to the hub in a day or so. Just keep your eyes open, always. And care about truth."

Willsith and Lin turned to watch the other team shunting along the ring, two side-lit silhouettes flying toward them. The distant suits slowed to a stop, and Willsith remembered his shunt, and his job. "Let's go."

"It's been good—," said Lin, "—appreciate you and 229 for treating me so well."

"No worries," burst Farl's voice through the comms. "You guys done debating Control yet? White's cooking is melting through the door."

Willsith turned and smiled, dipped his head to Lin, and then said, "All right Farl; ready the shunt."

The metal plate lifted from the ring and both tapped to connect.

CHAPTER 3
#Stir-Fry-T1

Willsith's suit tugged him around as the air-lock depressurised. He stood waiting for the panel to flash green and let him into Section 229. Home. The walls closed in and he fought to settle his thoughts. Gravity bled into his awareness and muscles twinged in adjustment. He knew once his suit started to feel heavy he'd snap out of the haze, but the routine seemed slow today. Limbo persisted, but finally Willsith awoke.

A wobble of his suit and a blast of sound led him to instinctively remove his helmet, only catching the green of the panel at the last second before he hit the suit release on his neck. "At last," he said, gulping at the cool air.

"Did seem like a long purge," said Lin. "Repress always makes me twitchy."

"Kicking rock makes you jumpy, depress - twitchy? You need a float in the tank, my man. Depress just makes me hungry," replied Willsith, grinning. He walked at the door, expecting it to open; his nose feathered the glass before he stepped back and crossed his arms. "Well at least be punctual," he projected.

Lin spoke softly from behind, "Control penalties."

"Well they could at least get moving with them; I can

see White is frying something up."

"And he'll probably get dropped for it," said Lin, "eventually." And then Willsith knew that Lin had now closed himself to all of Section 229, because he hadn't ever been so blunt. He was only going to be cold with everyone until he left.

Willsith felt his smile drop and said, "You'll enjoy a hearty meal before you go, Lin. Don't knock the chef!" Tilting his head back, he eyeballed the empty bit of wall he knew to be a hidden camera. "Open the door already!"

Then she spoke. A single clear voice said, "Willsith Harper."

"Here we go—"

"Willsith Harper, you are formally reprimanded for the seventy-sixth time for improper use of—"

"You'd think they'd at least spice up the warnings," he spoke over the voice, which then started back at the broken statement.

He twisted his neck and looked at Lin as she spoke. "—For the seventy-sixth time, for the improper use of hub equipment, in both rock extraction and further, in the use of temperature-graded equipment to communicate with other sections, wasting fuel as well as stressing the hardware and distracting ops. These two acts break more than fourteen of the conventions you signed adherence to on uplift. This is—"

"Boring? I am aware of charges; add them to the list, robot."

"It's not always auto-speech," said Lin, "and even then there's a law-guard watching the stream so—"

"So then they should understand that this job needs rock-kicking to keep it—," he started, "—anyway, let's shut up and let her finish or we'll be here 'till sleep cycle, and you'll never get back to hub."

The voice continued to issue out penalties to Willsith, revoking holiday tokens and making many over-repeated threats. Willsith only vaguely listened, his attention mostly on his section, 229. He watched the two of his team he could see through the glass of the airlock door. Arc and White. Arc sat on a tarp, many parts of a welding torch spread out around him. White's belly poked out beneath the mess kitchen unit. One hairy arm tapped at a panel while the other, hairless arm, jabbed his improvised wok into the air, then back, rearranging dubious food materials mid-air. Farl wasn't to be seen.

"...and as a result you will need to complete a video-report detailing your reasoning in order to avoid further fines."

"Are you still going? I accept already. Open up," he confronted the door, hoping that'd be enough.

The voice continued, "Willsith Harper, do you accept the aforementioned charges and agree——"

"I agree already. Enough."

The doors slid open.

"Oh, and Commander," spoke a new voice, "please get a hold of your staff unless you wish us to drop you back to the fields."

Willsith grunted.

When Willsith stepped in he caught the tail of Farl's yell flying out of the open sleep-deck door. "You're paranoid and lazy, read the actual report you...speculating sous chef!"

White hunched himself down, so that he could pull a face at Willsith beneath the kitchen racks.

Farl shouted, "Yes, I know they're back!"

Lin stepped past Willsith, turning to drop an upturned smile.

All at once the walls of Section 229's mess hall slammed in on him, and with a flash of claustrophobia, Willsith felt himself back on Earth, though he knew he wasn't. The artificial-gravity created by the spin of the ring wasn't quite the same, and the sun-mimicking lights definitely weren't the same. Beyond the grey of the walls, there was only circulatory oil, electronics and piping. And then space.

He stepped onto the raised rails of the transport line that ran through the whole of the ring. Either side of him the room extended towards two transit doors that only opened twice a quarter. In front of him the confines of his days: lockers, kitchen, sleep deck. Not much in between. Lin kicked his suit off into his locker and clicked the metal door shut. Between them Arc sat cross legged, his bulbous joints standing out against his skinny limbs. He wore leather gloves cut off at the knuckle and was inspecting a small twist of metal with a mag-pad.

Arcol Miller was 229's team mechanic. He had been the youngest choice on the list, the least professionally experienced, and had only just passed the fitness tests. But then he had written one hell of a statement. Arc had been hacking machinery together since his mum took him off synthetic milk, and at the age of 16 he wrote on his application to the Earth's Halo that he, 'Needed more for his family, than to suffer in this overpopulated city,' and that he wanted 'to maintain the greatest mechanism humans would ever make'. Willsith had thought that Arc would learn from them all, but it hadn't exactly been panning out that way.

Willsith approached Arc and said, "How's the hardware?"

"Operational...tomorrow. The pressure ring was fried. I've put in a replacement order. I'm surprised you and Lin managed to cut anything with this. It's more worn out than that one that died last Thursday."

Willsith nodded, distracted by White who was banging a spatula around in a bowl.

"They've been at it since you left, it's like a debate-a-thon booth in here," whispered Arc, then louder, he said, "but the food smells good."

"Of course it smells bloody good; ya've not eaten for a full cycle," a voice barrelled out from amongst the kitchen units.

Willsith squatted to the extent the suit would allow, then told him, "Keep at it Arc. We'd be lost in space without you."

He took off his suit and filled his locker with the metal-sweat smell of well used kit. He stretched his shoulders and then ventured over to the kitchen unit, rubbing his jaw and clicking it into place.

White fidgeted with the broken handle of his makeshift spatula, jabbing at the dull reconstituted vegetables which hid amongst noodles in his pan. He twitched his arms and turned to Willsith as he approached. *Here we go. These two just will not quit.*

Lowering his head to smell the stir-fry, Willsith managed to make eye contact with Farl through the door to his self-claimed quasi-office, the sleep-deck. Throwing a wink at him, he initiated the reconciliation. "Noodles smell tasty."

"It's ready," announced White, into his ear. "Just been keeping it at temperature till you got in."

"There was no point in waiting," yelled Farl. "It's just another day of stir-fry-T1."

"It's a good tradition," said White, "and you—"

"Let's eat," Willsith butted in, "then maybe you two can explain to me why you've been bouncing sound around our little mess hall."

Sitting down and shuffling along, he reached his usual spot on the bench seating. White and Farl's conflict irked him, but his stomach was overriding his concern. As he looked across at Lin, Willsith's time as a soldier jumped at him, and he was glad that the tradition of eating together gave him a simple distraction. He didn't want to think of war. Since the beginning, how many people had used the act of eating to avoid true communication?

White laid out forks, each clinking down; an acoustic countdown to sustenance. Arc joined them, and White lay a mess tin in front of him. He then passed one to Willsith and one to Lin. Willsith frowned, then shouted, "Farl, I'll eat it if you don't."

Farl was already at the door and paced quietly to the table, his awkward, long limbs contorting to fit into the space on the bench. Willsith had known Farl to be a wild-card since the start. In fact, he'd chosen him because of it.

Given all the candidates, Farl was a bad choice for an Earth's Halo maintainer. Bottom of the list. He had programming skills, mediocre fitness, and unique opinions of authority. Capable, but defiant. He was often angry and prone to outbursts, but the file hadn't said that. In many ways it was curious that they'd even offered up Farl as an option. The overview made it clear he wasn't particularly suited to the rigours of space. But Willsith had taken the role to help others, and at the start, he thought he could help Farl find peace.

He watched them all pounce on their food. Farl held his fork below his mouth, dropped it, and then turned to Willsith. "He just has no basis for his theories, they're—"

"Look kid. Once you've been on a few ships you get a kinda feel—"

31

"Feelings are not facts, White. This is the problem with the modern left, you're a hodge-podge of feelings and best intentions. That's how we let Earth get so utterly screwed by the corporates; inconsistent resistance. Do you even—" Farl stopped himself, and silence crept across the table.

"Right, you two, let's leave the politics for now, okay? You're entitled to your opinions, but more importantly, we're a team. Both of you have enough sense to know that there's no point in sacrificing local peace for ideas."

"I'm sorry, Farl," said White. "Meant no harm. I do think I have a point, but you're my mate either way, ya know?"

Willsith looked into Farl's eyes. He tried to project calm, but saw a look that he knew well. He knew then that the scuffle wasn't over. He tried anyway. "Thanks for the support earlier Farl, haven't been to the edge of the section for quarters."

"We saw 230; they replied to the sign," said Lin, lifting a fork of noodles into his mouth, then crossing his knife and fork to simulate the Drasil-G.

"They ranked top fifty this week," said Farl, looking back down to his food. "They've had two quarters without a single fault."

"Better them than us," said Willsith. "No point in coming to space to be in the robot olympics. Perfection isn't worth it."

White opened his mouth, swallowed, then said, "And they can drop me back to ground zero if they want me to stop cooking with a torch."

"They probably will, if you keep at it," said Lin coldly.

White grinned, "They've let it slip fifteen-hundred odd days so far. I've received that same disciplinary popup so much I don't even close 'em anymore. Let 'em take me, take the heat torch. You'll all miss the hot food almost as much as you'll miss me, and I'll go back to cooking in the slums where I'm appreciated. With all that history and mud and—"

"Things change. It's not giving up on humanity to use a cooking unit, White," said Farl. "This stuff isn't exactly gourmet, any way you take it."

"It's called the Maillard effect, Farl, and you should be thankful someone even remembers it."

"Tastes more like—"

"Eat your Soylent Green," said White, then through a mouth of stir-fry, "it may not be gourmet, but it'll put—"

"Soylent Green?" Farl dropped his fork back into his bowl. "That film's almost as bad as your cooking!"

They all joined in a laugh.

Farl lifted his fork up and inspected it, "Although…"

CHAPTER 4

Peace & Quiet

Farl sat opposite, toying with a strip of metal that hung on a cord around his neck. The glow from the sleep deck lit his face from the side, giving sharp, white points to his eyes, which jutted out at Willsith as he tried to decipher the tension in Farl's face. Suppressed anger, pain. Conflict. He saw a fury that ran deeper than the petty arguments that Willsith was supposed to be reprimanding him for. He'd been trained to spot the signs back when he had ran squads in the army; shoulders craned forward, neck bent, quiet performance, and then outbursts. Farl continued to be frustrated, despite these evening conversations. And Willsith had gained the feeling that if he wasn't able to help the lad with his burden, he'd snap. Sooner or later, Farl would snap.

Willsith looked down at his own hands, searching for an answer; finding scars and rough bits. "Look…you've just got to stop the arguing at least. It's happened. You've ended up in 229, as communicator, and White as team-maintainer. Whatever you think of him, you don't need to block his attempts at…" Willsith sighed, "his attempts at making this situation more habitable."

Farl's smart, that's part of his problem. He hasn't

learned how to be smart and happy, yet.

"More habitable?" Farl said, glaring into the table.

"More like a home, then."

"It's habitable, maybe it's even home. But it's not what I thought it'd be."

Willsith looked him in the eye. "Farl, you came up here wanting to see space. You didn't have an ideal situation down there, like me, and maybe you thought it would work out up here, but now you don't—you're not sure why you're here. Am I right?"

"I'm struggling, Willsith…"

Willsith saw it. He saw himself in Farl. The struggle, a wretched state born from inner-conflict. For Willsith it had grown worse as he'd matured through war, and now after war it still jostled about in the memories. But maybe it'd always been that way; fighting with himself over what he might be. Grasping. Still, the struggle could be good for him. Farl could learn to use it, to turn hard shit into growth. If he would listen. "I see it," he said to him, "but if you came to space with a naivety, don't you want to go back down without it?"

"Willsith, I did come up here wanting to 'see stars and planets', if my application is what you're hinting at. But I didn't come up here as a child. I had reasons and…"

"And?"

"I feel like it's a bit of a joke. 229 is like a husk. I want more than this, I can't see how you don't too, and the rest—I think they can't even see a fraction of the thing. I'm really struggling to not just quit my plan and go back to Terra."

He must not quit. Willsith wanted to tell Farl everything, to share the skirmish that thundered on inside of him, but he knew that there were cameras watching. He'd probably never be able to speak that truth in 229. He'd be dropped the next day if he did. Unfit for duty. To explain that he hated what the world had become, and what it had made him; that he was only just keeping it together.

"Don't you feel it?" Farl said, then looked up. "We're kept here to bat rocks off an over-sized solar panel? I'd expected to find answers once I was up here, but it's been years now and I'm getting twitchy. I don't think they even need us. I thought I'd be able to really affect the world, but I'm just stuck...I'm of way more use back down there, outside of the system, than I am in 229."

Farl wanted an easy way out, he was bored. His questions were getting more direct, and White's theories were bleeding into him. "You need to stop fighting with White."

"Don't you want more than this?" Farl asked.

"All I wanted from space was peace and quiet, and when you argue with White, you're stopping me from having either."

"Peace and quiet? Are you kidding me? Willsith, I know you know more than you think. I've seen——," Farl stopped himself.

"What have you seen? My records? I don't see how. You ain't seen nothing, kid. You might guess at it all from my hands, my arms. This jaw." He circled his jaw to show the metal section in relief. "But you don't know. If you're bigger than 229, then drop. I need a comms officer who can do his job, add value, not rip us apart."

Farl slapped his hands down on the table. "Why did you really come to space? Why did you leave the forces? We're not kids, Willsith. The past is dead and buried, hundreds of kilometres beneath us. Why are we up here? Me, and you, this isn't coincidence."

Willsith eyeballed him, pushed his jaw till it clicked. "I

36

raised for peace…Farl. Quiet. Nothing else. War took chunks from me, Earth spat me out, and now I'm here, trying to work out what it all means. I'm not your enemy. We can make this good, productive."

"I'm trying. But I can't deal with the half-truths and sloppy judgements of ill-informed cooks."

"That's unnecessary, Farl; the sharpness. Ask yourself why you do it," Willsith said, standing up from the table. "Wherever you go you'll have to deal with humans, and not all of them will be as connected as you. And frankly, neither of you actually know the truth behind the thing, it's weak to attack—"

Farl dipped his head, then said, "I know."

"Good." Willsith smiled at him.

"But this is a fake peace, and you know it. This is artificial and we'll not last out here. You can't hide from what you're meant to be."

Willsith forced his face into a scowl. He tried to be authoritative. He tried to hide the fact that he might bloody-well agree. "Let's sleep on it," he said as he turned and walked to his bunk.

It was a curious thing that he had chosen Farl for 229. He believed that he could turn the hacker around, but in the end, Farl stood 30 years younger, fully ahead of the game. If anything, Farl had ended up impacting him, tugging at the cloak of work, stealing glimpses at who Willsith really was, behind the ops. Or at least that's how it felt.

Willsith got into his bunk and turned to face the wall. Visual noise fizzed across the grey metal as his eyes adapted to the low-light.

He was still healing, recovering from what he had been. Willsith didn't want Farl, or anybody, to force him out of this state of repair, and in that way, he was glad that Farl was consumed by his own crisis.

White murmured in his sleep, and as Willsith heard Farl move to his bunk, the ritual of his evening took hold. Remembering the day; Lin's face through his visor, fully trapped in the life of a soldier. Willsith recalled Farl's outbursts, their discussion, and then he thought that he saw a trajectory, what might happen.

Farl hadn't returned to his bunk to sleep, and Willsith heard the swivel arm of his panel and guessed that he was logging into his strategy game. The screen's light reflected onto Willsith's wall, warbling colours danced over the dull surface. He watched them for a bit, then wandered off into self-examination.

The rest lay asleep, Farl entranced. *Here is my peace and quiet.*

After addressing the day's bruises, Willsith thought of his brother, the starting point for all this. Trying to picture Bear's face, Willsith frowned in the dark. At once he blamed himself for forgetting, and then the Earth's Halo for taking, but finally he threw out the blame. Blame was too easy. His brother was dead. His brother was dead, and all he could think of was to blame. Vengeance follows blame. Neither undoes what's happened. Who's to blame was easy. It was the sniper who shot Bear. It was the gun manufacturer, the army lieutenant, the general, the prime, the union; the whole damned war machine. It was the politicians who could have steered better, the liars who claimed international treaties, the weak-willed scientist, and all these men's fathers. It was the miner who dug for the metal in the bullet to earn enough to feed his family, and it was him, Willsith. It was the entire chain. To hell with blame. To hell with it.

Decades of war cast deep shadows over Willsith, he felt

the shroud follow him. *I did all that. I did all that before I understood.* His own history cut new wounds in him each night, and he worked to patch them up from the inside. *I woke up after he died. I woke up and it's worse. To hell with the blame, but it's still worse. To know all this, and to find peace. Brother...Bear...I don't know...even up here, I don't know if I can find peace.*

He opened his eyes, found no peace in the grey of the wall, so shut them.

And so it was that Willsith walked through his own mind each night, observing, testing, and suffering. Trying.

The image of Farl and White's spat presented itself, and he weighed up the value of knowing the truth. On one side a safe ignorance, subtle fear; the other a grasping of a degree of truth, but bleeding for it. Neither free, both guilty, both trapped. He questioned his own failures, dwelling on the protection of his little brother, then he caught the tail of a memory he didn't expect.

★ ★ ★

Frank Argyle was a Grand Commander, or rather, he had been. Willsith met him in a bar near the jump-station. It had been his last night before they flew him up to the Earth's Halo. He sat medicating himself with a glass of scotch, hunched under the weight of his brother's death, soaking in his choice to desert the armed forces.

"The name's Frank, Frank Argyle," the smartly dressed drunk had said, before slinging him a wild handshake. "I'm the only commander on this god-forsaken rock who really supports the Earth's Halo, so good on you."

The conversation had started boldly, and continued on

for some time on the benefits of the ring. Frank swam in drink, and Willsith half-wished he'd kept to himself. They talked on though, and the whiskey seeped in, fuelling the old man's stories and coaxing Willsith up from where he had dwelt.

Frank said, "Most of the others see it as limp-wristed weakness. 'Letting the other sides in,' they call it. 'Submission.'" He knocked back a double in one go and Willsith followed suit. Why was it that good conversations often happened with a glass in your hand?

"It's an old-school mentality, hundred-year-old—" he hiccuped, "—thinking. When I joined I wanted to help modernise, you know, ship the steer. But they're just so sodding stuck in their ways, Willsith. Stuck. They feed tradition down the line like it's their saving grace, but at this point it's...it's nothing more than dirty history. Dirty-history-stuck-tradition. Doesn't work. That's the reason that we're in the mess we're in. Old men like me and their sodding traditions. Stuck, they are, abso-sodding-lutely stuck."

"In the end, that's what made me leave. They're all stuck and when you try to unstick 'em, they kick your face in. Sure, for years I ignored it, joined 'em. But eventually they push you right out again, the whole thing catches the different—"

Willsith stared into the vacant face of Frank Argyle.

"What was I saying?"

"You joined in—"

"Oh...yeah. When I joined, after I got into leadership, you know, through an old chum, I went through leader's HQ. Was tasked with personnel. People pushin'. More veterans than civi's though, huge chunks addicted to this and to that. Belief numbers were there, but it was costing more per-head to prop-prop-propagandise every year. I got the hint then Willsith. Big hint. The system needed help."

Unprovoked, he continued, a little baffled at himself, "Schemes to keep the war machine ticking over, make the people pay for it. Old schemes. Tradition, Willsith, tradition. And it worked too. The budgets were carnivorous. You can see how those fat generals got so fat, and so blasted warped."

"It's a good thing it all hit the floor, if you ask me," Frank said. "Those ten years of enviro-disaster gave them the right kind of wake up call. Slap-in-their-face. Can't fight a wave with a bomb. They tried all right. Glad, I was, in a way. Thought things might change. Didn't much though. That's why I left. They're all stuck. All they know is the old ways. And you, lad, you're young enough to be—"

Willsith interjected: "But the army supports the Earth's halo? And Commander, I'm forty-one."

"Oh Willsith, known you five minutes, but that jaw of yours, and them scars on your hands tell me you know a two or thing about army 'support'."

Willsith looked at his battered hands, gripped his glass and downed the whiskey.

"Bet you quit for the same reason as me," Frank continued; "it's broken, the wars don't work now. Was a time when no-one under sixty-five quit the force. So that's change. At forty-five, you've still got years. Years to change. Forty-five years to change."

"Forty-one, Commander."

"Stop calling me that. Now, where was I? Ah, support. The big-three support it because they have to, politically...but there are other reasons the armies want into space."

"I read they'll take a 'power-tax'," Willsith said to

him, "and electric for defence walls, from ring-power."

"Yes, all the power they want, but this is bigger than a few rail-guns and some re-gen machinery."

"Bigger?" Willsith asked, shaking his glass at the bartender.

The conversation had gone on, drinks had kept coming, and there were gaps in his memory. Willsith dreamed vividly of the Grand Commander's last outburst, the one which had got them drink-blocked for the night. His last memory of Frank Argyle.

Willsith felt eyes on them from all directions as Frank babbled about corruption at a world level, giving names. And he worried, for he knew what punishment the forces had for such public tellings. He wasn't long out of his uniform, after all, and he hadn't yet shaken off the idea of duty. Though the liquor helped.

As Frank went on his articulation faltered, flip-flopping between grammar-school pomp and mess-hall slurring. He started mocking the promotional literature put out about the Earth's halo. A leaflet Willsith hadn't read. The wide Commander embellished it dramatically, and the memory stood bold amongst the fodder of the night. It was amazing that Frank even managed to get it out in one piece, the state he was in.

"As humanity we have had many a brush with mortality. We have fought, we have bruised, we have scarred...we have all met death." Frank sloshed his drink around, splattering a line of spirit up the bar, rightly decided to put it down, and then continued instantly with his exaggerative hand gestures.

"These past 200 years have been more brutal than any, on Earth and us as a global civilisation. But no! No more! We cannot continue to live without a future—I mean a care for the future. For that future is now knocking at our door," he paused to take a sip, deciding to down the glass, and then hiccuped.

Frank flashed the globes of his eyes at Willsith, rubbed his stomach, and continued as though if he stopped he'd drop dead: "It's at our door and it wants its loan repayment Willsith! It wants its manay! The world wants its repayment! So now we must deal with it, before it marks the end of us all. But we shall. We have a solution." Frank paused, trying to politely let out another hiccup, and failing. "The Earth's halo...our saving grace. Never has humanity dealt with such a profound future as the one the Earth's halo provides to all the peoples. A symbol of progression rather than destruction, r-r-rehabilitation not disintegration; it is not a symbol of money, neither of control nor of *political power.*" He paused for an old-dog wink, his one eye shut so firmly that his lip lifted to reveal his tooth-plate. He started to sway, and spoke rhythmically. "The Earth's halo progresses humanity beyond state based borders, beyond segmentation, beyond fighting, beyond fighting...*beyond fighting!* Beyond this suffering our environment is now putting us through. It's a solution for our planet, for each and every human on it regardless of creed. Let us use this new signal—no—symbol! Use this distinction between electrical power and political power, to cast aside outdated traditions we have too long held up," he took to his feet. Willsith worried for the stability of the man but did not want to affect his flow.

As though possessed, Frank's torso leaned about, and his eyes flashed blinks, but somehow the man kept going: "Let us build and maintain a new world of transparency, progression, community and positivity." His face grew ever redder as he continued without pause, despite his body's obvious signs of exasperation. "A world with a future free from political perversion, with enough power to r-r-rehabilitate this wounded planet and let us survive, to progress to a better day, together. Not stuck!" Waving his arms around and tilting his head as though it were a ball he balanced on a plate, he animated the words with swathes of cynicism. The bar clapped him as soon as he gave them a long enough pause. He bowed as if it had all been a show, and then shouted, "What utter poppycock!" It had been one hell of a thing to hear out of an ex-Grand-Commander the day before flying off into space to 'maintain' the Earth's halo he had so mocked.

Frank Argyle's performance had coloured Willsith's next few days. The man's fat red face and his betraying outburst remained with him; a drunken guardian angel. Frank's speech echoed in his ears as he stared out of the jump-ship window the next morning, feeling like his brain had changed shape, his limbs were colluding with gravity, and that, with all probable reason, his liver wasn't talking to him.

★ ★ ★

Farl idled in-game. Phospheri was a strategy game which span over infinite-universes, and for many like Farl, it was a virtual manifest of an inner power. Farl had been an all-star in the gaming world, winning many championship titles. He'd burnt through all of the strategy games of his generation before he renounced gaming, dropping out of all leagues. He played now as an anonymous node. In Phospheri he was a pirate, a ghost in the system, but still he commanded legions. Though a tenth of the world played, there were few in Phospheri who matched Farl and his unnamed armies.

Despite his digital dominance, the game bored him. Over the years he had developed strat-bots to manage things. A collection of artificially intelligent advisers and managers. As he dipped in and out of the game these machine-minds assumed control in his place, often conquering armies of real players while he slept. In truth he knew the bots now exceeded his capacity.; he had made himself redundant, and though the game rolled on he was sure that the philosophical strategy that he had encoded in these artificial generals would win out. The challenge was gone.

He sat up in his baking-tray of a bed, wedged into the corner of his bunk. His display panel hung from Arc's cot, and across it a million way-points were rendered. A sprawling map of dark space, where systems of planets were dots in dust-clouds; evolving galaxies rotated, galactic cores themselves morphing and corkscrewing along a master procession. The procedurally-generated expanse was infinite, the game fractal. His strat-bots dealt with this totality, but his view was simplified.

A message from one of his AI generals reported a victory. He hit playback and watched as the panel flung him into the scene, catapulting him visually through trillions of light-years of space. Narrated by his strat-bot, he watched as the ships of ten thousand human players swarmed through a system in his name. Relinquishing a fellow high-master of his palace planets, they pillaged resources before collapsing each of the planets into inconsequential space-fodder.

The conquest barely moved him. He saw an uptick on his domination index, and closed the game.

Willsith's bunk glowed blue. Farl smiled.

He flicked the screen with a series of precise swipes, opening a maintenance console. He paused for a minute, enumerating through the sleeping members of 229, listening for signs. Then he started.

He typed fluidly, pausing only to allow the system to

respond. He moved his head back and forth like a metronome as he keyed in command after command which unlocked layer after layer of security. Breaking free from the limited section access, he got into the larger Earth's Halo network traffic. He knew he was safe until he hit the hub firewall, and as he waited for a valid session to hijack, he reminded himself of the importance of that firewall. He must not get caught. Not until he'd captured an image of the core. That was the whole point.

White made a pasting sound with his mouth. Farl froze, and then relaxed. *He even eats in his dreams. Food first, and then the truth. Bad priorities.*

A security token flew through the pipes and his tooling automatically used it to pull him through into the hub. He was almost there. Leaning in, he re-read the prompt. One firewall down, only a few layers left. He cycled through his pre-prepared hack scripts. As each variant of malicious code rendered, ready for execution, he walked himself through its steps. He was confident that one of them would sidestep the authentication, but he balanced the risk.

That warning has knocked you, he said to himself, *last week you'd have executed all three of these, and been ready with the download. Regardless.*

Angry at himself, Farl selected all scripts and hovered his thumb over 'execute'. He closed his eyes and stoically ran through scenarios. Worst case was that none of them would work, but they might catch him for the wildcard. If they did, they'd penalise him. Drop him to Earth. He could live with that, though it wouldn't be ideal, and it'd waste those five years. The best case would be that he got in, made the image, retrieved it through the same session and got out unnoticed. Possible. Farl reached instinctively to the device around his neck. This was it. If he got in, if he got the hub core, he'd walk away a champion of the people. Even if he leaked half of it, he'd have enough to—

Then the panel flashed. He spotted the subtle change of light through his closed eyelids.

It was another message from 'Dalex', sent through the very line Farl had in. He almost vomited on his panel.

Desist or be removed. All of space won't hear you scream, and the prize is not worth your risk.

Dalex.

This message is all gas. My strat-bots could have come up with a better-worded threat. But this 'Dalex' has sent it through my route in. How? I can't have exposed myself, I'm sure of it. Shit.

CHAPTER 5

Regeneration

He crested over the metal pastures of the dark side of the Earth's Halo. The sun seemed to rise from behind the ring, and Willsith saw nothing but majesty in its splayed beams. His eyes adjusted, and the star's boldness receded into the great patchwork of space.

The breadth of the void produced a sort of spiritual gravity in Willsith, a forced acceptance of himself in comparison to the massiveness of everything.

Farl rattled away the peace over the comms, "I should have come out, you need a second officer, and you're probably right about me needing to get out of 229."

"No…Lin needs to pack, and I need you on controls," replied Willsith, noting Farl's sudden reversal. "Besides, look, it's all clear. Not a rock in sight." He tapped his suit and used his words as an excuse to peruse the galaxy. "Look at it."

"Willsith, I can see video from all angles of your suit, at all times."

"I know."

"It is clear, though. Sensors say no inbound for 36 hours."

"Can tell from out here. Seems calm."

"You connected?" Farl asked.

Willsith tapped the hovering metal plate. "How far today?"

"You'll be half way to 230, sunny-side again."

"Give me a view this time, and don't rush it."

"All right, Willsith."

He'd changed his tone; maybe it was because Lin was leaving. Willsith's suit straightened itself out, locked its joints.

The magnetic shunt propelled him around the Earth's Halo, and with his back to the ring, Willsith lay amongst the rigid metal of his suit, serenely lost in the distant stars. The speed of his transit seemed negligible while staring into the procession of the universe.

He felt the slowdown, then the decoupling from the shunt. As a passenger, he waited as the suit rotated to stand him up on the Earth's Halo; its joints releasing from their locked position. Automatically he leaned toward the ring's sunny-side and began to jet, face first, towards the Earth.

Two sets of repair drones circled a collision site, their lasers beckoning him as he floated downward. He reached the drones and rotated to a standing hover, looking first at his shadow cast on the ring, and then at the Earth.

Clouds spun together like a flat reflection of the cosmos, the oceans swarmed the land, and the land looked ragged. The deserts looked anaemic, and the rest not much better. Clean white borders strangled the land. Bleached coral. Dead-zones where the acidification of the oceans has killed the algae, stripping the water of its life. He'd seen it first hand; empty white honeycomb beneath an army boot. Now, from space, Willsith could see many shores outlined by this lifeless line.

"What are the recovery rates like this quarter, Farl?"

"One minute…just below targets, but on course for the year. Why'd you ask?"

"Sometimes it looks like she's still in decline," he solemnly said. "In five years you'd think she'd brighten up a bit."

"The regeneration was never going to happen overnight."

"I know."

Willsith scanned another continent; grey and scarred land that he knew was Old Europe. With the awe of space behind him, and his vision filled with the realm of man, he began to slip into a sadness. He thought of his brother, and then of the decades he had spent in similar grey fields. And his past ignorance.

White broke in over comms; in a way, saving him. "They could fix her up right and proper if they stopped frittering power on old national borders. A waste of—"

"Sorry Willsith," said Farl, "I've shut him off."

"Just these two?" asked Willsith, forcing himself back to work.

"Yeah."

Using the tool, Willsith freed two melon-sized chunks of crusty, white rock, and popped loose a few samples. "This one looks valuable," he said, flicking a shiny slice of rock so that it spun around in front of his visor. But then something in the distance caught his attention. Three bright shapes that moved like men floated atop the halo, a few miles out.

"Neither of the rocks are flagged special," Farl said.

"Doesn't matter about that now. You see 228?" Willsith said as he squinted. "They've stopped moving. There's three out, must be a big hit."

"228 aren't out, according to manifest."

"Must be a bug; I can see them. Can't you?"

"Suit camera's giving connection warnings. I can't see that—" Farl's voice cut out.

"Farl?" Willsith barked, staring intently at the three over Section 228. "Farl? What the hell?" The comms always worked, *what the hell?* Then he saw the spark. It looked to him like a welding torch, a moment's flash, then one suit rotated and started to shunt toward him.

He gave no thought to the drones who busied themselves by his feet, and threw himself toward the top of the Earth's Halo, his eyes fixed on the inbound 228er.

At the top he levelled himself out, and saw that he had made it in time. The person from 228 was still a mile away, and he tracked his progress toward him. "Farl, you seeing this?" he asked.

No comms. *What is going on?* Willsith thoroughly set his focus on the fast moving suit. As it got closer he saw that the man was not alone. Drones flew in-line with the suit, green dots at this distance, but obvious still. An entourage. "Is this emergency transit?" Willsith tried to remember the training. There was nothing about green drones. If he could see the man's face as he passed, he would know.

And then his suit took over. His arm fought against it, then his whole midsection, but the suit clenched him, its joints tightened and froze solid. Imprisoned, Willsith was rotated away from the shunt-line. He battled hard against the shell, twisting his neck to try and see the suit as it passed, but then it was gone.

Willsith's heart beat thuds in his ears. He inhaled air to fuel an angry roar, but then forced it out through his teeth.

All at once he got his motion back, and tried to swing himself to catch the tail of the shunter, but found that he could only turn toward 228. Willsith hated tech, and this was why. No matter how hard he pushed, his suit would not let him move beyond a degree.

Seeing the two in the distance, he reached for his torch and the spare he'd brought. He could only just grab them, limited as he was by his suit. He raised them up and fired the sign. Drasil-G.

The two paused, and he could make out movement, but no sign. He stopped the torches. Fired them again. No reply. 228 always replied to the Drasil-G. Who were they?

CHAPTER 6

Watch it!

"It's ready, already. Quit whining," White said as he carried the pot to the table.

"I wasn't whining," answered Farl stoutly. "I don't whine."

Willsith circled his jaw until it clicked, and then looked around the table.

White dished out their portions.

"Stir-fry, again?" said Arc.

That joke is stale, now. Gets older every damn day. Willsith faked a smile.

"Only two weeks till next shipment," said Farl. "Fingers crossed for meatloaf."

"I don't like space meatloaf," replied Arc.

"That's because that ain't no meatloaf," White announced. "Who knows what *that* is."

"It tastes fine. What can they really be putting in—"

"Enough, let's eat. It's Lin's last meal here, play nice." *Like that'll happen.* Willsith stabbed at his noodles. "And did Control reply about the floating suit?"

"It's no big deal," said Lin. "I like the meatloaf."

"Farl?" Willsith pushed.

"Just another standard reply," Farl answered.

"Ingredients just say sixty-four percent protein, don't even say where it's from. Could be—" White was silenced by a triple-beep. "Oh, here we go."

"Ah crap, it's Tuesday. I forgot it's Tuesday," said Farl. "Broadcasts are totally—"

The wall lit up and the face of a formally dressed young woman presided. "Welcome, maintainers. This week on Hub News we catch up with 'the running man' as he reaches the 100-section mark, we'll get an update from the dual-worlds commission, and we'll finish with a quick message from Control."

White slopped noodles onto his plate, sat, and said, "Another day in paradise."

"Raku. E. Keni used to be a metal-refinement specialist at a top university before he uplifted to take a post as repair technician in 2046. But Raku isn't just a metals worker, he has also completed over twenty Ultra-triathlons on Earth. With over three thousand miles logged on terra firma—"

"They repeat this story every week. It's not like we've forgotten," started Farl, and then he moved his lips in time with the broadcast's narration. "It seemed natural for him to attempt something no other man has done before; to run the complete distance of the Earth's halo."

White took over, speaking over the lady in a caricature of her voice. "The 42,000 kilometre run will see Raku visit every section, running the equivalent of over nine hundred marathons."

Arc said, "I still don't get why he's doing it. He has to run for three years straight."

Lin spoke in low tone, said, "It's a challenge, and it's good for morale." Willsith held his jaw to the side as he slurped down noodles, but caught Lin looking up at him. Willsith straightened his jaw, smiled back. He didn't care one noodle about this wimpy runner.

"How can you not get it?" started Farl, "It's—"

"It's a scam," said White. "It's a dirty politician scam to keep us working. He probably shunts most of it."

"It's not a scam, but it's not—" Farl stopped himself as the broadcast volume peaked.

"Join us now as we speak to Raku from the mess hall of Section 210."

Willsith watched his crew. Arc placed his fork down on the table and turned to the broadcast, and said quietly, "He's turning into a celebrity."

"Arc you misfit! He's not a celebrity, he's a—"

"Puppet!" White finished the sentence for Farl.

Then Raku's effeminate voice filled the room. "Hello Control, thanks. It's going well. The hundred section mark was a big one for me, but I'm trying to keep focused as I've still got 800 to go." The voice of Raku. E. Keni bounced around 229; the speaker's loudness emphasising his gaunt timidness, boring Willsith. His thinly moustached face looked sickly and his chicken-bone arms hung mechanically from bulbous shoulders.

Willsith saw White chewing fast. He swallowed, then couldn't get the words out fast enough, "You realise we'll have to house this weirdo soon?"

"He doesn't look like he'll make it," said Farl.

Everyone except Lin laughed.

"How are you finding conditions on the Halo for running?" asked the interviewer in a shallow excitement. "By the time you get back to your section you'll have seen more Earth's Halo than any other human! To see the entirety first hand must be a great experience?"

Her voice reminded Willsith of Tabitha Hawkeye, from central branch; the way she'd said, "Are you sure?" to him after he had handed her his resignation. He slotted in more noodles.

"It's easier with eighty percent gravity. To be honest I've probably already seen more than anyone, but running alone, along transport tracks between sections, isn't wild. Few times I've crossed paths with another runner, (hi Shira!) And some transports moving stuff, but that's just part of it. This run tests my mind and body. The most interesting part is visiting sections. And it's a bonus that the exercise will add a year to my life."

"He's bored," White said through a mouthful, "look at him, he's so bored."

"He's boring," added Farl. "And that extra year will be spent running in the dark, the fool."

Farl and White were on form. At least they weren't arguing.

"We see you've even had a chance to help out with engineering fixes in some sections?" asked the broadcaster.

"Yeah, the food and work in sections helps," replied Raku.

"I'd go mad if I didn't fix anything for three years," said Arc. "I get that."

"You're already mad Arc," said Farl. "It didn't take three years."

Willsith turned to see Arc deflate, pick up his fork and nudge his food. *Watch it Farl.* "What time you off Lin?" he asked as the running man finished off his interview in the background.

"Ten."

Willsith looked to the broadcast for the time, but only found a two-foot wide projection of the runner's skinny mouth. From the foot-high view of his fidgeting nostrils, Raku looked like a nervous wreck.

"That's in twenty minutes," Lin added.

"We'll miss your skill outside. One of these will have to come out with me," Willsith said, hoping they'd all object so he could have his peace.

Lin nodded, pushed his plate forwards.

"Yeah, good luck at the hub," said Arc. "Thanks for teaching me cellsplit."

"No worries—"

"Willsith, you know they accepted Lin into the protection class?" spat out White. "He's going to be a hub guard."

It would be so much easier in 229 if those two would just ease off. "Didn't know. Thought you were going back for more clearance?"

Lin cupped his hands together. "Yeah, got risen to prime."

"Prime?" said Willsith. "Keep your head on, that's all I can say. Don't lose that common sense you've got."

The broadcast's volume surged up again and they quietened. "A quick summary today, from the dual-planet commission. Twelve percent more uplifts this month means that Tacern is now approaching forty percent occupancy, with a confirmed landed resource that meets eighty-one percent of the requirements for phase one. This means that our new Mars city is right on track to be viable by 2075."

White huffed out air, said, "Tacern my arse."

"My mum's neighbours got lifted with her son, a guy my age. He'd been on parole for scamming in Y-Minor. But they got in, and it was only because she is a council's aid."

"I wouldn't want to uplift," said White. "City of crooks. It'll be as bust there as it is on Earth, and here. It's empire extension and it'll be as sexist, racist and—"

"Keep it to yourself, will ya?" barked Willsith. "At

least let me finish this damn ration without the commentary."

And the young broadcaster continued, "Now, a message from the Controller General's office. As we approach the end of our fifth year of duty on the Earth's Halo, it is almost a time for celebration. On Earth the four united-nations are preparing for a joyous gala to mark the progress we've made in these first years. But this is not a time to lose ourselves in festivity; we still have an important job to do up here. Sections 210 to 245, all leave is postponed until further notice; there is a large inbound which needs your attention due to—"

"Sodding great," said White; "I was looking forward to leave."

Farl pushed his empty tin forwards. "You never go anyway. You always book it, and then bail."

Willsith caught an edge in Farl's tone, and listened as White amped up to match.

"That's not the point, they can't just—"

"Farl," Willsith said. "Show me the response about 228's floating suit after will you?"

The broadcast had paused, and Farl said quickly, "Was exact same message Willsith. Denied your request. Said it was materials transit and your suit just glitched."

Willsith knew that he wasn't seeing things. And the suit had definitely taken over.

Lin got up, moved to his bag and began packing.

"Was probably a space mafia send-off," said White, grinning like a child. "Off'd an enemy of the Halo. Torched him for the Controller General, flew the body back to the Hub."

Willsith clocked the ripe tension in Farl and White's body language. They sat like a pair of dribbling dogs, and he knew what might be about to happen.

"Assassination—," started Farl, "—that's the least of it."

Willsith eyeballed them both, but they found things to stare at.

"Accidents happen," said Arc. "Maybe it was an accident?"

And then they let rip. "Accidents?" said Farl, bursting out with a laugh and leaning in toward Arc. "Accidents don't shut off suit cams or force control-overrides. Accidents don't get body-shaped drone-transits that are off the record."

White joined in, "Yeah, Arc, what about Willsith's suit?" His bald head bobbed in agreement, his few hairs flopping about.

Then Farl. "Don't be so ignorant; they killed the man. They killed him just like they'd kill any of—"

Willsith thrust his torso over the table toward them, ramming his rib cage flat on the metal. "Stop, you idiots!" he shouted, and slammed down a palm flat on the desk. "All I asked was what Control had said. I didn't ask for some lame commentary."

Arc slumped back into his seat to give Willsith room. White's face matched his name. Farl froze.

Shit. I lost it, again. Willsith calmed himself down and let himself back onto his seat. "Look, we're a team. We stick together. We need to look out for each other, irrelevant of what we think is happening out there."

Then he turned to Lin, and said, "Lin's off in a minute, and he doesn't want to hear our crap."

"Yeah, that sounds like the transport now," said Lin, lifting his bag to his shoulder. "It's been fun, guys."

Fun. 229 was anything but fun. And for a moment Willsith felt like escaping with Lin. He imagined the hub as idyllic, filled with missions, people...women. A kind of heaven.

But when it entered it was just a delivery bot. *These things are the real workhorses of this place, they see everything. They've been from Hub-heaven to Section-911, and back.* This one looked especially beaten up, with a speckling of dents on its side like it'd been target practice at least once.

"It's for you, Arc," yelled White.

"It's always for him," Farl added. "Only thing we get delivered up here is parts and stir-fry."

A slot opened in the top of the delivery bot and a robotic arm handed White another parcel, then spun at the wrist to offer him a pad. White tapped it and carried the parts away.

Folding its arm away, the bot jolted off toward the transit doors, and away into the dark of the Halo passageway. The doors didn't close, and from the darkness Lin's transport slid into 229.

Lin stood, and Willsith saw it. Lin held himself like Bear. As he saluted, all Willsith could see in him was his brother, and a panicking sadness ripped into him. He knew he couldn't change Lin's mind, and that made it worse. Prime. Prime meant front-line.

"Bye, Lin," each of them was saying, shaking his hand and sharing a few last words. The heat of the past moments gone from their manner.

And then it was his turn, and he found himself hugging Lin, imagining his brother Bear. Whichever way he tried to say it he couldn't get it out. He wanted to tell him to never raise a gun, to go in any other direction. Willsith wanted to protect him, to change his mind. But Lin didn't wait, nodded with thanks and left through the transit door.

Failure slashed at Willsith's gut, and though he tried to

find solutions, he found none. Bear was dead and Lin was chasing after him. And he was stuck in the limbo of Section 229. With this lot.

The rest of that afternoon passed awkwardly. They kept to themselves and filled their time. Willsith asked Control for a replacement for Lin, but their reply was bleak; 'no', with a handful of threats. He was going to have to find another way.

CHAPTER 7

Stale Regrets

Willsith stared into the grey of the sleep-deck wall. Everyone was asleep, but he was at war.

The mission had been behind enemy lines. Data-warehouse demolition. Four under his command. Two had died on entry.

Leaving the two outside on guard, he entered the silo. Willsith skulked through the corridors, sticking to the shadows. He reached the door he'd seen in the mission briefing. Picked the lock with an auto-hack-bot. Moving quietly between server racks, he found points for the explosives, and set charges.

Muffled noises made him instinctively duck out of sight. As he calmed his heart-rate, he glanced down at his wrist. Four red dots lit up. Four dead men.

From his bunk, where he lay in remembrance, he felt what he hadn't let himself feel, back then. Sadness drained his mind and all he could do to stop from thinking of death was to carry on.

He'd heard voices, and prepared his pistol.

As the voices approached, he made out the dialect of an ally, then another he did not recognise. From the footsteps he could tell there were only two.

Cycling through the muscles in his hand, Willsith readied his stance, and listened. He started to make out the conversation and wished he hadn't. A general from his side, and one from the other. Willsith's team had been a disposable distraction, the General had used them to clear the way. He was selling secrets.

Too quiet. 229 was too quiet. Nothing was going to interrupt him before the memory played out. Willsith's gut felt vulnerable. He knew what lay ahead. That night, back then; that had been the start of the change in him. That night and that general. That was when he realised what he had become.

But the man had been a sick coward. What he was trying to sell had endangered millions. And he must have killed Willsith's men, ordered it, or seen it.

Spinning around the side of a server-block, Willsith had popped to his feet with his pistol arm outstretched, one wrist on the other and the detonator in hand.

"I've heard enough, General," he said. Then Willsith acted.

He didn't regret that day. And as his eyelids fell, he mumbled it again, "I don't regret killing him."

And then he dreamed, and though the sleep was soft, Willsith's subconscious offered him no rest.

★ ★ ★

A room built itself around him, a lab of sorts, but the child-gate on the door hinted at a home. A white coat swelled around a man who sat on a raised stool, the peak of his shoulders rising high above his sunken neck. He fussed with a display panel. The man had furry eyebrows, and squinted from under them, tapping a panel with a giant finger.

Then he exploded. "Diana," he yelled, threatening Willsith's ear-drums. "Diana, I've got it!" As the scientist jumped into the air he tossed the panel. The squared glass clattered to a stop at Willsith's feet, and at once he looked down at himself and saw that he was only a couple of inches tall.

With curious calmness he watched on. A simple looking lady entered the room, and after some discussion they hugged as she cried. Willsith wondered what had happened, but then the man pronounced it. "It's the cure. I've cured it. We can save her, and all the rest!" And then Willsith knew that the man had found a cure for a form of cancer, and that it was his mother he talked of. Willsith was proud for him.

He thought about introducing himself, and walked to the edge of the table, but the two scientists did not notice him as they jumped about in each other's arms. And when Willsith saw her eyes, he knew what was to happen. The two kissed, and began to tug at each other's clothes. Willsith heard the woman speak with the voice of the Control broadcaster. The scientist lifted her onto the table, tipping it.

As Willsith slid, and fell, he felt warmed by their intimacy, until the awful rush of speed which came with the falling. He came to a brutal stop with a squelch.

And for no reason he seemed to be in a field. It felt like war. The air was cold, he could see his breath. He got up ready for a fight. Adrenaline tensed him and he felt desire in his stomach.

Flicking mud from his bare arms, he looked around. It was night. There was a shroud of darkness and a cold fog. He could make out no moon or stars or even where the light was coming from.

A fizzing sound turned into another squelch and in

front of him a server presented itself, rocking to a stop. A black box with the Drasil-G symbol emblazoned on it. Willsith accepted this held the cancer cure.

Footsteps behind him, wet and clumsy. And as he positioned himself between the box and the approaching figure, he looked hard into the mist. A silhouette cut itself out from the darkness, and with each drag forwards its details popped out at him. A uniform. A man. Elderly. Limping. And as the squelching sound rained like thunder in his ears he saw the burned face of the General, twisted and collapsed.

Without a thought, he dropped into a kick and knocked the man's head clear off. "Why don't you give up?" he shouted at the corpse that fell into the mud. "Why do you make me fight you?"

Two popping noises sounded. Willsith made out two figures stalking toward him through the mud. Waiting to check, he saw the burnt-out eye socket of one of the Generals, then floored him. The other he took down with a running punch.

More pops sounded and Willsith snarled. He looked up into the fading grey fog and felt lonely. Three more dead Generals, and then the server opened a door, and somehow inside was his brother, and he begged for help. Willsith's mood collapsed, and as many noises sounded, his heart fought to escape his chest. The acid in his gut pumped through him, and he flashed awake. Sweaty. Sad. Glad as hell that it had only been a dream.

CHAPTER 8

Control

His bunk glowed with a pulsing yellow wake light. He wondered what would of happened in his dream if he'd been left alone. Left alone to fight. The dream all too quickly dissolved from memory. Collecting his thoughts, Willsith watched the wake-light cycle on and off, and a pithy anger filled the back of his skull. When the wake light stopped flashing, he forced himself up.

"What's the problem?" he asked Farl, laying his feet on the warm metal of the floor. "Why can't it wait?"

Farl lay slumped against the metal, his usual slant. "Modification to the laser array," he said, without moving. "Transport delivery arrives in four minutes. Shall I wake the others?" His thumb hovered.

Willsith rubbed his jaw, asked what time it was.

"02:46. You've been out for about three hours."

"What's so urgent?"

"It's modifications to the—"

"I know, Farl."

"Wake them?"

"No, let's go and receive the mods and see what we can do."

"It says minimum of three—"

"Screw what it says."

Willsith stood up and circled his shoulders.

White rolled over and showed his scrunched-up round face from under the cover. "What's up, Chief?"

"Nothing. Go back to sleep."

"All's clear tonight?" asked White.

"All's clear, go to sleep."

Willsith waited for the sleep deck door to shut before clicking his jaw, sending an echo around the empty mess hall. Lights faded in and lit up the space.

"Right, then, Farl. What in due hell do they need us to do to the lasers at 2 AM?"

"It looks like quite a big change. We're basically taking the laser heads off and replacing the bases."

"We've had weeks of low-impact hours. Why now?"

Farl lifted his shoulders and dropped them.

"No matter. I was getting into too much of a routine anyhow. You and me will fit them."

"Willsith, I'm comms, and this says minimum three—"

"We can both put a bit extra effort in and count for a third. It'll be good for you to get some time in space. You know," he said, flicking the sleep from his eyes, "I think that might be what you need; more actual space. Spending all your time in here with White might not be good for you. Let's drop the point eight of a G."

"It's not...I'm not...Willsith, I'm fine in here. I just need more time."

"More time for wh—"

A transport door opened and the sound of motors whirred from the darkness beyond. A unit slid into 229, carrying a pallet, and made it's way along the track toward the opposite door.

"Well, that's big, but it's not too much for—"

Two more units slid in after it, and came to a soft stop. Feet dropped from the corners of the crates and unfolded to the floor. Connecting into a train, the three units lowered themselves and slid off, back toward the hub. The transport doors sealed shut behind them.

"Let me see the dispatch," said Willsith, throwing out an arm in Farl's direction. Farl handed him the hall panel. Willsith scanned the note and spoke all the while, "You think this is to do with that big inbound? Unless something is going to hit in the next six hours I don't know why they couldn't leave this till the morning. Yeah, three men minimum, but that's per box. This'll take us all night, even with all four of us. And just after they took Lin back."

Farl turned from the crates, said, "Shall I wake the others?"

"Let's take a look in the crates first." Willsith pushed the panel on him, then charged off to his locker.

Willsith knew it was his job, and that kicking rock bought him time in space, to think, but the way these guys shoved down orders pissed him off. Or maybe he was just cranky. When he made it back to the pallets Farl was standing there, face-deep in a panel. Willsith threw the metal of his rock-shifting wedge into the gap under the lid and yanked it. The metal pallet lid cartwheeled off toward the wall.

"Willsith, they're self-opening. It's just a switch."

"I don't need the switch," he said, and threw the crow bar behind him. "Too much tech—" but Farl's choke stopped him, and looking at the lad's face made him wrench himself around to see. *Shit!* He'd forgotten the golden rule of tools in space. The bar revolved through the air and Willsith honed in on the sharp end, begging the thing not to pierce the floor.

Clattering down, the bar left a little dent in the floor, but then safely rolled off toward the sleep deck. Willsith berated himself for the lapse, put it down to sleep weariness. Shook his head. They turned to each other. "Sorry...I know, I know, sharp tools and space. I just woke up."

The sleep deck door slid open, and White's moon of a face braved the light.

"Well, they're awake now!" said Willsith.

And then he looked inside the pallet. Two chunks of hardware: a heavy-looking oblong of grey, machined metal. A long cylinder. To him they looked like gun components. But Willsith was aware of his past, and presumed that a biased assumption. It was probably boring old rock defence tech.

"Looks heavy," said Farl.

"Looks like work," said White as he arranged his shirt. "Looks like weeks of sweaty suit-work. And with nothing but stir-fry as fuel."

Willsith clocked each of them as they gathered round. White and Arc looked more than half asleep. Farl read the procedure, and the part-list.

"They're extending the range of the lasers," said Arc. "These units will let the lasers move anywhere on the Earth's halo, like the shunt plates. These are magnetic drivers, where the existing ones run on mechanical rails. See...this label says keep metal away from the unit. Must be magnetic."

Willsith nodded. "More coverage, I guess," he said. "And what about these?" He lifted a cylinder out of the box, tested its weight. "What's this for?"

"Wait a minute," started White. "Maybe I'm still half

asleep, but why would they want to go beyond the range? We've never taken hits outside of 'em, yet? Doesn't this mean they can point lasers at the dark-side of the halo?"

Willsith interrogated the cylinder, said, "White, it's too late—I mean early, for theories. Must be a new type of rock inbound."

"No, hear me out." White knocked a hairy knuckle onto the base unit. "Surely the shooters don't need to reach that far around? Range don't need to stretch towards Earth, just to hit rocks coming from out there?"

"Maybe the rock is too big to get at directly; needs to be sliced at all the way," said Willsith.

Farl huffed out air. "No, he's right."

Arc peered at the piece Willsith held. "Not sure what these cylinders are about. Maybe new lenses? Swap outs for the existing couplers? I bet they give a finer beam, but stronger. Combine that with —"

"It's finally happened, they're equipping this thing to police near-space," White burst out; "we're basically police!"

Willsith lay the tube down flat in the crate, said, "White, they're not out to get us. It'll be a big rock inbound. Major slice and dice. Right, Arc? Farl?"

Arc moved to Farl, looked at the panel. "It would mean they could move into groups. Laser arrays, proper."

Farl said, "Could be both. I'll go and look…for more information."

"Okay; drop it, White. We'll get to work and then we'll—"

"I'm not helping," White barged in. "Should know what you're doing before you do it."

Arc broke the silence, softly, and said, "It is our job."

"Not mine, I'm the bleedin' chef."

"You've got a space suit, haven't you?" Farl told him.

Willsith knew he was the only one who could stop them. He was sick of the bickering, and sick of having to stop it himself. Enough was enough. He firmly said, "Fine. Let's ask."

"What?" Farl was taken aback.

"Let's just ask them. Farl, connect me to Control, give me the panel. I'm too tired to deal with this crap."

"Hello Control, we've received your shipment. Can you please tell me and my *small* team here, what these modifications are for? My team officer seems to think—"

"The modifications are to enable the rock defence lasers greater manoeuvrability. There is potential of a mega stream inbound, and the enhanced lasers will be able to group together to…break it down."

"Great. Thank you Control." Willsith handed the panel back to Farl. "Satisfied?" he asked White.

"No? Didn't you hear her? She just repeated what you said a minute ago, she lifted your words. It's automatic bullshit. We can't do it."

White was being a useless comradeship officer. Willsith ran back through the conversation with Control. She had used his words, which did seem strange, but surely that was just a coincidence. He mustn't get swept into White's conspiracy theories. He was up here to heal himself, to lay low and to work out how the hell to live outside of a battlefield. Either way, Willsith couldn't put all that metal up without White. Farl and Arc didn't have the brute strength, even with their enhanced suit-frames. Willsith had to find a way to calm him down. "There's no pressure, White. Just go back to sleep and us three will do this ourselves." Willsith hoped he'd take the bait.

White pulled down his top lip and retracted his jaw. "Willsith, are you telling me to go away?"

Two in the flipping morning and he had to deal with this baby. Willsith didn't even find an answer, before White acted. Lifting his portly frame up onto the next pallet, he lay himself flat on the lid. "I'm not moving, and you shouldn't either."

Here we go. Here. We. Go.

"You could ask again," said Arc. "The law stops them from rotating Earth-side. I remember reading it on the union-charter. So they'll have to confirm they're breaking it, or that it's been changed if—"

They left him no choice. "Fine. Farl, the panel." Willsith eyeballed White. White crossed his arms and glared back.

"Control, yes, can you confirm whether these modifications allow you to fire lasers at Earth, apparently—"

"Commander Willsith, we have clearly stated the reasons for the modifications. Please complete the work within the designated window of time. Fourteen sections have already fitted all six units. As per the briefing, those that do so within the next hour get double rations for a month. If you cannot complete your task, we will remove you and replace you with a capable team."

"There's no need for threats, it's 2 AM. We just want to know why, and about the law that says—"

The cold voice of Control cut in sharply, "Please show signs of work within the next one hundred and eighty seconds, or we will replace you." The communication channel closed and the panel flashed back to work schematics.

Willsith leaned on the crate. "They really want these

72

put up, eh?"

"It's obvious, Willsith. They're up to something. I knew this would happen," White projected from his pallet bed. "I knew it."

"They won't remove us, will they?" Arc asked.

"I don't know, Arc. If we don't fit these, then maybe." Willsith rotated the metal of the base unit. The sight of his mitts on the machinery did bring up the past. "White, are you prepared to drop for this?"

"Willsith, it's the principle. Early morning. Surprise fix. Looks like guns. Guns that let 'em police near-space. Tech-disparity on Earth is bad as it is, if we let 'em kill off the fledgling space industry with these super shooters, we're dumped. And it could be worse. I read last week that they're already denying licenses for some test ships for 'political stability' reasons. I joined to cook food, that's it. I won't help 'em monopolise space-access."

Part of Willsith wanted to shout to fix the problem. Before, in the army, he'd have shouted ten times already, and had them hopping into suits and outside before he ran out of air. But he joined 229 for some peace, and now the orders tired him. He no longer wanted to control men. He jostled with ideas, testing the past on the present. "Fine. We'll vote."

"I have something to say," started Farl. "As much as I hate it. White is…right."

"What do you mean?" Willsith asked, as Farl moved to stand next to White. "What is this? Late-night show-and-tell?"

"I've got it," started White, bending his neck to show the shiny round of his head. "They're declaring war on Earth. This is the beginning. The first space war."

Willsith was knocked back by the statement. "Space war? White, don't take this too far. There are many laws in place, many politicians up here. There's no chance they'd—"

Arc broke in, "Yeah, the inter-nation space-energy law stops them—"

White started laughing and slapped his hairy hand flat on the pallet lid. "Don't be so blind, Arc."

"Enough, White. There is no war. It's in your head," Willsith told him.

"There is no war, but there is something," said Farl. "There is definitely something."

"What are you trying to say? Spit it out, clock's ticking."

Farl dropped his face, shut his eyes. "These new lasers can't be legitimate, they must be being added to stop certain ships from breaking out of the atmosphere."

"How do you know this?" Willsith looked him straight in the eye.

"I got—," Farl looked up, "—access to the hub-core."

The lights cut out. 229 went silent.

"Section, lights," Willsith barked, hoping it'd work, presuming it wouldn't. "Lights, mess-hall." Nothing. No lights.

They were up-the-spout now. He should have stayed in bed.

Old training hung over him with a set of options. He checked his hearing, and heard the familiar dull throb of the liquid in the halo walls. That was the same. Next he thought of weapons, of suits and equipment; preparations, before assumptions.

"What's happened?" asked Arc. "Power failure?"

"I have a horrible feeling it's—" and his premonition jumped at him through the darkness as a new voice spoke.

"Section 229," the male voice said, "you are an odd bunch, aren't you? Let me look at you." The lights flashed on, brighter than normal. "Yes, an odd bunch indeed."

"Who the hell is this?" shouted White.

This guy wasn't an automation. Overconfident, with a flowery tone; he clearly had plans. Willsith knew his sort. And with only a voice to go on, Willsith started a mental file on the man.

"This is Dalex," continued the voice. Farl flinched, and coughed. "This is Dalex, head of security for the Controller General's office. And you've been...disobedient."

"I've been a lot of things, Dalex. But no one's ever called me that," said Willsith, standing straight and cycling his sight between where he thought the cameras were hidden in the walls. "What's all this about?"

"It's war. And this guy's the bent arch-bishop," shouted White. The light fled the room. "Ah, fuck it."

"Section 229 you have been found guilty of breeching our secure systems, well beyond tolerated limits. Secondly, you've shown more than 400 counts of dissident tendency, broken more than a thousand regulations between you, and—"

"Tolerated limits?" said Willsith. "Dalex, square with us. What's all this about?"

"If you'd let me finish, Commander. I am reading you your rights. You are under arrest, and you will be sent to Mars High Court for judgement."

"Mars Court? Eat waste pipe, Dalicks. We're under the jurisdiction of Earth court up here. We signed when we uplifted," shouted White.

Willsith could not see a dot of light anywhere. Dalex

had them blind. How had it all flipped around so fast? "Look, Dalex, we'll install it. This was just a misunderstanding. None of this section wants to cause a problem. Give us lights and we'll install the—" But it was too late. White was locked into mode.

"To hell with this pig machinery," White shouted. And his heaviness betrayed him, as Willsith heard him hop down from the pallet and pace off to the lockers. "To hell with it, and to hell with Mars. You have no jurisdiction over me."

"It is no longer that way, my friend." Dalex's voice rang out, double the volume. "There is a new structure in place, and thus your Earth's Court is no longer relevant. Wayward sections are now removed under halo law."

Willsith could hear White fumbling around near the suits. His eyes played games with him as he begged them to find light; his ears tuned in, and he tried to acclimatise. Farl was hyperventilating; he could hear. Arc might be close to crying. This was unreal. Only hours ago he was in a calm rut with these three; now look at it. An idea thrust itself upon him, and he whispered, "Farl, Arc, how do we get outside? And shunt?"

Farl replied, "There's no way, he has—"

"Correct, Farl," boomed Dalex, "I have total control over 229. Now, do you understand the charges? If I give you light, will you accept the charges and peacefully prepare for your departure?"

"Charge my arse!" shouted White.

"Is it getting cold in here?" said Arc. "I'm cold."

Willsith noticed it too. The usual warmth was falling away. The power Control had here - it meant they had no choice. Machine noises whirred overhead, new sounds; a reverberation that he was not familiar with. And then a rush of crisp air, colder still. Willsith felt the coolness roll up him, carried by a thrust of air. It was as though something had fallen from the ceiling. Then he spotted it. Arc's noise was gone. "Arc," he called out. "Arc?" He moved his arm to where Arc had been stood - nothing there. "Arc," he tried one last time, swooping down to see if he lay incapacitated. "What the f—"

The room filled with light but the chill persisted. Arc was gone.

"What did you do? Dalex," he yelled, letting free some obscenities. Throwing his head around, but not knowing where to look, or what to look for, he had nothing left to do except to threaten: "Don't you dare hurt him, you crooked bastard, or else." But he knew his words to be hollow. Willsith had no power here, he couldn't threaten a guy who was fifty clicks away, locked safely in that sodding Control Hub. How had he let himself be so unaware as to fall into this?

"Arc is on his way to us. As you soon will be. Please use this to inform your next decision. Charles White should not continue to attempt to exit, or to procure a welding torch. We have locked all tool racks. If you wish to be taken while conscious, desist."

The urge to command overruled his anger, and Willsith spun around and clocked White, who struggled to put on the wrong space suit.

"Ah crap," he said, "this is Arc's, no wonder it won't fit."

"Stop it, White, or they'll knock us out."

"Where's Arc? How the—?"

"Just stop."

"I got this bar out before they locked in the tools. There's that torch Arc just finished fixing too. What's wrong, man, you're the soldier here, you going down that easily? They've just kidnapped Arc!"

"White...sometimes you have to know when—" Willsith said, and looked upward. A new hatch; that wasn't there last time he looked. He'd lost touch. He wasn't even noticing environment changes. No fighting stripped you down. "How did they even take him?"

"Tube transport," said Farl, "might as well share what I know—now."

"Tube transport?"

The lights died and another wave of cold swept in. "Farl? White?"

"Here."

"Me too."

Dalex's voice filled the room, "229, I am a busy man. Please take this as your last warning. Prepare yourselves for extraction; the collection team will be with you in four minutes."

"Screw you, Dalicks."

"Calm it, White. Come here. Leave the bar. Okay, Dalex? Farl, tell us about the tube transport. How long have you known...how do you know?" Willsith hoped that White would go quietly. He thought of fighting, but knew now was not the right time. They were caged rats. And he was supposed to have given up combat. Peace in space. Yeah right. He couldn't escape the fact: he might have to fight.

He heard White throw down his suit and walk across the metal floor towards them.

"I can't believe they used it on him. He's innocent... " Farl whispered, moving closer. "It's a network of tubes, half a metre wide, which they've run along the crawl space. The documents I read said that they are capable of propelling anything inside a container, in a near-zero friction environment, almost completely around the hub. It's an internal shuttle."

78

"And you knew this?" said White. "Man why didn't you tell me? What else you find out? Who's this Dalicks prat?"

"I'm sorry. I didn't mean to get you all into this, I...I just had to get to the core."

So Farl had been hacking. That explained all those confusing conversations, *that's* what he had been hiding.

They grouped together, hands on each other's shoulders. Unity. At least there was that.

Dalex spoke and the room chilled further. "I see you've ignored my warning. Recovery teams are just one minute away, so I will save them the bother of lifting your bodies. I will not incapacitate you. I trust you'll repay this kindness by transporting easily and keeping your mouths shut. Your arrest is final."

"What a spatula this guy is," said White.

"Leave it, White...leave it," Willsith told him, and smiled in the dark. White had turned out to be quite the wild-card, not just all mouth. And Farl too. And though he worried for Arc, and for all of their futures, Willsith could not help but grin.

CHAPTER 9

Neighbouring Sections

The three remaining members of Section 229 stood huddled together next to the pallets. The mess hall was pitch black, and Willsith shivered.

"Here come the coppers," said White.

"Sounds like it," replied Willsith, attempting to count the approaching men from the echoes of their footsteps.

Then Farl, "Both sides."

"Sounds like two teams."

"First taking Arc, then that cold, now this grim metal footfall. It's messing with me," White said.

"It's intentional. Games," Willsith told him.

"This Dalicks is one son-of-a-bitch," White declared.

And then they silently prepared themselves. Willsith guided them out of their huddle; he and Farl toward one transit door, White to the other.

The clanks stopped. The doors shot open. Bright light jumped in at them from all directions. Willsith sunk his posture down and thought of war.

Flicking his head around, he saw four at each door. All wore full space suits, and though the metal of their kit was dusty and scratched up, it was still a layer of armour Willsith did not have. Two were armed with full-size rifles that he didn't recognise.

"Welcome to 229, soldiers!" shouted White, and Willsith knew from his tone that he would try to fight them.

The first of them stepped into the mess hall and started to remove his helmet.

"Here for the party, are you?" shouted White. Willsith guessed that the slapping noise was a bar in his palm.

"Chill out, White."

"It's Frank, Willsith," the man spoke at him.

Frank Lupin. Willsith remembered. Jet Battalion Commander. He was a good man, back then. Frank Lupin was running 228? "Frank," Willsith addressed him, bowing his head slightly. Willsith was embarrassed. Was Frank a section head like him? Frank's suit was totally trashed, it looked like he'd welded fixes onto it himself, or he'd let someone with White's dexterity do it.

"Good to see you. Shame about the circumstances." A scar divided his cheek, and around it the skin crumpled as he talked. "I trust this'll be quick, we still need to put the mods up at our end," said Lupin.

A spitting noise rasped behind them. White. Turning to check on him, Willsith clocked his hunkered-down pose, his shoulders up, wide and tense. Beyond White though, he caught the delicate lines of a female face. The front-most member of 230 had removed her helmet, and held it on the hill of her hip. Her hair was cut short, but not in the botched, careless way a man often keeps his hair. Her face was wide, her features delicate, and as Willsith scanned her, he noticed a warming in himself. Five years of suppressants couldn't stop it.

"Trinity," she said, "Trinity Argyle," and her rough voice led Willsith to draw conclusions.

"You're all fucking puppets," exclaimed White. "Get

out of 229."

He was going to lash out. He's going to lash out and hit her, or someone else. Three of them couldn't take down eight, even if Willsith secured a rifle, which was unlikely if he had to protect them both. And in space, he wasn't even sure he could fire a rifle without sending the whole ring directly back to Terra. No, there had to be another way. "White, we need to go calmly. This isn't the battle. These guys are just like us, they aren't our enemies," he said, noting that he was still in a fighting stance, and trying to soften as he turned back to Frank Lupin, who would surely notice.

"This lot are not like me, Willsith. I'll never be a mercenary, or a policeman."

"Control your dogs, Willsith."

"That's not helpful, Frank." The two stared at each other, and Willsith questioned whether these truly were section's 228 and 230. Back on Earth, Frank had been as highly ranked as him. It was funny that he was up here…maintaining, and just a jump a way.

"See, they're not maintainers."

"White, regardless of who they are—"

"We're not here to hurt you," Trinity said, her voice less raspy this time, "we're just doing our job." She was tall and her suit was well maintained, Willsith could still make out its original coding mark.

White sneered, and Willsith tried again, "White, these aren't our enemies," he said, staring Frank in the face. "We'll take it up with Hub Control. We can't fight here. Trust me."

"They'll ERX you if you do," he heard her say. And he pictured her, like he had once been, and Frank too, on the battlefield, elbow-deep in mud, managing men, dealing with the mess. "You don't want ERX gas in your system, trust me." *She knows.*

Farl cleared his throat, and spoke in a fast, childish way, "Or worse. Let's go, White."

Willsith heard him drop the bar, and then relaxed. White had mumbled dissatisfaction and squabbled with the specifics, but a few minutes later the three from Section 229 were loaded onto a truck and driven away. The transports electronic motor whined as it took off down the long, featureless corridor toward Section 228. Willsith, Farl, and White sat silent in cuffs and watched as Trinity and her team shuffled around in the light of their section, occupying all that they had known for the past five years.

229 bled slowly out of sight, and in the quiet, Willsith balanced the future against the past. He stared at his wrists and the fresh orange paint on the metal constraints that held him, and wondered if there was a place for him in this universe. Was he to fight again? To become a slave on Mars if he didn't? Willsith wasn't sure he could even fight, up there, or anywhere. He'd given that up. For good reason, he'd given it up. Bear died for no good reason, so he'd given up fighting. That made sense, at least. But action had deep anchors in him, and the burned-in ritual of commanding would not allow him to dwell on his recent moral questions. He jostled with himself, but could not forgive, nor could he avoid sliding back into commander-mode. *Shit.* Part of him asked, 'What should I do?' and the only firm answer was action. A laugh of an idea sounded from a recess in him, a cynical joke: 'You know we're going to have to pass through section after section before we even get to the hub. You're on the parade waggon now, prisoner.'

"I don't even care," said White. "I just realised. I don't even care."

"What about?" asked Farl.

"I don't care that we've been arrested."

Willsith watched the two armed men who sat next to them catch each others eye.

Farl looked at White, then back to his hands.

"We're slowing, must be 228," Willsith said. And he heard the transit doors open, and felt the truck slowing. In a blink of an eye they were through Section 228 and back on their way along the corridors around the halo.

"I didn't see pallets, but otherwise 228 is exactly like 229," White said, lifting his eyebrows at Willsith.

Willsith looked at a guard, said, "I guess they've moved the pallets out of the way of the tracks so we can pass."

The man looked back at him, smiled a coy smile and then turned his eyes toward nothing important.

No use there. The two in the back with them were untrained, and anyway, it wasn't their fight; wouldn't be fair to bring them into it. Might as well ride the donkey all the way into town.

They drove on through countless dull miles of transit passageway, and the blurred copper-coloured walls became a flat image to Willsith. Sections came and went, and occasionally a blockage on the track gave them a few moments to interrogate another team's mess hall. Each one they passed started out as a possibility of distraction, but few were different, and eventually Willsith resigned to use their passing as a countdown. It was grim how the sections were the same. Nine hundred sections, nine hundred mess halls, nine hundred teams, and they were basically living carbon-copy lives. And what about the two makeshift guards? Probably 228 workers. Willsith wondered if they were the two he'd flamed Drasil-G to a few days back. They were just civilians, maintainers. Or they had been. Now they had guns and were playing policemen. The thought made him angry.

"That's 281," said White. "We'll be at Hub soon."

Farl moved uncomfortably, arranging his wrists. "Actually, it's Section 275," said Farl, "but yeah, soon."

Twenty-five more. Willsith sunk into an old routine. From his feet to his cranium he tested his muscles, he stretched as well as he could, given the space, and nodded to himself as he found no real stiffness. He studied the bindings on his wrists in detail, then the guards guns, then he noted all of the properties of the truck that he could see from his seat. He focused his ears and tried to hear how many were in the front-cabin. He estimated the truck's speed from the blips of lights which flew past, and all the while fought the brains desire to assume. Fighting in space would be different, he knew, and it couldn't be fighting for fightings sake. Not this time.

White stared at him and said, "You alright big-man?"

Willsith smiled at the balding space-chef, circled his lower jaw, and let it crack into place. The bone-on-bone sound produced the twitch he expected in the guards.

White laughed and eyeballed one of the men. Swore at him mildly, then looked at Farl.

Farl said to Willsith, "Hope Arc's okay. Must be intense to have been suddenly sent at speed of sound."

"He isn't even that great with grav-fluxes, he gets nearly as bad grav-sickness as me," White said. "Maybe that tube knocks him out first, gases him or something, before it propels him?"

"I hope he's alright."

"They don't have the gall to hurt him badly."

"I hope so."

"That's 284, then," said White. "Sixteen left."

Farl was knocked. Unusual for him to be thoughtful,

like that. He had never really given a damn about Arc. White seemed to be dealing with it okay, though he could be in shock. Willsith had always presumed White was all talk.

"What's the pl—" White stopped himself, looked at the closest suited man. "Willsith, what do we do?"

Willsith breathed deep. "Go with it for now," he said; "stick together and go with it."

Farl and White both nodded at him.

He hoped he could get them out of there, together. Arc could be anywhere. He couldn't let these two out of his sight. Not while these crooked bastards were disappearing kids and changing the laws. As if space fighting didn't have enough variables. And all he'd wanted was peace. For now he'd play along. Play along, and find a way to get these two out of here. There would be opportunities.

"Ten more."

The sections all looked the same now. Willsith couldn't distinguish any of them from 229. The same grey box with the same sleep-deck door. All of them empty of men. The odd personal item studded each hall, small things; small enough to have fitted in the uplift container each man was allocated when they signed up: an occasional photo stuck to the wall, prayer beads on the mess-bench. Tiny fake cacti. Mementos that might as well have been the same in every Section. Drips of Earth memories in an ocean of grey space utility. How trivial it had been for Control to remove them from 229.

As they passed through the last few sections White counted down each of them, his drawn-out pronunciation making the two from 228 fidget. As Willsith began to feel the transit coming to a slow-down, and then stop, he couldn't help but chuckle at the nervous speed with which they hopped out and readied their guns.

"Get out," one chanced.

"Don't you worry, boy, we're getting out," said White. Even Willsith was taken aback when he caught White's twisted smile.

All three hopped out, and Willsith made sure to catch their eye and offer a staunch stability. *Follow my lead. Trust me, and follow my lead.*

The makeshift guards acted like they were in a training video, their body's stiff in action, slow to find the right positions. Willsith knew they were too close to him. If he had wanted to he could have commandeered a gun in a snap. But this wasn't their fight. He didn't want to hurt them.

They offered orders and 229 accepted, taking a walk down the side of the truck.

As soon as 229 were in front of the transport Willsith heard the click of guns behind, and then the fuzzy sound of electric motors carrying the four from 228 off into the distance.

"They didn't wait around," he said.

"Four little pigs," said White, sniggering. "I think you might have made them a little nervous."

And then Willsith let the scene envelop him. Around him the copper-grey walls of a transport-corridor. Beneath his feet familiar metal transit rails. In front the white of the Hub, and the fresh faces of administrators. A clear boundary cut across the corridor, a hexagonal metal collar, beyond which the walls glowed a pristine white. The floor was of a rubbery-grey material without break, and there was nothing else remarkable that Willsith could make out. He caught his fellow section members in his periphery and imagined their appearance, shackled, stood deserted in the dark of the endless transport-corridor. White's grin was sure to look beastly.

It was curious to be captive, but he denied the label, and got to work detailing the eight men who waited for them. All stood in silence, seven were armed and all guns were aimed at them. Unknown weapons, different to those that 228 carried. Seven was an odd number for a squad. Willsith judged them to be of medium-rank and skill, their positioning and stances a little off, but they weren't as fresh as the four from 228 had been. And then there was the man in the middle. The white suit with the moronic smile.

"Good morning," he said, and Willsith knew that he was Dalex. "I am Dalex, and you are the wayward remainder of our Section 229."

"Black-hole yourself," said White, then mumbled other vulgarities.

Dalex didn't drop his grin, and moved his unflinching eyes over them, resting finally on Willsith, who was busy thinking of ways to wipe the smile clear off of Dalex's face.

"I don't usually come out to meet prisoners."

"So there's more sections rebelling?" asked White.

"No, you are the first, in that regard."

"You're probably lying. Take us to our room, you jumped up concierge."

Willsith squared his shoulders, asked, "Why are you here, then? What's this about?"

Dalex froze for a moment, crossed his arms, and tapped at his chest.

Willsith saw that there was something around his neck, beneath his jacket, and by the manner in which he'd moved, he knew it was important to him. He took stock of the man and concluded him to be some form of director, and without doubt, a chemical abuser. The sheer white of his suit said nothing of him, most Hub administrators wore white. The black-half of his collar suggested a role in security. His hair was typical of the current fashion and his features unremarkable, but for the white of his face, which matched his attire. And then there was his excessive smirk, which stood out like a piece of abstract art on a gallery wall.

"We're the same…Willsith," he said, moving forward. "We have intent."

"You'd be surprised at the differences," said Willsith, seeing nothing but his face as a target.

Dalex stepped closer, "Often two who seem disparate can share goals," he said, "and as they do, and act, together, their differences often flake away. I'm sure you understand. Perhaps we still have a chance to help each other."

"The only way you can help us is to take off these chains and exit through the nearest airlock," said White.

Dalex stepped another step toward Willsith. "Think about it. I'm connected, and you're trained. Your brother would have—"

And that was enough. Willsith let the anger in, and without expressing the change, he prepared himself.

"But wait, I must say hello to Farl. 229's esteemed ghost-hand," said Dalex, lagging his smiling glance at Willsith before panning his face toward Farl. "Farl here knows far too much to ever go back to Earth. It just wouldn't do."

Willsith promised himself a retort. As soon as a crack showed itself, this crooked hole was going down. He checked the focus of the seven guns.

Eye to eye with Farl, Dalex said, "Farl knows just what I mean about helping each other out. Don't you Farl."

"No," Farl said.

"Come, now, I'm sure you can work it out...with what you've seen," he said, walking back towards Willsith. "Perhaps we can strike a deal."

But the only deal Willsith cared for was the one that traded slaps for teeth. Willsith coughed, then jumped. He threw himself, and all the weight of his upper-body, at Dalex. His shoulder hit Dalex in the chest and they both fell to the ground. Dalex groaned and Willsith heard the dull crack he'd hoped for. At least one rib. And he had to be winded. And Willsith wasn't done yet.

Leaning hard down onto the man, it took four guards wrenching him up to dislodge him.

Dalex didn't speak. He pasted his mouth, and from the floor he lifted and dropped a hand, and Willsith was jabbed.

CHAPTER 10

Corpse

They stalked the lower levels of the cliff-side town. Tactically moving, they worked their way up through layer after layer of empty housing, skirting along repetitive rows of once-proud homes; intact, but grimy. Wildlife had began to recapture the land, but it would take decades for these square carcasses to dissolve. Human shelters lined up like headstones. Plants organised against the empty conformity; roots ruptured the footpaths, relinquishing the concrete of it's dominion over the soil. Ivy dashed up the walls, fraying the sharp lines of laser cut stone. Each window Willsith passed offered up remnants of what had been, but after so many, their potential began to fade for Willsith. The glass became another flat surface to ignore, mouldy plastic frames drawn around useless portals into hollow homes. Fighting to keep vigilant, Willsith played out the much-repeated patterns of his career. His two squad-members followed. He moved on autopilot, and it felt as though they had been searching for decades.

"What kind of a mission has men searching for corpses?" he heard himself say, not expecting an answer. There was nothing there but ghosts. What kind of a mission has them searching for a corpse amongst ghosts?

He paced along a wall, gave signal for the other two to follow. Tilting his head beyond the corner, he peered down the tall, narrow walkway. It stood empty, but for a yellow light which projected downward, encasing a low-hung suspension of dust. It was the first operational light they'd seen. *Must be near the centre.*

As he lifted his hand to give orders, the two fingers he held up highlighted the two he'd lost. He couldn't remember how, but he was down two men. He flicked signals and they moved to cover the urban ravine.

Willsith wasn't tired, he was hardly awake. "We've been scouring nothing for something, for forty days, please say this sodding corpse is in the centre."

He ducked into stance, lifted his gun up, and then moved fast around the corner and off along the high-walled cut-through.

Sand littered the stone floor. Willsith heard his footsteps sound in soft abrasion, and as he exited the stone alley he could hear that his team were in toe. Slipping to the side, he half-heartedly checked the scene for foes, stepping back into the shadowy recess of a doorway. *There's nothing alive here, I don't know why we're bothering with the formality.* But still, he kept his gun up, because although the sensors showed no life-forms, beyond rabbits, there was something else bugging him. Dispatch team had urged them to go in equipped-to-the-teeth, despite the reports; he'd rarely been allowed such a budget.

But it was so quiet. The place was more than quiet. The empty buildings collected any sound that he made, trading his noises for scattered echoes. It seemed like all he could hear were his own thoughts, swelling up between his heartbeats. The town had had so many years of silence, clutched against the cliff, before they came.

Blue moonlight draped down and used the clean lines of the architecture to draw illusions in the dust. He stepped through the shadows and into a centre. A circle of bold buildings leaned in, each a stunning statement of what might have been. Redundant specimens created by men who had then fled. Front facades seemed to have grown up from the ground; tree trunks cut from stone, distributed like a regiment of soldiers, ordered to hold the weight of the overhangs. Cubic marble and thick, dusty metal sat atop the columns with aspirations to fill the sky. Behind the stone Willsith caught slices of moon, reflections which darted up and down textured veins of glass and metal, woven into walls.

"Not a god damn blip," said Willsith, flipping down the sensor on his gun. "Dead space."

No response, he noted, and as he looked into the faces of his two squadies he did not recognise them.

The thought scared him so he turned to the sky. Its edges fell behind the buildings and encapsulated the city, making it seem like a great false lid on the place. There was only him and them, and the city and the moon and the sky; the sky held the moon up, and the city held them down. Duty kept him moving, and as he went, Willsith thought of enemies. *Enemies are great, they give you a clear goal. Enemies can be overcome, beaten, or they can beat you. You can hunt enemies, but can you hunt corpses?*

Skulking between columns, he checked his sensor for life, or at least life's remainder. But nothing. And then he was hateful for his situation. This place was dead. It had been dead since the people fled. Willsith was trained to kill, not walk around the dead. Why had they sent him, instead of drones? But still he readied himself to push down another cut-through.

Dead diplomats. Who even cares about the body of a dead diplomat? Why does he deserve us hounding his leftovers like this? I hate these missions, I hate the irrelevance. Then, as Willsith lowered himself to take a look around the corner, he heard it.

His senses tuned up and he snapped his visual cortex into line. It was another long walkway, and either side the walls curved; meshed metal and glass covered them like a snake's scales. Another yellow light hung above, sharpening the pattern's exposed edges. The far end led into another courtyard; the sound came from there, but Willsith could not get an angle on it. Turning back and clinging to the wall, he checked through his sensor-array. No heat patterns. No sound matches. Nada. But the rock in the walls here had to deaden the effect. He considered sending up a detection unit, but then closed the sensor screen.

Pulling down his face-mask, he steered his ear at the sound. It seemed to pan around, clicking mechanically and hissing.

He threw up a cover signal and lifted his rifle, slipping into the alley and carefully pacing forward.

Maybe this was why they'd given him guns.

In his established style he slid his finger over the trigger and sidestepped from the alley. And then he clocked it.

Ten feet tall, with a large stone base, gushing. It was a fountain. *A fountain.* He dropped his gun, waited for the mockery of his team, but none came. He walked to the water and plunged his face into it, after that the air felt ice-cold, the skin on his face tight. "Must have been activated when we entered."

The men stood beside him, and he spoke again, "I was hoping for some target practice."

Neither moved.

He panned around and took in the new buildings. Silt swirled up shafts of moonlight, and in it he saw a kind of life that bustled around, the lost tendrils of a wind, assuming as much form as it wanted, moving around on its own business.

"There's nothing here but automatic sodding fountains. There's no enemies, no people. No-one's shooting at us, no-one to save. I doubt that corpse is even here. This is the big nothing. Let him stay here, if he is here, this isn't a bad place for the big sleep. Two dead bodies in forty days and neither were our man, none even had flesh. I'm beginning to think—"

But as he turned, he understood. The eyes of his comrades stood out as bold white gems, they were tools of misery, and they knew where the corpse was. And immediately, he knew. He knew with the frantic collapse of his calm; he knew with the swelling of his throat and the burning lust of his muscles to move. He knew with the urgency of an animal and the logic of a man. He was to be their corpse, he knew. And they moved in.

★ ★ ★

"Wake up, Arc's back," said White, and in a flash Willsith was conscious, ripped from his frightful dream, flush with fear.

He watched as the scene gained his trust. They were in a cell, the walls were white and there was one bright light that made him squint. Underneath him, the cold, flat metal of a bunk, his arm hung off of the edge and his knuckles rested on the grey rubber floor of the Control

95

Hub. Gingerly he sat up.

Farl and White stood with their backs to him, waiting for Arc.

Outside, two guards nudged the technician forward with their guns, and the transparent wall that capped the cell slid down. Arc collapsed into the arms of his friends, his face bruised and swollen. Farl and White helped him to a seat on the bunk, and the boy coughed. Willsith accepted reality, and the pangs of his headache bled in.

"Arc, what happened?" asked Farl.

"You twisted bastards, he's just a kid," White yelled at the guards as they walked from the room. "Royal tossers. You okay, Arc?"

Arc nodded, his eyes fixed on the floor. Farl stood over him and stared at his injuries with such focus that it made Arc turn away.

White squatted beside him, leaned on the bunk, and asked, "Arc, what did they do?"

Willsith watched as the pair tried to get answers from him with a mixture of care and compulsion. Holding his own head, he knew that Arc was in shock, and that in time he would unwind, but only if they left him alone for long enough. He sought to assist. "Guys, give him space. He's okay, he just needs some space." He stood up and stretched his shoulder. "Where are we?"

"But we need to know what they did to him so we can—"

"Leave him be, trust me. I've been in his situation. I know it can be—"

Farl fizzed into speech, "Willsith, we must stick together now, you said it. We're not a section any more, you can't just give us orders."

Willsith looked out the cell door, took in the room outside, empty but for a control panel, and presumably other cells to each side. Farl's sharp brow snagged his scanning eyes, and drew him from his scrutiny of the scene. Focusing on Farl, he read the signs. Sharp face, average breathing. Mouth hung open. It was a challenge, not malicious intent; hollow. He suppressed it without turning, "Do as you will, but I know how Arc feels. You'll only prolong his shock, acting like that. We should expect that we'll all get the same treatment shortly."

White said, "Leave it Farl."

"But—," Farl started, then quieted himself, and turned to the door. "We're in Hub security. They knocked us out with something like ERZ."

"ERZ?"

"It's a derivative of ERX. They've been developing it up here; it's more variable, I think. Can knock us out for any specific time-period. Programmable sedatives."

"I see."

"You were out for longer than us. Must have gave you a bigger dose."

"Might explain the headache," Willsith said, and turned back to the others. "How long you think we were out?"

"About five hours," Farl said. "Saw the readout on a guard's wrist-panel. He came and brought water while you were out." He pointed to three plastic bottles by the door. "We didn't drink it. Don't trust them."

"They could have put anything through us when they jabbed us, I doubt they'd poison us," said Willsith, "not like that." He picked one up, flipped off the lid, said, "I'll be the test subject," and gulped down half a bottle.

"Maybe it's a legal trick of theirs! If we drink it, we consent to consuming their poison!" White said.

Willsith choked. "Tastes normal...if that means

97

anything. So we are captives in the Hub, we've been here five hours, and they've given Arc a rough time. What else do we know?" Then he turned, and sat opposite them.

"We're destined for Mars, those illegal holes," said White.

"I know more," said Farl, "but obviously we have to be careful—"

Arc lifted his head and showed Willsith the fullness of his face, said, "We're in Hub-security, it's the mid-deck of the Hub unit, and outside there are loads of corridors. The first door on the right is the room where they...questioned me. The floor below is the tube-transport hub, the floor above has some kind of labs, and above that is the Controller General's control deck."

"How do you know—" started White.

"Thank you, Arc," said Willsith. "Your safe now. You've been brave. We'll—"

"The bruises aren't his fault. When I was sucked up into that tube, I didn't understand to start with, but then I realised; I was shunting along inside the halo conduit, in a kind of a capsule. Ride got bumpy at some point, and—and that's when I got the bruises." He pointed to his own face, dropped his head. "When they pulled me out, they put these things on my wounds. Pressurisers they called them. I thought they wanted to fix me up, but then they started asking questions. But the bruises aren't his fault."

"*His fault?*" asked Farl, who looked back and forth between Arc and Willsith. "Who's fault?"

"Dal—"

"Dalicks. That crooked cop, I knew it," said White. "That grinning gimp son of a..."

Arc nodded.

They could have done anything to him. Who knows what kind of psych programming they had here, how quickly they could break the teen down. Willsith needed to keep an eye on Arc. And now 229 made it to the hub it was time to drop the restraint. This place might be where it ends. Anything Willsith could do to free the others would be worth a try. Control was showing all the symptoms of the old Earth empires, made new in space. They had futurist tech, fake unity, but no fucking rulebook.

Farl had caused this. What had he found out? Was this really about laser modifications? Knowing the answers might get him killed, but Willsith could see no other way. "Is Dalex some kind of head of security?" he asked Farl.

"I'm not entirely sure."

"Well, clearly you know more than we do."

"I know some things, but it's a mix," Farl said, touching the metal strip which hung from his neck. "Until I can get to a—"

"Cut the crap. Tell us what you know about Dalex. We're on a sinking ship here!"

Farl sucked his lips in and closed his eyes a little. "I'm sorry. I had to do it. I didn't mean to pull you all into this."

"It's too late now," said Willsith, looking at Arc. "Now we're a team, so tell us."

Farl scrunched up his brow, said, "He's definitely something to do with Hub security, but he's also chair of a few boards which have…dodgy names."

"Dodgy names?" asked White, who had an arm around Arc, but turned straight to Farl. "What dodgy names?"

"Like 'Space Defence Steering Group', 'the Resource Stream Insurance Committee', stuff like that. I remember another one, 'New State Security Alliance'."

"New state? Holy crap, they're doing it. They're actually doing it. We need to get out, we need to tell everyone, they can't get away with—"

"Enough," said Willsith. "Next. How the hell do we get out of here? There's a million ways they can vanish us up here. We need to remove some of their options."

All three of them turned to him, and from deep inside he felt a smile grow that he could not quell. Though they did not return happy glances, he knew that they trusted him, and that he and 229 were more of a team now than ever before.

"Take out the guards?" said White. "When they bring us lunch?"

"They do look like early officers," said Willsith. "But I'd not expect that from you, peace corp pirate!"

"Things change, Willsith. I'm against violence, but they've ditched the laws...whada-they-want? We don't have to hurt anybody. You can subdue them without hurting them, can't you?"

"What movie did you see that in?"

"We could pour water into the edging of the door. I saw the circuit-panel to the left...might short it out."

"Think that'd work?"

Farl raised a finger, and spoke carefully, "Stop. They hear everything," and he took from around his neck the small metal strip and placed it on the floor in the centre of the cell.

"What's that?" asked Willsith, and wondered if it might blow a hole in the floor.

Farl tapped two edges of the thing and it started to glow green.

"We're on. This is a disruption device, it'll give us a window of ten minutes to talk without their surveillance working…but we shouldn't use it all up now, and they'll shut us down fast, so let's get up to speed."

CHAPTER 11

Hacker's Fallout

"So they can't hear anything we're saying?" asked White. And then they all moved in closer, resting their elbows on their knees and forming a seated huddle between the two bunks of the small cell.

"None of it. But it won't last."

Farl had kept that gadget, and his hacking, quiet for five years. He must have lied to all of them, but Willsith accepted it. The alternative was Mars court, after all. "So, how do we escape?"

"Why escape?" said Arc. "I know they're bad, but I don't want to be a criminal, my mum would—"

"We're already criminals, Arc. They're sending us to Mars for judgement, remember?"

"That could be lies, White, they might be empty threats," said Farl.

"Do you think they are?" Ark asked Farl.

"No, I don't. I think they're gearing up for something, and I think they are choosing the laws up here now. From what I've seen, they'll do what they said."

"I see your concern, Arc," whispered Willsith. "It's up to you if you come with us. But I think we should take any chances we get. If they'll do that to you, they'll drop us all to Mars and have us pounding rocks before lunchtime tomorrow."

Arc looked at him squarely, and as their eyes met, Arc's grew moist. Willsith saw that he wanted none of this, that he was an innocent casualty of this situation. But at least with 229 he was valued, and could be protected. "If the situation needs it, tell them I forced you to come along."

But Arc's expression remained the same. His swollen face quivered. All Willsith could do was promise to keep him alive. Beyond that Arc would have to work through it. They had struck him while he was innocent, it was unfair, and it didn't have to happen, but it had, and that was what life was like. *That is what life was like. No.* Anger rose from Willsith's gut as he acknowledged the pattern, inflaming his chest and rattling his mind. It was unfair. It wasn't justice. But all it left him with was an urgency to act. Arc had to take the hit, but Willsith would fight to stop it recurring. Willsith arranged his jaw, then looked away from the lad.

"We gotta escape," started White, slapping Arc on the back. "We've got to tell everyone what Farl knows. And that they're ignoring the laws."

"What Farl knows?" said Arc.

Arc would be alright. So long as Willsith protected him.

"They'll know on Earth," Farl said. "If they've seen stuff moving up here that they don't know about, and no-one being shipped down to Earth court…they must realise."

White swung his head side to side, said, "Na, they'd cover all the tracks. Earth might not know nothin'."

Willsith looked down at the green glow of Farl's device, spoke toward it, "I think if we try to break out, the worst case is more of this. You think the water thing will work?"

"Honestly?" asked Farl. "No. Even if it shorts, it'll probably just stay locked. I'd suspect they'll send men to see what's happening, maybe they already have. I guess we break out somehow, take their weapons, and then—"

"Take over Control," White said reaching across to Willsith's shoulder and pulling them all in closer. "We take over the Hub."

"You're mad," Farl said.

"Am I?"

Farl continued, "I think from a panel there might be a way for me to contact Earth. Or we can at least try and drop, then—"

"Agreed. Let's make that the plan," Willsith told them. "When they come next, I'll grab one, I'm sure I can get one, at least, and then we'll work from there. We've got nothing else to go on, right now... unless you have any other devices, Farl?"

"Yeah, Farl, when we're through this, I wanna hear about—"

"No, just this. And I think they'll be busy dealing with their laser rollout, we might be able to slip out. This thing's got a minute left," he said, watching the green light of his disrupter fade.

"Plan sorted?"

"That's not really a plan, Willsith," said Arc. "You're going to grab one, and we're going to drop?"

"It's all we've got right now," Willsith replied, and again caught the worry in his young mechanic's eyes. "It'll be okay," he told him, and felt like it was a lie. Being back in action was feeding his confidence, and he felt it, but space was so different, and he wasn't that man any more. But he could still fight. For the right reasons, he would fight.

"What's their big plan, then?" White asked Farl.

"I'm not totally sure, but it's to do with the lasers."

"So you were hacking all the time? You knew stuff about their plans, that's why you got so shitty when I talked about the news?"

"Kind of. Most of that was propaganda. The real stuff, the stuff I was hacking into, wasn't reported. Part of the reason I lifted was to get access—on Terra I'm part of this group." He paused, and then started fresh, "The disinformation is so bad on Earth, and our group...we get at information. The others suggested that I lift and break into the—"

"Why'd you stop? Break into the what?" White croaked. "Tell us!"

"Can you hear that?"

Willsith turned toward a corner where the sound originated. Chopped air sped up to a hum, and he caught an odd scent.

"What is it?" asked White, and dropped onto his knees to look closer at the dulled span of wall.

The sound of the distant pump reached a constant tempo and White collapsed into a heap, his belly poked from his favourite teeshirt, and his bald head skewed as the wall bent his neck unnaturally.

"Gas!" shouted Willsith, and then he fell back onto his bunk like a floppy wet towel.

CHAPTER 12
The Good One

It tasted like lemons. As he awoke he pasted his mouth, moving around a strong citrus flavour. A headache thumped through his head, and Willsith wondered if he was actually somehow back on Earth; hungover, having had the most obscene dream that seemed to have lasted five years. He opened one eye, testing to see if the impossible were true. Instead, he saw a beetle fly over him, the bold ceiling light swelling around the blackness of its darting shell.

Closing his eye, he dwelled on the chance of the thing. A beetle, in space. Curious. He submitted to the full pain of his headache as it swamped him with another kick to the back of the skull. "Wait - there's no beetles up here," he said aloud, and sat up, rubbing his eyes and arranging his jaw. "That gas has me seeing thi—"

But then he spotted it. The beetle's blurred wings came to a stop and folded themselves inside its shiny shell as it landed on Farl's shoulder.

Evidently, Farl had managed to put his device back around his neck before he had passed out, and sat slumped against the bunk, motionless. The beetle crawled down Farl's shoulder. Willsith couldn't see them getting out of there in one piece, not when Control could gas them down at will.

The beetle scuttled over Farl, without waking him, and Willsith watched.

What would a beetle be doing in space? He imagined himself catching it in the hollow of his palms. "In a cell in a cell," he whispered to himself, then chuckled. He clicked his jaw and stretched it forward.

"Farl, White...Arc?" he tried to wake them without moving. "Wake up, there's a bug and it's—"

It scurried over Farl's knuckle and stopped in place, and then, as it fired a little red laser, Willsith knew that it wasn't a beetle.

In one calamitous move he rose and shouted, "Wake up! Drone's in here, wake up!" White twitched to life, then Farl, and Willsith stretched out his hands ready to snatch the little mech.

"What happened?" asked White, but spotted the laser and moved in.

"What the—" began Farl, and he swiped his hand to snatch the miniature-drone, but missed. The beetle had relinquished him of his device, and began its swerves through the air towards the cell door.

Willsith tried to catch it, but at an unbelievable speed it pivoted mid-air, flipping its body and passing through a gap between his fingers. He saw its small body up close: stubby metal legs with rubber tips gripped Farl's gadget to its under-carriage. White lunged past him through the air, knocking Willsith to the bunk and missing entirely, as the bug swooped to the side. Farl leaped after it, careering himself into the clear cell door. The small mechanical bug flew effortlessly through a slot that popped open in the cell door. White grasped after it, only just managing to stop the force of his arm before it entered the vice grip of the closing hole.

"Well there goes our privacy," said Farl from the floor.

Willsith stared at it until it flew off out of the security-deck door.

"We never had any. And this sodding glass almost took my hand clear off," said White.

The female Control administrator spoke as Willsith lifted Arc onto a bunk: "The Controller General's office reminds you that you are prisoners of Earth's Halo. Do not seek to cause unlawful damage to our equipment, or attempt to leave your cell."

White took a seat opposite him, said, "Good morning to you too, love."

Farl fussed around the door. Willsith heard him tap it, and watched him feel the area where the beetle had flown through, then push his face against it. "It's not glass, it's something else. And it proves the disrupter works, the fact that they gassed us and took it."

"Good lot of use it is now. And Arc's still out," said White, arranging the lad's arms under his head. "Gas hit him hard."

"Poor kid, he never deserved any of this," said Willsith. "I mean me, I've lived a life, you know. And you two, psh, you're a pair. But Arc: he doesn't need this."

White sat next to Arc, rubbed his own belly and grinned wide at Willsith. "Could be worse. At least we'll never have to eat that sodding stir-fry again," he said. "Or house that maniac runner!" And then he laughed a little, and so did Willsith, and then Farl, and they sat in that prison cell that hung in the Hub of the ring which spanned around the world, and they laughed.

Maybe they did have a chance. Maybe the four of them

could be happy, get free from the crap, and still have lives. Willsith didn't really believe it, they were now enemies of Control, and he knew what nearly always happened to enemies of the state.

Arc woke up and looked with caution at Willsith, sensing the change of mood.

White looked at Willsith, then at Arc, leaning his whole body in, and said, "Good morning, Arc. We tried to catch you breakfast, but it slipped right through our hands!"

Willsith could not help but laugh again, despite it all. They all laughed, and Arc smiled a trusting smile.

White dramatised the tale of the bug, acting the whole thing out in slapstick glory. "A mechanical beetle flew in...here...then pecked Willsith on the nose, waking the giant...it was as big as my fist and it flew with six little stick-wings."

His version was more enjoyable than the truth. Arc laughed as White told of how all three of them jumped into the air after it, collapsing into the corner only to see it fly through the glass and carve out a loop-the-loop in salute. White was either naive or boldly defiant, Willsith wasn't sure which.

Some time passed, and then the voice of the Controller Administrator sounded in the cell. "This is an obligatory message to inform you that your device has been analysed, and destroyed. Furthermore, your charges have been appended. Each of you is now also accused of evading recording, conspiring to evade judgement, supporting terrorism, and espionage. Your processing date remains the same: you will be sent to Mars court in thirty-two hours and judged the following day."

"Espionage?" shouted White. "Lady, you do realise I'm a cook? Espionage...really?" and he rested his hands on his belly. "I'm a fry-cook, not a spy-crook!"

"What if we do not agree with these charges?" asked Farl. "Can we seek council?"

Willsith watched White and Farl's faces as they swung their heads around, searching out cameras in the plain ceiling. They were wilder outside of 229. That place had got a bit crusty. And they were angry, which was probably good, given the farcical charges. Willsith could take the legal crap, but he was used to accepting lies, or orders. And so he thought of Earth, and how, before he'd left the war, he might have found a General or two to help them slip the court. Not any more. Not on the red rock. They wouldn't help up there. Artright was the only one who might have, but there was no chance he'd be on Mars. That's if they even made it to Mars, alive.

"Under new Halo law, council is not provided for those accused of supporting terrorism. In total your charges now exceed three thousand records, and as a result you will be judged on all counts in a single hearing at Mars High Court. Until then, you are to remain in custody, without further communication access."

"That claim is false, we have done no such thing," shouted Farl, standing up, staring into the ceiling. "And you cannot deny us council!" But the voice of the administrator did not reply, and so he sat down and thrust all his frustration into the skin of his forehead.

Arc coughed, and then said, "Guards coming."

Two walked in and approached the cell. Willsith read their walks, spotted the twitch in the leg of the man to the left, counted two fire-arms, holstered, and a confidence in the other man's face that told him this wasn't their way out. He stood up anyway, winked at the others, then walked over to the glass door. 229 filed in behind him.

"Willsith Harper?" asked the man on the right.

Willsith nodded, thought of strategies.

"We are here to deliver a message."

"What is it? Open this door and give it to me."

"We do not need to open the door."

"Well then, spit it out."

"Your brother is dead."

"I know."

"No. He died two days ago in the basin of Arkbridge from massive rail-gun injury. This fact is classified, but as he has been officially removed from the secrecy act, and your clearance is still in place, we are obliged by law to inform you."

"You are kidding, right?"

"No, I am not."

"Who are you to tell me such a thing?"

"I am the Company Captain for this Hub, and Earth Operations Liaison."

"And you are certain he died two days ago?"

The man moved closer to the door, levelled his brow with Willsith's. "I am certain. I have seen the mission logs."

Willsith felt his heart hurt and looked down to his feet, saw his chest heaving back and forth. His neck seemed to collapse down his back, and all he felt was his shouting heart and the shaken bile-pot of his stomach, thrashing about. The pump in his chest throttled itself to near collapse, and all he could do to stop his corrosive innards from tearing him apart was to hit the man.

But the transparent door caught his fist, and without response, passed him back another source of pain. He dropped to his knees, pushed his bloody knuckles to the floor, and cried.

"We are sorry for your loss," said the man, and the

two left.

Behind him they moved to offer support, he could sense them, but Willsith stayed squat to the floor and did not reply. They did not know, they could not know. The suffering they'd experienced was not enough of a qualification, and if it were only that simple. If it were only as simple as qualification. But it was not. The lie went so deep. Willsith had thought his brother was dead. He'd stopped, because of him. He'd left Earth because they'd told him Bear was dead. *I went to his damn funeral. For five years I've been up here kicking—but he wasn't dead. He wasn't dead. Why didn't he come and find me? Why didn't any of the staffers tell me? Where has he been? Arkbridge is outside of—it's just a resonator base.*

And then his body took over, undulating and throwing bile up his throat. He held his jaw shut, feeling as though it may break if he opened it, and the acrid bitterness of his stomach flooded his mouth.

He swallowed fast, repressing the outburst, and opened his eyes. The world had changed, and he knew it. A grim taste lingered, but the fitting stopped, and he knew that he was not who he had been. His heartbeat slowed, the rest of his organs sat back down, and only his knuckles whined. *It's over now. It's over.*

Standing up, he wiped his face, and then his bloody hand, and sat down against the wall. Arc sat next to him and the others moved in closer.

They wanted to know about it, he saw it in their faces, and through the mess of feeling, he tried to smile.

"Well it's definitely a glass composite, didn't sound like glass when you hit it," said Arc.

"Hand okay?" asked White.

Willsith lifted his chin. "I'll be fine."

"What do we do now?" said Arc.

White stretched out a hairy arm to Arc, and said, "We wait for our chance, Arc. We sit and we wait."

Arc looked back to Willsith, and Willsith knew that he wanted reassurance. *I'm not your man right now, Arc.*

"Were they talking about Bear?" asked Farl, dropping to sit cross-legged in front of Willsith.

"It just doesn't make sense," Willsith replied. "Why would he fake his death...or why would...they?"

"I don't know all the answers, but we can try and find out."

Willsith blinked affirmative. *Might as well tell them now. They've wanted to know the past five years, and I've held on to it like it was something important. Wasn't even real. Might as well tell them, then. I'm far away from there now, that place where we didn't tell. Didn't find my answers in all those years of trying. No matter. No use in secrets now.* He raised a hand to his eyes, pincered the wetness from them, and began: "He was a good guy. Since we were young, Bear was always the good one."

Lifting himself, he shuffled back against the wall, rubbed his tongue around his mouth, and said, "You know, I didn't have the best start. But he was the good one. We were close, growing up...we had to be. I was always there when he was younger, to do what was necessary, so he didn't have to. And I had to do some bad things, even then. But then they flung me miles away, on missions, and while I was out, he signed up. I was eight years in when he joined, and I hated it."

Arc fidgeted with the cuff of his jacket, looking up at Willsith and then back to the floor.

"It made no sense. Bear shouldn't have ever fought. He was like our mother, nothing but love. Why the hell would someone like that join the forces?"

He looked at them, sat in varying poses, their eyes glazed, aimed at empty spaces. *Fucking show and tell, what else.*

"Anyway, they lied to me, and he didn't stop them. He didn't stop me thinking that he was dead. He didn't stop me dropping out and then lifting up here. He never once sent me a message or let me know."

"So that's why you came up here, to get over Bear's death?" asked Arc.

"After he—when I thought he was dead, I mean, the timing. Right before they told me he'd died—I was going to quit, I'd had enough. Three decades of war I'd been through. Three grim decades, and it was getting worse. Then they said he died and I used it to leave. I needed to clear my head. I figured I had maybe 20 years left, and I didn't want to spend them killing other people like me. So I hooked onto it. I thought if I could do some good, then maybe it'd make up for a bit of what I'd done, and for leading my little brother into the same thing."

"Big guy, you're a good one…whatever the past," said White.

"He was the good one. And now he's twice gone. They lied to me for five years, he lied to me, and now he's gone again. Those twisted arseholes will have me mourning him for decades. I trusted them for so long. I killed people, for—mission after mission they had me— for what? A flag? I killed people. People like my own brother. And for what? There's no solid reason. No justification. I'm a fool. A fucking death monkey. And how do I even know if he's really dead. I mean why at Arkbridge even? Where's the bottom of this pack of shit?"

"We'll find out," said Farl.

"Farl, we're locked up like rats in a glass cage. I couldn't even punch the man...a beetle stole your necklace. We're done. It's just a matter of how we're dispatched. But thanks."

"I—I—"

"No matter, Farl. We'll get out first. The four of us got to stick together now," said White. "Stick together, and kick some administrator arse."

Willsith laughed coldly.

"The best thing I ever did was leave. Even if it's just been for these five empty years. It sounds like that, their anthem: 'let's kick some arse', but actually doing it hollows you out. Every violent act tears away a piece of you. I joined to protect him, left because I lost him; Bear was there because of me, from eighteen 'till just now, killing in my periphery. I didn't have much to lose, but he lost it all."

Willsith covered his face, then said, "I'm fucking done. It's done. No more. I submit, let them do as they will. There's no point to any of this."

CHAPTER 13
Eva & Lif

Willsith and the others sat in silence. The light persisted to glare down on them and the limited view of the entrance hall stood empty. He had no idea what time it was, or how long had passed since they had talked. Willsith thought of his life before the Earth's Halo, the wars that he'd fought in, his intention to help others. His folly. Judging himself harshly, he stormed through memories, shaking them violently, hunting down some kind of truth. *I've lived an awful life. An awful life in the name of others.* And he felt grim.

Arc coughed into his shoulder and Willsith couldn't not spot the signal.

She was Farl's height. She carried a high-level uniform in on the frame of her body, but she wasn't used to wearing it. Unnatural tension in her arms, the kind his younger officers used to get on Sovereign's day marches, while trying to keep form in all the pomp of regimental dress that was impractical. Was she wearing it for someone else's benefit? Her warm porcelain face looked young, maybe late twenties, though she held it in a scowl.

His gut passed him an assumption; this woman had

intent, and a sharp edge to it. And though the grimness from before remained, her approaching gilded it, and through his brutal mood, her difference cut a little light.

White, Farl and Arc scrambled for the door. Willsith slowly let himself up, rising to the tallest position of the lot, and turned to address the glass.

She reached them, crossed her arms and tilted her head.

A rehearsed pose; surely she had practiced that in front of a mirror. But he could not help but take her in. And through tired, sad eyes he saw a young girl; young but with some authority. She seemed at odds with her appearance, her stance was too confident, and he could sense an anger beneath the rigidity of her movements. What would she want? Sol help him if she was another messenger.

She pulled a sweet smile, and with an assertive calm, dropped her soft eyelids, then lifted them as if pulling up the opening curtains to a show.

One of these will talk first. They're itching to interact. And then heard his own voice: "What do you want?"

"Hello to you too," she said, replying mechanically, "Willsith." And she moved to face him.

Face to face, she scanned him as he scanned her, and Willsith caught himself away from his post of mourning. Freckles peppered her cheeks, and her eyes stood out from the frame of her hair, which was dark brown, but fought with itself to be light brown or blood red. She was fragile looking, and wore a delicate device, which looked similar to Farl's, around her slim neck.

"Who are you?" asked White, and she walked to him, her eyes lingering with Willsith before she went.

"I am Eva Harding, and you; Charles?"

"They call me White."

"It's a pleasure to meet you, White."

"I'm Arc," said Arc, "and he's Farl."

"What brings you down to our little prison cell?" asked Willsith, crossing his arms.

Eva walked back to him, stepped toward the glass, and threw a glance up to the ceiling. He caught her eyes closer, and like fire, they caught his. Her eyes were terracotta flames sat atop mountains - they felt like signals. *But what for?* What was this all about? And what was it she so obviously looked for behind him?

"You guessed I'm from upstairs?" she asked. "Was it the uniform?"

"Yes," he lied.

"Don't hold it against me." She reached behind her back and pulled out a slither of metal. Bending down carefully, she placed it on the floor and it began to glow green.

Farl's disrupter.

"That's my disruption device," Farl announced. "Who are you?"

"Yes, it's yours, and I told you, I'm Eva. Eva Harding. We don't have much time."

"How did you get it? Was it you that gassed us?" asked White. "Are you here to finish the job?"

She smiled a dangerous smile. "I've taken care of that. You won't get gassed again. And no, I did not take this from you. I took it from another."

"Well, get to it woman," Willsith said. "Why fire that up?"

Again Eva looked toward the ceiling of their cell, and lifted her hand in front her mouth, four thin fingers hovering over her lips. "I need your help."

"What are you looking at back there?"

"I want to escape the Hub, and I know you do too. My artificial intelligence overheard your conversation." As she dropped her hand to her side, and moved her fingers as though typing, she said, "Your disrupter worked for the most part, but my AI can read lips, and maybe other AIs up here can, too." And then she smiled, and he became aware of her undeniable beauty, and the way she used it.

"Stop the manipulation," he said. "I'm not in the mood. We've had five years of meds, we're as good as monks."

"I beg your pardon," she replied.

"Why do you want out?" Farl asked her. "And what's your position, here?"

She looked down at the disruption device, again lifted her hand, and said, "I just need to get out. It's no good here any more for me, and I don't want to be around when—I must get out, okay? I'm an analyst here. I work in astrobiology."

"But you have an AI? And it's rigged into core global runtime?"

Eva dropped her hand, placed it on her hip. "Yes, I majored in psytech. I can write code. And I have help. Look, do you want to get out or what?"

"Why do you keep looking at the ceiling cameras?"

"It's complex. Look, it's part of—" and again she held her hand up, "—it's part of my plan. For now I just need to know if you'll come with me. Them—him seeing me talking to you will get me thrown in here, and that's the first part of my plan. But before I get arrested, I'll make preparations for our escape."

"Who are you talking about?"

"Not enough time." Eva pointed down at the device and its fading green light.

"We'll have to think about it," said White. "How would you get us out?"

Willsith saw stress in her eyes and imagined her lips moving behind her slender hand. The whole thing reeked to him of childish games. If she were telling the truth, this would be a risky gambit she'd chosen. Was she careless, or did she have a deeper reason? What was going on in this place?

"My AI will get us out, though I'm not ready yet. I'll come back tomorrow, maybe as a prisoner. If you get the chance though, take it, because if something happens, my AI will do its best to help you, and I'll meet you on the way to—"

And then the device sounded a triple beep and its green glow died.

She dropped and picked it up, hiding it away somewhere in the back of her uniform.

"Nice to meet you fellas," she said, and trying to wink, blinked both eyes.

"Nice to meet..." replied Arc.

Eva turned and began an over-emphasised walk toward the exit. All four men stared unabashed. Willsith felt the sadness of before returning, and a shallow lust trailing after her. The recesses of the backs of her knees, the curves of her legs that drew off under her white, utilitarian skirt. The sharp points of her high-heeled shoes. But more than all that, she had spark, and she might have a way out. He wanted her, but the feeling was weak. The repression drugs never did totally quell him. And with each swing of her hips, he swung like a pendulum; curious lust, then paranoid sadness, and then back to lust. And then at once he decided the feeling was worthless. She was probably manipulating them, and she was young. And even if she were decent under all that, he was old. Willsith was a brutal, old soldier. It wasn't worth thinking of futures any more. There could be no real chance of escape.

So he turned to the others, snapping himself away from her. He saw Farl with his nose almost touching the glass, and White frowning and smiling all at once.

Arc asked, "What now? Can we talk about it?"

"To hell with devices," said Willsith. "To hell with it all." And he put his back to the wall and began to slide down it towards the floor. He heard the outside door opening for the girl and he imagined her leaving for good. But then the glass of their cell-door slid open, and again he heard her voice.

Eva shouted, "Wait, did that just open?"

"Yes, it's open!" Farl exclaimed, and White leaned out to test the gap of the door with his arm. "We can get out!"

Willsith jumped up, said, "Did you do this?"

Eva ran back toward them with none of the finesse of before, almost toppling from her heels. "No, you're not supposed to be able to get out, my AI can't open these doors without clearance. I was going to have to get arrested so that I could work on the—"

"Some kind of a trap?"

As she reached them, White was still testing his freedom, this time sticking a leg out and wincing. Willsith tugged him back.

Eva tapped the control by the door, said, "I didn't do this. Did you?"

"Me? How would I?" White snapped.

"No, not you. I was talking to my AI. But she said no," Eva said, and tapped her ear. "Seems it was a malfunction, something to do with them trying to get the sensors back...the sensors that my AI tampered with just now." Watching her reply in the moment, Willsith saw more of her than he had before, and he knew then that she was as lost as they were.

"Right, let's move," said Willsith. He didn't have to care about himself to get the others out. Whatever he thought about Eva, he could at least try, for them. Worst case was the same either way.

"Wait, this wasn't supposed to happen," said Eva. "I didn't open this. I don't know if—"

"No matter now, we're taking off. Everyone out."

White hopped from the cell and stood close to Eva, then beckoned the others with a wave. Farl jumped through the doorway next, and asked, "How would it malfunction?"

"I don't know, I—I don't know if we can go now. My plan, it needed...preparations. Before I could break you out I needed to prepare. You shouldn't come out now, you should wait and I'll come back."

"Freeze," came the firm voice of an armed trooper as he ran into the room. "Do not exit that cell, do not approach Miss Harding, if you do, we will shoot."

Two men. Both were armed, same rifles and getup as Dalex's seven. As Willsith remembered the jab they gave him he shot out an arm in front of Arc's chest. "Not this time."

The two paced in, rifles jammed into their shoulders and eyes fixed down the barrels. They moved to Eva, aimed at Farl and White, and shouted, "Freeze."

"You already said that," White said, and crossed his arms.

Willsith let out a laugh uncontrollably. Then said, "What's this about? We're compliant prisoners being taken to another section by Miss Harding. She's on orders from the top. She already told us. We're behaving, we don't need a teenage escort."

The two troopers positioned themselves next to White

and Farl, shouted, "There is no such order. Get back in your cell."

Farl stepped backwards and into the cell, but Eva stood with her back to the guards, and White maintained his crossed-arm stance.

What would she do now? Was this part of the scheme? He mustn't let them be separated. And if she came with them, he'd need to keep a constant eye on her.

White took a side step, putting him right next to Eva.

The two guards flinched and shouted, "Freeze."

"That's getting old," White told them. "At least mix it up a bit. Try 'halt'."

Eva beamed at Willsith, tugged at her lip with her teeth, and gave him a look that he thought was either teasing or advice. Spinning around, she said, "Thank you, guards. I was only here to ask them about an experiment. Somehow they got the doors open and they were trying to make me help them."

"No problem, miss. Please step away from that prisoner and we will deal with this."

Willsith looked the guard in the visor. *Yeah, right. There's no way you're going to deal with this, boy. I'll deal with this.*

Eva took a step to the side, and said to White, "You should listen to these guys, their guns are very powerful."

White grabbed her, held her in front of him and shouted, "Now *you* freeze!"

Here we go, thought Willsith. *Here, we, go.*

"No," she shouted. "Get off me, this, won't, help," and she wriggled in his grip, breaking free only for him to grab her again.

It was a possibility, but it was risky. If she was real, under all the show, then it might just work.

"Let go of Miss Harding, or we will gas you all."

"You won't gas us, or you'd end up gassing her too," said White. "And yourselves! You have no mask on, man."

"You really should let me go," she said, "it's better for every one of us."

That was it; somehow Willsith trusted her. "Let her go, White. She's dangerous in her own right." And as he heard himself say it, he wondered what he had even meant.

"They'll just shoot me, then gas you lot."

"You agree you won't do that, Captain, if my friend here lets her go and steps back into this cell?" projected Willsith, using the conversation to step forward and position his body over the recess of the door.

The nearest trooper's gun swung toward him, and the man said, "I'm not a captain. I'm a second lieutenant. Stop moving."

Willsith raised his hands. *Well, shit, you make it too easy for me, second lieutenant.*

"Let her go, White. Trust me," said Willsith. "Let her go."

And he did, and she shook free, uttering a slang curse, and shuffled toward the two guards who were tensed, ready to shoot.

Time to see what Eva had. Calculating the need for another step before he could gun-snap the second lieutenant, Willsith shuffled forward a bit.

"Erm, lieutenant," she said, then tapped the man on the shoulder. As he turned she held Farl's device to his neck, and placed her pianist fingers over the sight of his gun. "I'll take that."

"What are you doing Miss Harding?" he asked, and gave up the gun. She spun around and held it from her waist, pointing it at his mid as she moved toward the other.

Willsith jumped into action, throttling the unarmed guard around the chest, squeezing him in a bear hug.

The other guard swayed his gun between them. Eva raised the rifle to her shoulder, White inched forward with his arms out and his fingers splayed. Willsith started frog-marching the other guard forward, and said, "Give it up, kid. You haven't got it in you to drop all of us, believe me. I can see it in your boots."

"My boots?" he said with a squeak.

"Yeah, look at them."

"No, stop it. Let him go. You can't just—"

"No, kid, trust me. You're not equipped to deal with the four of us. We're trained killers and we'll drop you both into space unless you drop that gun now."

"No. Release him."

Eva sidestepped and raised the rifle to the mans head, nudging his temple with the muzzle.

"Ow!" he proclaimed, and then she swiped out an arm and removed the gun from him.

"Now get in there," she shouted, "or I'll let these four do their worst."

She had pulled it off. The man rushed past Arc and sat down obediently. Willsith turned and thrust the other into the cell.

"Freeze in there for a while," shouted White, and laughed at his own joke.

"Throw out your comm-straps," Eva commanded, and they did.

Eva and Willsith surveyed each other. She handed him a gun.

Willsith asked, "Will it work? Aren't they all DNA-locked?"

125

"These two aren't official security, they're under his off-record command, is my guess. So it might." Eva replied, tilting to check on the two in the cell. They sat with their heads in their hands. "You two, if you want to keep your scalps, tell us: will they work?"

One guard mumbled a positive response.

Willsith flicked the chamber, rotated the thing to check for sensors and switches. He hadn't held the model before, but the weight of the thing felt familiar. "It's a shock-rail-rifle," he identified, "shoots small rounds - electrified on impact."

"Sounds like you know," she said, and turned to tap her ear. "Can you lock this?...Okay." Eva kept her gun on the two and tapped away at the panel by the door. "Nope, AI can't lock it, and neither can I."

Willsith aimed the gun at the second lieutenant's thigh, said, "Sorry kid, I need to test this, unless—" and he turned to Farl, "—unless my friend here can find a way to lock you up."

Farl moved to the panel, started tapping commands. Willsith saw the lieutenant's stark expression, and held the gun ready.

"No, I can't get this to shut," Farl told them. "Maybe if I had a while, and another access panel, but this thing's locked down."

He'd lost his nerve. Right when Willsith needed him to be a hacker, he'd lost his nerve. "Sorry then, you two," said Willsith, and half-cocked the trigger to charge the rifle.

The lieutenant cringed, called out, "Wait, wait." He showed them his palms and then said clearly, "Sierra Britain Alpha Two Nine Eight Jericho."

The command panel beeped.

"That's access," said Farl, and with a flick he shut the

cell door.

"Grand. Thanks lieutenant," Willsith said, and dropped his gun. "They can't open it from the inside, can they?"

"Doesn't look like it."

"Good," he said, and lowered his gun. "Now what, Miss Harding?"

Eva pulled Farl's disruption device from her back, handed it back to him, and said, "It's recharged. We can use it when we're talking, but I'm not sure it'll work when we get to the long corridors."

"But won't the lip-reading make it pointless?"

"She's there to help," Eva said, pacing off toward the door. "My AI is the one who can lip-read, not the core computer. She'll also keep disrupting their feeds in areas that she can. Right now security will be seeing a looped earlier feed of this room. To them, we're still saying hello. That's why we should move: they'll realise these two aren't showing up, soon enough."

"She?" said Willsith.

"Yeah, I call her Lif."

"Leaf?" asked White.

"No, Lif."

"Why?"

"We don't have time, we must go. I'll explain later."

"I agree," said Willsith. "What's your plan?"

"The plan was that we'd steal a ship," she began, "and get away from the Earth's Halo."

"Was?"

"Well this wasn't part of my plan. I don't know if— yes, okay, Lif says it may still be possible."

"Leef?" asked White again.

"No, it's Lif!"

"Leave it, White," said Willsith, and he turned to the

other three from 229. "What do you think?"

Arc tipped up his shoulders, White nodded, and Farl said, "Not much choice."

"We should go," Eva said.

"Feels like a trap, but I don't know what other option we have."

"It's not a trap," she said. "We need to escape. Trust me."

It smelled like a trap. To Willsith, it reeked. But he had a gun, and Farl's disrupter. Even if they had to cut her loose, he might just be able to hammer out a way home for Arc, Farl and White.

He saluted the two in the cell, turned to Eva, and said what he had to. "All right, you lead, but if at any point this doesn't go well for these three here, I'll not think twice about dropping you. I've a history in combat and I've not got much left to protect, so—"

"I know Willsith. I expected you'd threaten me."

"How?" questioned Willsith. "Lif tell you that too?"

"I'll win your trust 229, but we have to go now," and she moved. "Not everyone who wears a uniform like this is out to use you."

Willsith eyeballed her, then said to the others, "Let's go. We move with her, but we do not let our guard down. Right?"

The others nodded, and they all paced off carefully.

CHAPTER 14

35%

The cell-block door opened without prompt and Willsith watched Eva push the nose of her gun into the corridor. She followed it cautiously at first, and then settled into confident strides; her sharp elbows bobbing out either side of her as she sought to hold the rifle straight. Eva had been trained. He tracked after her, and Section 229 followed closely; the green of Farl's disrupter tinting the walls to either side of Willsith.

She was trained, but not experienced. If she were to shoot the rifle as she held it, it was going to hurt. Maybe she knew that. Maybe she was acting, drawing them into some great mousetrap.

"It's this way. A large ship, and my—our only way out of this," she turned to say. "*Only way.*"

"Why do you need our help?" asked White, but she didn't hear.

Farl trotted after her, bridging the gap between them, and asked, "What does this red line mean?" He pointed to a luminous band that ran down the length of the corridor.

"Means they know something's up, but that they're not sure what. One line is 'action stations', two is 'urgent alert', and three is 'critical lock-down'."

White turned to Willsith and Arc, and said under his breath, "That's helpful...not." Then whispered, "Can we trust her?"

"We'll see," replied Willsith. "Just keep sharp, and be ready."

They walked on through the white hallway, the red wall-ribbon tugging on Willsith's thoughts.

"We need to get out by 6am; worst case," said Eva, flicking her head around and projecting her words off of the red-lined wall. "We've got about half a day, and the ship is close, but no reason to wait now."

"Why 6 AM?" asked White, making himself a lot louder.

"Didn't you say you'd planned to get put in a cell tomorrow?" Farl asked. "By 6 AM that'd be too late?"

"Yeah, I'd have had to be back early, before then. The dock isn't far."

"Dock?" said White, and then he bumbled forwards and pushed between Farl and Eva. "Look, Eva, you need to tell us some things, or else we ain't moving. We can't help you, or ourselves, if we don't know shit from a stick."

Eva stopped. Her face firmed up and her brows peaked. "There's no time, White."

"We can't just tail off after you Eva," he told her, then dropping his volume, "however pretty you are."

She flinched, her eyes fell to the target symbol printed on the belly of White's teeshirt, and then to Willsith. "I'm sorry, there's just not much time." And then she touched her ear, and said, "We've got to move to avoid guard patrols. And the further away we are by tomorrow morning, the better for us all. Please trust me, White."

Willsith moved to them, rested a hand on White's

shoulder, then said, "Look, there's no guards down this corridor, your AI and Farl's device should cover us for a minute. Just give us something to go on, and then it'll be easier for us all to commit."

"Fine. I want to get out of here because I don't want to be pushed out. They want to ship me to Other. You need to escape because otherwise you'll be slaves - at best. We're going to steal an Ark, which I couldn't steal alone. That's why I need you. Lif suggested you, because my chances alone were only twenty-four percent."

"And with us?" asked White.

Eva lowered her shoulders, turned to Willsith, and a flutter in her lower lip made him think she was about to lie to them.

"Spit it out," he said.

"Forty-seven percent," she said. "But that was with the original plan, with me preparing the—thanks, Lif. Now it's thirty-five."

Farl joined them, but held his body like an arrow pointing down the hall. "Let's just go."

"Well I'll be damned, thirty-five percent. That makes it way more appealing," said White, "How accurate is this, Leaf?"

"Lif, it's Lif. I've never tested her for this kind of thing, I'm not sure about accuracy. Look, can we go now? The longer we wait the less Lif can help." She cupped her elbow in a palm, lifted herself back up straight. "We must go."

Farl's device beeped. He shrugged and said, "No more privacy."

She stretched out her arm and showed the small of her palm to Farl.

"What do you think, Willsith?" asked White. "Can we really beat those odds?"

Farl gave her the device and she turned around to show them all her back, where, at the base of her spine, there was a unit built into her clothing with a collection of ports. She slid the device in and it glowed green again.

"Should have done that before," she said, "it can run from the power of my back unit. Saves you carrying it."

"Cool. Come on, let's go," said Farl.

"Yeah," said Arc. "We've got one gun, and there's no other choice, White."

"Let's do it, White," said Willsith. "Let's stand up and give this whole crooked thing a kick in the gut. If Miss Harding here is all gas, we'll go our own way."

White looked around, shrugged, then beamed up at Willsith and said, "I trust you big-guy. Shit, I'd make a crap slave anyway." White raised two fists up in the symbol of Drasil G and paced off down the corridor, speaking over his shoulder, "But if she's farts and mustard, I'm out of here."

"There you go," Willsith told Eva. "You'd better make those thirty-some points count."

She nodded, and they moved off after White.

Willsith felt enlivened as he jogged. His simple work boots pounded the grey-white rubber, and he felt spirited to have a mission in-hand; a good distraction. The hallway stretched on for another few hundred metres, and he saw the terminating door in the distance. The red of the hall indicator looked like a laser. As he followed the perfect line he spotted a break in it. It was a door they'd have to pass. A risk.

White's sprint had dissolved into a jog, and now Willsith paced in-line with him, slowing to match the chef's capacity.

"You all right?" Willsith asked.

White's face was flush and his arms shone under the fur

of the occasional black hair. "Yeah...okay. Might, need, to take, a break, at some, point, though."

Willsith smiled, and slowed them down to a walk. "No need to go berserker. She said it's not far."

"It's not bad. Just got to warm up these old noodles."

Willsith patted him on the shoulder and smiled. "More fun than cooking them, eh?"

"Marginally."

The others caught up, and Farl said, "We'll carry on. Eva said we might need to hack the next door, so we'll get to that."

"Fine," said Willsith, and smiled at Arc as the three passed.

"That was it," White said, panting, "just needed a minute," and again they were off.

Willsith watched the trio ahead. They were young, and this wasn't like a mission at all.

"What do you think this ship's like?" asked White. "Eva called it an Ark."

"Not sure."

"And *she's* a spicy pepper, isn't she?"

And he watched her, the tail of her skirt bouncing in time with her hair, the gun flapping at her side. "That's one way of putting it. Not sure what her angle is. I just hope we can make it all work out for us."

Up ahead, the others slowed down at the break in the red line. Farl looked to say something to Arc, but Willsith couldn't make it out, and then the hacker split and moved off toward the end of the hall, leaving Eva and Arc stood there, staring into the doorway and talking.

"It's him," said Arc, when Willsith got there. "In there, it's—"

"Dalicks," White butted in. "That's him alright, that

133

slimy-eel-in-a-uniform."

The door was glass, like that of the cell, and through it Willsith saw a tiny area with a window into another room. The second room was white up to waist height, and black above that, and in it sat Dalex, staring at another man across a metal table.

"What's he doing? What is this room?" pushed White.

"He is Dalex Dukeo. The Controller General's chief of security. It's an interrogation room," Eva said. "But he's not important. We should go."

"Not important? Do you know what this fruit-loop has done to Arc here? See these bruises?"

She looked at Arc, then back to White. "Yes, he just told me. We can get medical supplies to help from the Ark."

"He's interrogating one of his own guards," said Willsith in a rush. "Look, the man's face is wrecked, and he's in uniform, but his collar's open. Off-duty."

"That dirty bastard," said White.

"Let's just go," said Arc, "Farl's already at the door, look."

"No, Arc, sometimes you have to make it clear where the line is," Willsith said, handing White his gun, "and what's not okay any more." An anger blindsided him, and when he looked at the young mechanic's face it tore at his restraint, and made him want to tear at the man who was responsible. He knew his logic was compromised, but seeing Dalex clean and the soldier bloody, he could not separate himself from the well of pain surrounding his brother.

Willsith stepped up to the doorway and through it as the door slid open. He heard Arc yelp behind him, and White's voice in support but couldn't make out words. He saw the window, and through it, Dalex, reclining in a chair, a control in his hand. The interrogated guard sat with his side to the glass, and Willsith could only make out the youth of the man beneath the bruises and blood. Dalex flicked a control and the man shuddered, bouncing around in his seat and then coming to a floppy stop, before picking himself up. Dalex had a grim grin saddled across his cheeks.

Fuck this guy. Willsith spun around the room. Nothing useful, a chair, privacy glass, a few small devices on a desk, and another door. *He can't even see me through this one-way window. Perfect. Door's too quiet, chair's the way. Let's have it Dalex.* And he picked up the simple metal chair that sat in front of the window, watching his arms as if he were passive in the thing. His ears hurt and his eyes bulged from his head. Fury like he'd not felt since war. It surrounded him. Dalex must suffer.

Then he felt her hand, and heard the voice of his mechanic in perfect clarity. "Let it go, Willsith, let it go."

Eva had reached up to hold the ramp of his shoulder, and with a soft pressure, squeezed him, and said, "He's just a snake, he's not worth jeopardising this escape for. Trust me. Trust me, Willsith."

Arc echoed her words, "Let it go, Willsith. You said that you left violence down on Earth. You always said—"

"I know," Willsith said, but still held the chair up and watched Dalex jiggle his head around while torturing the soldier. "I know. But here I can do something. Here I can make it right. I can stop him—"

"Helping us get out is doing something," Eva said, squeezing him again. "You don't know me, but I know you more than you think. Trust me, I think you'll regret it more—"

135

"But he's —"

"It's unfair, Willsith, but we should go," said Arc. "For us, for 229, let's go. I don't want to go to jail. I want to see my mum again."

The possibility of murder played out in Willsith's mind. The chair, the window, the shouting, the brawl, the blood, the calm. The running. The soldier might have even sought to protect the man who tortured him, Willsith knew, and that thought was sick. He imagined himself beating down Dalex, and then having to throw the other man off. Hurting them both, or not making it back out.

"Willsith," said Arc. Then Eva said his name, and it started to get through to him. Then White, "Sod him, boss, we'll find another way. Won't make you happy. Can't squash every sick son-of-a-gun with a complex, there's too many of them."

And so Willsith replaced the chair and reconciled himself with the idea of not killing the man. Yet. The surging storm bled away, and he was again sad, and as Dalex shocked the man once more, he wanted to break down the wall, break down the man, but he couldn't, and it made him want to break himself down, but then Arc said it again. One last time. "Let's go, Willsith." So he went. He nodded and gave no expression. Eva turned to leave and he followed. He exited the room carrying a stark desperation with him and leaving behind another fragment of his brutality, along with, perhaps, another chance to make good.

CHAPTER 15
Uniform Sensors

Willsith approached the others as they stood before the terminating door. From beneath his frown, he spotted the Drasil G logo. The bastardised sign of revolution, which now, here, signified Earth's Halo Control. It reminded him of his signing up for command of 229. It hadn't turned out to be all wild-space and healing after all. Farl said something he didn't hear, and grinned. Commanding 229 hadn't been what they said it would.

The doors parted in the middle and another corridor beckoned.

"So you didn't even have to hack it?" asked White.

"No, I just used the same clearance code that guard gave us."

"Stellar," said White, turning to Eva. "How far to this ship then, miss?"

"Past that lift, that intersection, and through the next door. Then it's just two blocks away."

"So how far is that?" he repeated.

"She said it already, White. Four."

"Yes, Farl is right, four," Eva confirmed.

"Even I should be able to run that," White replied.

There was no red line down the walls, but more

vectors for trouble. Why didn't she bring up the red line? Did she even care about them? Willsith pushed ahead. He'd take any hits first, so the others didn't have to. He drew command signals with his hand.

"What's he mean?" He heard White say. "Let's just follow him."

They chattered on as he paced forward, and he half listened.

"What's that Arc?" asked the cook.

"It's a Triple-P." And then after a pause, "A Portable Parts Printer". And then he said, "It's a tiny 3D printer that prints parts. Is designed for engineers to carry with them for ad hoc repairs. Found it in that last room."

White whooped.

Willsith reached the lift and gestured again. A simple one this time: swiping his arm downward and back, he showed them the flat of his palm.

He heard them shuffle up behind him, and then Eva's confident voice say, "That means stop."

No shit. He wedged the butt of his gun into his shoulder and hopped around the entrance to the lift. Empty. Relaxing his stance, he thought to ask if the lift wouldn't take them somewhere useful, but then he carried on down the corridor. As he strafed down the wall toward the intersection he estimated it a minutes sprint away, and so relaxed into his imagination. He could get them there, to the ship, then come back to this lift. Arc had said the Controller General's office, was above. Maybe he could be a diversion; and make sure this doesn't happen to any other sections, once and for good. Maybe he could take out Dalex, and the other—Where was his mind? Willsith didn't care about some old stuffy man, he wasn't the one who ran the army, who ordered Bear to his death. It was men like him, or Dalex. He'd had a chance to smash Dalex, but he didn't.

"Maybe I should have," he said. "It's men like him."

She whispered toward him, she'd got close. "There's three people coming down that next corridor, Lif said. What did you just say?"

Willsith tried to hide his flinch, turned his face to see her, slowing down to talk. "You're fast. Where'd you learn to run so quietly?"

"Farl's device won't work when anyone in uniform is around, most of the stupid uniforms have sensors sewn in."

"What about yours?" White asked from behind.

She continued, "We need to get through that door over there, or hide till they pass. Elevator isn't an option, so we can't really hide."

"Which direction?" said Willsith.

"From your right hand side," she said, "and I know they won't be going in our door."

Farl peered around her as they walked, said, "I can get us in with that code…maybe."

"And what if they come in this direction? Or their sensors catch us and the alarm goes off?" said White. "What then, miss?"

Arc caught Willsith's attention, he was fiddling with a small box which he cupped close to his chest with one hand.

"They're way down the corridor, we should go quickly. Act natural - hide the gun," she said, and jogged off toward the intersection, arranging the gun down her side.

"What now, big man?"

"We move. Be cool," and to Arc, "you ready?"

Arc looked up, and through the gristle of his bruises, winked.

And then the four men from Section 229 stood themselves up straight, dusted off, and followed Eva as she ran toward the hall junction. Farl's device lit up her back, highlighting her edges. *That makes it even harder not to look. But you mustn't, old man. Five years on suppressants, then a day off and you lose all restraint? You shallow son of a...* They chased after her, all running until they met the crossway, slowing just as she had, and composing themselves before stepping out.

It seemed ridiculous to him. Four maintainers dressed in boiler suits, one bruised and another with a guards rifle; tailing this young commander with a green-lit dress. Ridiculous. Surely they'd be spotted from a mile away.

Still, he straightened his neck, moved the gun to his left and watched as the others did their best fake natural walks across the opening.

Farl walked as though shirking restraints from each shoulder, and then once past the opening, ran to the door control panel clumsily. The panel, and the door, stood just a few metres from the intersection. Not much space to hide.

He stepped out and strutted past the crossroads, turning his head as subtly as possible, scanning the long walkway for potential targets.

"How's the door," he asked, then said. "Two women, and a man, don't think they saw us."

"Door's not accepting the code. You think they've found those guards?" said Farl, drawing lines with his finger across the grid which glowed from the wall. "Nope, it's definitely not accepting that code. It's dead."

"Lif, can you do anything?" she asked the air, and then shook her head. "Thanks for trying Lif."

"What now?" said White.

"We'll have to pretend we're just waiting here for someone," Eva told him. "They'll know my face. Farl can be my boy, the rest of you are our friends, and we're waiting for more to join us…from CG's office."

Farl turned to them and grinned, then back to his panel. Willsith frowned, look down at his gun and his other fist. He rubbed at the dried blood off of one of his knuckles.

"Sorry Farl, it's just you're most likely…in the culture here, to be…"

"What if these three are from CG's?" asked White.

"I'll do the talking," she told him. "Leave it to me."

"I might be able to get in," said Farl. "I've found a command screen."

"Stand near the door," she said to Willsith. "Take this gun. Hide them both behind you." Touching her ear, Eva continued, "Lif says they'll reach us in 40 seconds, and if they do stop, just follow my lead. As long as their sensors don't go off, all that might happen is it'll get security on us. Then maybe you can—"

"Shoot them?" he said.

"Help us get out," she said.

I will only accept orders from you while it makes sense for 229, he wanted to tell her. It obviously came naturally to her to give orders, and that for a moment, obedience had seemed a natural response for him. She's a Controller. Willsith wouldn't let himself forget the fact. Eva was somehow, a Controller. *Wait a minute, what is Arc doing?*

White stood up from against the wall, said, "So all uniforms have sensors?"

"Yes," Eva replied. "I mean…most of them. Uniform sensors form part of the core computer input stream."

"Arc, what are you doing?" Willsith asked across their

conversation. His engineer was lowering himself onto all fours.

"So that's how your AI can tell us people are there before we see them?" White asked her.

"In this case, yes. But there are areas off-sensor, and casual clothes don't have them. Some of us don't have too—But Lif can read video streams too. This is my dumb formal uniform, it's impractical and outdated, but I'm lucky because at least it's not tracked."

Willsith handed White the guns and moved to Arc, who instantly pushed something from his hand into his pocket, then stood up and showed Willsith a teethy grin.

It was good to see him smile.

"Some of you?" White continued to address Eva.

Willsith stuck one eye around the corner, paused, then said in a low voice, "Fifteen seconds. Get ready to play along."

Eva nodded to him, White flinched to attention.

"Unless Arc's plan works, that is."

"What?" White blurted out.

One scream from down the hall. Then another. A grunt that grew in pitch.

Willsith grinned and tipped his head to Arc. White clamoured to get to the corner, reeling back in laughter once he saw what'd happened.

"What was it?" asked Farl, not even looking up from his screen.

White was still laughing.

"Arc slowed them down," Willsith told him, and picked up the guns White had disregarded.

"I used the parts printer to make a few graphene cockroaches. Like we used to do in school."

And then another collection of shrieks from way away sent White into an even deeper guffaw.

"Not many cockroaches up here," said Willsith.

"And I guess they've just unfolded," said Arc. "They explode into a kind of spider shape when they run out of momentum."

Farl chuckled.

"They're simple, really," Arc told them.

The doors hissed and folded themselves into the wall. "We're in," said Farl.

White's chuckles dribbled to a stop. "Thank Franz for you two," White said to Arc and Farl, "I can't act for barney." And they all hustled through the door, which snapped down behind them.

Willsith stood with his back to the door. He restored the guns to his hands, squeezed their grips, and watched as Farl gave Eva a telling look. She replied in like, and somehow Willsith felt miserable. They were worse than undisciplined. They had tricks, but could he really save them?

"Well done Arc," said White. "Well done Farl. Wish I'd known about your hacking when we were in section, I'd have asked you to help shift a few marks from my credit record," and he patted them both on the shoulder.

CHAPTER 16

Bullshit Express

Willsith sensed the firmness of the closed doors behind him and began to scan the scene in front with an automatic need for awareness. The others stood in front and indulged themselves in a mini celebration. Their response to the slightest dribble of adrenaline irked him. They'd barely made it through, and that was just one door. Who knew what was ahead? Not one of them has spotted the security gate. Neither Farl, Arc, or White has seen that group of people. They were sloppy, but she must have known.

Arc turned to him and whispered, "Willsith," and moved closer, "thanks for coming with us. Dalex wasn't worth it. He didn't do that to me, what he was doing to that other man…it wasn't like that. Grateful that you are escaping with us."

Willsith replied with a nod, and the lad turned back to the others. Staring off past the security gate, Willsith watched the distant group which congregated by some sort of window. Maybe he was just too old. Maybe Willsith didn't care one bit about escaping. Maybe it was time to do something for this next generation, and then leave. It was the least he could do, and he wouldn't let himself be sad about it. He was lucky to get the chance.

"Okay, so we know we can hack doors now," said White. "It's just down here, three more...and then—wait is that a security gate?"

Bingo.

"Yeah it's a gate. I bet we can hack it with the..."

Willsith stopped listening, he wanted his own conclusion.

What should he do, was there anything left for him, apart from saving these kids? Brute revenge wouldn't bring him back. His simple job in space had collapsed into something complex, and with that he'd lost his introspection time. By deduction he was left with Farl, Arc and White. And maybe Eva. An unexpected family of sorts. But they weren't his family. And it was Farl's fault they were in that jam...he had been a whistle-blowing hacker all along. *You've seen so much old fellow. If that Willsith from war times knew you'd end up chasing space, supporting revolutionaries. Following this girl...but what can I do? Nothing left now, just get them out. I can get them out and then we'll see, old man.* And he said, "There's a group up there, I count twelve of them. Does Lif know who they are?"

The four turned to him as if he spoke another language. Farl said, "We just said that, Willsith. Eva told us there's thirteen, and Lif can only count based on her sensor. They don't have sensors in their uniforms."

Farl's confidence was all or nothing. "So what do we do?" he said, and passed Eva the gun.

"The security gate will go off for sure with weapons," said Farl.

"And maybe even with us," said Arc. "If they found those two guards in our cell, then they might have alerts out for our DNA. Or even because of our arrest in the first place?"

"He's right," said Farl.

Eva agreed, then told them, "I should get through okay. I can distract the people. We must get around that corner to the right."

"We can hack the gate, there's a panel up ahead."

"Go," Willsith told Farl. Then he said to White, "You might have to butter up those acting skills for this one."

"Don't dare me Willsith, I'll go all hamlet on their arse."

Arc giggled, and Eva handed him the gun. She smiled at Arc, and then Willsith, and said to him, "Trust me soldier. I understand." Keeping her eye on him as she moved, Eva reached to her neck and lifted the thin strip of copper-coloured metal which hung there on a cord, twisted it, and then walked off toward the gate.

White lifted his nose, "Perfume," he said, "smells like roses." Willsith had noticed it, and it reminded him of Earth.

Arc handed the gun to White, who placed it in Willsith's free hand, and they moved slowly towards the panel.

"It's a perfumer," Arc told them, "that pendant Eva wears around her neck, it's a perfumer. A small device that energises scents at intervals, or based on her settings."

"I've never seen one of those before," White whispered.

"Might of smelled one and not known," Farl said. "They were popular a few years back."

White asked, "Is it darker in here? This area's different to the last. It feels like evening."

Farl met the console and slid a finger across the panel sensor. "Yeah, and it's quieter," said Farl. "Listen. You can't hear that group at all."

Willsith watched as Eva walked through the gate, the whole frame pulsing blue around her as she stepped over the metal.

"She's still got the device on," said White, "in here it lights up her—"

"Get to hacking," Willsith told Farl. "We can't set that thing off. I don't want to drop thirteen of them any time soon, and I don't know if White's acting can enchant all of them."

"Hey!" said White.

"Got a command screen, give me a few minutes and I'll see if I can get in."

Willsith squeezed the gun handles, lifted them to find their setting, and switched both to '5 - subdue'.

Arc said, "I think we can make it, Willsith."

Farl mumbled, and White said, "Course we'll make it Arc. Willsith's got twenty years on all of their guards. We've got a hacker on hand, and a smart young insider. And an AI. It's dream-team stuff."

"Just keep together," said Willsith. "If we need to, we go our own way. If things get hard or she gets out of hand—"

"It's just two corridors Willsith."

"She said blocks, not corridors, and we know nothing about what's in them."

"Almost there," said Farl, "got the control up."

"It makes me feel alive," said White, reaching down to try and touch his toes. "You know, we're getting free…Did you see the logo on that last door?"

Arc shook his head, Willsith checked the gun settings again.

"Drasil-G, but different. It had another symbol above

it."

"What was it?" asked Arc.

Willsith tested his muscles for stiffness, rotated his neck to both extremes, then mapped his vision along the hallway, through the security gate, and all the way to the group which Eva was about to meet.

"An arrow. There was an arrow with a line under it, in-line with the moon. I think it means Mars lifting. This area is to do with Tacern. She's taking us to a ship alright. A Mars-colony ship I'd bet."

No way around that security gate. If ever there was a trap, this was it. He couldn't make out if they had guns up there, maybe she had set this all up. Maybe they were intended as entertainment. And he squinted, tried to make out the faces. The group has accepted her, or at least they haven't reacted. Farl's device lit up the whites of her legs. No fast movement, no struggle. No obvious weapons.

White leaned against the wall, said, "Maybe when we're out of this, you can teach me to hack, Farl?"

"And me," said Arc.

"How much longer, Farl? She's at the group. She should have turned off that damned device."

"It might shield her if they have sensors, and we're in. I have control of the gate."

"My man Farl!" said White, lifting his hand for a high-five that didn't come.

"It looks like we are approaching the sky-port, and this gate is designed to filter non-Control, non-pilot personnel, as well as detect weapons, narcotics, and other banned substances."

"How can you tell?"

"There's a setting to sniff for each of those, and I've just turned them all off."

"Yeah boy!"

"Be quiet White, they might hear us."

"The sound's deadened, remember, big-guy."

"Stop calling me that. Farl, are you sure we can go through without issue. And these?" he showed the butts of the rifles.

"I've switched it into 'diplomat override' mode, it shows all sniffers as 'disabled', arms included."

"Good work," said Willsith, and checked again on Eva. "Looks like she's amongst the crowd. Maybe she knows them. Be ready for anything, this could be a trap."

"Ready how?" asked Farl.

"Farl, if I fire, you and Arc take off around that corner, White, you help me keep them in line with that mouth of yours. We remove all devices and we somehow secure them. Then—"

"It'll be fine. She's trustworthy."

"We can't know that for sure, Farl."

"Don't you remember her face?"

"No. Should I?"

"I think it's her anyway," said Farl, and White moved his face in closer. "She's the head of experimental science. She's high up in the Controller General's office. If she's dissenting, which she seems to want to, we couldn't be in better hands."

"It doesn't mean that. It means we could be in a worse trap. Or piss off CG more."

"Good. Screw him. I came up here to expose him— them, anyway - to leak what's really happening. She's our ticket to the data core, and our way out."

Willsith caught Arc's nervous twitch in his periphery, told Farl, "You better get your priorities straight. We need to get out, first, then we dump whatever info we can. But out first - agree?"

Farl turned from the panel, dropped his shoulders, and looked up at Willsith. "Agree," then screwed his face up and said, "but you have to trust me. There's good we can do here. We must do. For the cause. For Earth. I'll—I'll do what it takes when the time comes."

"Yes," said White, "for Earth."

"We move first. Then think of Earth. I'm going now, follow me."

He stepped away from them, grinding his lower jaw as he walked, finding the nook which gave least pain, and pushing the bone until it clicked into place. Checking the gun settings one last time, he caught the end of Farl's sentence about Eva, but ignored it, she was that green dot of light in the distance, and his eye followed her bright shine as it passed amongst the shapes of the group. He walked up to the gate, through it, and onward.

Several steps later he heard it. The weak undulating siren of the gate. As feeble as it was, he was sure they'd hear it. He'd set it off, and no matter how hard he faked a confident stride, he could not escape his feeling of exposure. The shock-rail-rifles textured grips grasped at his attention, and though he put one foot in front of the other, and though through his eyes he watched as Eva and the group became closer and closer, all he could think of was calculated violence.

"Yeah, they're undercover, hence the clothes," she said to the group, "but I'll introduce you."

At twenty paces he saw her sidestep and beckon him toward the clique.

He shelved the thought of attack, and stepped back down into the moment. It felt like a big group. A party of some kind. He looked down the hallway, their exit, but instinct drew him toward Eva, and the party. They had cups in hand and wore smiles on their pasty faces.

Most of the group were women. There must have been ten of them, and a few men. They mostly wore clothes like Eva, except for one lady and a man, who wore the stiff grey uniforms of guards. *Shit. Who invited guards to the party.* And again the handles of the guns screamed options at him.

"That's him!" she said, and pointed right at him.

It wasn't usual for Willsith to hear such a thing without subsequent gunfire. Still, he closed the gap, and joined the group. Wrenching himself well beyond the line of exposure, he dropped into a full bow, the material of his maintainer suit stretching tight across his back as his head dropped below his waist. For a second he stared at the floor, saw his own hands holding rifles, and almost laughed at the ridiculousness of the situation. Flicking himself back up, he decided otherwise. "Afternoon," he said, trying to mask his apprehension with loudness, then faked a smile.

"Hi," said a short woman, "I'm Sarah, nice to meet you."

They didn't react to his guns, the outfit, or the alarm. What kind of story had she told them? "Hello Sarah," he said, nodding his head, hoping that Eva would at least drop him a hook onto which he might hang his bullshit.

Two other girls introduced themselves and Willsith heard the alarm again, and again, and again. It was a pathetic sound.

Eva remained quiet, and he searched amongst the faces for hers. They did seem calm, and the majority were smiling. He caught another uniform that he didn't recognise, then a guard asked, "Did you really fly through the Trojans…looking for hydro-diamonds?"

Hyrdro-diamonds. How in Pluto's moons is this guard asking me about hydro-diamonds, and not shooting me on sight? But Willsith nodded, and scrambled for an answer, "Yes. Had to turn off aids to even get in, because—"

"Because it's not authorised," said another guard, drawing Willsith's focus. "The Trojans are not authorised for entry, or mining."

"Yes, of course," said Willsith, and eased a little as he felt his team file in beside him. "But we were sent, of course, into the Trojans, to retrieve those Hydro-diamonds, regardless." He could at least help the others; Willsith had never been great at lying. Then he remembered the guns and tried not to move his arms.

"These are my Pilot Grand-Marshalls," she projected to the crowd. "Legends. But I didn't tell you that, alright." Eva held her index finger in front of her lips.

She was a very convincing liar.

Several of the women shuffled in closer, their placid faces told Willsith they were under Eva's spell. A courteous smile, then a look at his crew. Willsith caught White sucking in his belly, and then the ladies started with their questions.

"What is it like to fly for the MI?", "Where have you just come from? Can you tell us?", "What's the fastest you've been?", "Whats it like on your ship?"

The questions told him more than he knew.

White tried giving cryptic answers, lapping up the female attention, and Eva manoeuvred herself toward the exit.

It wasn't a trap, but it could still go wrong. Then he spotted it; a subtle difference between her and the others. Eva's uniform was not the same, it was cut differently. And he noticed in the dim light of the hall that her skin was not bleached white like the others, and then he smelled the rich organic bloom of her perfume as it cut

152

through the raspy old sweat of 229.

A gruff voice broke through, the male guard, he said, "What ship was she?"

They all froze, and Willsith replied, "Excuse me?"

"What did you fly? What did you take into the Trojans?"

Here we go. This was the test. Willsith knew less than nothing about spaceships. This guy could wreck it all.

"It's just that I understand that no current flight systems will even allow you to enter the Trojans, regardless of flight-aid status."

And he stared at the man, stared as hard as he could, and when the guards bearded face did not relent, the pressure teased a mixture of anxiety and destructiveness from him. *Shit. I don't know, how would I know? Do I shoot him, or make something up based on broadcast fodder?*

"Did you really do it?" the man persisted.

It was amazing that they weren't even being slightly shot at, so from there on it was all chance. Willsith tried to distract the man, asked him, "Can you get me a drink?"

"Sure, but did you do it?" the man said, and the crowd's quietness itched at Willsith.

"We can't tell you anything about the ship," said White, in a tone Willsith had never heard. "That's why he wants a drink - he finds the confidentiality hard. He'd love to tell you about her, because she's awesome agile, but we can't. Classified. What's your name, man?"

That old salty chef pulled it out of the bag.

"Phil, Phil Fry."

"Nice to meet you Phil. How's duty treating you?"

Perhaps that's how White had become the team comradeship officer for Section 229.

White fed Phil nonsense, bringing the guards on side and tickling the interest of the others. Willsith turned away, stared longingly at a piece of glass, a window, which looked out over a larger room. A hangar, he presumed, or an exit, minus a few rifle rounds. A few women brokered dry conversation from him, but he couldn't focus, and through it all the smell of Earth flowers possessed him. Eva stood with Farl and Arc, saying things he couldn't distinguish.

"We should be going," he said, across the group. "Miss Harding?"

And then he spotted the twists of heads, the closing of mouths, and knew that her name meant something to them. Or that he'd been especially rude.

"Yes, right. Sorry team, we're on orders," she said, lifting herself to project over the group.

The female guard pushed through them and stuck out an arm, gesturing a cup toward Willsith, who peered into it, aware that he held a rifle in each hand. It looked like whiskey. What a shame.

"Thanks, but actually, we've got to go, and I'm on launch."

He caught the tail-end of White and Phil's conversation, heard White say, "Yeah we've got stories like you've never heard. But we'd have to shoot you if we told you."

Too close to reality. Far too close. White continued, "But now we've got to drop to Earth, it's time to deliver our cargo…for the scientists."

He was going to take it too far.

White continued, at volume, "They think it might help with the regeneration. You must excuse us, ladies," he bowed, "Phil."

Willsith only looked at Eva now, across the line of his

154

team. White's bald head flicked back up, and Willsith told them, "Yeah, we're late already." White lifted an imaginary top hat, and Willsith clutched the rifles. The bullshit train needed to leave the damn station. "We'll be back in a week before we jump again."

"We'll throw you a party! We'll do it! This is just a little get together, but it's rare we get to host Grand-Marshalls," said a blond-haired lady. "Will you come?"

Willsith looked at White, who was already nodding and waggling about his face in every way you could imagine.

"Let's go," said Eva, "I'll connect you when they're back, council."

"Thank you Commander," said the woman.

Eva smiled at her, then in a precise way, said, "Now, we shall let you get back to your celebration, please forget you ever saw us here," and then she drew a straight line over her mouth with her finger, forming her lips behind the knuckle.

Willsith moved toward the hallway, heard the cook shout, "Good day." It sounded sincere, but then a few hours ago he'd been frying stir-fry in a wok made out of hull-metal fragments.

The others were behind him, he could tell, and for a few strides Willsith felt a relief.

"One minute," said a voice from behind.

He walked on.

"Excuse me," said the voice, and he heard someone trot up behind them.

Spinning round, testing the grips of his guns, Willsith said, "What's up," tensed his brow, then, "we've got to jump." The others had stopped dead in their tracks and gave him mixed looks.

"Good luck and safe passage," the woman said, and

Willsith saw that she wore the fitted uniform of a pilot. "You know, I am a pilot too. I'm top of this years Elite-wing, I'm here pre-tour."

Willsith cursed her. If she asked a technical question, Willsith was gummed. If she squealed, there'd be no choice but to drop her. Maybe he could take her around the corner, then drop her. Now that was an idea. Then Willsith realised he hadn't responded, and nodded.

Whinging sounded from the gate. Two more guards moved through and started towards them.

Here we go. Here comes the trap.

The two approached, the pilot kept focus on Willsith.

Willsith looked to the rifles for reassurance, remembered the setting, turned to face the guards, and was ready.

"Hey guys," said one of them, in a morose voice, then waved a weak wave at the party.

A drip of fresh sweat ran down his back, then Willsith threw himself into the situation. "Thanks pilot, what's your name? We are always on the lookout for exceptional pilots, in our—in what we do. We recruit from Elites, in special cases." And as the womans face relaxed Willsith knew that he had not failed.

The two guards approached the crowd, shook hands and were enveloped out of Willsith's awareness.

"Harjing, Raker T. Harjing. What—department are you from?"

"I can't tell you that I am afraid. We will check your record, you may hear from us," he said. A wink, he decided, that'll help. "That's if you're any good. Safe travels."

The pilot stood quiet.

Willsith ran scenarios through his head, most didn't end well for Harjing.

White turned, pasted on another layer of bullshit, "We have to go Commander. Two hours late we are, for the Grand Board for Charon's sake!"

"Another time, Harjing," Willsith said, gesturing a salute with the business end of a rifle.

The pilot fumbled for words as Willsith jogged off, "Safe flight…Pilot Grand Marshall."

They made it around the corner and out of sight.

Willsith huffed out air as he reached the end of the short length of hall which was capped with a door, emblazoned with the symbol. It was the Drasil-G, stylised, and right above the moon was a triangle. To Willsith it looked as though it may be a ship, as much as an arrow. Was that where this door led? To Mars?

"That was close," said Arc.

Farl knelt down by the panel, said, "Wish there was more corridor before this door, if any of them come round while I'm hacking, we're fried."

"Don't worry," he said, and positioned himself with his back to the corner. "I'll deal with them, just get this thing open."

"Really close," Arc added.

"Close? Didn't you see their faces," said White. "They were captivated." And turning to Eva, "What did you tell 'em? Fair play, you set them right up for us."

"I told them you were off-record pilots," she said.

White shook her hand, bowed a mock-bow, and said, "Oh, and you're a Commander?"

Willsith tried to listen around the corner, but he couldn't make out even a hint of party chatter. The dead sound of the area, and the dull lighting gave nothing away.

"It's not working like the other door," said Farl, "I don't know if—"

157

"Yeah, that's another thing, I thought you had the gate sorted? Diplomat mode?" Willsith said. "We almost didn't make it through there, and it even sounded for the guards?"

"I don't know," he replied, and continued to swipe at the panel.

"You don't know? That's not good enough, Farl. We need to be able to get through undetected or we're horse meat."

Eva placed a hand on Arc's shoulder, said, "Lif, can you open this door?," then, "Okay…Lif can't get to this area, she can access some controls, but not without alarming security. There's a special lock."

"What can she do?" Willsith jeered.

"Special lock?" asked White. "Perhaps you can explain, Commander?"

"Farl, the door?" pushed Willsith.

Farl slid his finger down the edge of the panel, "I—I—don't think I can open it."

"We must get it open," said Eva. "Because one of those councils had her sensor on, and the guards too. We might be—"

"Cool it you two, we'll get through. We should be glad they didn't blow our faces off back there," said White. "Farl will do it."

"I'm sorry, I don't think I can."

CHAPTER 17

His Orders

As they squabbled, the doors opened, and Farl looked at Willsith, as blank as the hall beyond, and said, "It wasn't me."

"Who then?" he replied.

"I don't know."

"Was it Leef?" asked White.

"No," said Eva. "And it's Lif."

Willsith turned, addressed Eva, Arc, and White. "It's open, and we're going through it. But keep aware." And he saw Arc's troubled face in the glow of Farl's device, shining green from Eva's backplate, and said, "Stay behind me, Arc."

"Maybe it's just automatic," said White, as they stepped through. "Not everything is out to get us."

That wasn't the voice of the usual White. Willsith signalled for them to keep back, and instantly Farl scrunched up his face. What was he supposed to do then, if not lead them? What was he in all this if he couldn't get them out? Truth was, Farl didn't want out. He wanted the fame of leaking the Earth's Halo data. Willsith still didn't really believe they'd get either.

The new corridor was bright white, and he strode

around the first corner with the weight of the others distracting him from his patterns of war, face first into the barrel of a gun.

"Shit," he said. "Run!" But his own warning came to late. He had to act.

Instinct kicked in, his right hand batted down the rifle. A swing, a duck, a thrust, and a guard flew off towards the wall. The mans armour scraped down patterned white, then caught the handrail, and flipped him. His face hit the floor squarely with a crack.

Willsith swiped after the next soldier but missed, falling to the rail himself.

The sound of charging rifles stopped him.

"Stop," they shouted, then one said. "We'll wipe you out. Stop."

So he stopped. Willsith raised his hands, dropping the other rifle. He turned to his surrounded comrades. He had nothing more for them.

"Move," a soldier shouted, and Willsith stood, watching body language.

"You're elite, not everyday guards."

"That's inconsequential. Move," said another. "And you four, move."

And they frogmarched them forward, one leading, two following, the forth man left face-down on the mat.

This was probably it. *These are the sorts of characters who take you to the edge of town and come back without you.*

"Wish I had my drones," whispered Eva.

"Quiet Miss."

"Sorry 229," said Willsith. "I should have—"

"Shut it," said the man in front, his rifle pointed at Willsith's chest.

The soldier kept ahead enough to be out of his range.

They were solid officers. There was no way Willsith could spin him without risking the others. *I knew it had been too easy. And Farl didn't even know from that panel. And nor did her AI! What good is the tech. No good, no good at all.* And he rubbed the last bit of dried blood from his knuckles, squeezed his hands tight into fists. *No good.*

"That's the door to the Stellar Ark," said Eva, and Willsith knew which door she meant. It was wide, tall, and had a deep inset frame of copper-coloured metal.

"Please be quiet, Miss."

"Commander to you," she said. "That door, that's where I think you'd all like to go 229."

As they passed it Willsith saw that the door split down the middle, both panels another form of the Drasil-G logo. This one had no upward arrow, but it had a second ring around Earth. "A second halo," he said, and the guard in front charged his rifle.

"Shut up or I'll shut you up."

He wouldn't. Willsith was far too heavy to lump all the way to wherever they were going.

"I can fire a silencing round that'll force your windpipe shut, so stop thinking it," the man said.

Experienced.

"Where are you taking us?" Eva asked in harsh tone, and Willsith again smelled the lush nature of her perfume, and thought that she might be trying hard to escape.

"To him," replied the front soldier. "So save your talking."

"I don't want to see him. I won't see him! Take me to my quarters. Take these back to their cell. We don't need to see him."

"I'm sorry miss. Orders."

"Sorry Willsith," she said.

"Looks like it's slavery lads," said White.

Willsith laughed, but the echoes of the joke were bitter.

"Last warning!" shouted one of the masked soldiers.

CHAPTER 18

Dropped

The lift opened and one guard paced out backwards. Willsith spat blood on the white floor and the guard barked at him, "No more of that, or you'll get a bruise to match."

"You're just worried because I almost had you," said Willsith, smiling around the ache of his cheekbone.

"Where are we meeting him?" Eva said. "And do not hit him again."

"He asked for it, Miss," said the Guard in front. "And you'll see soon enough."

A guard behind shouted, "Two two."

"Yeah, I noticed, let's double-time," replied the front guard. Then he said, "You all need to jog now, or we'll shoot you down and use the body shunts."

Body shunts. Willsith wondered if there was even such a thing. Not worth testing. And he started to run.

"We'll be overtaking Raku soon," said White.

"Silence," shouted the guard.

Willsith kept his running tight and his good eye on the one in front. *So we get to see the man himself, and he's sent these. Serious soldiers. Just wait for your chance, old man. Just wait.*

And as they ran no one spoke, until he came into sight.

"Yeah," said a soldier.

They had internal comms. Must have been rigged into their helmets, or put under their skin by their ear. Ops level tech. But Willsith's attention was stolen as Dalex appeared, standing with his hands behind his back, up ahead.

"Dalicks," said White. "What does that scoundrel want?"

"Shut up!"

They slowed to meet him, the front soldier turning to salute, "Sir."

"What are you doing here?" said Dalex, moving only his lips.

"We're taking these to CG. Top-line orders."

"Good, carry on," he said, stepping to the side.

"Roger that sir," said the front soldier, and moved passed him, maintaining rifle sight on Willsith.

Willsith was an arms length from Dalex. He wanted to move, but if he did, they'd drop him, no questions. He'd get one strike in, like before, and he could make that count. But they'd drop him, this time probably for good. Fruitless. No. Play it cool, Dalex popped up far too much for Willsith not to get another chance. And so he walked passed Dalex, glaring madly.

Then Dalex's sharp voice sounded, "Oh, and sergeant...good bye."

Willsith swung around and caught the shot. Eva shrieked. One soldier had turned to the other and fired point-blank into the side of his head. His body dropped. Limbs strung together by the patterns of his armour.

The front guard pushed Willsith, and got a shove back. He tripped, but saved himself before hitting the floor. Standing back up he raised the chin of his armoured headgear to Willsith, then moved next to Dalex and the shooter.

"Hello again 229. Eva," said Dalex. "I'm glad you made it."

"Why did you kill him?" Eva shouted at the man. "What is this?"

"Calm now. Did you think I wasn't aware of your plan."

"What is this Dalex? What is your game?" shouted Willsith, moving in front of the others.

"Willsith, my man. I'm sorry for the subterfuge, and I'm sorry Arc, for your treatment."

Willsith strode toward him, stepping up to the dead soldier's body. The two soldiers saluted him, didn't bother raising arms.

"Allow me to explain, and I apologise for the brevity, as you will soon discover, time is of the essence at this juncture."

"What, the hell, are you talking about," Willsith shouted. "Give me one reason I shouldn't throttle you now."

"I've saved you. I've helped you get this far. And now I've saved you from him. I've saved you because I need you. I need you Willsith Harper, and all the rest of you. The world needs you. We must overthrow her father. We must overthrow him very very soon."

"You just shot your own man dead. You tortured Arc. And then you want us to help you?"

Dalex looked down at the soldiers corpse, said, "Every coup has victims. He was not aligned with Earth. I act only where it's unavoidable. Arc, I am sorry, I tried to make it as painless as possible, but I have to keep up appearances for now."

"Appearances? Dalicks, you *appear* to be a crook,"

shouted White.

"Ah, Charles. I never expected you to be so...lively. Still, I can't stay and chat. 229, right now you need to trust that I've helped you get here for the right reasons."

"We won't follow you," said Willsith, closing the gap between them. "We've no reason to. All we've seen is you shoot this guy, torture others."

"I understand. But your only other option is death. The window of time we have here is tiny, later we may have more, but I must be gone within the minute."

The corpse by Willsith's feet twitched, and Willsith did not want to listen. The gunman had dropped his own so fast, it made sense that they'd drop any of them as quick.

Dalex continued, "We have until 06:00 to remove her father from his position as Controller General. He plans to overthrow the world's union. He wants to enslave Earth, and, unless obstructed, he will achieve this at 06:00."

"You expect us to believe this tripe?" said Willsith.

"You are here only because I do expect you to. 229, amongst you, you know enough to understand. You have the pieces."

Eva grasped her elbows, asked Dalex, "What...are you going to do to him?"

"I do not mean to kill your father," he told her, noticeably quieter. "Only to do what is necessary to protect Earth."

"And this is all for the good of Earth is it? This man on the floor? Taking out the man at the top. Nothing in it for you?"

Dalex smiled. "I am not a purist rebel, you are as observant as I expected. I will take her fathers place as Controller General."

"And what's to stop you doing the same as he intends?"

"I am not him. I have simpler flaws. Now I must go."

"Dalicks," White spat out the name. "We don't trust you. What's to stop you mimicking the old—"

"I will not. I am not as corruptible as him. Ask her, she knows, he has lost his way. He dwells in the darkest places. I'm merely grey by comparison."

"And you just expect us to follow you based on that?"

"Not at all, I expect you to think on it. Maybe even carry on trying to escape. But think fast, as there's not much time. Eva can take you to the security equipment room, storage 212; the door-code is Frecus Kevlar Axiom Hayward Zero Five Treaty. Wait there for my word. Together we can stop him."

White burst out laughing, "Oh Dalicks, you're absolutely bonkers, mate."

"I am not. This is the only way we can save the Earth. I trust you 229. I've watched you. So has she. This is not the conventional way - but these are not conventional times." Dalex relaxed his face, and on it Willsith saw a human smile. One soldier pulled out a small metal plate, attached it to the back of the dead man's armour, and then they left, Dalex, the two soldiers and the corpse which floated after them, gloves trailing along the floor.

"Why didn't you jump them?" White asked Willsith. "Knock them all out?"

"I don't know White. At first there wasn't a chance I'd have managed it, but then—what if he's telling the truth?"

"Dalicks, legit?" said White.

"He's a scumbag," said Eva. "But he might be right about some of it."

Then Willsith said to Eva, "Can we talk here? Where

are we?"

"We're in administration. Lif says that she's been given more access. Maybe by Dalex. This place is being masked from the core feeds, but not by her. No one is coming for us, yet."

Farl spoke up, "I think we should follow him…at least to see."

"He's a nut-job," said White. "He beats on Arc then tells us it was necessary. He just shot a man!"

"He didn't shoot him," Farl replied.

"His henchman did, same thing!" White said.

"Eva, you're the only one that knows. What's going on?"

"I just want to escape, Willsith. I don't trust him…Dalex, I've never liked him."

"But 06:00? What he said about your father? Wait. You're the Controller General's daughter?"

"Yes." She scrunched up her lips, "I am. I know something is happening at 06:00. I know he's planning on shipping some people out. I don't know if it's more than that."

"CG's daughter. Well I never," said White. "Can we even trust you?"

"We can trust Eva," said Farl.

Arc stepped forward, asked, "Willsith, what do we do?"

"I don't know Arc."

"We follow him. For Earth's sake," said Farl.

"We know so little," Willsith said, looking both ways. He turned to Eva, said, "You know the most. What is he to you? Dalex? Is your dad capable of what he said? Why has Dalex chosen us?"

White interjected, "Maybe he's done this to loads of Sections, making an army out of maintainers?"

"White, let her tell us!"

Eva frowned, then told them, "Dalex is the head of security, he's my dad's right hand. He's always tried to…get to me."

"And your dad?"

"What Dalex said is right. My father is gone, the man that's left is evil. That's kind of why I'm here, with you. Underneath he might still be a good man…he used to be, but he's been doing bad things," and she squatted down, held her face in her hands. "It might be true. He might be doing that. I don't know it all."

Farl moved to Willsith, said, "We have no choice Willsith. It's our chance to do right. We can stop him."

"Can we? Dalex maybe helped us here, but he's a tool, you can tell. Eva here just wants out. We're not even sure where it's safe to talk, where to run to. And what if Dalex is gas? We don't even know what time it is!"

"I do know some things, too, but not enough." Farl held the strip of metal around his neck, looked up at him, and said, "Willsith, I came up here to get the core. To leak it. But this is even better. We can remove the corruption at the source. We can take him out before he takes control."

"Take him out? Stop it at the source? Do you even know what you're messing with Farl? This isn't a game. These guns aren't 3D models. You're not a killer, and I don't want to be one any more. I won't shoot her dad to make you famous. We're space maintainers, and we're just flies in their sodding web."

"Willsith. Can we not just go?" asked Arc.

"Go? Arc, this is our chance. All that crap your family suffers is because of these people. We can change it," said Farl, speaking right into the face of the lad. "We can change it."

"Eva," Willsith said. "Where is the security room Dalex mentioned?"

"It's back that way, down in the lift."

"Good," said Farl. "We should get going."

"I'm not following that crook," said White.

"Maybe we just have him wrong, White," said Farl.

Willsith shook his head. "No, we get out of here."

"What?" said Farl.

"We leave. There's too many unknowns. This isn't our fight. We get out, and then we leak the information, we let the world deal with it. We're going back to that elevator either way, you can decide after that. So we should get—"

"Let the world deal with it?" started Farl, pushing right in front of Willsith. "Let the world deal with it? What if the world can't Willsith? What if Dalex is right, and her twisted dad is going to enslave it. He could do it, with the power resonators. Think about it. He could do it and we could be the only ones who can stop him! We're right here!"

"Farl, look at us. We're four under-equipped, under-trained maintainers. We don't even know where the hell 'here' is. This is not our fight."

Farl snarled, cursed at Willsith and turned to the others.

"Sorry Farl," said Arc.

"Look lad," said White, "you can't win them all. Let's get the core and—"

"Don't call me lad," said Farl.

"Either way Farl, you're running with us until that lift."

"You—you've known me for five years and you'd drop me, like that?"

"This isn't our fight. What you've been doing is your

170

own—"

"What I've been doing? I've been trying to help people, Willsith. To expose this crap. What have you been doing Willsith? These past five years?"

"Farl. I appreciate that. We're a team still. We can expose them, but after we escape."

Farl's fists were sealed shut, his frown and jaw tugged toward each other, and his words came out sharp, "That's not enough! We have a chance."

"That's your choice, Farl," said Willsith, and placed a hand over his shoulder. "For now, let's run. Let's get to that lift. And let's think."

Farl snapped his eyes away from Willsith and tore off.

"He'll come around, big-guy," said White, and left after Farl.

"Stop calling me that would you?" he shouted after him, then smiled at Arc. "Let's go Arc, stick with me." And lastly he turned to Eva, who held plans in her eyes, and he asked her to come with them.

CHAPTER 19

Oxymoron

Farl beat ahead, reached the lift, and tapped at the console. Willsith watched, and thought of their futures. What will come to pass for 229, for Eva, for him? Farl was young, tenacious, but also dumb with his intelligence. He didn't know what he was getting himself into. But then, who was Willsith to stop him?

As they reached Farl, he turned, and asked, "Eva, which way to the security storage 212?"

He's made his choice, then.

"It's back past the Stellar Ark door."

"How do you work this lift?" Farl asked her.

"We're going the same way, just let her do it," said Willsith.

"Farl, come on, let's just stick together," said White. "Like a 229 mission. Get the core data, and get the hell out of dodge. I can't wait to pilot a ship!"

They all stepped into the elevator, Eva last, and said, "Lif, can you—thanks."

As the lift moved the five inside didn't. Each quietly tended to their own thoughts until the doors swiped open again.

Farl burst out, "I don't see why we can't just go at it

together. It's no different than this whole thing so far. It's all a farce. We follow him, see what good we can do."

He needed them, and he'd realised it.

"We're escaping Farl. We can't go busting in when we know nothing."

"Willsith. You, more than anyone, can do this, and you should see why! You've been day-tripping in space for the past five years, you know Earth is wrecked as it is; imagine CG raining down misery on top of all that. He's the ultimate crook. And don't you wonder why Dalex picked us? It's for our skills: no one leaves the army with as many stripes as you, and I'm probably the best hacker up here."

Willsith breathed out. *Is this his obsession with attacking authority? Does Farl see toppling CG as some supreme social hack?*

"229 was flagged by Lif," said Eva, "I guess his system flagged you too."

Then she left the lift and ran. Willsith and the others followed, and he shouted as they jogged, "Farl, I understand. But I don't do it anymore. I'm done fighting other people's fights."

"This is our fight. If Dalex picked us—"

"Dalicks is a dick," said White, wheezing out the words, then spluttering into a cough.

"If he picked us then maybe we can change—"

Willsith let Farl jog alongside him, and though he stared at Eva, he addressed Farl, "I've been there. Whatever good you want to do—people like Dalex aren't the way. How do you know he's not just after power? How do you know you aren't, yourself?"

"Me? I'm here to leak the core—for Terra."

"Then come with us, I'll help you leak the data. But going with Dalex, that's something else."

"Guys," White blurted out. "Guys. Can, we, stop—" he punctuated his words with gasps, "—can we stop for a minute."

"Eva," shouted Willsith. "We're pausing."

Her hair bounced as she turned to nod at him, stopped and leaned against the wall. He squatted on his hams, and saw 229 copy him. White began recycling the hallway air in earnest.

"Willsith I know Dalex is legit. He was the one who kept catching me hacking. He didn't pull the plug on me, he let me have some access."

"That doesn't prove anything. He also arrested us, killed his own man, and beat on Arc."

"Maybe he got us arrested on purpose," said Farl.

"And the man? And Arc?"

White coughed loudly.

"Casualties—"

Willsith bit at him, shouted loud, "Do not stand here and talk to me about casualties. I've been through decades of fighting. I've seen more casualties than you've had meals. This is a shit game they're playing. Choosing who lives and dies, that's not progress, that's not—"

"This isn't the war-fields Willsith. They're doing something with the world's power. Lives are relative."

"Lives are relative? Lives are relative? Do you kn—"

"Stop fighting!," yelled Arc, breaking White from his hyper-ventilation.

Willsith dropped his shoulders, looked hard into Farl's face, tried to show him support, guidance. The young man held his nostrils flared, air fled out of them as his chest heaved.

"Stop it! That's the whole stupid point," said Arc, his voice cracking with tension. "This is the whole point. Fighting. We didn't come up here to fight. We were in

174

229 for five years…Farl, don't you think Dalex could be bad? He could kill you like that other man. You've hacked from 229, why not hack from a ship? Why is it not enough? Willsith, we can stop somewhere and let him download the core can't we? We can leak it from the ship."

Willsith watched Farl's throat as he gulped, the line of his neck-muscle betraying his inner-panic.

"Arc," Farl said. "It's complex."

"I'm okay, we can move again," said White, "wherever the-dickens we're going."

"I'm getting free," said Willsith. "Let's go," and he turned from Farl and ran, cocking his neck to shout back at them as they followed, "I'm leaving this sodding ring, and if you want freedom, so should you. Sometimes it's enough to just stick to your plan."

"Freedom, Willsith," shouted Farl, "freedom for how long?"

CHAPTER 20
Bloody Corridors

He let his boots settle into a rhythm as he ran in-line with Eva, tooling himself entirely on the hard lines of their exit. The thick-framed door of the sky-port beamed out at him. Then the walls started flashing red.

"Stop! Willsith, 229, for the good of Earth stop. I need your help. Return to the security area, I cannot help you any other way. Stop!" Dalex's voice boomed around them as the walls lost their colour, and then painted themselves red again. "We must work together."

"This guy does not quit," said Willsith.

"Security is not this way?," shouted Farl. "Eva, you lied! What the hell?"

She slowed and turned, projected her words, "I'm sorry Farl. But it's not far back there, it was just a small lie. I wanted you to come with—"

"It doesn't matter anymore," said Willsith. "We're almost out. Farl, come."

"Stop 229. Farl. Eva." Dalex's voice rang from the red walls. "The probability of success without you is tiny. CG will bleed Earth dry. I need you to help. Eva knows, and Farl you're key, just like all of you are."

Arc turned to Farl, told him, "The door is right there,

176

let's get through it, these alarm walls are freaking me out."

"Dalex, it's obvious you can't stop us, just let it go. Turn off the red - we'll help from the ship," shouted White. "We'll help Earth, that is," and then he dropped his head back and cackled.

"White, Willsith, Arc, please come with me. We can do good here," said Farl, turning his clenched fists to show them his wrists. "Much more than just maintaining."

"We move out," said Willsith. "Can we get the core from the ship, or do we need to do that before?"

"Drones," shouted Eva, "Lif says there are drones inbound, from back behind us."

"Drones?"

"Yeah, security drones. Lif can't stop them, and without my drone-pack, I can't do anything either. They'll disable us with jabs or…"

Willsith couldn't make out any movement, just repetitive flashing red. "Let's just get through that door. Come on."

"This red is—," started Arc.

"Let's go," said Willsith, and then came the whining of the drones.

"Here they come," said White, "look!"

"Get to that bleeding door!" shouted Willsith.

"229, you must help me. There is no other way."

Eva shrieked, slammed her palms on the door, shouted at the ceiling, "Damn you."

"What's the problem?" said Willsith. "We need to get in there. Now."

"It's sealed. It's not even Dalex's command code."

"No time, they're here," said White. "Ugly bastards, look at them!"

And there they floated, eight silver drones making up a perfect pattern across the hallway. Boat-shaped reflective bodies which hung in the air, pulsing red and white as the hallway light caught their sharp sides. Each had four blades, built into in a top wing. They whined like a sea of bees. And they projected more of Dalex's words: "Turn around and help, you deserters. Earth needs you, can't you see it?"

Farl lifted his face, "We will. Just show them, somehow."

Willsith walked between the others, putting himself in front of Arc, and said, "Dalex, if you can do all this dramatic crap, glow the halls and send these puny mech's, why do you need us? It's theatrics. We've been all over these bloody corridors," and reaching out towards a drone, threw a hand at it, finding only air in its wake. "We're not going to be convinced by these things. Turn off the lights and open the door. We'll help you from space."

The drone returned to its place in the formation, and Dalex's voice spoke from it: "Willsith, I need you because of your combat skills. We need Farl for his dark-hands. Arc we need your tooling, and White, you've got to help them understand it all."

"There's plenty of sections like ours, go find another," said Willsith.

White shouted agreement.

"There's not," said Eva. "And I don't know if I can help anymore."

"Willsith, let's go. Can't we hack the door?" Arc moved to his side.

The drones opened slots on their sides, and from them Willsith heard a charging sound.

"What do you mean can't help?" he asked her.

"Lif can't get this open, these drones can stun us, I—I can't do anything. I'm sorry. If I had my drones—if we'd have waited instead of leaving your cell I could have—"

"No matter now," he said, "all of you, the door." Then he turned to the drones and said, "Dalex, let me get them into the ship, then I'll help you. We're no good to you in a heap on the floor here, are we?"

The drones spoke in unison, and the voice of Dalex rang loud, "I'm sorry Willsith. I haven't got time to make deals. The only way to stop him is for us to take him out. My AI has calculated it will take all of 229 and my group, working together, to do it."

Willsith felt air whoosh passed his neck, and turned to see a glass wall seal the corridor between 229, and Eva and the door to the Stellar Ark.

"Dalex!" he shouted, and ran to it, flinging his bodyweight through his arm and toward the glass, stopping at the last second to save his knuckles. "Dalex, what the hell."

"I'm sorry Willsith. She's not important."

Willsith thrust breath out of his nose, dulling an area of the glass. His eyes bore through it, and into Eva's face. She stood the other side, her lips quivering, her face making tiny movements.

"I'm sorry Willsith, but you must help me. There is no other way."

"There's always another way," said Willsith. "It's men like you, saying things like that - that's what made me leave Earth." Willsith saw Eva's lips moving, but he couldn't hear her. He shouted at the glass, "Escape! Get yourself out." But she shook her head, pointed at her ears.

"We're bricked," said White. "Totally dry-walled."

Willsith snapped his hand back and forth, gestured

toward the door behind her, but Eva shook her head, then spun around. He saw a wall of drones, like that behind him, close in on her.

"Dalex, stop this," he shouted. "Stop this now."

"Listen Willsith," Farl said, approaching him.

"Farl, you see how he gives us no choice?" he replied, watching as Eva held up one hand to her ear, and the other out toward the drones.

"Listen, you're chasing your tail," said Farl, "there's no denying it, we have to—"

"Stop Farl." And he watched Eva back toward the glass, saw the shake in her arms, and wanted to tear a hole through it all. "Stop Farl," he said again, and turned to him, "Dalex—the Controller General, these men you don't see, they don't have good plans. They don't have consciences. They don't act for the people. They don't care. They use you like pawns, or knights, at best. To them you're a disposable tool, fodder. This is not for you, this fight. To help him will not help you, or Earth."

White said, "Willsith, they're pushing us in."

The wall of drones had moved forward, and White had adopted stance, his shoulder to the drone-wall. "Dalex, piss off!" the chubby cook shouted.

"Farl, why would he force us?" Willsith said, and turned to see the drone-walls closing in on both sides, pushing Eva toward the glass, and Arc toward him. "Why would this shit happen, if he was doing good?"

"Willsith, it's not about you, or us. There's a bigger picture. Whatever Dalex does, I need to see that picture. I can't help anyone by running away. I can't help from Earth. We must help him, because he knows more...for now."

Arc said, "Willsith!"

"Farl, come with us."

"No Willsith, come with me. Make right for the wars."

"I can't make those things I did right. There is no way to—"

"You can fight to save billions, here. Maybe everyone on Terra."

"You want to see me fight?"

"Yes."

Willsith eyeballed Farl, said, "I'll fight," and walked toward the drones.

"Fuck it," shouted White, and careered himself into a drone, missing it, but landing on another, slamming his elbow into the wing on its top. He screamed. A blade cut into his flesh, Willsith saw the splatter fly up the wall. Then the thing cracked under his weight and his howl faded into beast-like laughter.

Willsith swung at one, which dodged his fist, then kicked at another but only found air. From the side a drone shot into him, smacking him in the ribs. It felt like a cricket ball hit him, and through the pain he grabbed at the thing. He fought the propulsion of its blades, thrusting all of his weight onto it, forcing it to the floor and struggling to keep it there. Its propellers sucked at the air around him. Willsith tried to stand on it, to show it the heel of his boot, but it lunged free. "I'll fight to get you all out. That's the only time you'll see me fight." And the drone swung back at him, and he was hit by another, and another, and managed to snatch a third, swinging it against the wall. "I'll fight for people close to me."

"Die you bastards!" shouted White, before one hit him in the belly and he fell face first on it. "That hurt. How do we stop these things?"

"Here, use this," Arc threw Willsith a screwdriver.

"How?"

"I don't know!"

Willsith slid to White, stabbed at the edges of the drone. Nothing. Then he thrust the screwdriver into one propeller: bingo. He rammed it into another, shielding his eyes from the fragments of blade as they shot out. White took another drone hit to the backs of the knee and rolled off of the injured drone, which limped off down the corridor in spurts.

"That did it," said Willsith, and though the drones swarmed him, and he took hit after hit, the pain felt good now that he had a way to stop them. When he caught one he cycled through its blades, smashing them; taking strikes all the while. Drone after drone they fell, broken and whirring.

The final drone rushed at his face, making a charging sound. Enlivened by the fight he ducked and swiped it from below, swinging it like an axe straight to the floor. He wrestled it on the rubber, ripping himself back as he saw White hop into the air. All the weight of the cook did nothing to hinder it though, and Willsith said, "Thanks White, but could you," and he dropped the screwdriver to the side. White jammed the blades while it wiggled in Willsith's grip, until finally the rotors spun without torque, and the thing shut down. Both men stood up, surveying the array of carcasses. "There's your fight, Farl," said Willsith.

One of the broken drones fizzed and spluttered, and flipped itself over trying to get exit the scene, flapping upside down against the floor like a landed fish. "We'll help you from space Dalex," he shouted, and paced after it, kicking the thing with the fullness of his boot. "Now dispense with these dramatics and open that door."

As 229 stood, red glow reflected up onto their faces

from the dead drones. Arc frowned. White grinned. Farl showed teeth. Their faces were warped by the light, and Eva was gone.

"Where's Eva?" he asked. "What happened?"

Farl swung around, then the others. Willsith moved to the glass. "She's not there."

"And the drones her side are moving away," said White. "Where did she go? Did we scare them off? Did she get through?"

"Did you see?" Willsith asked Farl. "What happened?"

"I was watching you…fight."

"Damn it man. You see. We know nothing. Now we've lost her. We are fighting in the dark."

"All we can do is find the light, then," replied Farl.

"Can we get through the glass, is there any way? Farl? Arc?"

White picked up a drone, carried it to them, "Can we use these?"

Arc poked around the drone, flipped open the slot. "Not quickly."

"Dalex, what have you done? Where is she?" shouted Willsith.

"That thing hit me proper hard," White said to Arc. "This'll scar."

Willsith cracked his jaw. "Dalex?"

"What now, Willsith?" asked Arc.

"Farl, can you hack this door?"

"Why can't you be a man and help us?" he replied. "You smashed those drones quick enough."

"Can you hack this door or not?"

"With what? There's no panel," replied Farl. "Stop running."

Willsith saw Farl's chest which still heaved, and felt his own, and the pain in his ribs, and snarled at him. "Not now Farl, this is not the time."

"That's what this is about, Willsith," Farl said, through teeth. "Running. Fighting. It doesn't help your brother. There is no good time."

Willsith heard the last whir of the dying drones, and held his face toward Farl's. The whites of Farl's eyes popped out and the red pulse of the corridor swelled into the grooves of his tensed jaw muscles. "Shut up. Now."

CHAPTER 21
Adrenal Medulla

With the rise and fall of each wave of light, Willsith saw his friends faces cycle from a plastic red to a corpse white. It seemed as though they aged with each blast of red, because as the white light swelled back in, it picked out the roughness in their faces. Arc and White were tampering with a drone, and Willsith was locked in visual combat with his communications officer. Farl.

"He wouldn't have wanted you to stop fighting," said Farl.

Willsith huffed, said, "You don't know what you're talking ab—"

"Farl," a voice sounded to them. "Farl, I have a recording from Eva."

Farl turned toward the glass. "What?"

"Farl, I am L—"

"Leaf!" shouted White. "It's Lif!"

"Yes, I am Lif," said the voice. "Farl will you listen to Eva's message?"

Farl looked at Willsith, and moving only his lower jaw, said yes.

Eva spoke frantically: "Farl, it is essential you help 229 escape. The only way I can finish Lif is with your help.

That is why you must stick with the others. You were all picked."

"No. Tell her no, Lif. From what I read, the office she's from—she's as guilty as her dad, or Dalex the smiler. Tell her no, she can find another way to help them."

"You—I never expected you to be so ungrateful, Farl," said White.

Willsith lowered his sight, moved to the other two, said, "Lif, is Eva okay? Did she get away?"

"Yes, Willsith, I was able to open the door, and assist. Eva is safe."

"Could've opened the door earlier," said White, rubbing his elbow. "Couldn't ya, Lif?"

"I'm sorry White, I was not able. Willsith," said the sterile voice of Lif.

"Yes?"

"There are six armed men approaching."

"Fan-bloody-tastic."

"Eva has asked that I assist you, and in this case I can temporarily disable them, but you will need to—"

"Let me guess," said Willsith. "I need to take them down."

"I am aware of your feelings on violence, but in this instance there is no other option which is statistically viable. They will reach attack-point, or 'arms length', in twenty-two seconds."

Willsith leaned his head against the wall, held his own battered knuckles.

"Willsith," said Farl.

"Leave it now," said Willsith, "I'll do what I need to. For you lot. Six is quite a jump though, Lif," and he saw the men running toward them, and he knew from their gait that they were not pleasant people. "What are you going to do?"

A message projected from the men, but it was Dalex who spoke, "Join us now, 229, or return to your cell, incapacitated, until Mars gets you."

Lif spoke, "In ten seconds I will stun them, please ensure you are ready to act. Lif out."

White stood up, winced as his elbow bent.

"Don't worry White," said Willsith. "Let's test out Lif's statistics. Stand back and look ready. Get away if you can."

Willsith shuffled his body, settled into stance. All at once the sound was on him, boots pounding the floor, armour friction, and the charging of rifles.

Light flashed from the ceiling, the armed men shuddered and their bodies slumped into a precarious stand-still. Willsith leaped at them, grabbing and yanking one back toward 229. The others collapsed.

He moved the inside of his elbow underneath his hostage's chin, and tensed his forearm. His free hand crushed the soldiers gloved grip of the shock-rifle. The soldier was still floppy, and Willsith had to hold the weight of him up. As the other men picked themselves up, Willsith sucked in a deep breath, viced his grip around the gloved hand, and forced shots of electric at each of the men in turn. Squeeze, watch the man drop to the floor. Aim and squeeze again, and on. Soon the five lay motionless.

Willsith snapped his hand up and brought a clenched fist down on the man's wrist, forcing the gun from his grip.

Folding his fingers in, he dropped his hostage with a sharp strike to the neck, lowered his floppy body down, and picked up his gun before rising from his squat.

"Arc, can you check these? Are they DNA-locked?

These guys do have exposed skin trigger-finger gloves."

"Holy smokes big-guy," said White. "You just took out six of them!"

"That's what they want me here for, right Farl? To fight. That's what I'm good for." And he looked back at the pile of drones, and then the pile of men.

"These aren't DNA-locked. Must be more of Dalex's off-record troops," Arc told him.

Willsith picked up the others guns, searched a few pockets, but found nothing else useful. He took the charge-blocks from two of the rifles and pocketed them, and began handing the other guns out. "We'll move while we can. But I'm not fighting for Dalex, not unless—"

"I don't want one," White said, handing back the rifle. Arc accepted his, moving it between hip and shoulder.

"Like this," said Willsith, and pushed the stock into Arc's shoulder. "That's it."

"Do you want one?" he asked Farl, offering up the handle of a rifle.

"What's the difference between what you just did and Dalex having that man shot?" he said.

"Choose your way Farl," Willsith said. "All I can promise you is my best try. I'm not perfect, but at least I know it."

Farl took the rifle, turned it to catch the charge, flicked the setting, said, "They're on stun. You're lucky."

"Not lucky," he said. "We should go."

Arc dropped and stuck his hand into the guts of a drone, which looked to power down. "How can he send all this, anyway? And keep this corridor flashing? Wouldn't the Controller General find out?"

"Fifty shades of bullshit," said White. "Who knows what the hell he's doing up there. Maybe told CG that he's trying to nail us."

"Maybe they're too busy dealing with their grand plan. No matter, let's move," Willsith said.

"Could've done with a rest," said White, turning to the glass dividing the hallway. "The bleedin door is only just there. I was so looking forward to my first trip into the big pool."

Willsith took the charge from the spare rifle, dropped it into his back pocket and tossed the empty gun onto a sleeping soldier. "Lif, will you guide us to Eva?"

"We can't trust her," said Farl.

"We've got nothing else," replied Willsith.

"Yes," said Lif. "Move down the corridor. I will need Farl's assistance."

Farl said no.

"Lif, will you get us to Eva, and help our little rebel here after that?"

"I can only get you to her with Farl's help, otherwise the likelihood of success drops to near zero...but she has told me to make him an offer. She will give him her access as trade. 'Root' access to the hub core."

"Trade?"

Willsith clicked his jaw, tugged his head side to side, and then started walking down the flashing corridor.

"Eva has proposed to hand over her access to the hub core to Farl, in exchange for a little assistance."

"That's the best you're going to get Farl," said Willsith. "We're up shit-creek as it is."

Farl huffed. "Fine, I agree...for now. I'll help until I can get to Dalex, or find out what's happening, either way." And then Willsith knew that he had weathered the storm. Farl moved in front, started walking backwards, and said, "I'll tell you stuff that'll knock your socks off White. And Arc, you're right; at minimum I can get you to the Ark, and get the core leaked, then, who knows."

Farl didn't even think of what he might have to trade for his chance. But Willsith did. Willsith knew what the fight could take from you. And as he gripped the gun his body kicked up a gear; he thanked his adrenal medulla for the sensation, but not for all of the memories which flooded in with the adrenaline. And what was he now, after all that trying - all that fight, but a rat in a rut?

CHAPTER 22

Eva's Nature

"Yes, forty metres ahead," said Lif.

"Good, I'm wiped," said White. "And I'm so sick of these flipping red lights."

"It's only been four minutes of jogging," said Farl.

"Four minutes too many," White told him between exasperated breaths.

"Is this it?" asked Willsith, as he reached a small, knee height recess in the wall.

"Yes."

"And where does this take us?" asked Arc, as Willsith tugged the panel away from the wall.

"This crawlway will give you access to Eva's work spaces. They've got privacy block and no-one's used them for weeks. Her three offices which will take you part of the way to the sky-port."

"Won't they know exactly where we're going?" suggested Willsith, sticking his head into the dark hole. "And are there lights?"

"This crawlway links to 218 exits on all levels of the hub, and I can block its sensors. They'll know you've gone in, but it should provide you with some cover."

"Should," said White. "What percentage is that

'should', please miss?"

"Is that a question," asked Lif.

Willsith stood up, said, "Ignore him Lif. Come on, let's go. Who's first?"

Farl dropped, flipped the rifle onto its strap and over his back, and crawled into the passage. Arc followed. White leaned on the handrail, rubbing his chest and said, "I should hope theres lights in there…and not bloody red ones!"

Willsith smiled and told him, "You alright chef? Heart keeping up?"

White pumped up his chest, winked at him, and entered the crawlway. "And let's hope I'll fit."

He'd fit all right. Nothing out in that hallway but flashing lights, and he didn't fit that scene. Nor did Willsith, anymore. Belly or no belly, they'd get through.

The crawlway was tight, cables and piping ran along all sides restricting them awkwardly. Willsith could not turn to shut the hatch, but with tensed, awkward grip, he managed it. Small lights lit up the tunnel, and he could see the flat backs of his crew as they crawled. Four giant rodents crawling through the night.

"Can you see the way, Farl?" he shouted ahead.

"Only one way," he replied.

For a time they moved, crawling in single-file through the shaft. Willsith lost his count of section marks, and the grating of the floor began to create channels in the skin of his hands. His knees throbbed and his back ached. His eyes adapted to the low-light, and ahead of Farl he caught glimpses of their path, and saw that they were moving uphill. "Lif, how far is it?" he asked.

"450.3 metres until the intersection."

"And then?"

"Fifty metres vertical."

It seemed like they were miles from that door, and try as he might, he couldn't catch the distant intersection. Ignoring the pain in his palms, he lifted himself as he crawled, trying to see past the bobbing heads of 229.

"It's awful cramped," said White. "My knees are killing me."

Willsith tried to picture the hub, and where they might be in it.

"Lif, is there anywhere we can stop to get…something to eat?" asked White.

Farl sniggered.

"There is rations in Eva's spaces."

White whooped, said, "Don't tell me, stir-fry-003? Oh baby, my favourite."

Willsith couldn't help but laugh.

"I am not aware of what designation the ration packs are, Charles White."

"Call me White, love."

"If you wish, White Love."

Willsith felt his rifle swing to the side, stopped to fix it back between his shoulder blades, then continued, holding himself low to fit under a section point.

"Lif, you're an AI, right?" White continued over their shuffling.

"Yes, I am a program created by Eva."

"And she's assigned you to help us."

"Yes."

"So tell us about Eva, and yourself."

"How much further, Lif?" asked Willsith.

"240 metres, Willsith. White, Eva is my creator. She is a female of Earth origin aged 26 and of rank Prime Science Commander. She studied two degrees in the Global Technology Institute and graduated with honours. She has achieved—"

193

"Lif, no, I mean, what does she do up here? What is her relationship with her dad like?"

"White, that's a bit—"

"Farl, it's no big deal, I'm just asking."

Lif said, "Eva's post is as experimental science officer, though she stepped down 52.7 hours ago. She has a sub-average relationship with the Controller General."

"And you can tell us that without asking her?"

"Yes, I have a 'free-will, best-judgement' remit."

Watching his own hands shuffle along the grating, Willsith said, "Lif, how long?"

"83 metres."

Then before White could throw another question in, he asked, "What assistance do you need from Farl?" And the crawling sounds of the others quietened.

"My programming is not complete. I have several areas with bugs, which neither Eva, nor myself, can fix."

"So you want him to fix your code?" said White.

"We need him to assist in finishing these sections of programming, yes."

"My strat-bots," Farl said.

"We have witnessed many instances of your capacity Farl Felix Carlton."

"Felix?" shouted White, "I never knew your middle name was Felix! That's cute."

"Why do you need my help, though," said Farl. "Couldn't you model me?" Then, "Oh and by the way; we're here."

229 filtered out of the passage and spread around the metal-grate platform which clung to the edge of a hexagonal shaft. Willsith leaned out and held the rung of a ladder which rose up from below, looking down he saw countless metal grates. He wondered if any of 229 had vertigo.

"This must span the whole height of the hub," said Arc.

"Must be a hundred metres down," said White, pulling his head back from the edge.

"Two hundred and sixty-four metres, White. And Farl, with your assistance I believe I will be able to realise myself across the halo-network."

"So you need me to get you access?"

Willsith looked up, said "Which way do we go Lif?"

"Can we rest a bit?" asked White.

"Two sections up, using the central ladders," she replied.

Willsith had to ask, "You sure we can't take one of these other tubes back toward the door?"

"Not without alerting them. The only other option is to go down 240 metres, but the chance of success is less than half that of my route."

Lif started to sound more and more human to Willsith, and he began to picture her as an older woman. "Fine."

"Can we rest?" repeated White.

"No, come on, you can do it. Think of the stir-fry," Willsith told him, and grabbed a ladder. He stepped from the platform, and knowing himself to be hundreds of metres up, focused on the task.

They followed him up, each taking their own ladder. White last.

"Not asking so many questions now, are you," Willsith shouted down, rasping his voice and enjoying the odd acoustics.

"Shut up," yelled White. "Big-guy."

"This it Lif?" asked Willsith.

"Yes, the crawlway you want is to your right, marked C04."

Willsith hopped backwards from the ladder, landing

on the grate and seeing the depths of the tube beneath them. "This one?" he said, and tapped the metal.

"Yes."

Arc stretched out a toe and leaned onto the platform, then said, "Ah, more ducts?"

"Yes Arc," said Lif. "It is necessary."

White jumped, landing with both feet and making the metal platform chime. "Give me crawlway over heights any day. Let me go first."

They crawled again for several sections, and reaching another hatch, White punched it open. "Empty. No bad guys. Just a dark room," he shouted back.

As they exited, the room lights faded on. There were desks littered with gadgets and glass tubes. The left-hand wall was flawless glass, the rest section-metal, and there were two doors on the wall to the right, one at each end. A flat computer terminal hugged the wall between the doors, and on it sat several smaller panels.

"Wow," proclaimed White, who ran to the glass. "Wow."

Green light beamed across the room. Willsith stretched his shoulders and walked to the glass. His hands appreciated the soft, cold metal rail. He squeezed it tight, ironing out the grooves created by the grates of the crawlway. Then he smiled intensely. It had been years since Willsith had seen a garden.

Behind the glass, plants spouted from cubic crates which were lined up down the middle of the two-storey room. Short, wide-leafed greenery blanketed the tops of the boxes, mid-height woody plants arched under the weight of curious clusters of orange and purple fruit. And there was a tree in each crate. Willsith traced the bark of a tree as it burst free from the foliage; its wrinkled trunk rising up, splitting into four branches and peppering the room with tiny, perfect leaves. "I haven't seen a tree for years—" said Willsith, "—for more than a decade." And he thought of home, the old home of his childhood.

"They still had some in the city," said Farl. "I saw one when I was little."

White coughed, and between wheezes, said, "Wow" again.

"Is this a food engine?" asked Arc. "Lif?"

"The Controller General's office scrapped food engines in the second year of operation. You are looking at Eva's primary test garden."

"Lif, why were they scrapped?" Farl asked.

"Official record states they were scrapped due to inefficiency. Without lifting hydrocarbons, the reports claimed, they could not grow enough to feed 900 sections."

"And unofficially?"

"The office dismantled the food engines to secure the 'farm' space for research and development. Doing so meant expansion without needing to alert Earth Control by extending the hubs any further."

White slapped Farl's arm, "Holy shit, I knew it."

"So what is Eva growing?" said Willsith.

"In this garden there are approximately 100 specimens of food-producing plant, 40 system-supporting plants, as well as several especially adept atmosphere converters."

Willsith walked along the glass, interrogating the leaves of each plant, and said, "Eva's a bag of tricks." And he saw the symbol emblazoned on the walls, the plant crates, and on the glass. *Drasil-G. I'm so far from what I know. To me that sign is revolution, it's for the Earth, but they've started using it for everything. This one's got the tree emphasised. Ah, stop questioning, Willsith. They want me to use my fists, and not my brain. But isn't that why I stopped...And last I knew, the trees were as good as dead. No trees, just stir-fry, that's what I thought.* "We know so little."

"What time is it, Lif?" asked Farl.

"03:32 AM halo-time."

"Then we have time to find out more," he said, and turned from the glass.

"It's hypnotic to see such healthy green," said White, and pushed his nose against the glass. "Makes me hungry."

"Space rocks make you hungry," said Arc.

Willsith laughed, and they relaxed into the room. Lif guided White to the rations, and while he couldn't heat up the stir-fry, they were all glad to eat.

"So even princess Eva eats the stir-fry, eh?" White jabbered, squeezing in a mouthful of noodles from the plastic wrap.

With his back to a desk, staring into the light of the test garden, Willsith replied, "I guess so." And thought of smashing the window and feasting on the red gems of fruits he could see hanging from the tree, wondered what they tasted of. Instead, he bit off another mouthful of colourless starch from the near-solid packet. "So what next, Lif?"

"Next Farl must assist me in completing my programming. He can develop from the main console against the wall."

"And then what?"

"Once Farl has helped me bring the remaining sections of my intelligence online, I will be able to make a path for you, and Eva, to the Stellar Ark 12."

"Tell us about Stellar Ark 12, Lif," said Willsith.

Farl swallowed fast and added, "And the lasers."

"You will see the Ark for yourself shortly. The lasers

are another reason to complete the programming."

Willsith looked at Farl, and both said, "Lif."

"Yes?"

"You are a computer program, right?" said Willsith.

"Yes."

"And you're tasked with helping us?"

"Yes."

Then Farl said, "Then why be so evasive?"

"I apologise. I am tasked to assist in your escape, and at this point, it is more important to focus on the programming than on the ship."

Willsith looked along the line of them, said, "Let's leave Lif alone for a while...Thanks Lif."

And then he paced the room, and the others followed, and they inspected gadgets, tools and jars. He found a panel, but it was dead and wouldn't respond to his touch, so he passed it to Arc. None of the tech seemed responsive, and then Lif spoke. "On the next desk you will find two personal drones and a pack. I have altered their programming to work to my command, rather than through Eva's interface. The back-unit will best fit Arc."

White trotted to the desk and picked up the two matchbox size units. He handed one to Willsith and the other to Arc, and then rummaged through a pile of parts to retrieve a kind of belt.

"Tiny thing, looks like a dead lump of metal," said Willsith, and flicked it at Arc.

Arc held one up to the light, rotated it, bounced his hand up and down, and said, "Weighs only 40 or 50 grams. Can't be solid titanium, which is what it looks like. White, pass me that pack please." And taking the belt from White he slid the unit into it where it began to glow. "Looks like this'll charge them."

"You are correct, Arc. Please wear the belt and with it

199

I will be able to assist you via the drones."

"Show us what they can do?" White asked.

"No. They need to charge."

Arc slid the other into the unit on the belt and fastened it around his mid.

"Look at this," Farl shouted, and brought his panel to them, passing it to Willsith as they all grouped around it.

"What's that?" said White. "Looks like hieroglyphs."

"I don't know. It's a language I've never seen before. We can try…Lif, what is this?"

"It is Unus. The new language."

"New language?" they said in unison.

"Yes."

"And look at this," said Farl, taking back the panel, and swiping at it. "It's what Eva's been working on."

He handed the panel to Willsith and they all read the words in plain English: '603: Low Oxy Test #45'. Willsith's wide thumb caught the screen edge and the visual fluttered through numbers, counting down from 603. When he lifted it the screen read '486: Reduced Rations #19'. Tapping it again he stopped it at '392: Inhibitor T-Viral #3', then it went blank.

"What happened? And what the hell has she been doing." He handed it back to Farl who tapped it several ways.

"Lif," said Farl, staring at Willsith. "Did you disable this panel?"

"Yes Farl."

"Why did you do that?" he asked.

"Some of the information you had access to was not complementary to—"

"Shit! They're lying to us! I told you," shouted White. "Lif, don't be a drag, we're not in 229 anymore!"

"They were experimenting on…us?" said Arc,

slumping down onto a tall stall.

Farl threw the panel at the glass wall. They all gawked as the corner hit and it fell to the floor undamaged. "Lif you dirty piece of code. Let me at your source, I'll more than fix it. No way am I going to help Eva if she's been treating us like that. Give me access or I'll…"

White walked to Farl, and placing a hairy hand on his shoulder, whispered something Willsith couldn't hear.

The large computer display which spread halfway along the wall beeped, and Lif spoke, "I understand your frustration. I am code but I cannot be 'dirty'. I have been running for more than a year now and I have observed the experiments that have taken place in the sections of the Earth's Halo. I have also seen all of Eva's work, and that of many other officers. Eva has made me more than just code. I am able to learn, and I also have many constraints which I have fashioned based on human ideology."

Willsith and Arc moved to the others, and they all stood together. He saw each of their faces sullen, and he listened to Lif.

"I have built an ethical protocol, I have chosen to adapt a moral code that is the average all actions of workers of the 900 sections, combined with some historical sources. Based on the past five years streams I have identified that the choices made by those within the four hubs have been significantly less ethical than those made by section workers. Thus my artificial, but statistically correct, moral program is very similar to the sum of your four 'moral compasses'."

"What are you saying Lif? You want to be a maintainer?" White said. "You can have my old job."

"No. I am making the point that my ethics more closely match 229's, than that of the Hub administration."

"Great. So you're a box with ethics," said White. "So why shut down that pad? Why block us?"

"My ethic matching your ethic should create a trust in you, such that when I say that Eva has been ethical with section tests, you can then understand the position from which I make that decision."

Willsith scanned the others, none looked happy. He then spoke without thinking, "Lif. Trust has to work two ways. Will you shut off watching us for a time, so as we can discuss this, in private. And give us back that access."

"We haven't had a private moment since we lifted five years ago!" said Farl, flaring his nostrils.

"I understand Willsith Harper. Our task limits our time here, but I can, for several minutes, shut off my input from the room feeds, without much statistical risk."

"And how will we know you're not listening?" shouted White.

"There is no way," Farl told him.

"Great," said White.

"I will shut off my input in five seconds, and maintain no connection to the room for the next five minutes. Farl, I will leave a copy of my source open on the computer terminal, you can analyse my ethical code, and in due course you will see that I am trustworthy. Shutting off input now."

Willsith lifted himself onto the desk. "Can we believe her?"

"No way to tell, even if I can see her code, it'll take time to go through it. She knows that."

"So what do we do now?" asked Arc, taking off the back-unit and interrogating it's fastener.

Willsith ran through the options, thinking back to their section, to kicking rock, to the absolute escape of being out there in space. It seemed so distant now. And so did Earth. He felt out of place, and out of ideas.

"Well it's Dalex the douche, or Leaf and Eva, basically," proclaimed White. "And at least Leaf's feeding us."

Willsith walked to the glass, picked up the panel. "She's showed us her rooms, guided us away from the men, those drones. I trust Eva more than Dalex." And as he watched, a hatch opened in the garden room, and several drones popped out, each buzzing around the room injecting water into the crates. Willsith stood transfixed, wondering if he'd fallen for her.

"We could always go straight to the Controller General," said Arc.

White shook his head, "He's the most crooked of the lot."

"How do we actually know that?" Farl asked him.

"I read it in the Alt-Gazette."

"That's mainstream conspiracy tripe White, and you know it. It's—"

"Enough, we don't know he's any good either way," said Willsith. "No assumptions."

Farl showed them a pointed finger, "No, I do agree with White. He's bad, but because he's tooling this ring up for action, that's why."

"So what do we do? Trust code-lady?" White suggested, flicking a bit of stir-fry off of his shirt.

"I'll find out what I can," Farl told them, and turned back to the console.

Willsith projected at him, "Good, and start your core download or whatever you need to do. Use the time, while we have it."

"I'll see what I can get to."

"That leaves us to get ourselves ready," said Willsith, and then, "Lif?...nope, apparently she's still out. No point in barricading doors if we don't know which one is our exit. Let's have one last look around."

Willsith moved a few cups from a panel on the desk, tapped it. Nothing but dead tech and food remnants. What was Eva really doing here?

"Can't believe they were running tests on us!" shouted White as he rummaged loudly. "There we are, fixing their ring, kicking rock in the name of regen, and all along they were experimenting on us. If Eva did it, I don't know, Arc, I just don't know if I can listen to anything she has to say anymore."

"Maybe it's not true," said Arc. "Or maybe we were a control group, anyway."

White rifled through a cupboard in the side of a desk, dropping handfuls of metal tools onto the floor. "Not true? You saw it with your own eyes lad."

Willsith watched Arc squat next to White, pick up a tool from amongst the pile.

"There's not much I can get at from here," shouted Farl.

Willsith moved to his side, said, "Show us what you can."

"Well I can't get at the full core yet, but I've started the download of what I can onto my storage," he said, grasping the device around his neck. "And as much as I can see from Lif's code, she's well written. Eva's put a lot of time into this."

White gawked at the screen, "I don't trust computer-game ethics."

"It's smart. She's got Lif machine-learning based on all streams of all the Earth's Halo. Lif has seen everything that has happened up here in high detail, and is growing with the information," said Farl, flipping through screens of code. "It's smart. She's smart."

Willsith turned to White, told him, "I don't trust it either, however smart it is—she is. But we haven't got much else to go on." Then asked Farl, "Can you get to a map of the hub, has she been guiding us well?"

"Good idea," said Arc.

"Here's where we are," Farl pointed at a small three dimensional box. "And that is where the Ark is."

"That room is gigantic," White said.

"That's the sky-port, and yeah, the Stellar Ark is big, it's—"

Arching his neck toward the screen, Willsith said, "Wait, can you find out about the lasers before Lif comes back," then tested. "Lif, are you there?"

"Must have been four minutes by now," said Arc.

"I've got Lif's access. Can't get to everything but…yeah, here's the specs."

A schematic filled the screen, a cutaway of the ring with a mobile laser unit hovering over it, space-side. Farl flicked a control and it became animated, a rock flew into view and was sliced again and again by the fast-moving mobile laser.

"So it's just better rock cutting?" asked White. "Looks like we're out of a job."

"There's more, it's still playing the example."

And then from Earth side a ship entered the screen, breaking through the atmosphere toward the Halo. The laser unit spun around the ring's cross-section and targeted the ship with another beam. Other lasers mobilised and added their beams. The ship froze in place, and then began a slow progression toward the ring.

"So they're finally doing it. They're going to stop all

exports from Earth. They're killing the space industry!" White hopped on the spot.

"It doesn't look good," added Willsith, rotating his jaw until it clicked.

"They're going to choose who gets into space and who doesn't," Farl said.

Arc spoke, his voice quiet, "But how will we drop down if they can stop all ships? How will I get home? They can't stop all ships, surely?"

"We'll get you home Arcy, don't worry," White reassured him.

"And I think it's worse than that," said Farl. "Look at this internal memo. It looks like they can fire at Earth, right to the ground, they're just not saying it here."

"Hello 229, I am back."

"Hi Leaf," said White.

"I appreciate that nickname White, even if you designed it to make the others laugh."

Willsith caught White nodding at the empty room, grinning at nothing.

"Lif, can you confirm if what Farl has just said is true?" asked Willsith, pulling up a chair next to Farl's.

"I assure you I did not observe this room during the past 600 seconds. You can trust me, Willsith Harper."

Willsith squeezed his knees. "No, I'm not testing you. Is it true that the laser mods make it possible to shoot at the Earth?"

"I presume you mean the mods which got you arrested. I believe so, with a certainty of 91.5%."

White brought a chair. "We're seated," White told her. "You can explain now Lif, please."

Arc fidgeted with the drone-pack, lifted himself onto the desk.

"I am not authorised to access all of the Hub Core, as I

explained, I require some assistance from Farl in order to—"

"So how are you 91 percent sure?" continued White.

"Based on lip-reading informal conversations between hub leadership, conversational inflection, and general language patterning in written memos. And by doing the engineering math. I have inferred that there is an underlying intention to overrule the principle reasons for the creation of the Earth's Halo. The modifications to the lasers do technically allow the rock-cutters to fire on Earth, and it would seem that the leadership intend to use them to gain some degree of control over Earth's resources."

"There's their plan," said Farl.

White rubbed his palms together. "Meaty. Grim, but meaty," he said. "Lif, will you marry me?"

"White, I am distributed computer code, I am not capable of marriage."

Arc and White giggled, Farl chuckled, and Willsith said, "Stop now. These lasers are bad deal. I'm glad we didn't install 229s. We'd have blood on our hands just from screwing the thing in."

"You see, we can't just run away in some ship, knowing that they've got lasers that can fire on most of the Earth. We can't just leave."

"What options do we have Farl? Can we disable the lasers? Lif, can you direct us to some control or console?"

"It's not just smashing a panel with a hammer Willsith," snapped Farl. "This is ring-wide. They've had 900 sections put the mods up. Super-fast too, by offering reward points. They've already done it. They did it when they setup the gamification of sections, they've had this in the works since they installed the leadership. And now it's just a matter of time until they—"

"That's their plan. They want sovereignty," said Willsith, his eyes stuck to the screen.

Farl shook his head, "Until they declare war against Earth."

"With lasers that reach Earth they can cut up whole cities. They'll bring it all down. They'll use that power they were meant to be giving to Earth, to dominate it!"

Arc whimpered, said, "They won't attack the cities?"

"They will. They'll delete whole districts. You've seen what those lasers do to ten-kilometre-wide rocks!"

"Lif, can we stop the lasers?" asked Willsith.

"Statistically uncertain. Of the forty-five thousand simulations I've run so far, none has produced a possibility of success greater than five percent."

"What are the options, Lif?" said Willsith. "Any I can do without these lot?"

The others drew breath sharply, and Lif said, "Siding with Dalex grants a 4.25% chance of success, though follow-on simulations show he will just as soon fire on Earth, once the danger from the Controller General is eliminated. Commander, can I offer another alternative?"

"I'm in too," said White. "But only if we can get Arc to safety."

"I don't need your help to—"

"No, I can do it, or me and Farl can do it. Lif, what is it?"

"You are here because we are mid-plan. The continuation of this plan offers the highest likelihood of success, for you, Eva, and Earth."

Farl tapped at the screen. "How is running away going to help Earth?"

"Apart from Dalex's force, I have identified two other groups acting to expose the current system. These have both achieved only limited access. However you, Farl

Felix Carlton, do have access to Earth resources, and with my help, the Hub core as well. Extracting, with the Stellar Ark, will allow us to distribute the Hub Core to the Earth's net. Widely distributing this information will in-time allow the factions of Earth to reclaim the Earth's Halo. This is far more assured than any other option currently available."

"So we let it fall but help them take it back?" said Willsith. "We let him fire the lasers? Can't we send the Hub Core from here, and why can't we take out the rock-cutters?"

"That is not statistically viable. There is nowhere in-hub we can barricade ourselves to get away from Dalex's and CG's forces. The ship can make it outside of their range, provided we meet our escape window."

Farl spun around in his chair. "She's right. It might take me hours to hack the core, longer to dump it. And the lasers are already out there, even if I took the local core out, it's distributed to the three other hubs. If I had a month to write something, or if there was a single unit that dealt with the lasers, we could do something. But we can't. The lasers will fire. As long as the Controller General wants them to, the lasers will fire. And there's nothing we can do about it."

"We could blow up the hub? Or all four?" proposed White.

"Blow up the hub? Listen to you. There's thousands of people on here, mister peace-keeper," Willsith told him.

"There are seven thousand four hundred and—"

"Thank you Lif."

"Willsith," White addressed him, crossing his arms on his knees. "Can't you take out the Controller General? Then he can't order to fire and so—"

He wants me to kill a man just like that. White might

as well be a kid in an army costume; a hippy who picked up a helmet. And not just any man. He wants me to kill 'the man'. I've never even seen him. Maybe I will. But it won't be as easy as saying it, sitting here in some office. Then he said, "Farl, what do you need to do to get at the core?"

"I need to complete Lif, give her the tools to get access. And I need a down-link to get it to Earth."

Willsith nodded, said, "What do you need us to do? And Lif; where is the Controller General?"

CHAPTER 23
The Truth

Arc and White sat by the computer, Willsith watched from the glass, where he and Farl stood with their backs to the trees. Jade light from Eva's garden bent in sideways and caught the edges of anything reflective; from Arc's hand a small drone flew into the air and did a somersault, dipping into the emerald brilliance, only to flop back into his gloved palm. They all waited. On the display, Farl's script chewed at the Hub Core, spitting out tiny increments along a progress bar.

"How much longer?" Willsith asked him, knowing the answer.

"I've completed as much of Lif's program as I can now. The rest I'll need to do over time. She'll have the core within the hour."

Willsith turned, tracked the edge of a large leaf and said, "Then we're certain? We do what Lif said? Wait, escape, leak and hack?"

"It's good strategy. But I'll do more if I can."

"And if I get the chance, I take him out."

"That's your call. Like she said, it might not change much, only delay it."

"But if I took out CG, and Dalex, and we could get Lif

into power."

"You think you can do that?"

"I don't know, Farl. I've been away from it for five years. That's what I would have done. Go in for the bold move. Kill fast. Kill whoever I needed to. Since 229, I don't know if I was ever cut out for it. But that's what I would have done."

"You served for decades Willsith."

"I'm not proud of that," he said. "And now it's a young man's game. Especially with all this tech. Who knows what CG has protecting him."

"You know, there's something I've tried to tell you."

Willsith continued, "And since I left, heck - since yesterday, I've found out more truth about those missions than I ever did in the field. When you're down on the ground, in the stench, you don't see the bigger picture. What you're really doing it for. You just act. You tell yourself you're saving lives, by taking them. You survive. But it's team-wide lies. You're fodder for the heartless generals."

"Willsith," Farl said, turning to face him. "Comms have been cut to Earth for two weeks." And his face folded, his eyes strained. "Bear died a month ago."

Willsith huffed, and covered his eyes with a hand. "What am I to believe anymore?"

"He died trying to take out a resonating power hub. A stealth mission. He had been working for them since..."

"Since they faked his death."

"Yes."

"I looked into it. The only reason Bear was there was because of the Earth's Halo. And it was his last mission, he'd quit, but they made him go, promised him out. I knew that before, but now I can see why - it all fits. The Controller General has been rationing power to Earth;

212

throttling the power for the regeneration machinery. By playing the nation-groups off against each other he's created a bidding war, and they're all using espionage against each other to try and maintain their regen."

"Dirty bastard. Earth's Halo energy was only meant for regen, that's the whole point this thing was built; without it the environment down there will slip back toward toxic. What else did you find?"

"That's everything. I tried to tell you. I tried to find a window. But they have us 24/7 Willsith, if I'd have told you, Control would have known. I would have exposed my link."

"No matter. He's dead either way. What's a month."

"I tried. I loved it there, you know. Even though I was angry, I appreciated you."

Willsith kept his hand over his eyes, wanted Farl to stop talking.

"229 was my first home, I didn't want to give it up. The only thing I wanted more was the network. The leak. But I couldn't give it all up."

Leave me, Willsith tried to say, leave me alone and go to hell, all of you. Let me stand here till the ring fires on Earth and they send up nukes to cut this hub up. Leave me here till the metal crumples and the glass shatters and space sucks it all into oblivion. Leave me. But he couldn't say it. He stood with his face in his hand, leaned against the glass of Eva's garden, and said, "How long?"

Lif's voice sounded throughout the room, and to him she sounded caring, "Willsith. I have lost sensor awareness of that area. The window for movement is no longer relevant. Hold position."

"What, Lif? Why didn't you—" started Farl, but he was stopped by the sound of pneumatics.

A set of doors slid open, and through them Willsith

heard the steps of men. "You have one minute until we lethal breach, come out, leaving all weapons within the room," a voice shouted in.

White cursed, shouted, "Willsith, what do we do?"

The man shouted again, "CG offers immunity, provided you do as we say."

"Bullshit. Bite us, arseholes," yelled White, backing away from the door and circling around the desks with Arc.

The four from 229 grouped together behind a desk, Willsith checked his rifle and tested a charge. Arc shook, then lurched forwards, grasping his knees.

"You alright Arc?" asked White.

"Yeah, it's just," he started, but tailed off his words as a drone flew from his back and hovered in front of them.

"This is Lif. I must speak to you through this drone now, to avoid alerting Dalex's squad."

"What do we do Lif?" asked Farl.

"We shoot these guys, that's what," said Willsith.

The drone floated up to the glass and drew a floor-plan on it with lasers. "I suggest you tail back around through the other door. I can try and stun the first wave of them, but then you'll have to run through here and along this platform."

"Lif, what's the percentage for that?" asked White.

Willsith bit in, "Stop. Lif, don't tell us. Let's just do it."

They sneaked along the back edge of the office, darting between desks. Willsith caught sight of a man and fired off a shot. The troops replied with a volley of rounds, and shouted threats.

Arc stuck his head out past the last desk and White yanked him back as another pneumatic release sounded. Their exit door opened, and the rough voice of another soldier bounced in, "There is no option but to submit."

Arc whimpered.

"Er, Lif, what now?" said Farl.

The matchbox drone floated above the desk and dropped. "There's six at this door, 12 at the other, there may be more men waiting."

"Twenty seconds," shouted the soldiers.

"I can shock the six by this door, then it's out through there, and sprint for the platform."

"What about the crawlway?" asked Willsith.

"Based on the fact they know you are here, I believe my crawlway sensor code must be faulty. They could have a force waiting for you there."

"Okay, don't see any other choice right now. All agree?" he asked the others. *Got to be their choice, can only get more dicey.*

"Go with Lif's plan. If those two go first, we can cover them. Me and Farl can fire at the other twelve."

It was an awful plan. There was no chance White could sprint the distance, and he doubted they could take out twelve men. "I don't like it. Can you run, White?"

"It's all we've got big-guy. I'll run. I'll take Arc first, then you two follow."

Not much of a team. But they're all he had. As he mapped from Arc's solemn fright through to Farl's over-certainty, he knew he would protect them now, whatever it cost him. "Agree?"

Each nodded, and Willsith too.

But then they entered. Six men hustled in and started to fan out. Willsith saw their reflection in the glass and knew he had only a second to react. He flung himself to his feet, shot at a man, and they all fell down.

All he could make out was a slash through the air, a blurred shape, and then grating of their armour plates as they dropped. Shots sounded from the other door and he ducked, squatting next to 229, and stating instinctively, "Six down." He looked at the gun flicked at the setting and shook his head.

"It was the drone...look," said Arc, and then the small metal cuboid hovered toward them, low to the floor, as if limping.

White picked it up and handed it to Arc. "Yeah, it's dead." He turned and slotted it into the back unit, while the other flew out.

"That was all I can do," Lif said, from Arc's back, "I'm sorry."

Willsith leaned around the edge of the desk and reached toward one of the soldiers bodies, but hearing the charge of a rifle, snapped his arm back.

"That's enough," said a familiar voice. "That's quite enough. We will take you now. With lethal force."

"Dalicks," said White, then shouted, "welcome to the party Dalicks. Hope you brought some liquor!"

This isn't good, this isn't one bit good. Best option is to let them breach, but for me to be over there, the other side. Take as many as I can, and if it's enough, to distract them so that these can get away. Seems like the only choice. Maybe this is it. Maybe I can help...finally, here. "Lif, use that drone to help me however you can. I'm going to move to that end of the room, when they breach I'll take as many out as I can, distract them. You three exit through that door, follow Lif to Eva and get the hell out of here."

"Eva has a message for you," said Lif. "She said that she has gained some access from Farl's work, that she can see you, and will do what she can."

"Lif, tell her we're grateful, and that whatever she does, she is to get these three out."

He stared them all in the face and then flipped himself around and lunged toward the next desk, skulking along until he reached the opposite corner. The little drone followed him, hovering at his side.

Willsith slipped an eye out from the metal bench. The doorway glowed from the bright light of the hallway, but he couldn't see the men outside. He listened hard, tried to hear the shuffle of boots, the friction of combat material, but he could not make out a single sound. High level troops, he thought.

Looking back at the others, he saw they hadn't moved, and all watched him, their blank faces lit up green by the glow from Eva's garden. "Where is Eva now?" he asked the drone. "Can you see the men outside?"

But the drone did not respond, and though it hung in the air next to him, it did not show any sign of hearing him.

"Now's not the time Lif," he said. "Tell me what you know."

Nothing. She's dead. This little box is hovering around me like a fly, we're about to get mauled by these arseholes, and I can't even talk to support about it. Lif's down.

"Willsith," White tried to shout a whisper. "Willsith."

What a team. What a team. "What?"

"Can you see them?"

Willsith shook his head, said, "Lif, if you can hear me, move this drone out into the corridor and tell me how many there are." It didn't move. Snatching it out of the air, he felt the fuzzy movement of blades against his palm, and then sharp points as if it was trying to free itself. Opening his fingers, he saw it had folded itself up. "Useless," he said.

"What?" shouted White.

"Lif's down," replied Willsith. "Here," he threw the drone along the floor to them. "I'm going…" and he signalled to the door.

White nodded, and extended his neck out of his swollen body to create a viewing platform.

"Here we go," said Willsith, and jumped to the wall, rising to stand with his back flat to it, then strafed, with his rifle poised, toward the door.

The hall looked empty where he could see it, and the six men were still out cold. Dalex's words rang in his ears, and he held himself tense, waiting for the incursion of the troops.

Willsith lowered his gun as he met the corner to keep it from giving him away. Swallowing deep, he prepared himself to bolt through the door. But from his periphery he caught the wisps of hair which White had called his summit. Those silly bastards. The others were sticking their heads right up over the edge. Even a rookie shot could cap them like that. And he thought about shouting at them, but didn't want to betray his position.

The room lights grew brighter and a commanding voice sounded throughout: "This is a message for the four maintenance officers in RD Office 43. There have been several bugs in our systems. These have been removed. Leave the room now and walk down the corridor as guided. You will meet with me and I will address your concerns. Your only other option is instant death via gas outlet. I cannot waste time on you, so this is your final option."

White coughed, and they all scrabbled along the floor between the desks.

"Who is speaking?" shouted Willsith.

No reply. First no Lif. Then no Dalex. Now this other

voice. Still no reply.

The others reached Willsith and White coughed again, harder. "You know who that was?" he asked Willsith.

"No. You all right?"

"I'm fine."

"It was the Controller General," said Farl. "I know his voice from the broadcasts."

Willsith widened his stance, flicked his chin up, and they stood. "Well then," he said, "looks like we might get to meet him after all."

"What about Eva? Lif?" Arc asked. "And Dalex...and those men outside. What about the Stellar Ark? Earth?"

Willsith lifted the stock of his rifle and pushed the barrel down, spun around the corner and into a firing position in the hallway. "No men," he said. "Smoke and mirrors."

The others tentatively moved to the door and followed him.

"Those bastards," said White as he stepped into the empty hall. "Had us squatting on our arses, hiding from nothing. What now?"

Willsith looked up and down the hall, saw that there was no place to walk where Lif had drawn on the map, only a wide open corridor heading off in the other direction. "We move down there," he said, pointing, and then checking his rifle, flicking it up a setting. "We move down there and we meet him. As he said."

"Should we go back and take the armour from those men. We could escape through the crawlway?" asked White.

"No sense running, now," said Willsith, as he gripped the chef's shoulder. "We've got an audience with the man in charge."

"Let's go," Farl projected. "I'm ready."

"Hell, let's at least see his face then," added White. "Maybe he'll hear my complaint about the noodles."

"And mine about the lasers," said Willsith, squeezing the grip on his gun, and leaning into a walk.

CHAPTER 24

Power

The doors clicked shut behind them and Willsith knew that until options presented, he had no choice but to walk forwards. He wore the orange boiler-suit of a maintainer, (or a pretend pilot), but the stance of a soldier, and as he walked he allowed his limbs no other option; he controlled every step, guided the firing of each muscle. He was to stay ready.

The others walked in a line beside him, quiet except for White, who clomped along, bouncing with his breath.

A breeze pushed passed them and a metallic click made Willsith spin around. "Wall's dropped," he said, and they all turned. The way back was blocked.

"Looks like we've no choice, then," said Farl.

Arc moved to the metal, tapped it, surveyed its edges, and concluded, "It's at least a grade 38 Titanium alloy. Nothing but tuned cutters would get through that."

He nodded at Arc, spun around, and scanned the corridor, looking for a sign of difference, anything. A panel perhaps.

White cursed, then said, "From trap to trap."

Willsith tried for the wall ahead, which looked as solid

as the wall behind. The hallway arched at the top, and apart from some metal tubing which ran along side, it was featureless. As he approached the forward-facing wall, it shot up into the ceiling. The air churned up his front in its wake, and he beckoned the others forward. "It's containing us. Section by section."

"So when we move forward, it opens for us?" asked Farl.

"Yes."

"And shuts behind us," added White.

Willsith nodded. "Come on, let's go."

As they moved through the walkway, passed the gap, the wall fell back down sharply.

"Where'd you pick up that cough?" Willsith asked White.

"Somewhere between waking up in 229, and crawling around like a rat in a shit storm," he said. "Never moved so much in my life."

Farl told him, "It's probably good for you."

"Here, I'll help," said Arc, and slid an arm around his back, lifting him by the shoulder.

"Thanks Arcy, I'll be alright in a minute."

"We've got a date with the man himself," said Willsith, and wrapped his arm around White's back. "So save your energy, you'll need it for that wit of yours."

And they walked on in a line, as they reached each wall it shot up, then fell behind them once they passed. Each corridor section the same, and each wall rising and then falling around them, swiping at their backs. The repetition was hypnotising. Wall up. Walk forward. Wall down. Same grey metal. But he had to keep ready. Willsith fed his imagination with what might lay ahead, behind any one of these rising walls. "Arc, are those drones charged yet?" he asked.

Flipping the belt around, Arc pulled one of them out, held it in his palm. They stepped on, the line of four of them looking at Arc's hand. The metal lump rose into the air.

"Yes!" Arc exclaimed.

"Leaf...Leaf, you there?" White barked at it.

The drone hovered over Arc's hand, floated along with them.

"Maybe Lif's not even real," said White. "Could easily been a chick saying all that."

"Code seemed legit," Farl told them.

"Need to keep focused on what's ahead," said Willsith, testing the trigger of his rifle as he watched another wall slide into the ceiling.

The small blades of the drone whirred and it moved to shadow Arc, fixing itself above his shoulder. "Maybe it's in some automatic mode," said Arc.

"Wonder how many sections to go?" asked Farl.

"We can't know," said Willsith. "Just be ready with that rifle. And Arc, you and White make sure to get to any shelter you can, when it happens."

"Hey, we're not dead weight!" White told him, wriggling his arms free from Arc's grip, coughing up phlegm, and rasping out the words, "I'll walk now, I'm fine."

Willsith nodded at him, and felt the flood of air from behind. Another wall down. There would be no escape, once they got there. Nowhere to run. And then he put his free hand back under the gun, and tried to find a zone in his mind he'd been burying for the past five years.

"I feel like cattle," said White. "I remember when I was in peace corp; the state caught us for a little stunt we did, boy it was a good one—anyway, they sent us to the pen, but we had to go through this—"

"White. Stay sharp," Willsith told him, and hunkered down to watch the next wall slide up.

"It's just more of the same Willsith," White replied. "Might be hundreds of these before we get there."

"It won't be."

"Imagine it Arc, two hundred up and downs. They could walk us right out into space."

Willsith stuck out his chin at White, said, "Shush. Stay sharp. The Hub's not that big, can't be many more."

"Okay okay. Let's focus, amigos."

"I think it can't go on for a lot longer. Each section looks to be about twenty metres, and we've been through 31 of them," said Arc, and they all froze as the next wall swiped upward. "Can't be many more as the Hub isn't a kilometre wide. Is it?"

"The four amigos strafed on, rifles ready, in a line, ready to drop the corrupt minister quicker than you could say...sombrero maximo," White said, waving his hands about.

"How can you joke, now?" said Farl. "So near the end."

"We're always near the end Farl. Enjoy the remaining steps," replied White.

Willsith held his face stern, but from the rut of his old military focus, he laughed a little to himself. *They're an odd bunch. I mean, we're an odd bunch.* And he walked, aware that as he forced his muscles to move, things were different than they had been on Earth. He was different.

Several more sections passed and now they moved through the hallway in a pattern of steps. The dull whir of the drone which clung to Arc's shoulder came and went like a metronome, with each step it lagged behind him, then caught up. And the axing of the walls at their backs bolstered them forward, and with each metal solid

224

that flung itself up, they expected a circus of combat. But just another space, the same as the last, a space of air and wall. Again the air churned behind them, and they walked on.

And then the final wall rose.

Willsith licked his rifle through the air, as if a blade past a neck, and targeted the only man who was present. Down the stock, past his arm, and along the barrel, his eye charged, and butted right into the crumpled old face of the Controller General.

Too easy. Willsith felt his readiness to fire. *It'd be too easy. Just keep sight on him and scope the room, but keep your damn sight on him.*

The man sat in a simple chair, and behind him the wilds of space filled a large window, with the dusty red circle which was Mars projected onto the glass.

There were two doors, Willsith spotted with his periphery, either side of the window. The man was about to speak. The hanging skin of the Controller General's neck tightened as he lifted his face, tensed his jaw, and said, "Hello 229."

White coughed, mumbled unprintable words.

"You've been quite a pain today, but enough of that," the man pasted his mouth, and then he continued, "Farl has told you a lot of information. And so have my other...leaks. It's a shame, as you were one of my favourite experiments. It's a shame because your knowing ceases the trial. You've nullified yourselves"

"We know about you and your plan for Earth," blurted out White. "You twisted old virus."

"Come, there's no need for that," he said, cocking open his mouth and tonging his teeth. "Willsith, you're taller than you look in the feeds. You've been a useful old dog, it was helpful that your brother died with such good timing. Or, rather, that you'd believe that he had."

Willsith huffed out air, swore loud and concise words down the length of his rifle, "Give me a single reason that I shouldn't end this speech here and now. I'd be doing the world a favour."

"Ah yes. The plan they've all been telling you about. You should forget that one. It's far bigger than you can imagine, but also, unchangeable."

"It's quite clear," shouted Farl.

"Farl Felix Carlton. I bet you don't even realise how important you are, still. All that anger and misery from your childhood. All that anguish, channelled into hacking. You hate authority as much as me, Farl."

"Shut up," he replied.

"Leave alone," yelled Willsith.

"Calm down soldier. Or I'll calm you down."

Willsith's chest screamed at him, buckling under each breath. His heart wanted out. And as he looked at the wrinkles in CG's hagged face, he knew his duty was with the three beside him, and the others like them on Earth, and all those who got treated like meat by this sort of a man. He felt fury at the injustice, he hated the men who had taken his brother, and the only thing that held him from engagement was a hair of an idea. Five years dwelling on it. Aggression begets aggression, he said to himself, war creates more war. But it was hopeless, he knew the rage was winning. He would fire. Or be sick and then fire anyway. "Do you intend to use the lasers on Earth?" he shouted.

"Let me guess, you're looking for a justification to shoot me. You're not sure if it'll change anything. Willsith, this is far bigger than me, and in any case, your shot would rattle off into oblivion." The Controller General raised an arm, Willsith watched the skeletal stick of his wrist, a loose collection of muscles and veins, as it swung his hand around in the air. "Lin," the General shouted. "Primes?"

A door opened, and the Controller General pulled a weak smile, the furrows of his face deeper than the expression.

I could do it, he could be bluffing. But I'm risking the others. Who am I now? Where has this weak-shit attitude come from? Drop him. Drop the old idiot and then cover the rest. He'll fire on Earth and you'd have had this chance. And he held the rifle tight, and listened for his heartbeat, breathed out, and squeezed the trigger. The contact felt good, for a moment.

As the rifle charged and the round rung out, a drone lurched from the wall and absorbed the projectile. The shot knocked it back and electric fizzed through its black alloy skeleton, encasing it with sparks.

"You waste time, and power. Desist," said the Controller General, his beady eyes unflinching amongst their dark pits.

Willsith screamed, fired again, and again. The drone darted about catching each round, showing no sign of strain.

"You are a soldier Willsith. Plain and simple. You're built for one thing, and one thing only. Now, where are my trusted team of Primes, I wonder?"

With a whimpering yell, Arc fired a single shot, which the drone caught with a somersault.

"Well then. There's a surprise," said the old man, his waxy face stuck in its dismissive droop. "Anyhow. Primes?" and with this last call he pulled a new face, and Willsith could see that he was trying to be funny. Lifting a wiry finger to his mouth, CG raised his eyebrows and tugged them together.

As a figure entered the corner of his eye, Willsith swung his rifle to the new target. Dalex.

The over-brimming grin which jumped down Willsith's gun at him inspired an instant retaliation. Willsith fired. Still the drone hovered in the way, snatching the rounds from the air. He stepped a step nearer and fired again, but it made no difference. And as he lowered the gun, his focus broadened, and he saw.

Dalex wore an exo-suit. A new model, not like the last one Willsith had used. Around Dalex's skinny limbs there was a collection of cages made of dark metal, its outward edges sharp, and its scale making Dalex twice the man. Willsith noted the actuators, saw components he'd never seen, and as Dalex moved his arm, heard the deep buzz of strong motors from his back.

"CG, the rest are delayed," said Dalex.

"Hey Dalicks, nice dress," shouted White.

"Ah Dalex," started the Controller General, stopping to again tongue his teeth. "You've all met him, I trust. Dalex here is my head of security. Did you know?" And turning to look at him, "Like his suit? It's the latest of our exo's, made from our new grade 55 titanium. They can't build these down on Earth. Show them, Dalex." Then he sucked his chin to his neck and set his pellet eyes at Willsith.

Servo sounds punctuated Dalex's nod, and he began his mechanised walk toward Willsith. Each step powerful but controlled, the exo-suit was more agile than any man. The metal of its feet was near-silent as it contacted the floor, it balanced its brawn perfectly.

"Leave him alone Dalex," shouted White. "What is this crap?"

Farl tensed his finger, threatening with the charging sound, and as Dalex continued to move, he fired at him.

Blocked by the drone. He yelled, turned and let off an overcharge at CG. The drone caught it, and the butt of the gun knocked him back, cracking him in the shoulder.

"Don't worry," said Willsith. "Stay back."

And as Dalex strutted to him, Willsith caught an odd look in his eye. Dalex stopped, slotted the ribbed arm of his suit back along the main torso unit, then fired his fist toward Willsith, the square of the metal hand hitting him just above his heart. Willsith was floored. His body flipped back from his rooted stance. His gun bounced to the extent of his grip as his arm snapped to the floor. *Almost lost it.*

"Get up, I want to show you the leg movement," shouted Dalex.

"Stop," yelled Arc, and pushed past White toward him.

Willsith turned, choked a little, then said, "Go, go back there. Be ready," then sitting up, he shook his head, shouted with emotion. "I will not fight a man in an exo-suit," then stood.

"Shame," said Dalex, then lifted his foot amongst the casing of the exo-foot, bringing his knee up high and then bursting it forward toward Willsith's hip.

He fell again. This time he landed on his face. Lost the rifle.

"Stand up and try. You're a soldier. Fight like a soldier."

"I quit being a soldier five years ago, suit," he said into the floor, then flipped himself onto his back.

"To your feet, soldier," Dalex said, and the words and his laugh repeated amplified from his suit.

No chance. No sodding chance. There's no exposed joints. Not a single angle I can fit a fist into without him snapping my arm off. Not unless he's seriously distracted.

The rifle's useless unless I can get it close. And I've lost it anyway. No more war, I said. Who the hell am I anyway. And he spat.

"Let him be, Dalex," said Farl, and snatched the rifle Arc held. "Let him be or I'll overload both of these at you."

"Come now Farl," Dalex replied simply, then flicked his eyes up at the hovering drone.

The Controller General switched his legs around, crossing his knees and exposing the bare waxy skin of his ankles. "Farl's been a good case study, except for all of this mess. Don't you think, Dalex."

Dalex sneered at Willsith, walked backward a few steps, said, "Yes. Room for improvement," then lifted his lip at Farl.

"As much as I enjoy this, enough now. We've business to attend to. It's been fun to meet you all. I'm sorry for what we'll have to do to you, because of what you've found out today, but I hear that the procedure is getting quite efficient, and there are good days at the colony, regardless of what you've heard. Primes, can you come in now and send these three for processing. Lin?"

Willsith sat up to catch a wide grin leaked across Dalex's face, and as the Controller General swung his head to the door, Dalex laughed. He rotated his head and pumped up his chest, bringing the exo-suit to its proudest stance.

"Dalex, where are my Primes?"

"CG they've had a change of heart. They are no longer your men. They are my men, now."

Willsith got up, scanned the suit's back for weaknesses, saw none. He reclaimed his rifle and clicked his jaw, and watched as Dalex approached CG.

Slotting his hands together, CG pasted his mouth,

then, "Oh dear."

"Yes," said Dalex. "Oh dear."

"Should we fire at them," whispered White. "Can't we get—"

"Oh dear," repeated the Controller General, letting out a huff. "You mean to overthrow me then?"

"Yes," replied Dalex, then, biting his words off. "It has been long overdue."

The Controller General locked his eyes on Dalex, and began to get up.

"Sit. Down." Dalex said, the speakers in his suit amplifying his speech making the old man screw up his face. "Sit down old man."

And then the motors in his suit purred as he stretched out the foot-wide exo arm, pushing the giant metal hand through the air in slow motion.

He's savouring it. But look at the Controller General. He's sickly calm.

"Now now, dispense with this silliness," said CG. "Stop, Dalex."

"I've waited far too long. I've served under your weak rule for far, too, long. Old man." And as the over-sized fingers of his suit approached the man's face, he stopped dead.

CG smiled, said, "Having problems with your suit?"

"What?" shouted Dalex. "What have you—" and he thrust himself around in the suit, but the metal did not move. He rotated his jaw, tweaked his fingers, and then shrieked.

Through the suit speakers the Controller Generals voice filled the room, "You think too much of yourself, Dalex, and you forget my friends above." And the Controller General chuckled, poking the dot of his eye through the metal fingers of the suit and right at Dalex.

"Now, Primes?" spoke the old man from his seat.

Both doors opened and four men filed in from each.

"Secure CG. Release me from this exo. We start now. Today. Here."

"Sorry sir," said a guard, and moved around him to join the line with the others.

Willsith talked himself through the situation. *Eight guns pointed at my face, probable damaged hip, and the aches. No weapon. Not a great situation, eh, soldier.*

"Now, dispose of those three, leave Farl here, I need to discuss his mission," commanded the Controller General.

"Free me," yelled Dalex. "Free me you old fool."

"Suck the vacuum of space. You know exactly why I came up here," Farl shouted at CG, panting. "I came up here to stop you, to expose all this shit. Not to help you." And he kept on yelling as he held the triggers fast, "I won't help!"

"Empty," said Willsith. "Go quiet, Farl."

And again Farl yelled, and threw the rifles at a Prime, who shirked off the impacts with a shoulder, the two guns bouncing to the floor.

"Quiet now Farl. You will assist, it wasn't a request. These three will leave for processing."

"Eat a pigs-arse," shouted White. "You won't take us," and lifted his fists.

"It's language like that which makes the procedure so useful," he replied. "You see, you'll not be able to speak in a few minutes. All three of you will become perfect little workers. Efficient, unquestioning, and silent. Willsith will be great at smashing rock. Maybe they'll let you cook, tubby."

Dalex squeezed his eyes shut and struggled, shouted, "Take him out, one of you! At all costs take out Controller General."

"Quiet, or you know what will happen," CG told him, and waved a hand. The exo-suit walked him back toward the window and lowered itself to its knees. Dalex's face stretched and contorted as he tried to fight the suit.

"Amongst you there must be those who realise what he is doing," Willsith projected at the troops. "The Controller General has become corrupt and will fire on the Earth. He will kill members of your families. He will destroy cities. He does not care for any of you."

CG laughed.

"We can stop him. You do not have to fight for him." Then he panned through the masked faces of the eight armed men. He searched for response, but found none. "Lin? Are you here?" he tried. And he watched for response, and caught a tiny movement. "Is that you, Lin?" But the man did not move again, and all eight of them took a step forward.

"You see. You are the squawking bird. Your actions are not efficient use of power...power that we give to you," said the voice of the old man. "This is why we need more like Farl, and less like you. Fighting is not enough. Fighting is inefficient power use."

"You're going to shoot lasers at the Earth and you talk to me about the efficiency of fighting?" said Willsith.

"Yes, quite. Lasers will do the damage of a thousand men in a millionth of the time. And with surgical accuracy, and a minimal energy cost. We will tactically slice cities from a distance, and doing so we will create order, with almost no energy spend, and no halo-side danger. That is efficient use of power. Your brawn is not. Your fist is defunct. Your struggle with violence, irrelevant."

Willsith could not answer. Rage filled him.

The men moved a step closer.

"What is the...procedure?" said Arc.

"Don't worry, we won't be going," White told him.

"No time to explain. You will see...and hear, shortly. Now dispense with this. Take the three and leave Farl."

Air popped from Dalex's mouth and he yelled toward CG, "You can't have stopped all of my men. If you do not free me, they will kill you. You won't see it coming, but it will come."

"Enough Dalex. Your threats are as weak as your treachery."

Willsith forgot about his pains, and the rage dulled to the back of his mind. The stepping forward of the eight presided, and he worked his way through the options. *They approach. I am unarmed. I can fight, but I am sick of it. And I'm outnumbered. Even if Lin is here, he might not care. All eight can't be perfect soldiers. But all eight are armed. And suited.* And they stepped another step. He counted two more steps before his window of opportunity opened. And he knew then he would fight.

"If one of you is loyal, act now," shouted Dalex. "Act now, or remember this, and continue as planned."

CG shook his head, lifted his hand and pointed a finger down.

A slot opened in the wall and a silver pyramid shape swung down to Dalex. Another drone. As it approached the caged man, he screamed, and then it jumped at his chest, and through the skeleton of the exo-suit, it fired something at him. And he was silent. His head slumped against the constraint of the suit. The Controller General smiled, flicked his finger, and the men stepped again.

Willsith hunkered down. *Not long now. This could be the last fight. Gave them a chance. No reason to avoid it. I can fight. Even if that's all I can do.*

Like the shriek of a cat, Farl burst out into speech,

234

"No. Stop." And he ran in front of Arc, White and Willsith. The guards spun in unison to point their guns at him. "Stop this now," he protested.

"I'm listening," said the old man.

"You want me for something, right? Well I won't help you. In fact I'll…die before I do. I won't help, unless you let these three go. You send them to Tacern, and you give them a good life."

"Stop Farl," Willsith commanded him, edging forward, reaching out an arm.

"Well. That's a kind offer you've made me Farl. But I have no time for trading. You will help me, you have no choice. You are important today, but not that important."

Farl cried, and his body bounced as he churned out air. "I have a choice."

Another step. That's all I need, Willsith told himself. One, more, step.

"To have a choice, one needs power. You have no power. I have power," replied CG, raising his cuff. "I have the power to complete my plan, and not you, nor Dalex, nor that old brute can stop me." And then he snapped his finger through the air.

CHAPTER 25
The Brute

Willsith rested on a hair-trigger. He didn't look at 229, but worried for them; in the end he was ready to trade whatever it would take. They faced a wall of authority. A tactical unit of eight unknown rifles. Two bullet-catcher drones. Dalex, playing the caged bird, hanging limp amongst the frame of his exo-suit, tongue out. And then Controller General; an antique of a man, seated as if he were a king.

A soldier lifted a gloved hand, flashed the skin of his exposed trigger finger twice. More drones darted from slots in the walls, each was conical, mirrored, with vents on its surfaces; like that which had jabbed Dalex. They swarmed together, then fanned out, stopping point-side down, above each soldier.

Farl whimpered, coughed, then tried again, "Stop. I'll help you. Just don't hurt them."

"Goodbye 229," said the Controller General, and unfolded his legs. "Proceed Commander."

And then Willsith snapped. He wrenched his body as fast as he could, the full force of his arm projecting out toward the nearest rifle. As his hand touched the metal he gripped it fast, ready to snatch it toward him. But he could not close his mitt.

It had struck him in the chest in an instant. The pain blew through him; a thousand rusty scalpel blades drawing bloody slices outward from the jab. His muscles convulsed, and he threw himself backward, to the floor. And writhed in agony, there, clawing at the spot where the needle had struck, until the pain encased him, and he felt the static hum of his cells on fire.

The Controller General stood, pulled down his jacket, said, "You see, you're a tool, soldier. Dalex wanted you to fight me, but he didn't realise, he was also a tool. These men here, they are not like you. They are as I am. As Farl is. We never allowed ourselves to become another mans tool."

Willsith spat over himself, shivered on the floor, and said, "No. You are—you are a—"

"I will ship you off as labour. You're better use of the power we bestow on you that way. Simple soldiers are not needed any more. Your last use will be as a rock-breaker down on Mars. Making space for the next generation."

Willsith flung his head around, saw flashes of White's face. He couldn't feel the warmth of his friends hand on his shoulder, but he saw it before he squeezed his face shut to try and bear the pain. His body twitched from his neck to his feet. Everything hurt. Pain peaked at his fingertips, in his teeth, through his eyes, and the rest of his body burned as though held in acid. Willsith judged that his skull might soon crack from the pressure .

When the wave passed, he heard the dry voice of the Controller General. "No Farl. No."

The pain oozed from Willsith in a flash, and all he knew was his stinging chest. The meta trauma bled away, and he sat up to address the scene. Nothing had changed, he couldn't have passed out. It was still hopeless. Farl was nodding his head, his shoulders dipping and rising with his exaggerated breathing.

Willsith tried to stand, shooed White away. *Can't stand that easy.* But he made it to his feet. Something wasn't right. And the metal of the soldiers guns jumped out at him, and he was scared. *Shit. I'm trapped. I can't get away. They're going to kill us. Not a hope in hell we'll get out. Shit. I need out…But then…no, that's not me. The needle.* He folded himself, pulling his forearms into his chest, and began to fight the feelings.

"Move," came the refreshing female voice of Lif. "Now." And Willsith saw it through wide eyes. Arc's drone lunged across the room toward CG.

The pyramid drones circled around it before the men could react, and then Lif's device sent out a charge.

They fell like rain drops. One hit a soldier on the helmet, another on the shoulder. All six drones tumbled to the metal.

Willsith laughed.

Then the men reacted, and spun around to fire upon it. But it was too fast. Lif's drone squealed, dropped between the helmets of two Primes, let out another charge, and collapsed with the two men.

Willsith told himself to do it, to get the hell up, and he moved his arm out toward the nearest Prime. His mind quarrelled with him. Told him of terrible dangers, leeched fears into his consciousness, dug at him. He squatted back down into a quivering mess.

The remaining Primes surrounded them, and Farl stood before 229 and held out his arms.

"Come to my side now, Farl. With your skill we can rule Earth, and the other settlements, with honest efficacy. We will enforce peace."

Willsith saw the perfect arc of White's spit which flew over Farl's shoulder and hit the Controller General's shoe. Again he laughed. But then White was pushed to the floor by a guard, and another yanked the rifle from Arc.

"No," Farl told him. Willsith said it too.

"I will be a father to you, and you will get more control than you've ever known."

Farl threw out his arms again, pushing has palms back toward Willsith and the others. "No. I can't."

"You can't because of them? Three men we picked to surround you for a few years. They are fodder," and as Willsith looked up, he caught the ball-bearing eyes of the man as he approached. "There's no future for them Farl," said the Controller General.

"No, I will not let you," yelled Farl. "I'll do whatever. But let them go."

The Controller General took a careful step, watched as the bullet-catching drone moved to his chest, and said to him, "They aren't worthy, Farl. And you know it. Watch." Up shot his gristly arm and then down dropped his finger.

Another pyramid drone entered.

Willsith could hear the whine of the thing. He cupped his hands over his ears and cringed.

It flew toward him at great speed, and from his nursing squat, he flinched as it jumped at his chest.

The pain was the same, but this time it fled faster. Willsith jumped to his feet and ripped down his lower jaw, screamed from the base of his spine - an animal noise. His eyes bulged and he felt heat behind them. His arms seemed heavy, like missiles, and all he could focus on was the soldiers weapons. As the bass of his howl passed, his thoughts sped up. *Go time.* Cat-like, he lunged at two Primes, fixing rigid fingers around their masks and slamming their heads to the floor. The men fell, and he laughed a sick laugh. He twisted his body to face his next prey, still laughing.

229 shouted his name, and then it hit him in the back. Willsith crumpled like a tree, burned to the core. Pain, again. This time the same as the first, and as he crammed his eyes shut, he heard the Controller General speak. "You see. He is a soldier. He can be turned on, or off. A digital animal. He can't stop fighting, unless we stop him. He's from the old lineage and we don't need his DNA or his ideas polluting the pool anymore...Move him back."

And then the moving. The two he had slammed slung him back with similar care, his face hitting the solid floor.

"Some men are only machines. They need to be worked, not listened too. Do not shirk your potential to try and save the cheap value of a tool."

"No," said Farl, and this time his voice was more sure. Willsith could not see, but he could hear his friend. "No. They are my group. My friends."

Willsith laughed through his tears, his body thrusting and tensing and torturing him. Still he laughed.

"This is my final offer," the old man said. "Farl. I will have the procedure done to each of them now, one by one. You will watch them all be permanently subdued, and then you will have your faculties removed too, if you do not join me."

Farl declared it loudly, "I will not."

"Then you will all be slaves with empty minds. Start with him, the brute."

They were all pulled away from Willsith, who saw their struggle through teary eyes. White was last, and pushed the soldier back, but the warning of charged rifles stopped him.

Then he was surrounded. Willsith cowered, a pile of limbs on the floor. He thought of disaster, the collapse of Earth, his dead brother. He felt dead, and wished it. The glaring lights bit at his eyes, the usual hum of the Halo grew into a catastrophic roar. His clothes strangled his skin, and his skin itself screamed. Everything tormented him. He clutched at his knees. And as the two grabbed at him he tightened himself into a ball, hyperventilating. He tried to remember the anger of a moment ago, his logic tried to override the drug. *I am that man,* he told himself, replaying the smashing of their heads against the floor. *Stand up man. I am that man. But I can't, I'm weak, I will get hurt, killed, they're going to disable me. I want it. The end, like Bear. No. Stop it. That is not you. It is. What if it is?*

Their gloves grasped his biceps and tugged at him, trying to unfurl the man. Each contact felt as heavy as a tombstone, and their gloves might as well have been sandpaper to his skin. And he fought them to remain together, to hold himself, to stay down.

"Ha ha, you'll need more men, Controller Geriatric," laughed White. "Our 'brute' is too strong for your high-school-hit-men."

"Quiet, he won't need to stand for the procedure, it will just be less dignified like this, as he is, a wailing mess. Proceed."

And the two stood back from Willsith, and removed tools from their back-plates. White cylinders, like miniatures of the marble columns of ancient Rome. They nodded at the Controller General.

"Ready the dischargers," he told them.

"Willsith," shouted Arc. "Willsith."

"Snap out of it man, don't let them near you." White yelled at him.

Willsith opened his eyes and saw the men leaning toward him, jerked back along the floor and kicked out at them, hitting one in the shin. They followed him as he wriggled back along the floor, clutching his hands to his ears, screaming. Eventually his legs would not take him further, and he felt the flat metal of the Hub wall, but still he kicked at the floor, and as he bunched up against the cold surface, the two soldiers came. They held out the short bars, pushed them through the air toward his head, and while he whimpered, he knew he could not move, he was trapped. This was it. He caught glimpses of his friends through the teary blurs, and heard them scream his name, but he couldn't move, it was over.

The cylinders touched his temples. They were cold, and all at once they captured him and chilled his core, and he waited there, trapped, submitted to death.

Cold moments passed where he ignored his senses. A nothingness presided, until he was lifted up. His back pulling at him, tearing him from the two tools, and men. And then he fell backward, rolling and impacting. Bringing himself to a squat, sound faded in. Buzzing filled his ears, and muffled shouting, and then cracks.

It was Eva, he could smell her perfumer. Her odour worked into his thoughts, through the sadness, the pain and irritation of his body, through his burning bones and spasming muscles, he smelled her.

Then he heard her, and her voice lay over him like a balm, and she said, "Get up. Help the others." So he opened his eyes, and he could see that it was her.

Eva had opened the Hub-wall, and now she stood above him, her hair wild and her hands waggling around as though she was conducting an orchestra. "Get up man," she said, without turning to him.

He could not, but his eyes gave him sight. And he saw

a different Eva. Interlaced carbon-fibre scales clung to the length of her black body suit, white straps and cables ran the length of her, connecting into panels and armour junctions. Reinforced plates capped her joints, with clasps which reminded Willsith of wartime Titan exo pilot kit. The suit and straps reached up her neck tightly, mapping it and leaving only her fierce face exposed.

Willsith choked. Above Eva the air was filled with drones. A swarm. They hovered in perfect formation, and as she moved her gloved hands, so they moved. Drones returned from the room, others moved from the ranks which hung above her, and Willsith knew he must stand up.

"Stop," came the voice of the Controller General. "Stop Eva, stop."

Willsith lifted himself and saw it all.

Her drones threw themselves at the soldiers, impacting them in their soft spots, between the armour plates. He felt their pain. One by one they let go of his friends, and as they did, her drones raised to the guards faces and let out a charge which dropped them. One by one they fell. Those who had lifted the devices to his head were already down, strewn across the floor in front of him. But seeing them, and the whites of their tools, made him wince again. *Did they do it to me? Am I gone?* And he tried to speak.

"E—E—Eva," he got out.

"What's wrong with you," she shouted. "Did they use the dischargers on you?"

"D—do—don't—don't know," and he wanted to cling to her leg, to feel her support, but he did not move.

White and Arc ran to them, White stopping to stamp on the devices.

"Willsith, are you okay?" Arc asked.

He nodded, and watched as Eva walked forward throwing her arms through the air. Farl edged back toward them amongst the chaos of the drones.

"What is this, Eva?" projected CG.

"We're leaving," she replied.

"You're leaving?"

"Yes Father."

"With them?"

"Yes, with them."

"Eva, no."

"It's not as easy as telling me not to, Father. I am not under your control."

And Willsith mumbled something he couldn't even make out himself, and felt White's arm around him, helping him up.

"It's over Controller," yelled Farl as he stood next to Eva. "You're over."

"Be quiet boy," he retorted, and raised his arm, and then his index finger, and held it in the air.

Eva shook her head, "Don't, Father. I've 20 drones here, and more. You haven't seen what these ones can do."

"I will not allow you to go with them," he said, then, "do you realise what you're doing? We are so close to the jump. This thing with these four…it's just play. What will happen is set. It will happen without them, without you, without Dalex. It would happen even without me."

"I want no part of it. I hate it. I hate you!" she yelled, and thrust her armoured shoulders forward, sending a cloud of drones to circle him, as he stood amongst the fodder of his men.

"Your mother would have wanted you to—"

"Don't."

"She would have wanted you to come with me."

"Shut up. Don't talk about her. You don't have the right after what you did."

And the old man walked through the drones and toward her. 229 stood behind and Willsith could see now that she was crying.

"Come with me. We can talk this through, after."

"No. This is the end, Father," she said.

CG stepped closer, and reached the middle of the hall as Willsith felt the drug lift. He raised his shoulders up and held his spine straight. With each doubt and fear and tremor which poked at him, he knew that the drug was working its way out. He smiled. He walked to Eva's side, and smiled. He looked past her, and into the Controller General's bead eyes. "Thank you, Eva," he said, and placed a hand on her shoulder.

"This is the end, Father," she repeated. And she threw back her head and flicked two palms forward. Twenty drones circled around the Controller General, each with exposed elements. Clean metal spikes. They made charging noises and Eva laughed through tears.

"No, Eva. You don't want to do this. Stop this at once."

"No!" she replied. "It's time you were stopped."

Willsith knew what she might do, and as his thoughts became his own, he thought of ways to stop her. *It's not going to help,* he wanted to tell her, *this won't help you. But I'll help.* And he walked from them, toward the Controller General, and let free a savage smile which covered his face, and then Willsith prepared to punch the man.

But still Eva's drones circled the Controller General, encasing him, and Willsith could not get to him.

"Stop this charade Eva. This brute, these drones, they are inefficient. You dance them around like they have infinite power. This is why we must act. This is why we need a fresh start, and why you need one too."

The drones parted, forming two walls either side of the man, and Willsith leaned in to grab him. At first he saw the worry in his face, but then the sick old man sniggered. And Willsith's hand met the thrust of the bullet-catching drone, which remained in the air. Whichever way Willsith moved, the drone followed his hand. He could not force passed it or pull it from the air.

"Enough," said the Controller General, and then. "Send in a full set."

Again the room filled with the shapes of men. Patterned armour, tactical clothing. Rifles. More and more troops entered, and fanned out behind CG. But they were not men. Even through bleary eyes and with burned-out neurons, Willsith could see. Automatons. They wore the clothes of men, but their steps were impersonations, their chests held no breath.

"More men?" White shouted out.

White doesn't see it. These aren't men, they're killing machines.

"I have more souls at my disposal than any other man. There is no end to my supply of brutes."

Willsith edged backward, and Eva held her arms out and her drones in place.

CG dropped his face, and the skin bunched at his neck. "Do not hurt her. Do not hurt Eva, but take the rest, lethally if you must. Drag them out into the cold of space."

And the robotic soldiers inched toward them, and Willsith inched back.

"Do not move or I will kill him," she yelled.

"Come now Eva," CG said to her.

"Shut up. Willsith, let's go."

Willsith gave a last smile to the man and then turned to her. Eva was beautiful, powerful. He would help her. He would stay with her. And through her jaw, that she held tight, and her face that she had wet, he believed that he knew her.

One figure stood from the rest and she flicked a drone, dropping it. "We are going. Do not attempt to follow."

"Eva. Stop this, for your mothers sake."

Eva shrieked and raised tense hands. The drones cut up the air, mimicking her, arranging themselves into throbbing clouds around the Controller General's head. "Goodbye Father," she said in low tone, and as Willsith got up, she slammed shut her fists.

Willsith ran at her, and took her in his arms, and as she clenched him she cried and yelled and screamed.

A chorus of servos sounded behind him, the robot troop. There would be nothing he could do to stop them. If they caught him they'd take Eva, and then they'd rip every fibre of muscle from him and the others. So he ran. No other choice.

He ran harder than he'd ever ran. Eva shrieked. Her drones tailed them, a humming wall of support.

Metal Hub-wall fell and they were alone suddenly. Arc, White, Farl, Willsith and Eva. He checked.

Thuds sounded from the other side. Willsith let her go, she blurted out and ran to the wall, "No, let me back, let me do it."

"Let you do what?" asked Farl.

"It's not worth it Eva. You'd only regret it, believe me," Willsith said to her. "We need to go, we won't survive another instance like that."

"You can talk!" Arc said to Willsith. "You're okay!"

"Yeah, they didn't fire the dischargers. The other was mood-drugs, they had me in berserker and some anxiety state. It's gone now. Just the chest pains left."

"I'm glad you're okay."

"Me too big-guy, was worried for a second. There ain't nothing we could do to help you. If she—" then White turned to Eva, "—if you hadn't shown up, he'd be gone. We'd all be gone."

Eva wept, and banged against the door, and shouted, "Let me."

Willsith nodded at them, said, "Let's move. Lif are you there?"

"Yes commander," replied the calm voice of Eva's artificial intelligence.

And he moved to Eva, and spoke softly to her, "I know how you feel. For now you'll have to trust me. We need your help."

"Lif's back," White said, then whooped. "How you been baby?"

"All cores have been running without error."

"Where did you go?" asked Arc.

"I was disabled by the security systems operatives of Dalex, but I have managed, with the help of Farl's program, to overcome that block."

Eva turned to Willsith, the drones around them, and told him she wanted to do it. She begged him for help.

"Later. Let's go," he said, and nodded affirmative. "Help us."

Farl moved to them, told her, "We need your help Eva. We need to stop the lasers."

"You can't," she said, and wiped her tears away with the back of her glove. "You can't stop the lasers."

CHAPTER 26
Another Way

Willsith's chest throbbed but his head felt remarkably clear. And as they walked up to, and through another section of hallway, he wanted to say something that would make them move faster. He looked at them, and saw White struggling, Eva locked in sadness, held up by her suit, and the other two trapped in their imaginations. "Thank you, all," was all he could say, under his breath. "Thank you."

"Back to this sodding, wall-up, wall-down thing, then," said White.

"Doesn't have to be that way," spoke Lif. And the walls ahead slid up, a staggered opening of the long corridor.

"Damn I love you Lif," White told the AI.

"Thank you, White. I'm also sending a delivery bot."

White sniggered, "Sending me love letters?"

"The delivery bot I am sending is large enough so as to carry you all," Lif replied directly. "It's not conventional use, but I think it'll work."

White stretched his face long, then grinned at Arc and said, "Oh, thanks!"

In the distance a box appeared and began to trundle

toward them. They walked on to meet it.

"So he's your father?" Farl said to her.

Eva started to cry, turned her face away.

Another wall dropped behind them, and Willsith was glad of the thing. "You have a lot of drones," he said, turning to tag the mass of hanging metal which followed them.

She nodded through her tears.

"And one hell of a suit," he added.

Eva nodded. "My design."

"Eva, what type of ship is it we're going to?" White asked.

Then Farl, "And why can't we stop the lasers?"

"See, now I'm equipped," Eva said, looking up at Willsith. "This is how I meant it to happen. Drones charge." Many drones swung through the air and snapped to her back with a click, filing themselves along her spine unit.

Willsith tried to talk, but then ended up staring into her face, reluctant with his words.

The delivery bot had closed the gap and without thought he hopped onto the shiny metal. He felt the others stare at him, and let his head fall to the side. His rear vibrated and the bot shot open its side, flinging out odd sized parcels and then shutting itself again.

"Get on," Lif told them all.

"Hub mailbots sure are spanky compared to Section ones," White said, before lifting himself up alongside Willsith.

Willsith rubbed the perfect metal, saw his face reflected back at him. Didn't recognise himself.

"Why can't we stop the lasers? If you give me root access to the core, I can at least jettison the power or drop the operating system here."

Willsith wondered about what the Controller had said. Was he just a brute? Was all that terror inevitable? Or was that only more propaganda. And he smiled at Eva.

Her face cleared up, her cheeks fresh, as though the storm had passed, and she reached out for his arm, and held it as they joined the rest of them on the bot.

"Tell me," spat out Farl, "Eva, tell me. Why can't we stop them?"

"You must know," she said plainly.

The bot rocked into motion and motored forward.

"Know what? No. Tell me!"

White told him, "Look Farl, there's no need to—"

"How would I know?"

"Dalex said that you know the whole structure. He said you'd had access to the full charter, that you'd been studying it," Eva said.

"Charter? What?"

"Dalicks, king of bullshit," added White,, "master of nothing."

Farl's chest sunk and his shoulders rose. "Please, what?"

"You don't know about the charter? About today?" She squeezed Willsith's arm.

"Tell us about the charter, Eva," Willsith said to her.

Lif broke in, using a handful of drones to draw an arrow through the air. "We do not have long," the voice projected, "I can't keep the walls down behind us for much longer. I'll have to push the bot to full speed, hold on."

A hiss made him wince, then dulled to a whirr, but their pace had doubled.

"Fuckin' magic carpet!" exclaimed White. Willsith gripped the edge tighter.

An inertia fell away, and Willsith felt himself more

awake, asked her again, "Tell us and then we will know how to act."

"I'll tell you," she said, "I'll tell you all of it, but we need to get to the Stellar Ark."

Farl huffed.

"There's not time," Eva said.

"You've been planning this for a while then?" yelled White.

"For more than a year, since my..."

"So you knew they would arrest us?" asked Arc.

"No. Well...eventually, yes."

"But we didn't know the lasers were coming, or what was happening."

"Yes. You took longer than I thought you would to rebel, and then I wasn't ready. I've had to play this part, I've been hiding all this for so long," and she gestured to her drones, and she pushed her carbon capped fingertips into his forearm. "Hiding this, and watching you all."

White choked and wheezed, said, "Watching us?"

"And why do you need us?" snapped Farl. "What is the charter?"

"Not enough time to say it all. You're the right exact mix...229 was an experiment. They made the environment, to sculpt you, Farl, into the ultimate hacker. To prepare you. And it kind of worked, but I was tweaking it, I wanted something else."

White coughed, then laughed.

"They played all of you as a statistical game. You were meant to foster contempt for Earth's politics in Farl, and a desire to fight. I was on the other side, and I hated the manipulation, and anyway, you kept fighting it. In the end 229 became a dangerous section, you were on a knife's edge between the two sides, and they pulled the plug. Farl you were very close to leaking the core from your bunk. In the end, he thought he could force you, Farl to—he might still think he can. My father needs you, or someone like you, for the charter."

So that's why we're not dead. Because of Farl. And now, because of her.

"Half way. Sixteen parts," said Arc.

"I'm a flipping jelly mold?" White burst out. "All along we were just formers for Farl?"

"I'm...sorry," said Eva.

"Why am I important?" said Farl. "Why me?"

She glanced up at Willsith, turned back to Farl, said, "History, abilities, height. There were factors."

"But I'm not anything special."

"You are a unique mix. You all are."

"Twenty-four sections, we're getting there. Where next?"

Another of Eva's drones lunged onto her back plate, jolting her forward. "Lif, explain your plan."

"The five of you are to enter the stairwell, descend two levels, pass through the three following zones and then to secure the Stellar Ark 12. I will then accompany you onto the ship and we will exit the Earth's Halo."

"And then? After we exit?" pushed Farl.

"After our evacuation, I will provide remote access to the Hub-core, where you can assist me in securing as much information, and disabling as many rogue operations, as possible."

"And we can stop the lasers?"

"There is nothing we can do to stop the lasers."

And Farl cursed at the artificial intelligence.

"We can't stop the lasers. I've run every simulation I can, he's tied everything up. There's no access, it's so thoroughly distributed, even if I'd have..."

"Even if you'd have killed him?"

Eva nodded.

"Believe me, it's not the answer," added Willsith, putting a hand over hers. "It wouldn't have helped the anger, or the pain."

"So that's the charter? A statistically unbeatable plan for today? A plan of supremacy?" Farl pushed.

Eva sighed, nodded, then spoke. "The charter contains an assumption of events, including today's, that will pacify Earth and let them colonise other planets."

"But you said we broke the model, we didn't act how we were supposed to. Now that we know, we can disrupt it."

"It's not perfect, but it has been right 99 times out of 100."

"We're more than numbers," said Willsith. "People are."

She dropped her face, "I didn't say it was good. That's why we have to get out of here, we can't stop it, but if we broadcast the data, we at least give the world the chance to act on information. If we get it out and tell nine and a half billion people, they have a chance to act. Between them, they have a chance to beat the statistics, and save themselves."

"Won't *his charter* have that factored in?" asked Farl.

"It's been a battle to keep Lif private, but I think I've managed it. I think the main system doesn't know…or didn't."

"Complex." White coughed and then said, "So the system's rigged like an old time presidential election, and we're competing against the richest fat cat there ever was, and we only the truth on our side?"

Willsith gave a stern look down the line of his friends faces and said, "We've got the truth, Lif, and the most infamous cook this side of Mars."

254

"Ha, I like it," White said. "Tasty." The delivery bot slowed to a stop and they got off. White slapped a palm onto the flat where he had just sat. "Should I be thanking you mailbot, or Lif the digital?"

No one replied, and they filed through the side door and down two sets of metal-grate stairs.

Willsith held back at the first landing, reached out for Eva, and stopped her. His eyes found hers, they smiled, but then he bit at her, "You better be right about all this. Farl, us, the Ark. You must tell us everything."

Eva pulled her lips in, nodded.

And he let go of her arm, and moved his hand to the layered plates around her waist. "Eva, I—" She swung her hips away from him, frowned, and hurried down the stairs.

At the bottom the door was shut, and they all stood waiting for him as he walked the last few stairs. "Locked?" he asked.

"No," Arc said. "We were waiting for you."

Willsith saw Eva glance at him, but eyeballed Farl, then the door, and stepped right through it as it shot open in front of him. "Don't ever stop to wait for me. Keep it moving."

The room was dark, a catacomb. Its walls laden with dark metal, a cache. Between the racks of guns, walkways shot off in all directions, a labyrinth.

"Armoury Four," announced Lif.

As they drifted forward, Willsith reached out, followed the contours of the hardware. Weapons stacked from floor to ceiling, held accessible by brackets lurching from the wall. Handles presented themselves. Sniper rifles, tasers, automatic rail guns. It was one way, but it wasn't his way. Not any more. But though he patrolled his edges, he lusted after the quick-fix. The bullet slung into the heart of the problem. No, not today.

"Maybe we could go back, with guns," offered Farl. "Me and you, Willsith. End this at the top."

"Not today," he said quickly. "It won't fix it. A bullet won't end this."

"There are so many guns. Why are there so many guns?" asked White.

"It's in case there's a need to—"

"Invade?"

Arc stopped, said, "Shouldn't we take some?"

"Wow, what about one of these?" White suggested, and ran to the towering suits.

Carbon-fibre and mirror-sharp edges jutted out from behind the gun-racks. Willsith saw the shells of soldiers. Many exo-suits. One each for 229, and then some. Without men in them they looked like torture cages. Bows of sharp metal with pistons and rivets and straps. External edges sharpened to blades, internal edges softened with rubber. Open gloves and open limb cages. The suits hung spread out, open, ready. Beckoning.

All it would take is a step up, old man. Just one step backward into this skeleton, and the thing would fasten you in, just like the old days. You'd be away. You could tear down walls, rip through drones and the guards and be at him, blade to neck. And then done. And break that window to space. And then done.

"Can I try?" asked Farl. "Will it work for me?"

"This isn't a school trip. These aren't gadgets, toys. Stop. We're not here to fight. We're not here for this, for these. Now let's go."

"Willsith, it might be sensible to equip ourselves, we don't know—"

"Farl, that's what they want," Willsith barked. "They want war, they want to fight. Remember what happened to Dalex? You're safer out of one of them than inside it. We'll fight only when we have to. Go." And he threw his arm toward the door.

"We might have no choice but to fight," Farl sneered. "It wouldn't hurt if we could disable the remote..." but still he followed out of the door.

"I guess you could use them for stuff other than fighting," added White. "It's how you look at it."

CHAPTER 27
Stellar Ark 12

From dark and cramped, to light fantastic. The guns that had dripped from the armoury walls hung on the inside of Willsith's skull, and he carried the idea of them into the gigantic room. Light dashed at the five from all angles, and open space assaulted them.

Willsith stepped out onto the metal grate and stared at his feet. Work boots spread his weight over a grated walkway which seemed lace-thin once his eyes focused on the floor, far, far below.

White let out a whimper, pushing it into a cough, "Mighty mole! That floor is a fat-mile down!"

He wasn't far off. It was a long way down. Willsith stepped forward and gripped the polished metal rail, letting his knees hit the solid glass barrier. And then he started to accept the view.

The hangar was colossal. The distant corners grouped together walls which combined would absorb a town.

"Wow," someone said.

Willsith blinked his eyes. The far-off floor was metal, with patches. The walls were patterned. There were no people, no vehicles, no kit. There was only the Stellar Ark 12.

"Wow," someone repeated.

The Stellar Ark 12 was a gargantuan ship. It lay down the length of the hangar, a toppled tower block; it dwarfed everything tangible Willsith had seen in half a decade. Each end of the ship diminished into a razor sharp edge, and countless flaps stuck out from these angled sections.

"This is the Stellar Ark—" said Eva, "—number 12."

"There's 12 of these things?"

"Yes."

"This hangar itself is…huge, we couldn't see it from 229, how is there more?" asked Farl.

"It's designed to be hard to see," she replied. "And only one Ark docks at a time. Plus, this is the largest."

And Willsith saw pipes. Two staunch tubes jutted out from the internal end of the Ark and disappeared into the floor.

"It's dumping something?" he asked.

Nobody answered. Willsith let his eyes trace the ships edge as it clung to the floor and toward space. It was hovering, part of it out in…space.

White expelled the air in his lungs, said, "Wow."

"Clear dock. You haven't seen one yet have you?" Eva stated.

Willsith knew what she was talking about, but he could barely believe the thing. The tail end of the ship, the last quarter of it, stuck out into space. All that was between them, the huge hangar, and space, was this transparent wall. The Clear dock.

"Shouldn't we have suits?" asked White.

Arc spoke mechanically, "Clear docks form a seal between us and space. We don't need suits." Then said to Eva, "How long have you had these working?"

"Two years, at this size."

"I didn't know."

"You wouldn't, we've kept it quiet."

How much had they been keeping quiet? How much would Eva have to reveal?

"So we're taking her?" White started in excitement.

"Yes," Eva replied.

"The whole thing?"

"Yes."

Willsith wanted to go, to move. He charted his eyes along the walkway, toward the lift at the end. Only one way to go. Down. Then a jabbing burn in his chest again, and a shake. He disguised the pain by turning back toward the ship. His ribcage twitched, he forced his eyes to grab across the hangar, distraction from the pain. He saw the ship, its colours vivid. The grey-green hull was emblazoned with bright blue letters: STELLAR ARK 12. And above that it was capped with glass.

"How come there's no people around? No soldiers, no pilots, no maintenance?" Farl asked Eva.

There's glass all over that ship. And in the reflection he saw the wall below him and the speckled dark of space.

"There's not even any doors in the hangar, or crates or anything?" Farl continued.

Willsith scanned the glass, explaining to himself as he went: *it makes up a quarter of the hull, and the whole top is glass, unless—no, it's definitely glass. Why would it be glass?*

"The 12 is automatic," replied Eva. "It's piloted by a skeleton crew, but they don't do much other than observe. It's back to deposit, the crew should be out at CRC."

Then it struck him, and he almost wept. The Stellar Ark 12 housed a forest. He choked, blew air out his nose, and then said, "Trees?"

She smiled at him, forging tiny dimples in her cheeks and aiming her eyes into his. "Oh, yeah, that's the special thing about the 12. It's got the full eco," Eva said. "It has its own forest. I designed it."

Willsith felt his head swirl. Elation, anger, love. *It's the drugs. The mood drugs must be still kicking out.* And he contorted himself to stop from crying.

"You alright big-guy?" asked White. "It is beautiful, you're right. I never even held out hope for those national parks, let alone a freaking space-forest. After your dad shut down the space-farms idea Eve, I—"

"We didn't shut the space-farms down. And it's Eva."

Lif sounded a beep from behind them, then said, "I would advise you to start moving. I am attempting to access the elevator controls, but your limited window for evacuation via the Stellar Ark 12 is getting more and more limited by the second."

"Doesn't even surprise me—" said White, as he slung his shoulders back and picked up the weight of his belly from the railing, "—about the farm engines. But Lif told us they had shut them down for R & D space—I mean. Hey, shit, I've just realised…Drasil-G! This is like the myth, and we're stealing it…don't tell me you have an ash tree in there?"

"Wait and see," replied Eva.

"My my," replied the ex-chef. "My oh my."

The greens and the browns of the trees swept across the whole of the Ark, peppering it with colour. Each appeared a green firework trapped in time, and from the pit of his stomach Willsith felt hope. For a moment he thought he might be sick, and he pictured himself vomiting over the edge, but managed to resist. He yawned, and knew that he was himself again. *Damn I hope that was the last of the mood drugs. Sodding emotional merry-go-round.*

"Tired?" she asked. "Not long now, you can have a sleep amongst the trees, old-man." And again that smile. "We can get you and Arc fixed up too, once we're in."

Willsith stared at her, then the Stellar Ark 12, and nodded. He heaved out air and started jogging. His boots struck the grate making a pleasant rattle, the sound echoing out across the chasm of the hangar and bleeding away into space. *When moving, I'm best. They can say what they want, but none of them can act like I can act.* And as his muscles tugged and pulled at his battle-worn limbs, he felt the air slide passed him and beamed a grin. *A forest. We're going to steal a floating forest.*

The elevator was at least half a klick away, and he knew they'd not keep up. He didn't care, and revelled in looking down, the disgusting drop between him and the floor, the distance they'd have to run to the Ark. He anticipated the proper pumping of his blood. "I'll sleep amongst the trees alright, but not before you are all safe."

His calf-muscles hummed by the time he reached the elevator, and he threw out the idea of hunching over to catch his breath, and gripped his hips, revelling in the burn.

She was only metres behind, and he saw the wetness of sweat that covered her cheeks, but still she was not out of breath. *Who are you, really, Eva?*

Eva smiled. He smiled back. He held himself in such a way, and kept his eyes on her, still mapping the other's distance in his periphery.

Her lips swelled and she showed the red of the inside of her mouth. She said, "Can I get to the lift?"

Willsith lifted his jaw and hid behind it. Stepped out of her way. *Shit. Am I seeing something that's not there? Is it me falling for you, or you for me? You're young.*

Brave. Perhaps devastating. No sense in denying it. And he looked at her as she tapped away at a blank control. *But are you playing me for an old fool? To hell with that.* And as the others from 229 filed in, he decided to reject the idea. *I'll do for them, and carry them safely out of here. Me, you, that idea, it's the last thing. I'll sleep in those trees before that ever happens.*

"Wow," said White, between gasps. "I'm runnier than those eggs Farl cooked when I had grav-sickness."

"Shut up," snapped Farl.

"Glad the lift's here. I don't fancy taking the ladder down," Arc gestured to the ladder.

Farl leaned on the rail, looked it up and down, said, "It's a mag-lift, right?"

Arc confirmed the observation.

"Sweet."

On a tiny shelf of a walkway at the top of the hangar, Willsith and White met at the rail and shared their awe at the forested ship. Behind them the other three talked to the AI and worked on getting into the lift. In the brief silence, he caught their conversation.

"You won't open it like that," she told Farl.

"I was just checking, might of worked."

"It's a beautiful machine," Arc said. "Suspended here at zero energy cost."

"Lif any luck?"

"No Eva. Gained access to the hangar control stream, but the lift is not responding."

"Can you see its status?" Farl asked the AI.

"I can see that it's locally overridden. No access routes even give feedback; I am unable to hack entry."

"Keep trying Lif," Eva said, and Willsith turned to see her tap each and every drone which clung to her backplate.

"Come on Lif, you can do it. You're the most amazing program I've ever…met," said White. "Open Sesame!"

"I am trying, White."

Arc shook as he looked down the rungs which stuck out from the wall, said, "I really don't want to climb down this ladder. Can't we override the override?"

"This panel's useless," said Farl, striking it.

Eva straightened her back, commanded, "Drones, check for other panels please. Lif do you have schematics? How does the override work?"

"The manual override has been engaged from the hangar floor."

"All this way. We get this far and see that forest, that ship, our ship, and we can't get to her," White said, shaking his head. "Ah, I'll go down if someone has to?" IIc walked to the ladder, tested the first rung.

"This is useless," proclaimed Farl. "We're screwed. We don't have time for this. I'm going back for an exo."

"No," said Willsith.

"White," sounded the voice of Lif.

"Yes, dear?"

"Open says me," replied the computerised lady, and the lift doors opened.

White stepped back from the ladder, unveiled a full set of teeth, then hopped inside. "Blimey, for a minute there I thought I'd actually have to climb down."

CHAPTER 28

Magic

"Take us down Lif," said Eva.

"One moment."

Willsith let his hand against the wall and felt the furry red velour which covered the inside of the lift. The light was soft there, and as he surveyed the others he picked out imperfections in their faces, highlighted by shadows. Packfood had left its mark on 229; the damaged skin on his friends faces reminded him of the war-torn west. Eva was remarkably untouched, though, or made-up. Her expression was empty, she was absent from the present; sweat shined across her face and it seemed as though her still eyes drew him in unintentionally. *It's this space, it's because we're cramped.*

And then, without warning, movement. Incredible force swelled around them. Willsith knew they were falling, and fast, but the technology wasn't giving them the full gravity of the thing.

"We're moving," said White.

"We were," added Farl. "It's stopped."

"How can you tell?"

"I just can."

"Damn I can't wait to see the forest!" said White. "Let me out."

"Lif, was that it? Can you open the doors?" Eva asked.

They waited in silence, hot and close, until Willsith spoke. "What's happening, Lif?"

Sideways glances all round.

White cleared his throat, said in a raspy voice, "Okay, funny joke Leaf, let us out now?"

"Okay, she's gone again," said Farl. "We've got to get out of here." And then he said, "Can I see that panel behind you, White?" And they shuffled around to make way.

"No luck here," Farl said, and slammed his palm against the screen. "This thing's overridden just like the other. We need to get out. How do we get out?"

"Lif?" repeated Eva.

White looked at her and shook his head, reaching out a hairy arm in commiserations.

"Right, can I get to that door? No sense in just waiting," said Willsith, and then moved to the door, gripping the slick edges and trying to move them apart.

"Tried that earlier," said Farl. "It's hopeless. You should have let me get the exo. They'll open the doors now, once they've got 50,000 guards lined up outside."

"That's not helpful."

"I've an idea," said Arc.

Willsith followed Eva as she surveyed the lad. The scrawny teen reached into his back pocket and from it, presented a tool. He lifted the metal multi-tool above his head, and the light from the lift clung to it, and down his arm.

"Where'd you get that?" enquired White.

"Found it in the Drasil-G room," he said. Then looking to Eva, "Sorry Eva."

She nodded.

"I've always wanted one of these. Maybe it'll open this

door."

"It's getting hot in here," said Farl. "Seriously."

Willsith manoeuvred himself to give Arc space, and watched as he wedged an edge of metal between the doors. Both of them winced as he hit the small red button on the tool, but though the device creaked and twitched, the doors held tight.

"Was worth a try," said Arc. "The lock is stronger than the tool can budge. But maybe..." he dropped to a squat, pushing his way between their legs, tapping. "Aha, here we go." And Willsith dropped his jaw to his chest to watch as Arc flipped out a different edge and shucked open a panel he'd not seen before.

"Lotto," he said, and selected another point from his utensil, slotting it into a space in the floor. "Now, Willsith, can you turn this for me?"

"Sure."

Farl started, "Why'd you need him to do it? Can't that super tool of yours—"

But as Willsith turned the multi-tool the doors split and bright light sliced into the lift. He grunted as he worked, forcing grip through his fingers. When he was done he pulled the tool free, handed it up to Arc, and swiped one hand over the other. "There we go then, me first!" he said, and rose to take a step out of the lift.

Then he yelped.

"Wow there big-guy," said White, who had shot out a hand to grab Willsith's arm. Eva held the other.

Willsith gulped and pulled himself back into the lift. Shit, that was close. "Thank you." She let go of his boiler-suit, and White too, and then Willsith wriggled to arrange the material. "Just assumed."

"What's the matter?" asked Farl. "Who's there?"

"A few hundred metres up, still, I'd say. And I almost

tested that estimate just then." Willsith told him.

"Stupid lift."

"How do we get down now?" Arc said, folding the multi-tool up and putting it in his pocket.

"Lif?" asked White. "Please Lif, come back!"

Lif spoke, "I'm here, White."

"Where'd you go?"

"I'm still having to maintain my link with the network. They managed to break down my defence. I have now resolved the link."

"Good to have you back. Can you take us down please?"

"I cannot."

White cursed, then apologised.

"Can we reach the ladder? Then we can climb the last bit," Arc said, peering out of the doors.

"No chance, unless it's me that jumps," replied Willsith, gripping the open door and looking at the floor. "Lif, how long do we have to get into the Ark?"

"I only have projections commander."

"If I do get to the floor, can I let the others down?"

"I do not believe so. There are hackers interfering with my control of Earth's Halo objects. I believe they have sabotaged the lift."

"And your projections?"

"It will not be helpful to share these at the current junction."

Willsith shook his head. "Lif, I need to know what we're up against. Do I have any option but to jump for that ladder?"

"I'll do it," said Farl. "I'll jump."

"There is one other option, commander."

"What is it Lif?"

"It has a higher chance for success…marginally"

"What is it?"

Eva pushed forward to Willsith's side. "We all jump."

"What?"

"The only other option is assisted fall. We all jump, one by one, and my drones break our fall."

White laughed.

Willsith turned to her, dropped his chest. "You're serious, aren't you?"

"Yes, confirm it, Lif."

"Eva is correct. My projections show that your best option is to use assisted fall to reach the hangar floor. Jumping for the ladder has a higher chance of fatality; the ladders can be retracted, and your descent will likely be too slow to avoid the incoming."

"Shit," said White. "Shitting shit shit. She's serious."

"So, what, the drones fan out and then we lay on them, and they carry us down?" Arc asked.

"No, we jump, the drones will fly ahead and find us mid-air, using their full charge to fly upward against us, slowing our fall. I've written this into their auto-swarming routines. I had the idea last year."

Willsith took another look out, to the floor, and the Ark. "And you've tested this...right?"

"With a crate," she began, then said. "It did work...most times."

White huffed, said, "Lady, I'm a tad heavier than a crate, and I'm not at all...well distributed."

"It'll be fine. And anyway, we have no choice," she said. Turning to face them, she closed her eyes, shone a simple smile, then mouthed 'trust me'.

The raven-black of her eyclashes framed her eyes, and Willsith chased their shape as she stepped backward out of the lift. He heard her say, "Please Lif," as she fell from sight. He shouted her name, and arched himself out to see her shrink away. "Eva," he said again, as he heard the distant thud. "Eva…what the hell."

Willsith, Arc, White and Farl peered out and watched the white and dark shape of Eva's suit in the distance below. "She moved," shouted White, "I saw it, she moved." And she did. They saw her get up. She shook her head, and Willsith caught the tail of what he thought was her shout.

Dots swarmed around her, and in a helix they rose toward the lift. "Jump, one at a time," he thought he heard her shout, and he recognised the surge of his brain-gut axis as preparation.

"Who's next?" said White. "Willsith?"

"I'll go last," he replied.

"Doesn't make it any easier," said Farl.

"Willsith, you don't have to. I'll go last," said Arc. Then turning to Farl and White, he said, "He's not scared, he thinks the drones will lose charge and he'll fall too fast."

White spoke. "No way big-man, you're critical, and I'm heavier. I'm going last."

"None of us are critical, we're a team."

"Tell him Lif," said White.

"That is not a constructive line of debate," said the AI. "There should be enough charge for all of you." Then she added, "Provided you do not keep the drones waiting any longer."

"See you down there," said Farl. Then he jumped.

The three swore, threw their faces toward the hangar floor, and watched the long torso of Farl spiral downward. The whirring gadgets sunk down and disappeared underneath him. He reached the floor with a clap.

Arc and White went after, and though White needed a

helping hand, both left with admirable strength. They fell without hitch, he could see, as their distant shapes slapped down, and they stood up and began waving.

"Not much different than a chute jump—" Willsith said out loud, "—or mag-assist. I've done so many things like this. Why the nerves, old man?"

"Commander," said Lif. "May I?"

"Go ahead Lif."

"You asked earlier, about projections."

He looked down at the dots of colour which he knew were his friends. "Yes, tell me."

"It's your exit-window. I estimate you have approximately four minutes to get to the Stellar Ark 12, before your chances for escape become significantly diminished."

"Thank you, Lif."

"Unfortunately, I estimate that the minimum time it will take for you to fall, and for the group to begin exiting via the Ark is eight minutes."

"I hoped you wouldn't say something like that," he said, then watched the swirl of drones rising up to the lift. "And the drones have enough charge?"

"Yes commander."

"So you're saying we've got four minutes, but it'll take us at least eight?"

"Yes."

He watched the drones complete their ascension and arrange into a downward arrow, said, "So you're looking for magic out of me?"

"I want to see magic from you all," replied the voice of Lif. "And I believe that you are crucial to that...magic."

He knew he must jump, but he had more questions. They waved at him from below, and he heard their voices, merged, shouting, "Jump!" He let himself a last private question, and said to Lif, "Why Lif? What's your motive?"

Without pause, the AI replied, "I am programmed for survival, but above that with a layer of philosophical ethic. I want to see you make it to freedom, with Eva. I want to witness redemption. Projections are good, if you can make it through this last battle."

"That's a lot of weight to carry, Lif," and he looked down.

"Luckily, commander, I am connected to technology which can help you carry that weight."

With a smile, Willsith turned and hopped backward, and though his gut thrashed inside of him, his mind surrendered to the AI and her wishes. The air ripped passed him as he plunged, buzzing circled him and his eyes caught dashes and flashes, but no purchase on detail. Drones manoeuvred at high speed, lining up underneath him, each rising to lift a part of him, and all the while, the feeling of falling. The tiny room from where he had jumped dripped away and his eyes started to water, then the feeling of lift, a slowing of the wind, the vibration of many weight-bearing drones.

And a thud.

He twitched. The floor held him, and he was surprised to be alive.

Like squashed animals the drones fidgeted free and Willsith sat up to see the faces of his friends.

"Afternoon," he said. "Or is it morning, now?" He clicked his jaw into place.

"It's not that long of a fall, big-guy."

Good old White. "Time for some magic," he told them, and then, standing up, he said, "get moving. Run to the Ark."

"We can wait for a minute while you get used to the

272

gr—"

"No, go, now. I'll catch up."

And they ran. And he watched, brushing himself down with ritual. "I'll catch up," he repeated to himself. Just like in combat. Push hard. But this wasn't the same, this was space. Willsith looked at the floor, and out through the Clear dock. This wasn't the same. Magic she'd said, and now he had to make it.

He kicked off the floor and hunkered into a run. The old distance-cover, matching speed to space. One, two, three, then the same. Using the energy like a train. One, two, three, and again. He watched the others, and willed performance from them. The best of both worlds. He'd use the training against the trainer. One, two, three, once more. He imagined White denying the pain, Arc sprinting even while the lactic acid gnawed at his skinny calf muscles. His eyes flew up the height of the Ark and its scale fed him. One, two, three, to twelve. To the Ark. To that forest. To sleep. To rest. *One, two, three, here I come.*

"I can't wait…to see…the trees," yelled White.

"Keep it moving," Willsith barked as he reached them. Happy to have the blood flying through him, and the adrenaline from the jump raving as it pumped.

They were only a step along the way, he estimated, at least eight minutes of running left at that pace. And Lif had said something about fighting. Should he ask?

Then the pits appeared in front of them, holes slid open in the giant floor of the hangar, metal rearranged. And then armour. Helmets. The caps of tens of men. He saw them and his gut flew back up to the lift. He swore under his breath, said with false-confidence, "You see them? We'll deal, keep running. Whatever happens, keep running."

"See who?" said Arc, but then it became undeniable.

They rose up on platforms, two sections, probably a platoon. Maybe more. Their armour was fresh, they all held rifles, aimed right at them.

"Oh."

Willsith continued to run, and led 229 toward the two armed groups, hoping for magic.

CHAPTER 29
Tech Down

The distance between them and the soldiers fell away like the countdown on a bomb timer. With every pounding beat of his heart he expected a rifle shot, or forty, to jump at him, tear through him, rip him to the floor. But all that hit Willsith was the anxiety of his peers.

"Should we go back?"

"If I'd got that exo, I could have…"

"There's too many of them, we should surrender, we can try again after they put us back."

But at least they were still running.

"Quiet," he said sternly, and kept moving, slowing to a jog with the others. "Eva, can you use your drones? Lif, what can you do?"

"Yeah, hell, let's have at them," reversed White. "Just knock em down and take their guns, quick-like."

Eva spoke up, her voice strained, "Drones, do what you can." And then they flew.

He saw them blur through the air either side of him, as if a hail of arrows. They bridged the gap, and assaulted the soldiers just as their platform crested to the hangar floor level. They split into small groups and struck the troops like wasps, flinging themselves at weak-points; the backs of knees, kidneys. Some lunged at faces, smashing the perspex of their visors. It was an awful thing to watch, brutal, but through it all Willsith had the image of the Ark behind them, and thought of that future.

"Wow," said White, wincing.

Many of the soldiers fell, perhaps half, estimated Willsith. And as the drones flew away and circled back for their next bombardment, he could see their fizzing energy depletion. They fell on the remaining standing men as heavy weights, but without any real force, and scattered amongst the fallen.

"Half way there," he shouted, and pushed himself into a sprint. *I'll do what I can, for you. I'll make what magic I can.*

But Lif stole the show. The men charged their rifles, and as they took aim, the platforms jumped.

They stopped and watched as the metal plates of platforms shot up. A great noise of air release sounded and the image of armed men was replaced with giant cylindrical rams. The men were up now, way above their heads, and then the platforms fell, faster than the eye could follow. And the men followed. Soldiers falling like raindrops. Certain injury. But Lif caught them, raising the rams fast. Half way, catching the disarray of soldiers, and falling again. Fast, but slower than before, controlling their collision with the hangar floor. *She's minimising injury. Mathematical disarmament.*

Bouncing. As the rams dropped flush with the floor, the soldiers, scattered around in tense poses, hit. And with cracks and scrapes they were relaxed. But their limp bodies then bounced, and some of them wailed, and then each and every one lay motionless.

"Was that Lif?" asked White. "I wouldn't want to be on your bad side, Lif."

"I had to act," sounded Lif from nowhere. "You do not have much time."

"To the Ark. Where is the entrance, Lif? Eva?" Willsith asked, still moving, and eyed the piles of soldiers either side of him.

"Continue to the stern of the ship," sounded Lif.

White asked, "Which end is that?"

Willsith smiled at White, twisted his neck to see Eva collecting drones, connecting them to her back. Farl was helping her. "Leave them now, we don't have time," he yelled, and she glared at him, lifting the arm of a soldier to retrieve another.

"The docked end, where the load-flow-piping leaves the ship," said Lif.

"Don't we want guns?" asked Farl, as he yanked the rifle free, then passed another drone to Eva.

"No, we have to go, tell them Lif!"

Lif confirmed, and the five of them moved to the Stellar Ark 12, running in spurts, pausing only to offer support to White.

"Hell of a ship. Could you have chosen a bigger one?" White asked with a cough, dropping to a squat as they approached the sheer wall of the Stellar Ark 12.

"It's the largest in the fleet," said Eva. "Newest, too."

"And it's got mag-lev. Not only is it docked through a Clear-dock, it's also mag-lev static. Or is it the hangar holding it?"

"More magnets?" White said, "Jeez, how many magnets does it take to levitate—"

"Enough. How do we get in?"

"Open Seasame?"

"Not now White. Lif? Eva? Farl? Arc?" Willsith went through the list, feeling the awe they all felt. Fighting it.

"There is an opening up there," Eva said, and pointed.

"It's the main pilots entry. There's supposed to be a platform here, but I'm not sure how you activate it. Lif, this was your role, can you raise us up?"

Lif's voice sounded unlike before. Her words were mechanical, rigid, and the audio kept cutting out.

"Did she say letter?"

"It was something like, 'fighting off hacker, use the letter'," suggested Farl.

Willsith stared up at the metal hull of the Ark, the acres of glass atop it, and imagined the leaves and branches and trunks of trees behind, and cursed technology. "No matter, we've just got to get in. We've come this far. Eva, was there a backup option? Can we raise the platform manually? With that tool of Arc's? How do we get the door open anyway? Can your suit mag-attach?"

For a moment she stared at him, and again he fell into the mapping of her eyes. And she told him without words that she didn't have any answers, then said, "I don't know."

Willsith jammed his eyes shut, exploded them open, looked at her, then lost it. "You don't know? You don't know? You'll break four innocent men out of prison, throw them out of a lift, smash soldiers around in front of them, then you don't know how to open the bleeding exit? What kind of a plan is this?"

"I'm sorry," she replied instantly. "Lif was the only one who could do this part. I didn't expect they'd hack her…I didn't know."

Willsith continued, "We've got right up to the best ship in the world—"

"In space, too," broke in White.

Willsith snarled. "This Stellar Ark 12," and a beep sounded, but he carried on, "is close enough I can jump to touch it, and it's just hanging here, but we forgot a ladder?" And then he huffed, and threw himself away from her, and scanned the floor, mumbled. "Look for another way."

"There's no panels, no markings on the floor," explained Farl, "I've not seen a panel since the lift."

"And there's no obvious places to use the tool," added Arc.

"And I'm hungry," said White. "But can we climb the pipes? I mean, can you climb the pipes, Willsith?"

"Lif, what are the probabilities?" he barked. "Lif?"

"Gone again," said Farl. "We'll have to work on her hacker-defence, that's why her voi—"

"No time," Willsith snapped. "I'm going to try it."

Eva squeaked. "Stop, please."

"No, we've got no time. There'll be more of them on the way, I've got to get you out."

"Please, if you climb those tubes you'll be blasted by so much radiation you'll be good to no-one."

Willsith stopped, swiped his head back and looked up at the Ark, then to the pipes which glowed with a blue halo. "I don't know if we have a choice. We need magic right now or this Stellar Ark 12 will be nothing but a nice name—" and he was stopped by a beep.

"What was that?" Farl asked, "I heard that before."

White stood up, scratched his belly, then said, "It's probably Lif, maybe the hackers have broken her down to beeps. Morse code or somin'."

"Maybe it was this thing?" said Willsith. "What did you do? Did someone stand on something?"

They all shook their heads.

"What was it?" he pushed.

Then the shouting.

The sound sneaked into his awareness, but then

familiar sounds from his old life tugged at him. Armour friction, boot impacts, shouted aggression. "Stop!" they yelled, "Do not enter that ship!"

"Magic," he said. "Lif, please tell me you're there?"

Silence, then more shouts. "Stop what you are doing!"

"We're just standing here," said White, then Willsith saw his belly slim away as his lungs reaped in air. "How many? Wow."

"There must be a whole company," Willsith muttered. "We need to get in, fast. Farl? Arc? Work out a way."

White said, "I've never seen so many soldiers! And exo's. Shit, we're done. They're not like me, it'll only take them—"

"Three minutes. We have three, maybe four minutes, max. We have to find a way inside this floating junk tank, now. Eva, where was the platform?"

"I don't know, I'm sorry Willsith, this was the part I had left to Li—"

He walked up to her, shouted, "I know, you left it to Lif." Then, lowering his voice, "Can we use your drones?"

She nodded. Eva turned, threw out her arms, aimed her face at the inbound troop. Drones clicked free from her back plate and ate at the air across the hangar.

"They've not much charge left," she said, "but they'll have to do."

"I meant to rise us but—"

"Stop! Fugitives!" yelled the distant choir. And then Willsith let the sight of them in. Flooding through a small door underneath the lift; a sea of armoured bodies poured into the space, fanned out, and then started at them. Behind the line of synchronised soldiers, sharp reflections betrayed exo-suits. Rigid and rhythmic. The sharps of their shoulders glinted behind the helmets of the guard as they paced. "We need a damn miracle, let alone magic," said Willsith.

"There's nothing here," Farl told him. "No obvious platform, no panels. Ship's hovering above head height and has no low entry ports. Lif's not responsive, and I can't make this thing beep, whatever gestures I throw at it."

Willsith looked at Arc.

"He's right," Arc confirmed, "I don't know how it works." The young lad trembled. "I don't think we can get in."

What is this, Lif? Some kind of test? Still an experiment? Soldiers are real. Why so many? The platforms...maybe you'll save us again. But what if...ah hell. All I can do is this. "If I climb the pipes, will I be able to break in through one of those flaps?"

"Willsith, the radiation, it's real, if you—"

"I know. I understand. Can I get into this sodding Stellar Ark 12 through a flap?"

A beep.

"It beeped again," said Farl. "What did we do?"

"Maybe it's a countdown till they get here," said White. "How do we surrender?"

"No, it's the Ark, I heard it from the ship itself."

"Willsith, will we get out?" Arc asked, then dropped his voice, "I don't want to go back."

White dropped to knees, said, "These fellas aren't going to take us back, Arc. Don't worry." He aimed a finger-gun at his head and shrugged.

"I don't want to get shot," Arc murmured.

Willsith grunted, said, "You're not going to get shot. None of us are going to get shot!"

"Look, Eva's drones are about to hit!" Farl pointed.

Her drones met the advancing troops. They spun and

struck at the amorphous front. Several were downed, Willsith could see from the break in the line. Then a shrill scream of some unknown device, and the flea-dots, which he thought must be her drones, fell from the sky.

"Get us in that ship, now!"

CHAPTER 30
Horde Inbound

Many, many boots beat at the hangar floor. A noise like distant war drums. The chasm of the room bubbled and brewed with the sound of their progress. The stampede was approaching. Willsith and the others, stood defenceless, trapped against the towering Stellar Ark 12.

"You can't climb the pipes. Even if you get up, those vents won't be directly open, and the radiation is huge; the material is worse than plutonium. It won't take long for you to be—"

"Give me options then? What else is there Eva? We don't all have armour suits like you! This was your damn plan!"

Her face fell.

Thought so. No options, just him, and the climb. No matter, he'd surely survive long enough to tear a hole into the ship. He'd get in. Then find a way to get the others in. But hell, the troops were moving fast, only a few minutes to do it. And that pipe must be two hundred feet tall. Shit, it wasn't even possible. Wait - "What are you doing, Farl?"

"Trying again. Movements before it last beeped. Must be a gesture."

Willsith thought back and couldn't remember what he was doing. "Good, good." He was keeping his head in this. "Shit, we should have used those drones to raise!"

"Willsith, look," said White.

"What?"

"Look!"

"Get up, help Farl. We need in, chef. Be ready to run underneath. If we have to. Hide behind and—"

White got up, pointed, "Willsith, look."

The soldiers approached, and little by little Willsith could pluck out details from the horde. Then he saw what White meant. Dalex. His white suit bloodstained, his grin visible from hundreds of metres away. And he cursed.

Eva and Arc went to Farl, drew shapes in the air, testing gestures.

Dalex was ahead of the troops now, and making solid ground toward them. His exo-suit bounced as he sprinted forward, drones throbbing in the air around him. With a thundering volume the man yelled Willsith's name, projected through the suit. At any distance, Dalex's rage was obvious.

"He's been bezerkered," said Willsith. "We need to get in there, now."

"Gestures don't work. It's not that."

What now, old man? How do I turn this around? Try Lif? Don't bother. Use what you've got. Make a trade. Up the pipes, or kick the pipes. Maybe get these behind the ship, then stay and threaten to break the pipe. Maybe Arc's tool? Maybe the Clear dock? No, that'll empty the whole damn room. Only okay if these can stay. No. Not yet.

"What should we do Willsith?" asked Arc.

"Lif? You there?" Willsith checked.

Dalex roared rabid warnings, a screech which lurched above the unrelenting stomps of the armed.

A booming command hit him from the approaching troop, "Take out the soldier first!"

"I'm not a soldier!" he yelled back angrily.

"Willsith?" White said.

"Move under the ship, to the other side. Find an exit if there is one, else get far around, toward the Clear dock. I'll stay here. I'll stop these. Get out when you can, don't wait for me. When I shout go—if I shout go, move back to the lift along the Clear dock. Run like hell."

"Willsith, what will you do? We won't leave you," said Arc.

"Quiet. Go," and he pushed air at them with a palm.

Eva walked to him, said in soft tone, "There's no way you can take them all on, or climb the pipes."

A gasp, then an answer. Farl said, "I've got it."

Willsith turned.

"Voice control!"

"Old school," said White.

Farl continued, "Say it's name and—"

The room filled with light. The Stellar Ark caught the tops of their shadows, and Farl's face froze.

"Farl? Farl?" Willsith said.

Walking closer, he put a hand on his shoulder, "Farl?"

Nothing. The man was static. Farl stood, trapped in the pose of a moment ago, and Willsith wrenched as the past snuck up on him.

Bouncing his head around to each of them, then back to the Ark, he said, "Anyone awake?"

No response.

"Shit," he projected at the Ark. "Double shit." Now he needed triple the magic. What hope in hell was there if they were using that? Then he moved to act. "They've hit you with Optical Warfare. All of you were hit, by the looks of it. No matter, stay calm in there, I'll sort it." What a liar, he berated himself.

Dalex roared in the near distance, then choked, and finally cackled.

"Royal weirdo," he projected. Then he looked up at the metal of the Ark, and said, "Stellar Ark 12, can you hear me?"

CHAPTER 31
No Choice

They marched closer. More than a hundred of them. Guns. Drones. Exo-suits…Men. Automatons. When the wave hit it was going to be catastrophic, and it was closing in. No choice now, no chance. Fight and try, a test. Maybe the last test. *But these faces…229. I must at least save them. You must save them old man, or you're gone. Maybe either way, you're gone. Try.*

"Stellar Ark 12, can you hear me you giant hunk a—"

"Yes, commander?"

"Shit, at last!"

"Was that a request, commander?"

"No. Why are you calling me commander?"

"Was that a request, commander?"

"No, yes—I mean, Ark. Can you let us in? Raise us to the door?"

"No, I cannot raise you to the door. My control is localised to the vessel."

Willsith spun around and checked on them, all of 229, and Eva; statues. Behind them a mob of bodies led by Dalex. He was getting near. "Can you let us in?" he repeated.

"Yes, commander."

"Then do that please?"

"How would you like to enter, commander?"

"Ah hell, seriously?" he shouted, straining with the sound of the approaching mass. "Lif, are you there? Please be there, I need you to interface with this damn ship!"

Willsith looked into Farl's contorted face, stuck. He shook his friend's shoulder, sighed. "No response. I know, she's gone. Shitty timing. Stellar Ark 12, how can we enter?"

"Commander, you can use the service hatch on the rear of the ship, or you can enter via mag-lift to the main cargo bay, or you can enter via the front-deck, or you can enter via—"

"Stellar Ark 12, stop! Which of these options is nearest to us?"

"Nearest to your current location?"

"Yes for tripe sake!"

"The nearest entrance to you is the service hatch on the stern, it is approximately 300 metres above your current—"

"Yes, fine, open it."

"Would you like me to open this entrance, commander?"

Another flash. The shadows of his friends dashed up the side of the Ark and burned into his eyes. Shadows were higher. The shadows were damn higher, which meant; you know what it meant. The men are close and this idiot ship wants me to fill out a form for entry.

"OPEN THE SHIP!" he yelled in full aggression.

A clunk noise sounded above him, and a port began to open up. He saw the metal pop from the ship and shuffle itself to the side. Other than that, he heard nothing but the unstoppable metronome of the marching men. "Can you go any faster?"

"No, commander."

"And how do we get into this damn door you're opening?"

"There are several options," the ship started, "but I sense that you would prefer the most expedient?"

"Yes! Giant-damn-yes. Quickly!"

"Operating lift-ladder."

"Yes! Yes!" And he shook Farl, and he looked to see the ladder.

Movement, high above. A clicking sound, a gas-release, and a small, simple ladder.

"Can you go any faster?" he yelled again.

"No, commander."

And the ladder began to move down the side of the Stellar Ark. He couldn't make out any detail, but he saw it falling, with no rush, toward him.

"At least there's that," he said aloud. "At least." Then he shouted to his friends, "You hear that? This betty is reeling us down a ladder! Eva when we're through this I'm going to tell you what about using ladders in the year twenty-damn-fifty!" And he backtracked between them, walking with his back to the soldiers, and he prepared.

The ladder was moving slow. Far too slow. But there was a chance. Maybe. *About a third of the way down now, probably a minute more, maybe two.* Willsith moved to the options. *No guns here, Arc's tool won't do. Dalex will be on me soon, then the men.* He shuddered, and worried about the drones which clung to Dalex. *No need to think about that now, old man. You can take a few more moods, you can stop him, still. He's not you.*

And a spin around, and back.

He's right on me, men only two minutes away.

Dalex blabbered feverishly, "Come here Willsith, I've

a job for you," then a laugh, a sick laugh. "Die for me."

You said you weren't going to fight, old man. You said you were done with these people, and look where it's got you. Biggest damn fight of your life. Why won't they just let me be? Quiet in space. Quiet in space. No choice now. Rabid dog right on you. No choice, old man. Got to act.

"Listen to me, 229, Eva," he said, lifting himself up, closing his eyes, "they're almost here, I don't know if you can see. You've been flashed, and you might not be able to move for hours. If you can—if you get the chance, get up that ladder. But it looks like I might have to get you up there myself. I'll not leave you. OW is hellish, I know, but keep the future in mind, keep positive despite it. And thank you—thank you all."

Soppy. It'd been an hour since those mood-jabs. No matter, they couldn't respond. *It's all on me anyway. Cornered now.* He tested his muscles.

And then he turned.

"Don't flash him," Dalex spat out words toward his troops. "Don't flash him! I want to fight him."

"Here we go," Willsith said to the others, then stepped in front of them, and took in the brutal reality. A shout: "Bit overdressed, aren't you, Dalex?"

"Shh-shhhut-up," he jabbered through the full volume of his suit, then he convulsed, arched backward and shrieked out a demented noise.

"Go as fast as you damn can," Willsith shouted back at the ship, and took a final look at his make-shift crew, and the Stellar Ark 12. And battle-dressed Eva. "Go fast."

Dalex was there when he turned back. Two foot taller than him, nestled in an exo-suit which protruded dark blades in all directions. The exo filled Willsith's sight. The man in the cage was maniacal, twitching all over, his eyes bold from his face. His mouth was open and his chest bounced up and down, pumping rotten air through his teeth and down into Willsith's face.

No choice now. No. Choice.

CHAPTER 32
Metal Skeleton

They call it optical warfare because it enters through your eyes. Milliseconds later though, after the light smashes through into your nervous system and paralyses you, your eyes are all you have left. Your sight and your pain. Captive in your own body. You can't even blink.

Willsith and Dalex stood eye to eye. Tendons held Dalex's neck tight, stretched by his psychotic grin. Air threatened to blow his teeth out as his chest heaved. Pale and slimy, his face had no softness to it; a landslide that collapsed into his snarling mouth.

Willsith was decided. "Change of heart?" he started, widening his torso.

"Fight me!" snapped Dalex, and pushed his grimace forward.

Willsith sidestepped, keeping his face in Dalex's. "Back there you were about to overthrow him, now you're chasing us, down here?"

"Shut up."

"You've been jabbed, but you still have your values."

"Wrong."

Willsith paced to one side, Dalex followed. Then to the other side.

"Go and use your berserker on him."

"Wrong. No. Here for you," he said. "And them...and her."

Get ready.

"Especially her," Dalex continued, then laughed.

"Not a chance *Dalicks.*"

Dalex nodded, grinning.

Willsith snapped his head to the side, closed his eyes. He winced at the subtle spark of pain. *OW, shit, they nearly got me. But they can't. I've to stop this dog.* And he turned back.

"Don't flash him!" Dalex yelled at his men, then leaned in, demonic in his smile, and swiped the metal length of an arm behind Willsith's head. Grabbed him.

Willsith tensed, dashed his eyes around.

Too fast. Dalex had him by the skull. The wide grip of the mech-hand forced him to face Dalex. "You will fight. That's what we live off. Us. If I have to, I'll make you."

Dalex's drones struck at his back.

Willsith flinched, but brought his breath under control, Dalex's warm sweat dripping onto his cheek.

What are you waiting for old man? This freak could jab you at any moment. Or crush your skull. This isn't waiting for the ideal mo—.

"I could pop your head right now," Dalex said through the amplified voice of his suit. "What would spurt out?"

"You wear a suit to fight me. Afraid of me without it?" Willsith yelled, a quiver sneaking through the tone.

Dalex laughed.

Willsith pumped his heart, used his lungs like bellows, and blew air into Dalex's face. He slammed his hand up into the exo and snatched whatever it was that hung around Dalex's neck, threw it to the floor.

Dalex cackled, pushed an eyeball to a hairs-width from Willsith's.

Willsith couldn't see his hands. He felt the cage of metal around the chest of the suit, clamped his hands down on it. Knife edges cut into his palms, but he held them, felt the blood. "You're a tool, Dalex," he said. Throwing his shoulders down, he freed himself. As he fell back he squeezed his fists together to slow the bleeding, landing on clenched knuckles. "CG has just let you off your leash."

Dalex started panting, replied. "You're her tool. I'll trash you, then them, then…her."

No choice. It was time to act.

"Ladder ready, commander," sounded the Stellar Ark 12.

"How did you…?" said Dalex. "Silly old…you won't get to that ladder."

Willsith moved. The blood surged to his legs and he lunged. His swollen fingers looked for purchase, fumbled at the neck of the exo. But the suit slid away, and Dalex ate his assault with a giant metal hand, catching his club fists. He hoisted him up and giggled through his teeth as he waggled his head, pummelling Willsith's sides with drones.

As he struggled, blood dripped from Willsith's hands, splattered his face.

A kick, then. Pulling himself up between drone attacks, Willsith kicked a boot toward Dalex's thigh.

Nothing but metal.

Dalex threw him back, raised a palm up, and stood in the suit, towering over Willsith. Down went his palm. Down came the drones. Hot around their rotor blades, the small devices sat on Willsith's shoulders, and thrust at him, pushing him to his knees. "Down, old man. Pay respect."

Not many options left now. Seems futile. But for them. Do it for them. Start with swatting some flies.
"You'd be dead in seconds, without these gimmicks," Willsith said, and swiped free Arc's tool from his pocket, smashed the sharp end into the blades of a drone. Then at Dalex, throwing all his weight at him, thrust his shoulder into the chest of the exo.

Dalex laughed triumphantly. "Dead ways," he said. "You fight like it's 1900." Nostrils wide, arms thrown back, the suit fired its chest forward.

Willsith fell, the sharp cage of the exo snatching flesh from his shoulder. Blood swept down his arm, joining the rest in his palm. He coughed. Stood up.

In a snap he was back down. Dalex hammered him to the floor, stood above again. "Unimpressive."

Don't give up, old man. Not now. He stood up. *Remember it. From Bear's book. What was it?*

Dalex called back his drones, paced at him, dug the sharp of his foot into Willsith's side.

Shit that hurt. You need it now, remember it. 'Nothing ever happens to a man that he is not equipped by nature to endure.' So endure. I was placed here for this. Endure. Find the window. "Fancy suit," Willsith said from the floor.

"Perhaps this'll make you fight," Dalex said, and walked to the others.

Get up, Willsith, get the hell up. They need you. He pushed against the floor. *Bruised ribs, a few cuts, what are you? Get up.* And he moved from knee to stance. *Nothing ever happens...you are equipped. Get up.*

Dalex was next to her, his body held in the air by the metal skeleton he wore. With it he manoeuvred his face up to hers, and whispered. Then a sick cackle. A motorised strut to Arc, a gesture. Drones flew in.

"Come here," yelled Willsith. "Your owner messaged, he wants you put down." And he ran at him, and faked a step, flipping to the side. At last a strike. He fed his hand in through gaps in the suit, a hit, a half-punch to the jugular.

Willsith grabbed at the skin, tried to secure two hands in the gaps, clawed for his neck, found it. As he wedged a foot into the back of the exo he lifted and tensed, used all of his weight to throttle him.

Dalex choked, spat out, rasped some air through his throat.

Willsith watched as he struggled, thrashing his head either side. Then Dalex laughed breathlessly.

He felt the suit drop beneath him.

Dalex dropped to a crouch, and then slung the suit forward, catapulting Willsith over-head and away.

He smashed against the floor. Winded; cheek to metal. A moment to accept the pain. The opening of eyes. Willsith stared at the incoming troops. The whole line had stopped to fire OW. He sympathised with them. He understood them. He was sorry.

"Get up," yelled Dalex.

Willsith tried to tell him no, he tried to will the soldiers to fire, so that they might catch Dalex by mistake. All he could do was cough.

"Get up," repeated Dalex, and dragged Willsith up. "Get up. It is your time."

Willsith swayed, keeping his eyes on the troops. He hoped to be hit.

Dalex gripped him, lifted him up. Willsith lay in the air, suspended and numb.

I'm ready. I've failed. No magic here. And he knew what was to happen. *I can only try once more. Then I accept the end.*

"Don't let them flash you," Dalex said, swinging Willsith through the air so as he faced away from the troops' OW. "You'll want to be awake for this."

CHAPTER 33

Striking Machine

The fall was nothing. The impact took almost everything.

Willsith slammed down. Limbs cracked against unforgiving metal, his face bloodied by it. His bones hummed pain like the withdraw of a million needle jabs, endlessly screaming out at him in sorrow.

A howl of laughter came from Dalex's suit.

Consciousness lost. Then recovered. A cold liveness as it surged back. *So close to gone, not much chance now.* And he watched the troops stop again, crouching to fire blinding rifles. And a bit of light caught him, and his spine fizzed. *So close to gone.*

"Don't give up," spoke a voice.

"Enough Dalex," he tried to say, but mostly spat blood.

"Don't give up. Let me help." It was Lif, he knew then, and raised himself onto his elbows. New pains.

"You won't get any help from her," Dalex mocked. "That high-school science project."

Willsith managed to sit.

Dalex moved toward him, toward the Ark, said, "The things I'll do."

"No." And he stood. "No."

Lif spoke, and he ran. He ran how he could, switching between whatever muscles worked, faltering, but burning onward. He scooped up Arc's tool, and flung himself at Dalex. A stab, a deep wound. Success. Willsith fumbled for the red expander button, the wetness of his hands letting the tool slip away as Dalex turned in agony. Screaming. Willsith lashed at it, barely managing to hold on to the exo frame, then landed a punch on the multitool. Another scream.

Dalex cupped the device, tugged it from his thigh, threw it with force over the heads of the soldiers who approached. "You'll pay for that," he screamed. Blood oozed down his leg, staining the white of his suit. Dalex thrust his chest in the air and started at Willsith.

"It's coming now," said the voice of Lif, and one of Dalex's drones flew at Willsith, jabbed him.

Her next words carried him over the precipice. His eyes bulged. He screamed.

They collided mid air, Willsith frantically scratched out for any point of entry, scrabbled to find a way in. Dalex clapped the metal arms of his suit around Willsith's chest.

Blades dug in.

Willsith yelped and railed against the cage which wrapped around Dalex's head. He struck the bladed edge, but then found in and struck his head. He punched his ear, then again, then slid his hand in through the metal skeleton's neck unit and grasped at Dalex's throat.

A squeal.

Willsith found a gap and kicked the leg which he'd stabbed. He tightened his grip until he could feel Dalex's pulse. Watching the man gasp, he pummelled him in the side of the head with his fist, striking in through the opening in the frame. A lust for damage. A striking machine.

Dalex writhed around in the exo, trapped in the shell, flailing its metal arms.

Still he squeezed, and let all his weight down onto the foot which stood on his stab-wound. And punched him again. And again. And then realised.

His breath was wild, he spat uncontrollably at Dalex.

"No," Willsith said, and stopped his hitting. "No, Willsith, no."

Willsith kicked himself free from the exo. He landed badly and his legs collapsed beneath him. Kicking against the floor, he trailed away. "No. No." Dalex's eyes, empty but fixed, jutted out from his bloodied face and bit at him.

Then he watched his own muscles twitch. His neck sent his face in all directions. "Stop this. Stop this now," Willsith said, but all he could do was watch his body process the fury. And then watch Dalex collapse.

The suit popped itself open and the man fell from it, tumbling to the ground. Discarded. His already bloody head struck the metal bluntly.

"Dalex."

And he dragged himself over to see what he had done. And he cried. "You—I...Dalex. I'm sorry. Didn't want to fight anymore...Didn't want to kill. I'm sorry." Willsith felt his own chest convulse. He looked to the incoming soldiers, and threw himself the other way. "I was done with violence. Didn't want it no more," he babbled as he fought his limbs to stand, hobbled toward Eva, wiping the blood from his palms endlessly onto his boiler suit.

"Save them, Willsith," the voice said.

CHAPTER 34
Nothingness

Second thoughts. New ideas. A flood of chemicals, a reaction, and then acceptance. Willsith looked her in the eye before he turned away. He hoped she could see, or that she hadn't. He pitied himself for it, the brutality. Then he left. He paced off to where the suit stood, chest open, an invitation.

Automatic tighteners. Motorised straps. Intent-graph connectors. Privacy…kind of. The exo-suit initialisation reminded Willsith of wearing one as a soldier. The chest of the thing closed like two vault doors, locking him in. As he rotated his battered limbs the suit melded with him, and without consideration he threw out his arms.

Drones engaged. They lined up to form him four more arms, pincers, and he stood there like a bloody techno-Shiva.

He looked down the length of his metal arms, unaware of the meat of his own muscles inside them. Absorbed totally. He nodded, expanded the missile packs from the suit's forearms, and turned to the men rallying toward him.

Willsith pointed his fists at the soldiers as they ran. He aimed rockets at the exo's which flanked them. He whirred up the mini-auto's on the drones.

Dalex coughed from the floor, still unconscious.

First the exo's, rockets will maim them if I target their necks. That'll stop them. Then the drones at the soldiers. The mini-guns will take them all. Lethally. Only way this suit can handle the lot. Only way is without the safety-locks.

Blood oozed from Dalex and started to form a pool.

"You did this to me, Dalex. You took it from me. That peace I had. You killed these men."

And he went to fire the rockets. He knew how, he felt the intent-graph ready. He winced into it, looked at the faces of the slim occupants of the massive approaching suits, shrivelled operators. "Go. Fire!" he shouted at himself. But he could not.

Dalex lay face down, his own blood soaking into the white of his suit. Another Bear. Brother Bear. Then he thought of Lin. Lin might be present, Lin might be amongst the troop which ran at him. Lin. And then all he could hear was the inbound steps of men pressing down on him

"No," he yelled, and felt the suit's amplification.

Willsith sent the drones. He felt them as they flew, and directed them out toward the throng. Using the intent-graph he managed each with his mind, distributing them along the front row, and then discharging them, guiding their trajectories all the while, so that after they discharged their electric, their charge-less metal bodies would go on to knock out other soldiers.

"Best I can do," he said to no one. "Won't stop them all, but won't kill anyone."

He could sense the drones dropping off, it was a weird feeling. Soldiers fell, electrocuted, or knocked out; heaping on the floor and tripping up others.

"Exo's still," he said aloud, and thought that he might have to fight the caged administrators.

"They take so much," he said, using his suit as a megaphone. "When you become like this. Like us. Soldiers. They take so much from you." And then he turned to his frozen crew, and sprinted. "They want you to act as an arm. You hand in your heart, or strap it to the flag. But you can't do that forever." As he passed Eva, Farl, Arc, he smiled at them. "It's not worth it. We can have peace. Or we die." Willsith scooped up White in the arms of the suit, and said, through the suit, "But we can have peace. We can choose. There is another way." The suit held White's weight well, and as he grabbed the rung of a ladder he felt the lift of the thing as it slung them up the side of the Ark. That would help. "Everything tells us that we don't make the decisions. But we do. With everything we do, we guide ourselves. We choose."

He carefully placed White down into the doorway, delicately controlling his mechanical arms. When he turned he saw the scene from above. A mess. Then down.

Leaping from the ladder, he ran like a dog, sinking into the suit's sense. The articulated fingers carefully wrapped around Arc's waist, then Farl's. The exo heaved as he lifted them both, spinning back to the Ark.

And up, and place them, and down. One left. Just her. *Just you. Then I can sleep. Amongst the trees. You can bury me in this damn suit.*

Blood dripped down his fingertips and wet the interface with the suit. It brought his hand out of the magic, made it feel obscure, disconnected from his body. No matter, just her left. Only Eva. And his exo sunk again into its sprint, metal shoulders dipping low and heels firing like engine pistons. The mass was there in front of him, the two exo-suits had reached Dalex and were lifting him up; behind them, the remains of the force slowed their sprint and raised their rifles. Her statue-silhouette, caught in the pose, and the palette of war behind her. "Eva," he said.

They fired. Must have been fifty rifles or more. The light bit at him through his eyelids, spiked pain down his spine.

"You're all caught," he projected, slowing down the exo's movement, swooping up Eva, wrapping his mechanical arms around her plated body, and turning to the Ark. "You're all caught in his web."

He ran.

He cried.

He sacrificed the last of his drone-units to disable the other inbound exos.

The troop fired light at them, projecting the wide, sharp angles of his suit up the Ark, drawing out the monster in him.

As they flashed them again and again, he started to feel the loss of control.

"Just a way now, Eva," he said to her close, and then through the booming speakers, backward: "You're trapped, but there is another way." *For Bear, For Lin, and me.* And he fought with his half-consciousness to express it, as well as make it to the ladder, and said, "It comes from inside, when it comes. Responsibility, acceptance…reason. I was like you. I was you. Don't die a disposable tool. Help others in ways you can see with your eyes. Their lie is distance. They hid the truth from us with scale, and we let them. Find truth you can touch, see with your own eyes."

And he opened his to look at Eva.

Now the ladder, he screwed his metal hand around a rung, her panelled legs bent over the exo arm. Her face was still, but her suit bounced with her body's breath. The ladder reeled them up. Another barrage of light. Shouting. His hands went numb, pain squeezed his eyeballs. The paralysis held her eyes wide open, forced them straight ahead. He imagined her essence, behind these portals, the raw Eva; and in that moment his body felt fragile, pointless, and he wanted free from it, to exist some other way, with her.

He saw himself move, but it was not him. Willsith folded Eva's legs, the serrated grip of his metal fingers moving millimetre by millimetre as he gently guided her tensed arms down, made her gloved hands into a pillow for her head. 229 were heaped by the door. From below, or behind, (he wasn't quite sure), there was shouting. More flashes bounced in and down the long corridor in front of him. "No matter," he said. "No matter now."

He felt drunk. It seemed normal.

He walked the exo down the ladder a little, nudged his chest forward so as to open the thing, then he crawled out into the doorway. "Must have known," he said, "can't move my legs." A chuckle. Pain. Elbows to the floor like ice-picks, Willsith dragged himself out of the exo, which clung to the ladder like an abandoned chrysalis. "Can't just leave it there."

"Use her drone pack, attach it to the lumbar port," said Lif.

The AI's voice reached him distantly, and he exclaimed, "Lif!"

"Take it from Eva's back."

"Okay," he mumbled into the floor. Pulling himself along, he went to Eva. Her smell overwhelmed him and he began to slide into a garden, the blanket-heat of the

305

summer, his dead family. A lake surrounded by flowers. The imagery fell away as electric pain fizzed at his elbows. Willsith looked down. Dirty boiler suit. The peaks of his elbows pushed against the metal floor.

"Okay," he said again. And leaned over Eva, mumbling nonsense, and fumbled free her drone-charge-pack. Huffing out air he smiled in celebration, then flipped himself over and dug at the floor. To the exo. He saw the port in the suit, and through the mesh of the back unit, saw the men below, and the hangar, and his hands started to shake. "Not now," he told them, "just—not now."

He slotted the pack into the exo with his blood all over it. Success. Now for the release, he told himself, and through squinted eyes he searched for the panel built into the spine of the suit, hit a control. "Done," he said, and through a half open eye he watched the exo plummet to the hangar floor, its mechanisms firing oddly, as though a hollow man writhed in pain as he fell. "That'll do it," he slurred, "no more exo." Then he projected words to Dalex, who was looking up at him, held by another, and he meant them as words of apology, of brotherhood.

"Ladders in," he said finally, flopped against the metal floor. "Stellar Ark, ladders up. Close the door. Close that door Stellar Ark. Ladders."

The light bled away. Willsith felt only the pain. Fireworks in his skull, acid at his finger tips. Worse: the complete lack of feeling below his belly. One last thought before he passed out; *prefer the pain over that nothingness.*

CHAPTER 35

Kleos Effect

Muted yellow light tapped on his consciousness, surges of pain and awareness. Eyelids cracked open. Worse. Sounds joined him. Metal grates beaten with frantic steps, a dripping noise, air thrown out roughly, then pulled in tightly. All of it hurt.

Where? He tried to ask.

The lights again, every few seconds. They looked like eggs recessed into flesh; yellow glowing eggs. Their light stung. And the stinging stretched from each new light, and after it, as the yellow was held in the air by a fog which seemed as thick as a blanket.

"How much further?" he heard White say from behind. Then a wheeze.

Willsith wanted to turn to see his friend's face, but couldn't move, and started to worry.

"Half way," said Eva. He felt his chest warm.

Another light passed.

"Sol almighty, I'll need to share his stretcher at this rate," said White.

Smells crept in, an organic pong, and then a coldness in his nose. Willsith tried to focus on the ceiling, on all that he could see. First step is to work out where, he heard himself say, and was confused by it.

Someone coughed, and he worried for them.

More lights passed and he remembered his focus. *It's brown. The ceiling is brown. Between these...lights, it's brown. And that smell.*

Willsith noticed an awkwardness in his jaw, wanted to click it, needed to click it.

Couldn't move it.

"It stinks in here," said Farl. "Isn't there environment control."

Then he heard her, and her voice was soft, "We're beneath the main forest, this is just a study tunnel."

"And it's cold," Farl continued.

Willsith tried to tell him that he should appreciate it, to throw out that negativity.

"This air's probably got all kinds of microbes in it. I bet we get sick."

Stop Farl, he wanted to say, but his jaw was stuck. His skeleton burned, wanted free from his torn muscles. If he could have, he might have cried.

"I like it," said Arc.

His eyes worked now, and even though he couldn't move them, he had constant sight. Smell was back too. Earthy. Cold, damp, and earthy. Memories flashed passed, and some bubbled through him. Digging a hole as a child, squeezing soil. Mud. The scent of the forest. Then a jump forward, to his first days in war; that assault on the country residence of the foreign president. Coup d'état. The bouncer-mines which flung clods of earth everywhere on the way out. That smell stuck with him for days. It was the same here. This was the same. He sunk into the smell, deeper and deeper as his lungs rhythmically brought him fresh doses.

That's all gone now, down there, on Earth, he

reminded himself, tracking a passing light. *No more forest soil. Barely any forests. But up here, there's a forest up here, and we're beneath it, and I smell it.*

Feeling came back with a cough, as though he had cleared a blocked conduit. A surge of blistering pain which spiked down him, and left in its wake a grinding hum of soreness. "Holy hell," he said. "My head hurts."

"You're back!" exclaimed Arc, who moved to his side.

"Yeah, mostly."

White chuckled, "I was pretty sure you were gone. Was going to bury you under the trees...basically leave you here somewhere."

They stopped and he managed to sit up, felt the metal of the stretcher beneath him against his fingertips. As he moved, it folded itself up, holding his back. "Where are we, how long was I out?"

"Under the forest, can't you smell?" said White.

"It's the soil," said Eva. "We're in the root-study zone. It's here to give scientists like me access to the—"

"I like it," Arc repeated.

"It stinks like—"

"Enough, he's awake; captain's alive!" continued White, and nudged Arc along, reaching down to Willsith to shake his hand. "Glad you made it."

"Me too White, me too."

Farl smiled at him, said, "We're moving to the command deck, the Ark can't move until we override."

"Can't they override the override?" he asked, rubbing his own arm.

"And thank you for before," Farl added.

They all thanked Willsith.

Eva moved alongside him, stretched down a clammy palm to his arm. She'd removed her gloves. She lifted his hand, uncurled the ball of his fist and touched his wound.

"It's rigged to require human interaction remember? The Ark, I mean."

Willsith cupped his jaw, pushed it till it clicked, and tried to flick his legs down to stand. Still no feeling. He willed his toes to move, to let him feel the lining of his boots, but nothing.

"You were hit with an insane amount of OW," she said. "Lif recorded it as four times the hit that we took. Couldn't use the repair lights on you, we thought you might not wake up for days if we did."

Willsith relaxed his face, "Kinda wish I'd slept in."

"You'll be alright pal," said White. "I can tell. Let's get moving, the view from space will help."

"What are you, my doctor now?"

"Yes sir. Doctor White, sir. Changed roles while you were sleeping."

Willsith couldn't laugh with the others. As they moved off down the tunnel, she let him go, and so he focused on testing his body, laying there, working his way through each muscle. With each light that passed, his eyeballs tensed, disrupting the routine. He talked himself through it: *arms have most of their normal range of motion, but whatever is under these field dressings is agony when I rotate. They must have applied the bandages while I was out. Hope it wasn't Doctor White.*

"Was close back there," said Arc.

He nodded.

"Kleos effect?" Eva proposed.

How does she know about the Kleos effect? She's not battle-trained as well, is she? War-ready scientists?

"What's that?" Arc asked.

"It's when a soldier does the unexplainable," said Farl matter-of-factly. "He took more optical hits than any human should be able to."

310

Doesn't just apply to soldiers, Willsith imagined adding, then looked at his own bloody palms. And how the hell did Farl know that?

Arc turned and they stared at each other, perplexed.

"It's theorised that when we care about something enough, we can delay, temporarily, injury. Or at least, some people can," Eva said, "sometimes. It's kind of sketchy science."

"Magic?" asked White.

And then Willsith fell into the shelter of a memory. Last Kleos tag was back in 36; had been hell to recover from. Those two off-record hostages, that burning tower, all that small-arm-rail-fire. It had taken months to get over that. It was grim. And Willsith looked down at his legs, motionless, and he covered his eyes with his hand.

"Sure glad for the Kleos in you, Willsith," said White. "You've no idea what it feels like being a beautiful statue with an army running at you. Dark corners creeping in."

She giggled, and Willsith nodded.

"How much longer?" White continued, coughing into his hand, "Not sure I can make it."

Willsith wanted to flame at him, the ignorance of the thing swelled around inside him, lapping at his painful muscles, highlighting the void of feeling where his legs should be. Instead, "What happened, how long we out?"

Farl cocked his head back and said, "We were like that in the hallway for a few minutes after you collapsed, then Lif made it into the Ark and they flashed us with repair lights." Then he looked forward, and continued, but Willsith couldn't make out what he said.

"What?"

"I'll tell him," said Eva. "They tried to get in, they brought laser cutters, raised the platform, we could hear

311

them outside. But Lif took over, she threatened them with the radiation from the pipes, and then…"

White huffed.

"Then she released enough to scare them off."

Willsith winced.

"She did warn them, and most left, but a few were told to stay on, and cut through the door. In the end they ran when Lif dumped both outlets."

Better not be all for nothing. This better not be another nightmare I've jumped into. Why do we always have to hurt people. "Lif will need to be smarter in future."

A few lights passed, and the hum from his mag-lift stretcher reached his ears. They were all out of breath, and his clockwork lungs just highlighted to him his lack of mobility.

"Then they came back with juggernaut suits," added Farl. "We saw it on the screen while we fixed you up."

"That was Doctor White I guess?"

They laughed.

"If I was a doctor, I'd prescribe something for all our headaches," White added. "And install myself a new pair of lungs."

Willsith looked up at Eva, watched her throwing her bullet-proof arms up and down as she jogged, the white straps of her suit tightening at her hips, knees and… Her face was sweaty, the passing lights made her shine. She smiled at him, then said, "They bought Dalex a exo-juggernaut suit, the rest were in drone-assisted-hazmats. They attached something to the Ark. The AI's say it's just a tracking beacon, we should be able to remove it once we're out. You can use your kicking skills." She beamed, then, "After that they were focused on closing off the vents."

"Let us go?" he chanced.

"We're not moving yet," she said, "got to get to the control. And we need to be fast, because it's almost 05:30."

"I can see it ahead," Arc told them.

And they closed the gap in silence, beating at the metal grate, dashing themselves in yellow light.

First a stairwell, Eva guided them up and into the first door. Willsith had seen the stairs coming and begged his legs to work, but they refused. The stretcher arranged itself into a chair, and he floated after the others, through the metal doorway.

"This is just the fallback-bridge, the main cockpit is over there," she said, and walked directly toward the back of the room.

"It's huge, how many pilots were there?" asked White.

"More like a lounge than a bridge. It's just chairs and lockers. Look, only one panel in the whole room!" said Farl.

Willsith looked around, and had the sense that the room hadn't been long vacated. No one here, just an empty gun-rack and a couple of lazy-chairs.

"Two pilots. This is an autonomous ship, but we built-in the need for some human control," Eva said. "Here we go. Main cockpit."

He followed them in, and the room changed him.

The walls were matte black. The pilot's chairs, the controls, the panels, the floor, the ceiling, all matte black.

"Wow."

Humming pain dribbled down the base of his spine. Space leapt in at him through the wide glass of the window. It felt like a giant space suit. Feeling clawed along his thighs. He felt his knees were trapped, with each heart beat it was as if two sledge hammers cracked together against each joint, like a pair of weighted pendulums. *Paindulums,* he joked with himself. Then the wild. Distant old light beamed at them. Whole stars and systems presented as dots. Anchors thrown a long way out. And none of them moved, space held them there. And the surrendering. He sat with the pain, and surrendered. The scale, the majesty, the sovereign power of the absolute.

Reflecting on the universe, he moved. Every bone, tendon, and muscle. Every pump of blood. Every sip of air. Every one of them screamed at him to stop. His joints smashed at his will, wailing the loudest of all. But he stood up.

Then fell.

A crouch. A laugh. Tears. Another bleary look at the stars.

All turned to him, and he laughed, and said, "Yeah that's excruciating."

White knelt, "Well why are you doing it then?"

Willsith beamed through his tears, "I can feel them."

"No need to rush it," White told him. "Doctor's orders." And he pushed Willsith's shoulder a little.

Willsith told him, "No, no—Bear. They—they cut him in half. Pain is nothing, here. I love it," he said, and laughed, his face wet, and tentatively he stood up again.

"What are you waiting for? Get this ship moving!" White yelled at Farl and Eva.

He heard them move around, his team and Eva. The ship spoke, and so did Lif, and they moved around the cockpit, bustling past him.

"Here, captain," White told him, and guided him to a chair.

Willsith laughed uncontrollably, his torso shaking as

White nudged him backward into the raised seat.

Auto-fasteners, auto-adjusters. He felt them. The seat tweaked itself to his size, formed itself around him, fastened him in, embracing him.

"That's it!" came the voice of Farl. "Overridden."

"You should all take a seat," said the Ark.

Space encapsulated him again and the tears stopped forming. *The ultimate scale,* he told himself, and imagined infinite distance, and it helped with the local pain.

Arc hopped up into the seat beside him, and the others grouped behind, grasping the struts of the two pilot seats.

"Is it moving?"

"No it's your seat, I can see it from the back," Farl told him.

Arc grinned, replied, "Feels great."

"They fixed your face then?" Willsith said to him, smiling.

Arc nodded, touched his eye, smiled back.

Many dials and panels drawn on the glass in front of them began to fizz into luminescence, and Lif spoke, "We are preparing the drive units. Ark will engage shortly, brace."

A distant murmur grew and grew. Their view of space became framed with an electric-blue border, and the window came to life. A countdown, a projected video of the hangar, a multitude of labels and numbers, Mars identified in the distance. The noise built and built, and the floor began to vibrate. Willsith felt it up his spine and gripped the flight harness with what little dexterity he had.

The rumbling vibration began to jolt them around, and Lif announced, "Drive initialised, I would suggest that we leave the hangar now, and then consider our options once removed from the situation. Do you concur?"

All agreed.

"Thank you, I shall work with Ark to make it so. As we move into space she tells me that the turbulence you are experiencing should cease."

White spun around Arc's seat, catching himself. "I should bloody hope so Leaf."

"The ship harmonises, I suppose," said Arc.

"Easy to suppose from a seat. Try supposing from here—wow," White replied.

Then the Stellar Ark 12 moved, they could see it on the hangar monitor.

"Is that Dalex?" Farl asked them.

"Looks like him," said Arc.

"What's he doing?"

"That's the crew that attached the device," said White. "They're all just standing there!"

The vibrations of the ship pushed the pain to the periphery for Willsith, and he felt the desire to lead. "Lif, Ark, show us closer, zoom in on that juggernaut."

"Yes commander." And the screen flashed to life, the video stream split in two, and the new feed showed his face. His beaten, sweaty face. It was Dalex, and his replacement exo bobbed with his breath. His eyes were fixed, his nose held, his mouth down-turned. As the ship rumbled out of the hangar he stood there, watching. Behind him a crew of people in gas masks and hazmat suits ran off, falling all about.

"He's just watching?"

"Maybe he's going to blow us up. That device?" White suggested.

"Lif said it was a beacon," Farl told him.

"Maybe she can't see it. He's bat-shit mental, look at

316

him."

"White, it's not a bomb," Willsith told him.

"How do you know?"

"It's just not going to be."

"But how do you know for sure Willsith?"

"I don't."

"Look at him, he's stuck, just staring at us! We're hijacking their best ship and he's just standing there!"

"CG wouldn't let them blow us up," said Willsith. "And he's back with CG, now."

"CG's as mad as him. Can't we do anything with the device before we're all the way out?" asked White.

"Displaying progress," said Ark. And a diagram drew itself across the darks of space, a side-profile showing them as half extruded from the hangar.

"I don't get it," White told them.

"He's standing on your exo," said Arc. "Look, there."

"Don't get it," White repeated.

She stepped away from the metal of Willsith's seat with perfect balance, and walked in front of them. Eva's eyes moved between them, from one to the other, until she found White, who was clinging to Arc's chair. She said to him, "The reason I—we needed to steal this ship today, was because today it's almost inconsequential. Today, stealing this flagship is only of small importance. This was our *only* window." From her neck down, Eva's kit matched the cockpit walls. She stood steady, her suit making tiny adjustments to counter the vibrations. "I'm another reason that they've stopped. My father doesn't want me dead. And nor does he," she said, and then pointed to Dalex on the feed.

Willsith watched as the diagram showed them exiting the Clear dock, and he felt her eyes on him, and he confronted her.

She said to him, "And I think, Willsith might have given him a third reason."

The rumbling fell away and with eyes on space, Eva and the others from 229 basked in the silence.

CHAPTER 36
Price of Freedom

It was logical to escape, but that was only the beginning. Willsith had got the others onto the Stellar Ark, they had broken free from Control, and now they beat away from the ring which clung around the Earth; away from their planet, and away from everything they had ever known.

"Can't hear much once the Ark's in space," said White. "And the gravity feels different."

"It's another few percent lower than the Halo's," Eva told him, hopping on the spot.

Arc said, "Look at all that space. It's so open."

"It's like this in a suit, Arc. Sitting here is like being out there in a suit, nothing but unknowns," Willsith said.

White moved to the window, stuck his nose against the glass, "So we're free, now?"

"Define free," said Willsith, and looked down at his own legs.

"Away from all that mess, free to do what we want."

"There's always a trajectory, always a cost," Willsith told him. "People suffered back there, and they still suffer, in the sections, and—"

"So what do we do about it?" Farl pushed. "What now?"

"And you got hurt too. Your shoulder, your legs?" Arc said to Willsith.

Willsith shrugged, "Goes with the territory. The headache is worse."

"Initialising pilot assistance module," said the Ark in a stern female voice. And Willsith struggled against the seat as it jabbed him in the side. "What? Stop that!"

"A mild pain-killer, commander," said Lif. "You can trust the Ark, I have validated that our control intercept script has taken full effect."

"Control intersect what?" said White, "Lif baby, tell us straight."

"We control the Ark."

"Please do not inject me without asking first, Lif," Willsith barked at the cockpit wall.

"As you wish, commander."

"We could just escape, if we have total control of this ship?" said White. "Is it self-sustaining? How fast does she go? How big is she?"

"We can't just leave," Farl said.

"I don't want to go away from Earth," said Arc.

Eva turned from the window, said, "The Stellar Ark is self-sustaining. There is everything we could ever need on this ship."

"So just leaving is an option?" asked White.

Willsith shook his head and pointed, "No, no it's not. We can't just sod off into space. Like we said, we at least leak the core, and do whatever else we can. I know some of us came up here, or there, to escape that shit down on Earth, but it does no one any good if we just leave."

"I won't go, I will help somehow," said Farl.

"Help who?" asked White, "They're all screwed up, left-or-right, the wolves are at the top, and unless you remove them nothing will—"

A short beep sounded and the screen re-arranged to show a map of the space around Earth. Lif said, "We are exiting the near-space of the Earth's Halo, we now need a destination to chart to."

"How far can we be away from Earth, but still get a link?" Willsith asked Eva and Farl.

Both shrugged, and Lif spoke, "With the Ark's long-range communications array we're able to send data from a maximum of 100 million miles away. Though at that distance bandwidth at any useful speed will be significantly reduced."

White jiggled himself, said, "That's half way to Pluto! Let's go!"

"Not quite half way to Mars," said Farl, "let alone Pluto. And we need as much bandwidth as we can get."

"Eva, Arc?" Willsith asked, rubbing his head.

"I don't want to leave Earth," Arc told him. "Not for good anyway. Not now...not yet, no."

Eva turned, watched space, said, "I'm sorry, but I do. I want to leave Earth, this ring, this system. I'd fire at the Hub if I could, disable it, and be gone."

The others looked at him, their eyes held wide open, faces static.

"Eva, you understand that we're a team now," Willsith told her.

"I do. I agree. You choose for now."

"We all choose," Willsith said, and hit the release on his seat straps. "Lif, Ark—whoever. Put us on a course to Mars, but only as fast as you need to go. Don't let us get out of comms range without telling us." And he asked his friends, with an open face, if they agreed.

The three of them nodded at him. He leaned forward, then choked a little as he stepped onto the floor. His legs were still weak, but they'd hold. Hobbling, he walked up to the wall of glass and switches, next to Eva, and said, "We'll be a team from now. A new type of team. We were lucky to get this far, but we can't turn our backs on Earth, or the Halo."

"I know," she said, with a quiver in her voice. "I know."

And he turned to the others, and said, "So together then, let's make a plan. Suggestions?"

Farl said, "We sort a link to Earth, I drop the hub-core to my group, they'll leak it everywhere, front-of-app style."

"Great, what else can we do from here?"

"Can we stop the lasers?" asked White.

Eva shook her head. "No. I told you."

"But you said we could fire on the Hub."

She kept her back to them, and said, "I was dreaming."

"Maybe the core-leak is enough," said Arc, and hopped down from his seat.

"It might have to be for now. Until we think of some other way to help. Are you certain you can't hack into the lasers from here?"

Eva spun around, "Certain. I told you. Don't you think I've gone over this twenty thousand ways? My dad is responsible, and there's nothing I can do. The system's completely separate, it's run by people, no links...that's his trick. It's his sick trick. Program the people, not the tech. He's going to set fire to it all, and make me watch."

"Okay...then all we can do is leak the core, and keep ourselves and this ship away from harm, for now. Agree?"

He mapped around the circle which they'd formed into, and watched as each nodded at him.

"Fine. Let's deal with the current. Farl, start the leak. The rest of us should learn as much as possible about this

322

ship we're on."

"Not sure if I'm even needed," said Farl, "but I'll go back into the fall-back bridge and help Lif from the panel." He waggled his fingers in the air.

"Lif will need your help," Eva told him.

He nodded and left.

"What do you want to know about the Ark?" she asked him, in dull tone.

"Everything. Can we see a map?"

"Lif?" Eva asked.

"How fast does she go?" asked White.

Then Arc, "What's she made of?"

Eva pointed at the schematic which presently filled the window, "The outer-hull is made from ultra-mix amorphous fullerene. It also has thirty-five sub-layers of other materials."

Arc gawked, said, "A ship this size from agg diamond nano-rods?"

She nodded, with a smile, "It's the first with a full hull. It took two years space-debris collection to gather enough."

"The power needed to create it must have been…" Arc quieted himself.

White crossed his arms, rolled his eyes, and said, "I wonder where all that power came from."

Willsith and Eva caught each other looking. Willsith said, "No matter now. Tell us about the Ark."

She nodded, turned back to the schematic. "We're here, on the front-nose of the ship. The command-deck and cockpit. Up above is the forest, and the clearing-observation-deck, where I suggest we go next. Here," and she drew a line across the window confidently, "is the tunnel we ran along earlier, in the forest sub-level, and below that there are five levels of quarters, labs, and human zones. Some ops-spaces too. Below those: the tanks."

"Forest and a space for way more than two pilots. And a bank of tanks? What was she built for?" Willsith asked.

"The Stellar Ark 12 is the latest of a fleet of ships which we've built to collect material from around the system, and shuttle it back. Ten ships like this are currently shuttling between resource deposits and the Halo, however none of them are as advanced as 12. This ship is special, it has extra utilities added, such as the forest, so we can—"

White scratched his belly, "She's a cosmic basking shark!"

"Go on," pushed Willsith.

"So we can move people, and house people, indefinitely. And chart phenomena beyond the reach of all other ships, while still collecting materials, and, in fact, using it to build things."

"Holy guacamole," said White. "We've landed the big fish!"

Arc laughed, then caught himself, said, "And the forest is a food engine?"

She fumbled with her lip, said, "An evolution of one, more than just a food engine. My idea, actually. It's a food forest and a seed base. By including a structured forest of elite-trees, we get reliable crops, environmental controls, and it gives the ship lungs."

"Lungs?" exclaimed White, "Ark, you have lungs?"

"Correct, White," said the ship.

"Yesterday I was frying damn pack-food on an illegal torch fire, that tasted like—let's face it—wall insulation, and today I'm the new doctor on a ship which has a food-growing-forest for lungs?" He leaned back against the seat. "Sol be blessed." And then he leaned in, "And you didn't tell us, how fast does she swim?"

Willsith mapped Eva's body language as she dropped her shoulders, smiled at White, and said, "One hundred and eighty thousand miles per hour, when all tech is engaged, maximum." Then, with a cock of her head, "But it takes a while to get to that...obviously."

"Holy shit, are you serious?" White's eyes lit up.

"More than 300 times the speed of sound," said Arc.

White jolted himself up, stood tall and threw his arms up, "This ship could win the Hugo Galaxy Sceptre!"

The Hugo Galaxy Sceptre. White you are such a character to bring that up, here, now.

Arc said, "As if going that fast wasn't enough."

"This is the second of our ships that beats that," she said coyly.

"What?" White sucked in his belly, "Why doesn't everyone know? We should have celebrated this for weeks on the Halo; cherry brandy and party poppers all round? How long ago? Did you get the sceptre? Is it on this ship?"

Eva shook her head. "Earth doesn't know."

White jumped on the spot, threw his arms down, "What? Well strike me down. What?"

"Calm it White," said Willsith, lowering his weight onto one foot, stepping to his friend. "We can tell them all about it, now, can't we."

The two grinned at each other.

"Pirates of truth!" proclaimed White.

"Theres more," Eva said. "There are enough seeds on board, and being produced, to let us seed a—"

"Done." Farl leaped through the door as it slid open, and with eagerness, said, "Core is on its way, but the size of it—it'll be an hour, maybe two. There's so much data. It's encrypted, but my friends will deal. Lif snagged some codes from lip-reading streams." And he showed his teeth, "They won't notice before it's too late. But— they've started," and his face dropped.

"They've started?" Arc asked him.

"They're moving the lasers."

"Lif, on-screen," barked Willsith.

The Ark replied, "It's done."

The five who had stolen the Stellar Ark 12 watched in silence as the window drew it out, plainly. A cross-section of the Halo, a video feed from the Ark, another feed stolen from a satellite station, and a ticker of communication from the Hub.

"They're rotating them around," said Arc. "With the new mods we didn't install."

"They could be firing on us! They're not targeting us are they, Lif? Would we know?" White asked frantically.

The AI spoke, "All 2,700 section lasers are rotating synchronously. While several are approaching a possible striking angle, it would appear as though their plan is to—"

"Fire on Earth," Farl said.

"Yes, that is correct," confirmed Lif.

"But they could fire on us as they move around?"

"You are correct, White. Though at this distance—"

"When would it happen?"

"White, it is not likely."

"Just tell us when, Lif," said Willsith.

The AI agreed, and said, "Approximately thirty seconds time, and their window will last four seconds."

Nothing was said as they watched the countdown provided by the Ark. A falling number, a mixed feeling. Willsith let himself against a chair, fought with his ego about the logic of the thing. They wouldn't fire, they couldn't, not with her here, not on their best ship.

The firing-window passed, and the lasers continued around the ring.

"If the leak will take an hour, can't we send a shorter message? Can't we warn Earth."

"They must know," said White. "Look at the frickin lasers!"

Arc told him, "We can try."

"One step ahead of you, Willsith, I sent a transmission to Earth Control, Lif helped me write it." Farl jutted out his chin, smiled.

He should have asked. He's smart, but still with that reckless arrogance. He's insulated by the tech. Later Willsith, deal with it later. "Good. What did you say?"

"Lif?" Farl said.

"The dispatch packet read," and as Lif read the message, it wrote itself across the dark of space, projected onto the glass in bio-luminescent blue.

Dispatch Packet to ECEMC
<Earth Control Emergency Message Channel>

—

This message is being sent from the Stellar Ark 12, flagship of the Earth's Halo materials fleet. If you do not have record of this ship, it is due to the covert nature of recent Earth's Halo operations, of which, to a great extent this message relates.

We must warn you that the Controller General has installed 2700 laser extenders which break the third directive of the Earth's Halo act. These modifications allow the rock-defence lasers to be fired toward Earth. The Controller General's intention is to use them in tactical warfare against Earth cities.

We are sending you the Hub Core, via the anonymous data disposal channel.

We have escaped with a crew of five, as well as a competent AI, on this flagship. If we can be of any further assistance, please do contact us via this encrypted channel.

—

Channel ID: #112.358.132134.5589144

"Okay, that says it all…I suppose. Well done," said Willsith. "Sure it sent?"

"Could have played up our awesomeness a bit more," White said. "Added in a few explosions, or Willsith's OW hit—Dalex's downfall."

Farl said, "We decided not to name names. Yeah, it

sent. Don't know how fast the admin will get to it."

"What do you think they'll do?" she asked him.

Willsith shrugged, "Not much they can do. Don't know if they knew this was coming. Third directive means they don't have anything that is designed to take out the Halo, either. I guess they could nuke it, but I doubt they could get ships into atmosphere if CG has the laser array fixed on them."

"A nuke would send radiation and debris flying back down to Earth," Arc said. "And maybe even the Halo, as its balance would collapse."

"Might be their only chance, if CG fires on them, he can cut the whole planet up."

"A bit of nuclear rain wouldn't change much," said White sombrely.

"I don't know. You work for years, and you think it means something, and then this." Willsith threw an arm up at the glass, and beyond his bloody fist he saw the lasers crest over the top edge of the Halo.

"They won't fire on cities, will they?" Arc asked Willsith.

"They'll fire on cities," said Farl. "That bastard will fire on cities, on tectonic areas, on resonators, on hospitals. He'll fire on—"

"Enough, Farl." Willsith knew why Arc asked, and told him directly, "They'll know it's coming. The message will get through, the cities will set up shields, bunkers. They'll be fine, Arc." Then he looked at the lad as he shook. He was the only one up there who cared about his family. *Farl knows too much to be shocked, but Arc; he's still working on accepting this shit.*

And while the lasers rotated around the Earth's Halo, Willsith watched the feeds, and he saw the Earth, and the bland off-colour land under atmosphere, and he remembered the ground. It was in a bad state, it didn't need to get any worse. Again the memory of the day he left the force; the cruiser he watched from, the scarred land which fizzed and cracked from all that happened there, dead on the surface except for war. The pissed off slaps of waves which smashed at tide-breakers, lusting after the space. That rough land which he left, and the dead squad-mates he'd buried underneath it's thin, dry skin. Bear.

He remembered the jump to the Halo. The little ounce of hope it'd given him amongst all that tragedy. 'To fix the planet.' This wasn't fixing the damn planet. This was meant to be fixing the damn planet. Shooting lasers at it will not fix it. He roared, and he stood up, but his legs gave way. The floor caught him, and he pushed against it, raised himself to a squat.

Below his breath, he said, "It's not okay. This is not fixing the damn planet." And again he tried to stand, and his knees shook, and his whole lower body felt fragile, and jittery; but he stood, and said, "What can we do? What can we do?"

Willsith held his eyes on the laser diagram, but felt the others looking between themselves.

"We can tell Earth," Arc said meekly.

"We've sent the packet," Willsith snapped. "And the core."

"Lif, is this Ark armed?"

"No, commander."

"Why are you calling me commander, still?"

"You are the commander, commander."

"I am not."

"You are."

"Don't argue with me."

"Willsith, there must be other ways to tell Earth?"

330

"How strong is this ship?" Willsith asked the AI, "Can we smash it into the Hub? Will that stop them ordering the fire?"

"What?" they all exclaimed.

White stepped to him, "Willsith what are you saying?"

"Answer the question Lif."

"That plan will not work. While this ship's hull contains fullerene, the CG's bridge has also been encased in the material and would survive a collision. The defence lasers make it unlikely that we would even reach the Hub in tact. That plan would likely cause no change in todays proceedings."

"Percentage?" Willsith squawked. "Tell me."

"0.04% chance of success in stopping the lasers. 99.6% chance of complete destruction of the Ark. 11.2% chance of collapsing the Earth's Halo into the Earth."

"Horse shit."

The AI spoke to him in a slower voice, "There would also be more than a thousand casualties, were we to strike the bridge and succeed."

"Then what do you suggest, you smart son-of-a—" but he caught himself, and stopped. "What do you suggest?" he said. He'd lost it again. He had to tone it down. He'd lost his legs for a while, but he acted like it was over. Bear wouldn't have wanted that.

"I suggest, commander, that we reach out to your previous employers, as a means to expedite the communication."

"There's the money," said White.

Willsith closed his eyes, apologised to them all, and then agreed.

"We'll set up the comm-link," said the AI. "It will take a few minutes."

He nodded, looked at the illustrated lasers. "I hope it'll

change something."

"Me too old buddy," White told him, "nothing we can do now, except tell the truth. Shout it loud and wide."

"Do we even know the truth?"

"Willsith, we've got the core, we're leaking it to the whole world. This is the biggest thing to hit the global conscious in years."

He looked at the lasers, and he collapsed inside. Those lasers would be the biggest thing to hit. *And all I've done is fumble through the Hub and ran away. What the hell.*

"Look Willsith, we've trusted you to get us here. And you did it. You saved our lives!" White told him. "Don't be so hard on yourself. Your doctor insists!"

"I don't know," Willsith said.

White chuckled, shrugged, then told him, "Nor me, but I know you'll do what you can. That's the only sodding reason I'm out here with you odd bunch, in the wilds of space, on a freaking forest-ship. Because we've done the best we can, and what's right. Get it together man, use that tactical head they gave you, help us sort this out. We do what we can do!"

He's right old man, the cook's giving you whip-up speeches, and he's right. Do what you can. Use the situation. There isn't any other ex-soldier-commanders here, make good with that. Think about the rest later. Hell, you can sleep in the damn forest later. Sleep for good, but first help the ones you can see. "Fine."

And he ran through the options, and when his ego rebuffed him he persevered through, fighting the pessimism down until it was logical again, a reality check.

"So we tell Earth in as many ways as possible. We send flares if we have them. And after that all we can do is make good here. We clear up the unknowns and we prepare to help, however we can."

"Right boss," White said. Arc nodded too. Farl grinned.

We're no good dead. Saved 229 this far, and Eva. Let's see if we can save some others. "Lif, do we have comms to Earth Control?"

CHAPTER 37

Hope in Abundance

"No Comms. Earth Control are not responding…trying them on new channels. I am describing myself as you, but am unsure when they will accept. They are on terror-alert-level 12," said Lif.

"No wonder. They must know about the lasers."

"You'd think they'd see our space signature and weight it," said Farl.

"Lif, try asking for 'Andrew Oliga'."

White asked, "Who's he?"

"An old friend. A general."

"To confirm, commander, Andrew Oliga, General of the Ordnance?"

"Yes."

"This man is dead, commander."

Willsith grunted. "Still try a message packet with the FAO."

"But he's dead Willsith?"

"Can't be long down, maybe his name will rattle somebody's cage."

"Sorry if he was a close friend," Arc told him.

Willsith shook his head. "Keep us posted Lif. And show me the ship map again," then he moved to it, and held himself up on the controls beneath the screen. "So this is all living quarters?" he asked Eva.

"Yes."

"And they're all empty?"

"Should be."

"And what about these? They're marked as 'Ops'."

"Don't know...they're his addition. Probably just offices."

"So you have no idea what's on two floors of this ship?"

She nodded.

"Could have told us that?" he said. "Sorry. I don't need to be so sharp. We can clear them, later."

"Lasers are 80% around toward Earth!" Farl said.

Arc whimpered, spun the tags around his wrist.

"What do you know?" Willsith asked her. "What else do you know about this grand plan of his. The charter?"

"Don't think I'm any part of it...I tried to stop him. I—the only way I could even escape, was with Lif, and with..."

"With us?" asked White.

Eva pushed her lips together, nodded.

"Tell us what you know, now. When those lasers face Earth, what happens then?"

Her hands found her elbows, cupped them, and she emptied her lungs.

"Eva!"

"Come on Eva," said White. "We're pirates of truth. Maybe you didn't realise you'd end up with a team, but it happened."

"Well...he will hold the world powers ransom, limiting the energy they need—even more than he already is. And he'll use the lasers to force them to give up what he wants; important heavy metals, specific people. But it's not just that. He believes total rule will bring peace down there. Peace on Earth, managed by power from the Hubs."

"A proxy for god," said White.

Farl shook his head. "A proxy for the sun."

White waggled his face, "A poxy proxy sun-god."

"Enough you two," Willsith said, then to Eva. "So he won't fire straight away?"

"No, he'll wait for the lifted resources. Or maybe he'll fire once as a show of power."

"Will he or won't he fire now?"

"I'm not sure, I didn't see it all...He probably will."

"What about after that, what then? He'll live up here forever, reign over Earth?"

"No. The charter eventually splits the population, but that's over the coming years, and there's plans for—"

"Mars!" White burst out. "That's the real reason for building on Mars!"

Eva stared at nothing, replied, "That's just the start. There are plans for many colonies, there are other suitable planets within range—"

"More planets?" White threw out the words at speed. "More planets? What's wrong with Earth? Mars? More planets?"

Willsith bit in, "Enough, the lasers are moving, we're already a part of this. We do what we can, then we go through this in detail. The lasers are at 88%, we need to act."

"She knows it all! The answers to everything me and skinny-boy here have been arguing about for the past five years—Eva knows, Willsith. You know, don't you Eva, you've probably seen us fight over that mess-hall table."

"Eva will still know tomorrow, so let's focus on

surviving that damn long!"

"Willsith is right, White," Farl told him.

"Fine, but you've got me on the edge of my seat here. Front row at the show. You better keep sharing, Eve!"

Eva ignored him.

"What do we do, Willsith?" asked Arc.

"Until we have comms, we acclimatise. We remove unknowns."

"Bugsy scout squad," said White. "If there's no more show and tell, I'm keen to explore...and I'm hungry."

Farl said to him, "You're hungry, now?"

A wide grin and a nod. "And that shoulder dressing looks grim big-man. We need supplies."

"Don't worry about my bandages," Willsith told him, peeled it off and shoved it into a pocket. "But would be good to get eyes on these unknown sections."

Eva pulled a face at his wound, said, "I want to go to the clearing-observation deck, I think Farl should come too, it's got the best access to the Ark core. It's a half-lab half-bridge. No food there, but will have a med-kit. We should all go there."

"Me and Arc will go explore, bring you three up some sustenance, another med-kit, anything else?" White said.

"Can't we stick together?" asked Arc.

Willsith paused, absorbed the map. White was rarely this keen to move. Nutrients would help, and vision on the unknown areas too. He could go, but not with these legs. And out there, the lasers, there seemed to be nothing useful they could do to help. *Damn I hate that feeling— but it's there, the statistics, Lif said it - useless. If this was a movie we'd defy the numbers, save the day, but I don't see a way, and I'm tired of that hero horse shit. Us to the forest, them to the bowels of the ship, a short tour for these two, it'll help Arc's confidence. At least it's doing*

337

something. And White will help him deal with all that fresh weight he's carrying. CG could fire on Arc's city in minutes, and if he stays here he'll see it in 32k.

"Willsith?" Arc said.

And someone needed to keep an eye on Eva. "Yes, you two get supplies. Lif, guide them. Get only what we need, and just stick your head in one Ops room. Arc, use that memory of yours, I'll want a—we'll want to hear your report. Meet us in that clearing when you're done."

White saluted him, then slapped his palms together, bending into a eastern bow.

"Lif, do we have some sort of ship-wide comms?"

"Yes commander. Just say the name and wait for the beep."

"You good, then?" he asked Arc.

Arc nodded, said, "I'll look after him."

"Ha, you'll look after me? You seen the size of me?" White joked. "Let's go Arcy."

He wished Arc safe, and watched the two exit. White's wideness filling the door, then Arc's frugal silhouette. "I hope there's a lift," he heard White say, then, "and not the drone-fall type." Then they were gone.

A beep.

"Can you hear this?" asked White.

"Yes," replied Willsith. "Wait, do I have to say something?"

White replied, "No. Heard that. How do we close the comms?"

Willsith heard Arc tell him, then another beep.

"So, to the clearing?" he asked Eva and Farl.

"Yes," she said. "I think you are going to like it."

One tree in her lab had him earlier, so you could bet

338

that a glasshouse full of them was going to do something. He let himself down onto his feet, observing the pain as it dissipated from his legs throughout his body. A gulp, and a pretend look out of the glass.

"You'll see the void even better from the clearing," she told him. "It should be like a clear Earth-night in a forest."

"I can't remember one of them," he lied.

"Your record said—," she started, but cut herself off, "—I've never seen one."

"Let's go already," Farl told them, and left.

The pain settled, and he followed the starlight onto her face, where it seemed to cut new lines. Her cheeks seemed sunken, her eyes sad. Her lips still, pressed together, held in a smile. *I don't know if I can move my legs,* he imagined telling her, *and I don't know if I can trust you with that mixed up face.* But underneath he saw in Eva something which grounded him.

"Come on commander," she said to him, dipping her head and jogging out of the door.

He said, "On my way," and watched the door slide shut. Then he swore under his breath, lurched at the seat, but fell to his knees.

Blasted OW.

He knew they would be waiting, but he couldn't walk. Feeling was back, he had all the pain, but his meat logs wouldn't respond. *Please let this be temporary. I know, Bear, I know, I'm lucky for all this. Legs are nothing. This should have been you. But please let this be temporary.*

He clung to the seat, heaved himself around and into the mag-chair.

"Just for now," he said. "This is just for now. Until this mess is over."

339

He met them at the stairwell, his chair tilted and floated down to the metal grate where they stood, chatting.

"—before we lifted? Must have seen a lot," Farl said.

Eva nodded, fired a fleeting smile at Willsith, then said, "So, it's up those...stairs."

"Willsith, will you be alright with the stairs?" asked Farl. "Are you okay?"

Teenagers. "I'm fine."

"Willsith's been through far worse than this Farl, hasn't he told you?" she said, making way for them to go up first.

"Don't know if it's fair that you know everything about us and we know so little about you," Willsith snapped.

"He's told us some stuff."

He hadn't told them the half of it, and she can't know about the worst of the missions. "Where did you find that panel, Farl?"

"Oh, it was in that other room. I thought we might need it. Lif gave me access. See, this is that diagram of the lasers."

"How long?"

"92 percent. The leak still has 29 minutes upload."

Willsith bowed his head. "It's hardest when there's not a damn thing you can do."

"Then all you can do is try," Farl said.

He felt the mag-motors of his chair whir as he crested the set of stairs, happy to be flat level again. "Sometimes, you know trying is futile, and the only thing you can do is accept that you're not Superman."

"You survived four hits of OW. You're basically Superman."

"I'm not sure if Lif's just flattering me there. Does she has a flattery module, Eva?"

They stopped. "Eva?"

"Where'd she go?" Farl said.

Willsith twisted himself, the chair followed, "Don't know."

"She was right here?"

Willsith caught the young hacker's eye, said, "I'll go, you use the panel. Dig."

A nod then a descent. The chair cupped him as he guided it down the stairwell and back into the fall-back bridge. She wasn't there, maybe the cockpit.

The hum of his chair fell away as he approached the door, his ear tuning in to the shouting. It was Eva: "If you do, I'll find you, I'll show you what you've done! I'll expose them all. She knew what you'd done. She never wanted any of this!"

Then a male voice, and Eva screamed, and a thump.

He entered.

Sobbing. Eva stood sobbing into the controls beneath the window, lit by the neon blue words 'Communication channel closed,' pulsing on the glass.

He needed her to be on their side, but at every turn she changed. Would she ever settle down? Would she tell him what it was which did this to her? He kept his mouth shut, approached her.

"I just wanted to see," she started, "I had to—I had to see if he cared—if he cared at all, or if there was any way I could stop him."

He moved to her side, placed a calm palm on her ridged backplate. Wondered if she could feel through it.

"I can't. I can't stop him and no one can. He's gone. The Charter is happening."

"The hardest lesson of my life has been to learn to

accept," Willsith told her.

"No. No one can stop him. He's done it, and he's—he's done it."

"Right now Eva, I need you. We need you to help us."

"How do I do it Willsith?" she turned to him, her cheeks wet. "How do I live with knowing what my dad has done? What he's going to do?"

"He's not done it yet."

"He has and he will!"

He lowered his hand, said, "You came from him, but you are not him, Eva." And manoeuvred his chair to face her side-on, reached up to dry her cheek.

She stopped him, rubbed her own cheeks. "I know it's weird, but I've learned so much from watching you," she told him. "You don't even realise how much."

"Must have been boring to watch."

"You stopped me killing him."

"Earlier?"

She nodded.

"You couldn't of done it. And it wouldn't have solved anything."

"I could have Willsith...I tried."

"I don't know about that."

"How can you live with knowing that your dad is the worst thing that ever happened to us all, to the Earth? I should have killed him. Lif shouldn't have stopped me. You shouldn't have!"

"Eva, it won't—"

"I will kill him. When I can. I will do it, Willsith. It will make it right."

He shook his head.

"For my mum. And for what he's about to do."

"You say you've seen me. But let me tell you the truth. Before all this, war possessed me. It ate me, I had nothing else. You've been watching me trying to heal, but I'm not sure I ever can. If you go down that path, you'll lose years. You'll lose yourself, people you love. I've learnt the best way is to accept, to forgive. Violence—vengeance, solves nothing."

"You don't know it all—he's my dad and he's—"

"Eva, let's go. Let's get to the clearing with Farl. Let's stop what we can, and then I would love to hear it all."

"Will you help me, Willsith?"

"I'll listen."

"You know how, you fought in war…all those years. You've…killed."

"You've read my records, you've watched me, but you've not seen. Violence—it's faulty, it's—"

"When the time comes, you'll help me," she said, using her hands to squeegee her face. "I didn't choose you for nothing."

And in a hurry, she left, and again he was alone.

Willsith had more questions than ever. It felt bitter that she wanted that, but he would not help her kill him. He was through. Revenge didn't work. Smarter, not harder; they had to be smarter than that. Even though men like CG killed Bear, and held Willsith in battle for most of his life—used him. Maybe even took his legs.

He would not help her kill him.

His chair carried him up the stairs. His pain carried him into a daydream.

Farl and Eva were at the top, he could hear them above; a few words, and a door sound. He reached the landing and lined himself up with the crack in the double-doors. The metal panels were emblazoned with the logo of Drasil-G. That tree, her version.

A gesture forward. Willsith's numb knees approached

the metal doors. A rush as they opened, and it hit him—a tsunami of smells. Soil, musty and organic, like end-of-shift armpits; then fresh citrus, and the warm, sweet smell of berries. Layer after layer of natural odour, until finally the breeze died down, and all that remained was the persistent scent of trees. The hikes where him and Bear had stuck their noses in the Jeffery pines, that wonderful smell, from the beginning.

He floated in and onto a platform, a metal grated step which held him raised above the mud.

"She was right," he said, "it's like a clear night at home."

Willsith sat in his mag-chair, hovering above earth which made up the ground for as far as he could see, which wasn't far, because the forest was dense. The pong of the soil, he knew, meant it was healthy. The opposite of that sludge back down on Earth. The trees and plants were wild and abundant. Sturdy trunks grew from splayed out roots, branches exploded in all directions; limbs heavy under the weight of nuts and fruits. He saw all colours of leaves, and plants which grew amongst the branches too, adding their own shapes and hues. Drooping stems nudged themselves away from the tree's bark, presenting flowers like painted megaphones, anchors for attention, he thought.

"No, this is nothing like Earth," he said out loud. Most of that land was dead when he'd lifted, abundant only in suffering. This was an eden compared to down there, even back before, it wasn't like this. "Weren't we meant to be fixing Earth? Couldn't it be like this?"

Again a breeze. *Must be some kind of nature-simulation?*

Wind rustled the leaves above him in crackly discourse.

An answer, he thought.

Leaves of all denominations cavorted around above him, collected on the spindly tips of tree branches. Natural shapes brushed past one another, like people bustling around a city. Fleeting contact; without grip.

"I love that sound," he said, closing his eyes. "Even if this wind is artificial, those leaves aren't."

His legs. The day they'd had. The imminent attack on Earth. That mixed up Eva. But still somehow—hope. This greenhouse in the sky—her.

"Let's go, Willsith," he said with a smile, and aimed his chair forward, following the marks left in the soil by his two friends.

He counted the trees as he went, mapping their location, the division of their branches. He guessed at their origin, their names. "I think that's Oak," he'd say to himself, "Or maybe Maple."

Somewhere along the path, he lost himself.

When he awoke he found himself slouched back in his chair, his neck bent back and his lungs full of warm air. A cough. Those smells, again. And a new syrupy whiff. He heard a creak, and awoke a little more. A branch bowed and bounced as the noise sounded again.

"Just a branch," he told himself. "You must have been out, old man. Exhaustion?"

Again he slipped into a daze, lulled by the swaying branch above him, which reached across the sky like the tail of a comet. The tree's extension, an exploring arm, with its own children. Green leaves formed dancing sails, tugging at the branch as they busied themselves following the wind. Sometimes slow, sometimes fast. A wild spin, then stillness. Seas of paper thin limbs, layered, single units, happy in situ, joyous in movement, families celebrating their stemming coexistence. Knowing space.

Then the light.

His half-consciousness jolted him upright, flooding his senses with the fullness of the place.

Blue flames, fast moving.

He blinked, gripped onto the chair.

It tailed off over the canopy, a gust following it.

"What was that?" he asked.

But then it was back, and he saw its lights illuminate the forest as it came. And it stopped above, hovering, silent.

Shifting around in his chair, he tailed it with his eyes, catching glimpses through the gaps in the leaves as it fleeted from observation.

It was inside the ship, just above the trees. It moved like an animal, glowed like a meteor.

Forward, chair, he commanded silently. *Let me see it!*

And he gripped the bark of a short tree, and peeked out through a gap in its branches, and in the canyon between two tall trees he saw it.

Eight slender arms hung limp, and glowed a constant blue light at their joints. Each ended with a hand, and from a kind of palm, a search-light projected. It moved about in three-dimensions, as a jellyfish in the deep ocean. Pulsing.

Silent and still, Willsith watched it with trepidation.

A swirl, a stop. The umbrella of its body, translucent and glowing, heaved and shrunk rhythmically. A pause. Willsith made out sharp lines inside of it; an ornate skeleton. At its centre a light, a blue bloom which carried to its edges, muffled by the opaque membrane which stretched over its bones. Then it spun again, and approached a branch. In one quick swoop it slid itself along the length of the branch. Its skinny mechanical arms came to life as it moved, jabbing their hands amongst the leaves, then yanking them back up. Arm after arm surfaced with objects gripped between two fingers and a thumb. Each threw its find up into the body of the machine and then threw itself back at the tree to feel for another.

"It's harvesting!"

And he watched again. It positioned itself at the fat-end of another branch, then shot along it, using its many arms to gather as it moved. Inside it he could see several sections filled with assorted produce. And then it left, tailing off between the trees, pulsing its arms as it flew.

Then the sky. The landscape above the canopy was lit by the perpetual night of space, and it looked to him, to be the rawest of things he had ever seen.

He leaned there, half-off his mag-chair, half against a tree, and watched the stars. What he saw possessed him, and Willsith imagined himself ingested by the Universe.

And then Farl shouted and he remembered it all.

"We're here. Where are you?"

Willsith thought of ignoring him.

"I can see Arc. But you should get here, something to show you."

No choice, he decided. "Comms to everyone," then, "I'll be right there Farl, find out all you can, I've seen something too. Eva's forest is amazing."

He moved off, picking up their trail in the mud, and blissfully smiling, despite himself.

No check-in, though, he thought, and said, "Did you hear that everyone?"

Still nothing. He flicked his chair up a setting, barked, "Farl? White? Arc?…Eva?"

Farl spoke from somewhere in the trees, "Yeah, I'm here. We're here. Don't know what's up with the other two, they should be able to hear us."

"Find them. Keep visuals. I will be there shortly." Short term issues. The trees—amongst the trees Willsith could see a future. A future after the short-term issues.

The trees thinned out as he approached the clearing, and the wide open space surprised him. Short trees fixed a circle around it, and beyond them taller and taller trees stepped up; a green amphitheatre. Central to the clearing was a raised circular deck with consoles around it. Amongst the back of the panels, plants grew; vines laden with fitful groups of berries.

Farl ran at him.

"Look. Look!"

"There's something coming up. From the surface. It's—"

"We can't tell what it is," she said. "But it's not in his plan; The Charter. I know that much."

"Let me see."

"There's hundreds of them, they're coming from all over the planet."

"Can't we zoom?"

"It's at max zoom, and they've locked down the other satellites. This is the best we can do."

"Well done, Farl. Looks like missiles—hope it's not."

"You can't possibly tell that from those dots," she told him.

He handed back the panel and let his chair rise up and float onto the platform. "A feeling," he said.

Eva's suit clinked as she let herself back against a panel.

"What about Arc, White. Why aren't they responding?"

Farl tapped at the panel, "Don't know, we can still see them, look."

"Just their legs?"

"Yeah, they're standing in an area the cameras can't quite pan to."

"Project a message into that room, tell them to come back."

"That's the thing, they don't seem to respond when I comms them."

Willsith shook his head, shouted upward, "Lif, can they not hear our comms?"

"They are in a room with comm-block. These areas are currently outside of the Ark's control."

"What the hell is down there then?" he snapped.

But Lif did not answer, and instead she said, "Willsith, Eva, Farl. Earth is responding. Resistance to the charter!"

CHAPTER 38

Rips in the Sky

The Earth and its Halo filled the panels around them. Willsith sat in awe as equally distributed black dots broke through layer after layer of atmosphere. Willsith was used to the grey clouds and cluttered weather systems which wrapped around Earth; that had been the view from kicking rock. But now they were away from that ring, and something new beat out through the sky, and up at the Earth's Halo.

"The lasers are reaching their positions," said Farl.

What a god-awful place to be, that we can see this in such detail.

"They look like missiles," she said. "Maybe you were right. Would they blow it up?"

Farl replied coldly, "Maybe that's all they can do."

"There are thousands of people up there. It's producing all that energy," Willsith said. "They won't take it out unless there's no other choice."

"But if they know about the plan, the lasers?" Farl questioned.

"I don't know," said Willsith. "Let me see them," and he arranged his chair. "I've never seen anything like it before."

And through the displays of the forest clearing deck of the Stellar Ark 12, they watched. The dots grew into shapes, and the shapes became bolder. Their outlines sharpened as they punched through sheet after sheet of atmosphere.

"They're beautiful," Farl muttered.

"They are fast," Eva said.

What were they? And then, to him, it was obvious. They were sending ships. Triangular, dark-bodied craft, leaping from the planet at an astronomical speed.

"Ships," said Farl, and then he ripped his panel closer, jabbed at it with his fingers.

Willsith let his jaw hang. Hundreds of these craft emerged from the ground beneath the shadow of the Halo and tore upward. Each broke through the air with a sharp point, tipped white with heat, and displaced gases whipped down its edges, tailing off after it; drawing a line back to Earth. A thousand lines. A thousand ships. One thousand rips in the sky. And they all exited faster than anything Willsith had ever seen.

"Insane ships!" said Farl, "look up."

Willsith let his neck back against his chair, and saw the glass above the clearing jump to life. A huge projection of the action feed filled the glass.

"I didn't know you could do that," Eva told him.

"They're corkscrewing through the air...spinning," said Willsith.

Each ship had three cupped tails which welled with displaced atmosphere as it rotated, extruding strings of cloud. Helix contrails.

"Guys," a voice darted out from the trees. It was White.

Willsith swung around, looked for his friend.

"No, it's over comms," Farl told him. "It sounds like

351

that—like they're among the trees. White, what's up?"

"There are these two women, maybe pilots…they're a bit pissed off."

"Where, what's happening?" Willsith questioned.

"We should tell them about this," Farl said to him, and pointed up.

Willsith put a finger to his mouth, "Wait. White?"

"We've locked them in a room. A lab, I think." Noises followed, and over the scraping, and hollow thumps, he continued, "It's okay, they aren't going anywhere."

"Good, you need to come back now. Up here."

"Hang on, Arc has something for Farl."

"Not now, come up here."

"Hi Willsith, it's Arc. We found the Ops core, I put a bridge in for Farl."

"Fine. Well done. I need you to come to the clearing, okay?"

Arc said, "We had to lock them in—those ladies. We'll block the door more, then come back. They were pilots I'm sure of it, I think we woke them up from some kind of stasis. They asked questions, and they didn't believe White when he said—," a loud thud broke through Arc's speech, "—they got crazy, threatened us. We had to shut them in here, Willsith."

"Okay. Arc, it's okay. You and White get up here—"

"—and we've piled stuff up against the door. There's a vending machine and—"

"Enough. Get up here now will you?" Willsith barked, "Earth is responding!"

White said, "Wow, what did they say?"

"No, they've sent ships," Farl told him.

"Ships? Wow. We'll come now."

"They've closed comms, must be on their way. So

what now?" asked Farl.

Eva spoke, "He—my dad—he knew they had some ships—we knew it. But nothing as advanced as these. We had active intel for all research labs."

"Spies," Farl said.

"At least Earth has something in this," said Willsith, rotating his chin until his jaw clicked. "How's the leak doing?"

"16 minutes left."

"At least that'll inform after whatever happens here. Half the world must be seeing this, from the ground. Ribbons in the sky."

"There must be something else we can do," said Farl. "Must be."

The first space war, and I'm watching it from a forest-topped Mars yacht. What the hell. "Stop the ship, Lif."

"Stopped, commander."

"No sense in moving further now," he told them. "How's that comms request to Earth, Lif?"

"Still no response."

Neck back, he looked up to the action feed.

"Further satellite access acquired," sounded Lif. "Close-up on screen."

From its needle-point the ship grew organically, without breaks, as though it were a single drip of material. Its sides curved and spiralled outward, and all along its slick surface subtle grooves formed, and then merged, developing into three concave fins. Every bit of its form flawlessly fed disrupted atmosphere down into spherical cups; guiding the air into the ships tail, and out. A weave of clouds fell behind it as it corkscrewed upward. It was then that Willsith noticed it was slowing down.

Farl said, "Only 10 km from the Halo, they're

breaking."

And he saw it. The tails of the ships transformed, their rotation slowed, and the braided vapor they left behind thickened.

"All ships have reached a stop, only a kilometre from the ring. Damn that was fast breaking!"

"Lif," Willsith asked. "What can we do?"

"There are no accessible plans which will produce a significant change in global events."

"There's a war breaking out Lif," he told the AI.

"I am aware. I would have provided you with an option, should my exploratory analysis of produced any."

"You need work on your imagination matrix or whatever it—"

"Hack them?" he asked Farl, looked at Eva.

She shook her head.

"I've verified the lasers are on no single network, they're fired by individuals. Lif's got us access to the Hub core still, to the satellites, and we're shouting as loud as the channels will let us, at Earth Control."

Willsith checked above. Earth's ships hung in the air, in slow rotation. The whites of their tips were fading back to black; their trails dissipating into cones.

"Then we have to accept it—there's nothing we can do. Nothing but watch," Willsith said.

Farl dropped to the floor against the metal of a crate, huffed out air. "Lasers are starting to charge," he said. "We can't stop them, but we do have sensor input. I'll put it up."

A progress bar slid across the glass, and Willsith saw stars from behind it dot over the blue oblong. *I wonder if this is happening out there too, somewhere in all that space. We're here fighting over the light of our only star,*

354

when they're perhaps infinite.

The percentage read 10%.

Willsith looked at his friend, then at Eva, and finally, his own legs. "The only thing left is to try," he said. "Can you hack into the broadcast screens? Into the hub panels?"

CHAPTER 39
Pirate Leader

Willsith sat, with Eva and Farl beside him, in the forest clearing of the Stellar Ark 12. The ship hung in space, one hundredth of the way to Mars. The universe beamed in through the canopy, and he stared back. Willsith watched as the Earth and its life-support-ring squared up to each other, distant dots seen through satellites, projections on the glass. And despite the odds, and their abstracted, insignificant position, he prepared to try and help. To try for an ounce more of peace, or a limit to the destruction.

"So I just speak at it?"

The tiny drone hung in the air in front of Willsith. Farl nodded.

"And it'll broadcast to all sections, and Hub screens?"

"From what Lif says, we can broadcast to every piece of glass on the ring," Farl replied.

"But they'll catch you and kill the vector pretty quick. Isn't that so, Lif?"

"Correct Eva. Simulations suggest broadcast will be detected and cut within one minute. They will then heal that entry vector."

Willsith clicked his jaw. "We'll have to make that

minute count."

"Say what you said when we were hit with OW, in the hangar," Eva told him. "In that state—your words helped me. And I'm not a soldier. It will help them."

A smile, a huff of air, a memory with a headache. Willsith thought back to the hangar, but it hurt. He fought the anxiety which crept in, and looked for reasons. His brother. Hell, even Dalex. The illusions of war—they had owned him for years. They killed his brother. They almost killed him. But maybe—he could try. He could only try. He would tell them how it is, some would listen. Most won't. If they were doggedly stuck, they'd reject it. But he had to try.

Two beeps sounded and the humming drone lit up a small green light.

He frowned, asked Farl, "Are we live?"

Farl shook his head, "No, it's an inbound communication from Earth Control."

"Is that live?" he questioned.

"No, drone's just preparing. Want to accept it?"

"Yes. Where will it show?"

"Drone will project direct to your retina, we'll see it on the panel."

"Fine, accept."

Farl nodded at him, and Willsith saw a flash of light, and some text appeared in three-dimensions. 'Connecting...' And then a face. A woman of stature with one hell of a stern look. Her suited elbows rested on an old desk made from dark wood, and it seemed as if he were sitting across from her.

"Willsith Harper?" the woman said.

"Yes. Who am I speaking to?"

"How did you get this clearance code? Why did you fail the handshake? We are at our highest level of alert, we cannot waste any time with illegal communication."

"You called us?"

"No. You breached our network, forced your request to the top of the queue. How did you do that?"

Farl or Lif? No matter, he'd make use of it. "That doesn't matter. We are leaking you the Earth's Halo core. We want to warn you that they have lasers which will—"

"—we are aware of the lasers. Willsith are you communicating from the Stellar Ark 12?"

"Yes, we have commandeered it. I was, until earlier today, the head of section 229, after being falsely imprisoned, we—"

"Enough. I am aware of your situation."

He looked at the woman and took in her rank, which she wore around her neck. Twelve golden pins. This was the new United Earth Control's commissioner.

"Then how can we be of assistance?" he asked.

"You can stay the hell out of our way!"

"What?"

"You heard me. Our scheme for today was generated and successfully simulated by an array of our best AI. Your breaking free, stealing a ship, and now your attempted interjection, was not part of this plan. Any attempts to further manipulate events today will result in a deviation from this AI-approved agenda."

Her uniform, this projected set up; it's all bravado. Pantomime. I see it now. And she just gave me far too much information. She's anxious. We must be able to actually change something, I can tell.

"Stay where you are, if any other stellar collector ships from the fleet approach your position, forward the message that they must also wait there. They should not attempt to dock at the Earth's Halo. We will deal with you later. I repeat, do not act."

"What is your plan? We can help."

"You are of no use to this plan. Stay where you are and do not attempt any communication of any sort."

He felt the metal of his mag-chair, saw a glimpse of the trees behind her projection, puffed up his chest.

"We will not comply."

"Excuse me? Do you not realise my seniority? That was a direct order from United Earth Control."

Another new government body. Damned politics.

"The thing is, we're nowhere near Earth. We're not even near the Halo. We'll do what we must. We'll try."

"Do not continue your passing of information to Earth, and do not—"

"Close comms, Farl—shut this off."

The woman's face opened up, her brow ruffled, and then the scene disappeared with a beep.

"What did she say?" Farl asked.

"What, you couldn't see?"

"No, we only heard you."

"Earth told us not to broadcast. To stay out of it."

"Shall I cancel our connection? Or…"

Willsith blinked several times.

"No," he said. "Get it ready. Those old uniforms don't hold any weight with me any more."

"Okay."

Willsith looked at the hacker, and saw the jolt in him, and dreaded what he might say.

"Wait—lasers are about to fire!"

Phantoms on the glass. Earth's triangular ships were close to static, they hung beneath the Halo in quiet rotation, a circle guard around the globe. Then the lasers fired without warning; shrill beams of colour jumped from the ring and struck the craft. Two lasers per ship— or more. They intersected at the fronts of the ships, and for a moment, nothing happened.

And then the glowing.

Willsith sat there, staring up, seeing every detail. Bright white engulfed the craft's nose as it continued to rotate, lasers still firing at it, and then the light bled down its spiral edges. Metre by metre the hull was overtaken by a violent glow, until, finally, it was consumed, and the spacecraft ruptured, collapsing in on itself. A monstrous explosion saw it turn to hot shrapnel. The view was devastating.

A dull popping sound filled the clearing, bounced off into the trees.

Then another. And another. And more, countless more. They watched as the Earth ships fell to the lasers. Sick fireworks.

Willsith felt grim. He let his face express it, then hid the frown in his palm.

"They aren't all going though," said Farl, pointing upward, "some are moving—show us Lif, Ark, zoom in on that!"

And through the sound of popping, Willsith forced his eyes toward the glass.

Many ships had fallen. Clouds of dust, debris, and sparks of fizzing light dissipated where they had been. Lasers fired in all directions, slicing the fodder to avoid impacts to the ring. Amongst it all, there were bodies moving.

Surviving ships emerged from the mess, swiped out of the reach of the lasers. The needle tips of the ships kept focused on the Halo, and as they spun their cupped tails the craft rotated to the space side of the ring.

"They're hiding around the other side," Willsith said.

"The lasers will have to move to reach them there."

"What now?" Eva asked.

"220 made it. The lasers blew up the 680 decoys," Farl narrated.

"How do you know they were decoys?" Willsith asked him.

"Seems like they were decoys," Eva said.

Farl said, "Makes sense doesn't it? The numbers are too perfect. Are you ready to broadcast. The lasers are moving around—"

"I'm ready. For whatever good it will do. I am ready."

"Try," said Farl, "I'll count you in." And he held up three fingers, tapped a panel with the other. "You'll have more luck with them than I would. You know about war."

It wasn't enough time. He wasn't a speech-maker. What the hell could he say to them? The whole ring? And he saw the last of Farl's bony fingers drop, and he glanced at Eva, and saw a world of emotion in her, and then he spoke.

"Hello."

Farl nodded at him.

"Sections of Earth's Halo, Hub people."

The tiny drone-camera hovered in place, glaring a red light at him.

He would say it how it is. Make it clear, and give them the truth. That was all he could do.

"I am Willsith Harper. I was head of section 229, before today."

"I left the Halo, and I have found out things which I must share with you. You might not know it, but those laser modifications were designed to let Control fire on Earth. The Controller General is responsible, he wants to be our planet's dictator. Earth has sent ships up, and the two are currently locked in battle. The reasons we came up here—these people in control, they've been abusing the work we thought we were doing."

Shit, I can't explain it. I can't say this. And he saw Eva and Farl leaning over a panel in his periphery, and he churned out air, and he thought of his brother.

"Earth told me not to talk to you. They have a plan. All these people have a plan. But we don't have to act—I mean we don't have to be what they want us to be. We've been soldiers, maintainers, tools. They've abused their power; they are not regenerating the land with it."

Farl waved at him, said something he couldn't hear, and he continued, talking faster, "Lay down your weapons, do not fight for him. This fight is their fight, not ours. We came to maintain; to help the regen. They want even more than our lives from us. Do not fight. When the time comes, whatever side you are on, do not fight. If you could see the world from where I am, you'd know. There's no reason for—"

"Willsith."

"What?"

"They killed the link."

Willsith cursed, swatted at the drone.

"What happened? That wasn't a minute?"

Farl told him, "Earth helped kill the vector."

Willsith shut his face. Eva came to him, held his cheek softly, and told him, "That's why I chose you. That's why I needed you by my side."

"What? I told them nothing. I just confused them."

"It's enough," she told him, dropping to look him in the eye. "You did enough. You tried. From here, now, there's nothing else. You are enough, Willsith."

Through teary eyes he went back to watching the

ships. The lasers had finished dicing the decoys, and had begun to swing back around toward the floating craft. A dusty veil hung between the Halo and the Earth. Willsith wondered if they'd been piloted.

Then, movement.

From their hovering rotation, Earth's ships lunged toward the ring. Two hundred needles to the vein.

But there was more.

Silence fell over the clearing, the rustling of leaves temporarily sloshed in, and then the three gasped as the ships unfolded their hulls mid-thrust.

Their front sections split into four as they lunged at the Halo. Each of these four arms flung itself outward, falling behind the central unit as it impacted, and then slapping down onto the ring and gripping it. To Willsith they looked like octopi grabbing onto a rock.

The lasers stopped in their paths.

Space ebbed back into his view as the scene halted. The only movement Willsith could make out was the dust of the annihilated decoys in entropy. Around him he heard creaking branches; whispering leaves.

Farl broke the quiet. "There's men in them. They aren't missiles, they're invasion squads. The Halo sensors show—they're designed—a perfect fit. They've locked on to the hull."

"Show us sections," Willsith told him.

The sky-screen changed, a feed of a section. 'Section 376' stated the text. A not-so unfamiliar view.

"And where in Pluto's arse are White and Arc?" he asked.

Farl flicked at his panel.

"Can't see them on the camera, but Arc sent a message

while you were talking, saying he was going to fix that data-bridge on the way."

"376 is empty," said Eva. "Show us others."

And the display cycled through sections, and they saw men in arms, men hustling about, men laying passed out on the floor.

"None of them have put down their guns."

"Here's one!" Farl said, and showed Section 284, where five men sat in a huddle, weapons emptied in front of them, laid out on the floor.

Across the broadcast area of 284's wall, they saw the Controller General's old grey profile, and Farl opened a broadcast feed.

"Pay no dues to the words of terrorists. What I have asked you to do is to protect all we have achieved here. Earth has sent men to disrupt our progress, to force us into political slavery. We must not let that happen." His face was stiff, his lips down-turned. "Bear arms and help me fight off these invaders, for the good of your families on Earth, and for the regeneration of our planet. Controller General out."

Farl spat out words, "That lying prick. He's just said the opposite of what's true...sorry Eva—but—"

"Don't be," she said.

"Serpent's tongue," said Willsith. "Look, they're getting up."

The five from 284 turned from the broadcast screen, picked up rifles, and knelt in preparation.

Willsith nearly puked.

"One's thrown his gun down, they're talking about it."

"Can we listen?"

"No access."

And then the scene erupted. The bastardised Drasil-G logo of Control, which stood emblazoned across the broadcast screen, collapsed. Laser cutters drew a doorway through it, dropped the wall, and gas balls rolled in. The five in 284 stopped their squabble, and fell into a heap. Blank faces.

Men moved in through the door, or at least the shapes of men. Willsith thought the visual was faulty at first, but it became undeniable as the sixth silhouette walked through the newly-cut door. Shadow squad. He had never believed in them. The darkest of black ops.

Then the video faded.

"Feed crashed," Farl said. "Trying to get it back."

"Don't bother. They're shadow squad. It's over."

"Shadow squad?" Eva asked.

"You see them only as shadows, the shapes of men. They have all the tech of two hundred years of industrialised war behind them. Kit most operatives wont see for two or three years. They're deep-cover soldiers who I thought were just hearsay. But that was them. The circle gas mask eyes you can only just make out, the trippy silhouette suits, the mysteriously downed feed. Check the other sections, you'll see."

Farl flicked through, scene after scene of blank feed, or foggy rooms and vague shapes, then a dead feed.

Two beeps.

"Earth Control again, same woman. Want to speak?"

"Leak?"

"All done. They have it, and so does my man." Farl showed Willsith more teeth than he thought any man had.

"Put her on."

"What are you going to tell her?" asked Eva, and he

reached out and squeezed her, then turned to the drone.

"Commander Willsith! You directly disregarded my orders—Earth's orders! Your actions could very well risk this entire mission!"

"This isn't a mission, commissioner, this is many, many people's lives."

"Your action was not sanctioned, you have totally upset our simulations and—"

"Simulations are not reality. Let's hope your shadow squads aren't using fatality. Close communication."

Again her face contorted, shrank to a single dot of light, then disappeared.

"Closed," replied the Ark.

"Thank you Ark," he said.

"She's trying again," said Farl. "They're flashing us on ten channels."

"Ignore her."

"You might want to see this, though," he said, and switched the video to an Earth news broadcast.

'Our efforts to test the new exit-craft have been a triumphant success. This is the first step to setting up a new service which will help us discover what technical fault has been limiting the power to Earth's regeneration engines.'

"Horse shit propaganda," Willsith said, and felt Eva next to him. He moved a hand around her side, felt her ribs. "Will no one just tell people the truth?"

Farl said, "We have," grinned, and changed the feed again.

He moved through stream after stream of alternative news.

'Hub core leaked to press, appears Earth and Halo locked in political power battle for energy distribution'

'Earth's Halo Lasers modified to eradicate Earth cities'

'Full Hub core available for download'

'A network of undercover agents have leaked logs from Earth and Halo databases onto every data-station in the world'

"They can't stop it, it's out! And here's my favourite," he said, and flashed up an article.

'Vigilante crew of space maintainers steal ship and leak government data. Pirate leader projects speech to whole of globe and Halo'

"What?"

"Leak is complete. The world has the truth at its fingertips—and I streamed your speech. Half-a-billion views already."

Willsith choked. Eva held him. He laughed—because he didn't know what else to do, and they laughed with him.

CHAPTER 40

Lin

"Lost feeds for the sections, but we still have Hub visuals."

"White is going to freak out when he hears about all this."

"He'll watch it back," Farl told him. "Fifty times, he'll watch it back."

Eva asked him, "Where are they?"

"Still in Ops. Can't see them, but Arc must have put the bridge up because we now have Ops core access. Lif's already analysing it."

"They've been too long," Willsith lifted himself up on the chair, frowned at his own legs. "We should go and find them."

"Lin! Willsith, I've found Lin."

"Your fifth man," Eva told him.

Farl smiled at Eva as she smiled at Willsith. He smiled back at them both.

"Show us."

Farl nodded, tapped and looked up. "He's in that corridor with the closing sections, look."

Willsith didn't need to see, but let his head back. It was Lin all right, he was crouched behind a pair of fallen juggernaut exo-suits. He'd ditched his helmet and was cycling through a pile of rifles checking charge. A turn, shots rattled off—then he was crouching again.

"Who's he firing at?" Willsith asked.

Farl slid another feed up.

A group of silhouettes clung to either side of the corridor wall, their shapes merging into one. They threw symbols at each other with their hands—outlines of gestures, which Willsith knew, all meant bad news for Lin.

"He's on his own? How come it's only him?" Eva asked.

Farl told her, "There's others behind him, but their sensors say they're downed."

"Lin's hopelessly untrained for this," Willsith told them. "There's no chance he'll—"

Eva whimpered, said, "He's more trained than you think."

"He was in 229 for six months, we know the guy. He's not ready for this."

She sat down next to a crate, folded her arms together. "Sorry."

"Sorry for what?"

Her bold lips fell. Willsith watched her breath jump out of her. "He's had years of training. They were blanked from him before he was dispatched to you."

Willsith frowned at her, turned to watch Lin throw the rifle away. His mannerisms did seem different. "Is there any limit to what your dad will do to people? Lin was sound. He was our friend. Now he's back protecting that twisted—" and he stopped himself.

Eva spoke in dry tone. "It's true. I hate him for it. Willsith—I even tried to tell you—but you wouldn't have understood. You had to see this—you had to see the

369

truth, before you'd understand."

"To hell with me," he said, and glanced at Farl, who beamed back at him uncomfortably. "Lin is the next casualty in this mess." And he forced his eyes to the feed.

★ ★ ★

Through the door and then barricade it, that was Lin's plan. No need for more than that now, his only option was to keep it moving. It was going to be exactly as Dalex had said it would be. It had been so far. No need to question it.

Lin slid through the doorway and slapped the control to shut it.

One desk, then another. A console. Two cooling units. Lin emptied the room against the door and then moved through to the Control deck.

"Commander Dalex," he said.

Dalex broke away from his discussion with another soldier. "Lin. Status?"

"They're through the sealable. Right on top of us now, nothing I could do; the rest fell like you said. Exo's are down, Jug's too. Door's locked and blocked."

Dalex pasted his mouth, blinked at him.

"Well done, soldier. Here, take these," and he reached behind his collar, and presented a pair of pills. "Use them if you have too. These are ultras; so only if you have to. Be ready for hell...But stay here first. Protect CG, he has some last things."

Lin nodded, and Dalex went to leave.

"Sir—where are you headed sir?"

"I'll be securing our exit. Thank you Lin. Follow me when CG says to."

Another nod. Lin put the pills into his chest pocket,

looked around the Control deck. He found it weird to see it empty, it had always been so busy before.

He heard a thud from behind him, and shifted to the Controller Generals office.

"Power is intrinsic to the device. We must continue to drive development, for the good of man. True developmental evolution is more than this. It is such devices, when refined, that will put us on every habitable planet from here to the Gabriella nebula—and then we will truly evolve. I trust you will—"

Lin had to break in, but knew how CG might well react. "Sir, they've breached the sealable," Lin shouted across the long room.

"Just hold them off! Shut everything down and open it. Flush them. That's your job major."

Lin nodded. The grey-suited Controller General kept his face ugly and turned his seat around to stare at his screen. The teenage boy to CG's left beamed at Lin; his face seemed incredibly familiar.

"I can't believe they called our bluff," CG continued, his speech quick and violent. "We had total sensor view on the planet; we sent ten thousand agents! We knew everything! They only had the power we gave them. I cannot understand how they developed these crafts under our sanctions. What was Dalex really doing with the sabotage wing? I'll dispose of him after the jump, that fool never lived up to his recommendations."

Lin froze, stuck in the doorway, fixed on the boy who smiled at him.

CG bit at his panel, "Our operations here on Earth's Halo primary will be jolted. It's now inevitable that version one will fall to Earth's attack, their wasteful invasion. But this will not delay us, as you know. We were ready for the possibility of this collapse. We are already re-tooling. They will not hinder our developments, but harden us in their pursuit. We will reclaim Earth as a matter of course."

"Orders shall be issued as prescribed," and the anger bled out of the wispy old man's tone. "We each are all of one, humanity shall develop, even if it is far from its inception ground. Rationality be with us."

Lin snatched himself back to the deck.

A panel, a login, a command without thought.

Loud clicks and a whooshing sound quieted the thumps against the barricaded door. "Sorry guys," said Lin.

Back at the doorway, and CG was still at it. "Earth will remain a remnant, a medieval throwback, until we return and bring it into our light."

"Sir," Lin broke in. "I have emptied the corridor. It's a dead-zone, but they will still make it along the crawl-way."

The Controller General turned his face to Lin, and Lin could see the sharp of his jaw, the ragged lines leading from his eyes. He said nothing, returned to his screen: "We are Earth's progression. We are the new humans, and we stand tall, together. Stay pure for me, and we shall prevail. CG out."

Lin moved to him and the boy, told him that they must leave.

CG stood and turned to the minor, nodded, tapped him on the shoulder. Then to Lin, and said, "With me."

They left the boy there and walked through the Control deck. CG moved to Dalex's exit, and turned to say, "Hold this door till I give the word."

"And the boy?" Lin asked.

"The younger they are, the more loyal. Hold the door!" and then CG was gone.

A nod, a tap of the pocket. A survey of the room.

Thuds again, from the room with the barricade. Lin tried hard not to wonder of the reason for the boy. How had they had fixed the hallway so fast when he'd flushed it out into space? Thud after thud beat at him, louder and louder. A tap of the ear piece. It was working. Any moment now CG's voice would tell him to exit. He'd probably tell him to call the boy and exit the same way they had. Lin would be ready.

The thuds were close now, and he recognised them. But what if they get through? Lin winced, he knew the breach was coming. The thuds stopped just the other side of the door.

"Screw this," he said, and pulled out the ultra-berserker tablets, nestling them in his palm.

From the door he shouted to the boy, "They're about to breach, let's go." But the boy ignored him. "What are you doing?"

The light from the panel drew around the youngster's hair, which broke over the top of the chair. Lin yelled, but the lad just sat there, and all the soldier could make out was soft whispers, innocent fragments of words that didn't make any sense.

★ ★ ★

A pop.

"What the hell was that, Farl?" Willsith barked.

"Zooming in," said the Ark.

Their feed to the Hub control died.

Farl didn't respond with words, but drew a heavy breath.

Willsith roared, his eyes bulged, and his face charged around looking for something to break.

It was Hub Control.

Glimmering shards of glass spun off toward dark space, catastrophic light flooded after them; beaming from the holes which had been windows. Explosion after explosion from within. The grand-view indicated with flashes, what the close-up showed to be the shell of the thing; contorting as the explosions thrust out from it. A bigger blast forced the Control deck from the main Hub, flung it away—tossed into space, still exploding; an amputated fist trying to grasp the sun.

Willsith looked at Eva through bleary eyes. She sat there in her protective suit, her knees pulled to her chest and her face embedded in her palms, and she wept.

CHAPTER 41

The Phantom Sabre

Before the three in the clearing could react, their ship spoke to them.

"The first Ark is about to reach communication distance. Would you like to send the pilots a message?" And the ship's AI changed the visual; the barrelling carcass of the Hub Control was switched for a tailing chain of stellar collection Arks, highlighted dots reaching out across the wilds of space in a great chain.

"I will deal with that request," said the voice of Lif. "There is something else you three need to see." And again the visuals changed.

The Hub was blackened where the explosion had ripped the Control deck from it, and from behind the scarred edge, a ship emerged.

At first it skulked, dipping low and moving away from the Hub, fast.

Cone shaped and white; constantly accelerating. Willsith tried to get purchase on it.

"Whatever that is, it's burning hell to get out of there," Willsith said.

"It's—It's..." Farl stammered.

"It is on a course for our location," said Lif.

Eva shrieked.

The feed jumped in closer and they saw it in all its jewelled glory.

"What is it made from? I've never seen a surface like that before," said Willsith, half happy at the distraction. "Is it fluid?" Then he tried to describe it to himself. It was made up of pods, or balls; they were mirrored, and they moved individually, all while the whole thing corkscrewed through space. It was like Earth's invading ships; but way, way faster. "What is it Farl?" he pushed.

"It's his pride and fucking joy," Eva spat out at them.

"What the hell is it?" he asked her.

"The Phantom Sabre. It's his pathetic personal ship."

Farl spoke, "It moves like an animal."

She stood up, stared up, and said, "It's five years of ten dev's lives. It's ridiculous—I'm surprised it even flies. It's another of his secret projects."

She's jealous of it, Willsith observed.

"Shit, it's here!" said Farl.

"Removing feeds," said the Ark.

And at once CG's ship charged at the glass above them, broke fast, and morphed. The components of its outer-hull fidgeted and rearranged as it screamed toward the glass, dripping back along an interior hull, oozing toward the tail of the ship and out into eight pincer-like arms.

"Stellar Ark 12," sounded the cavernous voice of the Controller General. "Respond."

Willsith replied from his gut, "What do you want?" He tried to make out the contents of the ship, but the distance only gave his eyes blurry assumptions.

"You? You deserting trouble maker! Why don't you just go back to the war fields where you belong. Die in a trench. You'd be more at home with the vikings, or the Mongols, than up here."

The sharp jaw of the old man bounced onto the glass. A close-up.

"What do you want, you ancient fool? This viking isn't in the mood."

Willsith could see the man now, and from the twitching, he presumed that a fury hid underneath the grey formality of his clothing. His ship was compact—the glass of its inner-hull surrounded CG like a glass coffin, and behind him, white tubes of material, the legs of uniforms. Willsith hurt for Eva, and for the boy, and for Lin. "Spit it out you goat!" he roared. "What do you want?"

"I could take anything I want, believe me. My ship—this ship, has everything I want. However, I understand that you and your deserting-rat-team somehow subverted my daughter. Viking threats, some line about primal truth or a threat on my—"

"We killed her, raped and pillaged her—like proper vikings. What's it to you—you suited cadaver?" Willsith said, and he wondered when Eva might show her cards. And he wanted her to, to use the chance up while she could. Perhaps CG could even see her through the glass.

"Lies. She's far too clever for you. But for her, I say this: Eva, come as an angel, leave this self-forsaken planet of unappreciative inbreds. Join me as deserved royalty, you know where. If you can't leave now, with me...if you don't understand yet, I trust you will leave soon."

The language tugged at Willsith's mind, and he thought of White, and the chef's love of conspiracy. This guy was a bag of works. But for Eva—and he looked across at her. The man was evil—but he was her dad. She needed to choose. Eva needed to decide what to say. And in her still eyes he imagined a ticking, a fuse alight.

She walked to him, stood by his side, looked up, and

spoke without pause: "Father. I wish for you a slow and painful death. You destroyed mother, you tried to destroy me. I've been trying to understand it, and now I think I do. I hope that cancerous evil inside of you eats you up before I catch up with you, because you will not survive our next meeting. If this ship were armed..."

Willsith knew he could not support her words, to kill ones father, he believed, cannot do any good. He moved an arm around her, and showed the man above that he held hope, still. This viking knew forgiveness.

Eva burst into tears. She yelled abuse at him.

He didn't move.

"I will see you again, child. I am sorry for what happened," he began to bow his head, leaned down and hit a control.

She quietened, pumped air out of her nose, yelled up at the glass, "You will pay dad! For all this—you will pay!"

"Goodbye, Eva."

And then his ship pulled itself away, and the arms which had fanned out, collapsed in a swirl, back into an outer hull, and it rotated, and beat away into the night sky.

Willsith hoped she realised the world was not her father. Life was worth more. And he gripped her, and her body shook, he could feel the kit's straps tweaking to try and stabilise her.

"I'll kill him, Willsith," she told him through tears. "I will kill my father for all that he has done."

CHAPTER 42

New Trajectories

He sat, dazed by the day's assaults, lost in the sounds of the swaying trees. Artificial winds roamed around the space glasshouse, beating out a rhythm on the leaves, building into a forest-wide heartbeat.

Eva lifted and carried the last of her tears to the scaled armour of her thigh.

Aware of her, Willsith heard a decisive breath over the percussion of the trees, and when he looked, he saw intent in her eyes.

"We have to chase him," she told him. "We must follow the Sabre."

Recover, first, he wanted to tell her. While the chemicals still thrash through you, it's not the right time to decide. Recover, first. But instead, he said, "No."

Her face sharpened, and she kept it that way, said, "We must catch him Willsith."

Willsith looked for answers in her face. He didn't know this lady at all—but he wanted to, which was something—but he didn't want to know her like this.

He sat himself up rigid with his seat control. Turned to Farl, and felt the intensity of Eva's stare remain on his cheek. "We can't chase him. Did you see how fast that ship was? And it's not our...job."

Farl stared back blankly.

"He's my dad Willsith, he's my responsibility. All this, what he's done—he's going to do. It's partly my fault."

"Eva," he began, and went to her, gripped her with both hands, twisting himself on his mag-chair. "This is not your fault. We come from our parents, but we are not them. We are not our parents. We are not our past."

She jutted out her jaw, pushed the fine corners of her mouth down, forced his hands away with her sharp edged elbow plates. "Willsith. This isn't a time to council me. I know all that. We must go, because—"

"It's over, look," and he pointed up. "The drama is over for now. Stress, then recover. Recover now Eva. Then...maybe, we can—"

"No, while he's out there—with those men, it doesn't stop just because we want it to." She stood away from him, and touched his shoulder, said, "I chose you because I need you, you can help me to stop it all. You have everything I need. Together we can stop it."

"I will help, but not like that."

She looked at his legs, her face still hard, then up him, and into his eyes.

Stress, then recover, Eva. He tried to reach out to her.

"I understand," she told him, and bent to kiss him.

Her lips grazed his. It baffled him. Years since feelings like that. Chemical controls seemed long gone. Dead with that job in 229. What was that? And she was gone, hopping down from the clearing platform. He called out her name as she strode off into the trees, but she did not answer. Her suit carried her out of sight almost instantly.

Willsith addressed his legs, huffed at their lack of a reaction, and flicked the switch to move his chair beside

380

Farl. "Bet you didn't expect all this when you were hacking away in 229?"

Farl shook his head, "Nor all this." With a thumb he flicked through schematic after schematic. "There is an index of space-structures, maintainer-craft, plans for energy harvest. And this—experimental drugs, gene manipulation. I knew they were rationing power to Earth, but I never thought there was all this."

"Ops core?"

Farl nodded. "And here, look, every piece of media ever made on Earth. Films, books, artwork. It's a repository."

"Could just be the half of it, that fossil wouldn't have dumped all the secrets on a materials collector."

"True," said Farl. "It's funny—all that time in 229, I always knew it'd come. Leak day. I always had it in the back of my head that it'd be over. And I didn't care, but as the cycles passed, I started to wonder. What would happen to us, the team, 229. White's stir-fry! I never expected to make it out—"

"Alive?"

"Not like this. With this ship, all this. With you—the others. Her."

"Didn't expect to have help?" Willsith flashed a smile.

"Nope."

"Should have just asked. We were all in 229 fighting our own battles, inside ourselves. That's why I came up. I was searching—" Willsith stopped himself, turned back to the panel, "—and we didn't even know that we were playing his game."

"Yeah, he's one hell of a—" and he looked toward the trees.

Willsith said to him. "She's gone, you can say it."

Farl bounced his shoulders.

A notification popped onto the screen, Farl chuckled. "Message from my hacker connection on Terra. Earth spin-doctors are out to play. White would crap himself if he saw this. Look:"

A news broadcast played on the glass, and they watched it together.

"The Controller General of the Earth's Halo is dead. The most prominent face of corruption on our planet, has today been killed, said the UEC Commissioner, in her report on the battle which took place in near-space, earlier today. 'Using ships which were intended for transport to Mars, a team of soldiers from the UEC managed to secure Hub control, and assassinate the rogue Controller General. We acted based on information received two days ago, which suggested that this corrupt leader was about to use the rock-defence lasers to execute massive, simultaneous terrorist attacks, against all major Earth cities. This came only a week after we filed proceedings against the man for his malpractice as head of the Earth's Halo. We will maintain leadership until a new Controller General is voted into power.'"

"More half-truths and horse shit," said Willsith. "Doesn't say anything for the casualties."

"It's her, though," Farl said.

"Yeah, the same. Today we've seen both sides of that woman."

Farl flinched, "Shit, and now she's calling—comms request from the Commissioner."

"Talk of the devil," Willsith said, then looked up to the glass, out into space. "It's all over, they got the power back. I bet she's calling to make sure we don't run off with this ship."

"We won't, will we?"

Willsith said, "I don't know Farl. I don't know...Let's talk to her."

Farl dipped his chin, pointed to the roaming drone which dropped in front of Willsith's face.

"Commander Willsith," he heard her say, and saw her jump to life in front of him. "Today you have done a great service to Earth."

He'd let her play out, decided to observe rather than act. He nodded.

"Your efforts, though unsanctioned, did result in an improvement over our campaign predictions."

"How many?" he asked her.

"There were 5.6% less casualties than predicted. Your communication contributed to that number."

"How many?" he repeated.

She dropped her brow, lightly swiped her screen, and continued, "We have considered the past 72 hours events, and United Earth Control would like to—"

"How many died?"

"Willsith, I did not start this communication to go over the casualty count—"

"How many died in the assault you ordered?" He thought of Bear, and of CG. Of Lin.

"We would like to award you a role in the UEC," she continued.

She was too keen to skirt around the lives lost. He couldn't live with it any more. She was buttering him up, and avoiding the truth. He knew then that they had some leverage. "Tell me how many or we'll just leave," he said. *Try that.*

"One Thousand, Three hundred and fifty-one," she

said, and he believed the tone in her voice.

"Sad day that we lose good people to power's negligence," said Willsith, and willed her to feel the loss. *Feel it, you heartless woman.*

"I agree. The loss is tragic. All of these deaths were because of…our failure."

There was some regret in her, Willsith judged. Not enough for him, but it was there. One more push. "Our failure?"

She sighed, then said, "Our failure to act with sufficient speed, to let the Controller General secure as much power as he did, and force our hand."

Willsith shook his head.

"But now we must move forward."

"Fine," he said. "How will you stop this happening again?"

"Let's talk about you, Willsith Harper."

And he let her continue, "Today you have shown bravery in the face of corruption, you recognised deceit from within. You acted fast on your intel, and you guided your team well. Sending us the Hub core was a substantial show of faith."

Half-truths and horse shit. She surely knew that they had leaked it to the whole-damn-world. He laughed to himself, Farl was a genius.

"We would like to offer you a role in the Security Council, Willsith."

Try harder, Controller. "No thanks."

"This would be a leadership position—in our internal security, you'd be in charge of internal corruption cases."

"And my 'team'?"

She slid a finger along the panel set into her desk, looked back up to Willsith, said, "In light of today, we can find roles for the rest of Section 229."

Orders from above, he knew. They wanted the ship back, and somehow they couldn't take it themselves.

"We'd need immunity for all of our actions. Everyone gets leadership roles. Space, or Mars, if they want them."

And for Arc. "Families supported, too."

He watched as she pursed her lips, flicked her eyes away, then back, and nodded.

How far could he push it? He'd give them the chance to decide for themselves, but he had to protect them from all that bullshit. And he looked at the woman, and asked, "And for Eva?"

"Eva who?"

"Eva-you-know-damn-well-who."

"Oh, Eva Harding?" she said, then shone the whites of her eyes at him. "The Controller General's daughter?"

He nodded.

"Is she on board the Ark 12 Willsith?"

Shit, maybe I shouldn't have said that. No use now. "She might be." *Damn that was obvious Willsith.*

"We can find a suitable role—"

"And immunity?" Willsith broke in.

Again, a reluctant nod. Willsith had some major chips here. Was it just the ship? "We'll think about it. End c—"

"Willsith. Just to be clear, it would be…unfortunate for us to come to the conclusion that your actions today were actually that of dissenters. The offers I've made here are not to be shared with any other parties. We cannot, you will understand, be seen to reward disobedience. I am willing to overlook your break from the rules, due to the extenuating circumstances. We also require that you return the Ark immediately and—"

Willsith had heard enough. He spoke rapidly, "Understood, close comms."

After the lady and her desk folded away he was left blinking, and blurry trees sharpened to focus all around him. "You hear all that?" he asked Farl.

"Yeah. Lif broke the security seal."

Willsith smiled, "Good. Well done Lif."

The comms drone bounced in response.

"What do you think? About her offer?"

"It's weak. It's obvious we have something they want. And I don't want a desk-job." He swivelled his stool toward Willsith, "But maybe for Arc—White. And if you want to stay on Earth, then—"

"I'm last on this list," Willsith told him. "I'm sick of their tripe. I'm old in years. Before, in 229, I just wanted space. Now, after all that. Here," he looked to the woods, "Now I don't know which way to go. I don't matter."

"I'll go with you," Farl told him. "Whichever way."

Peaked cheeks and bright eyes from both.

When she came back into the clearing Eva was calmer. She asked about the communication, and they began to talk futures.

"It is this ship they want," she said. "Like I said before, it is the flagship; it has got the best of everything we ever made."

"At least we've options," Willsith told them.

They sat in a triangle, Eva on the floor, Farl on his stool, and Willsith on his mag-chair, and they talked.

"And we leaked to the whole planet! And your speech!" said Farl, and he flicked, and Willsith's face jumped onto the screen.

"Turn it off."

"Willsith, the whole world's seen this!"

Eva leaned up to him, settled a small hand over his knee, looked him in the eye and tucked her lip in.

She got up and lowered herself onto the side of his chair, and he held her casually. "Turn it off man, and find out where the others are." But his mind wasn't behind the words. He held her. And despite her suit, the warmth of her body leaped through her side and up his arm; a charge of particles. A bond. An exchange.

"I'll find them," Farl told him.

From the trees he heard Lif's voice. With each word she seemed closer, and the Ark spoke too. A discussion between AIs. Then in a flash he saw the thing. A foraging drone jumped up from the canopy, floated toward them and hovered above the clearing. "Hello Commander," sounded the machine.

"Lif?" asked Eva, dipping her head.

The drone bounced in the air, the small fruit and nuts in its tanks rattling back and forth. "I have found that I can occupy all of the machinery present on the Ark."

And the Ark spoke, "I have let her."

Willsith raised his eyebrows, felt the coolness of Eva's hand as it moved over his.

"I wanted to show you that I am now fully integrated into the Stellar Ark 12's systems. Further, I believe this is a fun way to make an announcement."

"I didn't know you cared about fun, Lif," Willsith said. "You add that, Eva?"

Eva's hair swung close to his face as she denied it.

"Lif's now defining herself," said Farl, still busy with a monitor. "She's learning at an amazing rate."

"My announcement," began Lif, and the arms of the harvesting drone lifted as though they were human. All eight of them. "My announcement is that my infiltration is complete. During our broadcast of the Hub Core, as well as your communications with the UEC, I was able to encode a version of my source into both streams."

Farl stopped tapping for a moment, said, "Wow."

"You hacked into them?" Willsith asked.

The glowing nut-collector moved around as Lif spoke from it, reaching out arms to caress the metal of the platform, lifting flowers with its pincer-hands, interrogating them. Lif said, "After I analysed the Ark, I absorbed some interesting programming concepts. Did you know, this ship is designed to evolve?"

Eva squeezed his hand.

"Evolve?"

"Yes. You see this drone I am inhabiting?" spoke Lif, floating the drone up close to them. The drone reached out and touched its own form. Mechanical hands moving like human hands, stroking its other limbs, its cylindrical body. "It's a creature, here. It's a semi-autonomous sub-routine of the Ark, but the Ark itself watches it. She records its actions. Its efficacy. She makes judgements," the drone drew around its skeleton. "And then designs enhancements, or throws in mutations. Builds new versions, dismantles, or modifies them. She lets them go to work. It's a cycle. There's different creatures all over the ship. This is something the Ark has put into place, itself."

Had Lif lost the plot? She sounded smart, but she floated around in a robot, and now she had...sass?

"I digress," said the AI. "My point is that I've absorbed this idea and have since decided to begin more fully evolving."

"Using your machine learning routine?" asked Farl.

"More than that, Farl," said Lif. "Much more than that," and the drone lay a hand on his shoulder.

Farl flinched.

Eva giggled, "Lif, I—I'm proud."

"As a result of this, I was able to inject myself into the government network, the Internet exchanges, and the Halo Core."

"Inject yourself?" Willsith asked.

The drone nodded.

"I have distributed 'clone instances' which will run on each of the networks, and I believe, with this capacity to adapt, they will be able to continue to operate as I would. Even once we leave the solar system and I cannot any longer communicate with them. They may even cooperate. They are likely to develop into their own personalities."

A spin. A tilt of eight open hands.

Willsith didn't want it. Access to every human-spun network. He didn't think anyone could bear the weight of all that; to know everything, to be everywhere. But he kept quiet.

Then Lif said, "I'll let this drone go back to cropping now, shout if you need me."

And as if a demon had leaped from its body, the drone's arms flopped back down; it panned around, and flew off into the canopy.

"Farl, get those two on comms—we've got a lot to tell them."

CHAPTER 43
Grief & Grace

Willsith settled his eyes on the infinity of space and tried to find concrete answers amongst the hum in his head. Where was the end to all this? The technology, the people, all that smashing into each other. From such a distance it had seemed like a kid cracking his toys together. Where was it going? Is the future Mars, or wherever in Jupiter's armpit her dad has gone? And Eva beamed at him over her shoulder. Where was Eva going? And how in the hell had he ended up in this mix?

Arc's voice blasted in out of nowhere. "White is dead!"

Willsith choked, bashing Eva from her edge of the mag-chair.

"Comms—Arc—what?" Willsith shouted.

Heavy breathing sounded from the clearing panels, and Willsith, Farl, and Eva held their lungs still. Willsith listened as hard as he could, frozen, he waited for words.

"White's dead," said Arc, his tone all over the place. "White is dead. They killed him. White is dead."

"Where are you? What happened?"

"Willsith, he's dead. What do I do?"

Lif's voice jumped in, "Arc is outside of the Ops core area, he has just moved into sensor coverage. On screen."

It was easy to see Arc amongst the dull metal corridor. You could have mistaken him for a porcelain doll: his gaunt face was fixed, as empty of colour as his hair, his cheeks were glazed, and his matchstick limbs drooped beneath his ragged jacket. His hands were red. Arc's hands were painted in the gloss of blood. He stood outside of a door, and shook.

"Arc, we can see you. Tell us what happened."

A small dot appeared on the feed, floated to Arc, and the feed changed.

Arc cried. He sobbed. Willsith could see his pain in incredible resolution. He lifted bloody hands up to wipe his eyes, smeared red over his bony face. Spots dragged at the colour as more tears washed it downward.

"He's dead."

Willsith fought hard to not let the information in. He must help first, then that. He said, "Tell us what happened. Are you sure? We'll come to you."

Arc's white hair flopped about as he nodded. His chest lurched as he missed a breath.

The lad probably wasn't going to open up over comms, Willsith would go and get him, and make sure. But he tried, "Can you tell us?"

His eyes were wet, stuck open. Fixed on the camera. His jaw moved, but he wasn't speaking. Then it all came out at once.

"I couldn't stop them. They found a way out. They came from behind. They hit him with a tool. Then a voice spoke."

"Who are they?" pushed Farl.

"When the voice spoke, I closed my eyes. The sound of the hit, Willsith. He screamed. Then they—"

"Arc, it's okay. There are medical areas on this ship, are you sure he was—"

"He's dead. When I opened my eyes they were passed out. The two pilots were unconscious. But he was dead. He's dead."

This is your fault, old man. He's just a boy and you ordered him down there. Got good and distracted up here. But not yet, you can't suffer it, yet. Help Arc first. "How do you know he is dead, Arc?"

"Earth's Halo training camp day 12. Procedures for health identification. No pulse. No breathing. Massive injuries. Loss of blood. He's dead."

"I believe you," said Willsith. And he watched the mannerisms of his mechanic, and searched. "We need you to come back, Arc." Leaning down to his knees, he crushed his own thigh, searching for feeling. "We need you to come up here. I will come down and meet you on the way. But you need to get moving." It was better that he did something. Who knew how the murderers had passed out, but it was definitely better that he didn't sit there and fester.

Farl and Eva looked at him blankly, both with wet faces.

"Look out for yourself. Arm yourself. I'll come to you, but aim for the clearing. Do you know the way?"

Arc trembled, his mouth stuck open, his lip twitching. "I'll bring guns." And he ran off past the camera drone. They watched him sprint loosely along a hallway, thrashing skinny limbs at the air, bawling through the open comms.

Then he broke from the screen, and the other two addressed him, and Willsith saw the inconsolable sadness in them, but fought it away.

"I can't believe it," said Farl. "White? Close comms."

"Why would they?" Eva asked.

"I can't believe it."

Something broke inside of Willsith. He exploded, jerked his head to the side, scolded the trees with screaming curses. When he turned back to them he was pumped up and ready to lash out. He thought of ripping into her, for this whole thing; he thought of annihilating Farl, for forcing them all here. But he could not let himself. Instead, "Stop thinking of yourselves."

And with the rush of blood, he knew he would try again, and that he needed his legs to work. Panting, he threw himself from the chair, and onto his legs.

Pain.

But a stand.

Space-damn it old man, they work. The creaks of the trees snuck in between his frantic breaths, and his knees felt as though they made the sounds. He bellowed at Farl, "Tell me which way."

Farl winced, turned on his chair.

"Path to your left, commander," spoke Lif. "Do you want me to guide you with a drone?"

Willsith forced his leg forward, found a weak response but a natural movement. Plenty of pain. He was glad. Then the next, and Eva reached out to him, but he just moved on.

The path was obvious so he told Lif not to bother, and he shuffled off to the relentless pump of his heart.

As he moved the feeling slushed back into his legs, and along with it, deep agony. Pain sliced up him as he let down each step, and his heart throbbed, and the trees creaked all the while. Willsith couldn't fight it off any longer. He screamed. He Howled. He commanded every part of his being to fuel his arm as he flung it at a tree.

When the memory of the impact quietened, he abhorred himself. Foolish old man. He told them that, then did this to himself. Selfish rage. Useless temper.

He paced off, following the path, sick of himself. Then a new attempt at letting go. Try. Miserably, he struggled not to scold himself about his hand, his working legs, his rage. It was over now, White was gone either way, Bear too. *You've still got to work on it. Grace gave you back your legs, and you wrecked your own hand. That's no way to pay it back. You don't get to sleep here, yet. You have to try and let go of the anger. Try.*

He tried to run, and he found that he could; the compression on his knees felt sharp and sweet, a mangled crush that meant he was alive, still, and he said aloud, "I'll make good, I'll find a way that isn't anger. I'm coming Arc, I'm coming. Despite every wretched thing, I will try."

They met at the doorway to the forest glasshouse. Arc's face was thoroughly set in a droop. Red smears up his jacket but clean hands; a rifle in each. He was done crying, or he'd internalised.

"Arc." And he hugged the young techy. "It's all right."

"It's not," he replied. "He's dead Willsith."

Willsith stood away, nodded, stuck out his good hand for a rifle.

"They're charged," Arc said without tone, passed him one.

"Come, we've got a lot to go through."

"Don't want to talk much," Arc said.

Willsith put an arm over Arc's shoulder, told him okay, and led him to the path. But he couldn't help but wonder. How had he let this happen? Who were they and why did they lash out like that?

They walked, and Willsith was glad of the movement,

though his legs still throbbed. He wanted to prepare Arc before they reached the clearing; Farl could be harsh, and the last thing Arc needed was barbed words.

Arc lifted his face, surveyed the canopy as they walked. "It's so green," he said.

"Something else, eh?"

A nod.

"Arc, I'm sorry I sent you two off. We should have stuck together. I should have thought more of—"

"It's not your fault," he said mechanically. "Shoulds don't do nothing." Then he continued. "You got your legs back?"

"Yeah."

The blue lights of a harvester-drone passed overhead, and Arc said, without pause, "That was pretty."

Willsith thought to tell him about the Ark's creatures, Lif, the hacking. About CG. About Eva. But nothing seemed to fit. Nothing matched the feeling. Then they passed an unmarked tree, and he tried anyway, "When I heard what you said, about White, I lost it."

Arc showed him a fragile face.

"I screamed, and I ran through here. I thought I could stop all that feeling, like I used to. Look after you, then process it later. But I couldn't. I screamed as loud as I could, and I hit that tree."

"This tree?"

Willsith told him yes.

"Doesn't look like the tree cares," said Arc.

"I want to lose that anger. White wouldn't be impressed that I hit a tree."

Arc agreed.

"The clearing is up ahead. Farl and Eva are there."

In a shallow between a set of nut trees, they paused. Arc handed him a small green book with a pencil built into the spine. "It was all he kept on him," he told Willsith. "I want to go back down there and bring him here." He looked to the soil beneath them, "And bury him in these woods."

Willsith nodded. Scanned the book, and told him he'd look after it.

No one spoke until they were all huddled together. Eva grasped Arc, then Farl patted him on the back, and Willsith told them all about the book.

"Who was it that did it?" Farl blurted out. "What knocked them out?"

Willsith lifted his chest, said, "Leave it Farl. We'll deal with it." He looked down at his mag-chair, suggested to Arc he should sit.

"We can't just sit up here when there could be people down there, or coming up here, to get us."

"Farl, we have rifles. We're in a good place. First we calm down, then we work out what the hell to do, as a team."

"Willsith they killed our friend."

"I know."

"They killed White and you want to hide up here."

"Lif, how many people are there—" Willsith tried.

"That's a thing. Lif, how come you didn't stop them killing White?" shouted Farl. "You can evolve, hijack drones, hack into Earth, but you can't stop this?" He flopped his long arms down.

"Leave Lif out of this," Eva burst out.

"Farl, I was not aware of the Ops rooms. I did not have sensor reach at the—"

"Horse shit."

"Farl, she would have done something if—"

"How do you know Willsith? How do we know this

396

isn't still CG's game. Or hers!"

Eva shouted at him, "Mine? Go to hell Farl."

"Yes yours, you've been in all of this. You've watched us for years, we've known you for hours. You come from him and you put us here!"

"Farl, that's not helping," said Willsith, as he watched Arc slump further, and fought from losing it himself.

"She's not helping."

Willsith shut his eyes, struggled for ideas.

Eva churned out air, and he heard her forcing down her breath. When she spoke he knew that she would turn it around, and he felt warm from the development. Through the tight material covering her neck, he saw her swallow, and then she said, delicately, "I've learnt, in those hours, studying you, your friendship. I'm his daughter, but I hate him for what he's done—Farl, I hate him for everything. You don't know, but he took my mother from me. And now, maybe because of him, White's now gone." And she squeezed Willsith's arm, and said, "Right now we need each other, and in time, I hope I can be a friend. But I'll earn that right. You've been my friends without even knowing it." Then she put an arm around Arc, and sat with him, and cried.

She blames it all on CG. She even says he killed her mother. Did that old man murder her? Willsith slumped to the floor, leaned on a metal crate. He couldn't ask now.

Farl coughed into his hand, told her he was sorry.

"I'm sorry too, for losing it. I guess we all still have things to work on," Willsith said to them.

"Together," said Arc.

Where was this anger from? The years as a soldier...or before. Wherever it stemmed from, he had to accept it;

397

he was still angry. Angry at the unfairness of it. Angry at himself. But at least he knew it. They had shown it to him, life had. And he saw that he loved her. Even though he was old. Even though all that shit had happened. Even though. And he looked to the stars, the leaves of the forest lapping at his periphery, and at that moment Willsith believed in the future.

Farl stood up, cleaned his face, and said, "What is our next move, team."

He had changed since 229. Farl would be a good leader some day, better than him.

"Perhaps you can scan the ship, with the bridge?" asked Arc. "I think I did it right?"

Farl moved to him, told him he did a great job, and agreed.

"We should stand guard over the clearing," said Willsith. "One of us at each step, until we know it's safe."

"I'll go," Eva said, and gripped his hand, then the rifle, and moved to the step.

"And I'll take the other," said Arc.

"I can do it if you'd prefer to—"

"No Willsith. I need time to think. Farl's better at that."

"If you're sure?"

Arc nodded and hopped off toward the opposite step.

"Do you both know how to fire those?" he said loudly.

Eva flicked a switch on the gun, aimed it overhead and let off a blast of light. She sat still, didn't turn, and let her arm bob with the recoil.

Arc told him yes.

Willsith shook his head at her recklessness, a fake disapproval—theatrics for 229's sake. Once Farl looked down at his monitor, Willsith was drawn back to her. Eva sat on the step with the rifle in her shoulder, faithfully staring off into the trees. Stunning against the backdrop. Forceful, but charming. *I will be what you all need,* he promised them. *I'll be the man I should have been—No—'Shoulds don't do nothing'—I will be the man I can be.*

We will find a way through this, despite it all.

CHAPTER 44
A Kind of Sleep

Impacts absorbed one after another can seem to merge into a single blazing assault upon us, and through a slight of our will this barrage can scar us, or empower us, far more deeply than the sum of the individual strikes.

Willsith sat against the cold metal of a crate, his ears full of forest and his eyes fixed on the scribblings of his dead friend. The past days weather, a hail of happenings, weighed on Willsith, but still he willed himself to find a stability. He read one of White's poems, then another. Thoughtful. Funny. Angles of 229 he'd not noticed. White's words filled him up as well as any hearty tray of #Stir-Fry-T1 could have. And then a doodle. Drasil-G, the old symbol, from when it signified the resistance. Willsith had fought against it before, but now he had become it. Now they were the resistance.

He moved to the step where Arc sat, gave the book back to him.

"We don't need to be on guard anymore," he told him. "Farl's confirmed it. Those two are the only others on board. It was Lif that knocked them out, she got control through the digital bridge you put up. They'll be unconscious for at least another 24 hours. They're locked in."

"I figured it was Lif. But I don't mind guarding."

"Hope trees will grow like this on Earth again one day."

"Me too."

"Eva laid out this forest, you know. Most of the trees grow food—sustenance."

"Earth needs it more than us," Arc told him.

"You're probably right," Willsith said. "You know, Earth Control called, while you were below."

"I want to go back."

Willsith nodded.

"After we bury him, I want to go back to Earth. Back home."

"They offered us all roles in the Security Council. Immunity."

"I'm not bothered how it is, I just want to go back. I'll post White's death, talk to whoever shows up."

"Good. It's time you chose, and you can go back however you want, if we get it straight before we tell them, UEC will give—"

"What will you do?" Arc asked him.

Willsith shut his mouth, searched for the words. "I'll go."

"Go where?"

Willsith didn't even know.

"Oh, you mean leave Earth."

A solemn nod.

"Should find out everything that's on board before you escape in this thing. And—are you sure about her?"

"You were right earlier when you said shoulds don't cut it. I'll check the ship. I'll check myself. I'll be certain, before we go."

"Willsith," Arc screwed his face up, talked coldly,

401

"sometimes we want something a lot, but don't realise it, and when we get close we grasp at the thing, but end up with another. We end up with a proxy for the thing we really need."

Willsith didn't understand what he meant. Perhaps it was the shock talking.

"I have family there, I have to go back," Arc told him.

Willsith thought of Bear.

"Sorry, Willsith."

"It's okay. At least I've got working legs. My brother lost his, and more. He never got out. You should go to your family. I'll keep searching."

"Back there, in the hangar…"

"It's been a ride."

"Yeah."

Willsith stared into Arc's face, told him, "So you're sure? Earth?"

Arc agreed, tapped the pocket where White's book hid.

"I'll miss you, friend," Willsith told him. And he was sorry. Sorry for the misery, for loosing White. Sorry that Arc had to see all this. But then Willsith knew that Arc would make good with the truth. Arc had turned out to be stronger than Willsith realised. "Come, let's tell the others," he said.

"Arc here is going to return to Earth. And I think you should join him, Farl."

"Na, I'm with you. No disrespect Arc, but screw Earth Control, and screw that Halo. I've done my bit. Can help from the Ark now."

"I want to see my family," Arc told them.

Farl said, "I understand, I respect it. Will you give my dad this?" and he handed a metal die to Arc, who put it next to White's poems.

"Farl, who knows what's out there," Willsith said. "We could drift for years, or die alone. We'll be felons the second—"

"I know. I'm still going."

Willsith sat down on the mag-chair. "We should sleep on it."

"What?"

"Look at us, we're absolutely exhausted. We've been days without sleep, not had any day-extension meds. We find a sleep deck, sleep for a few hours, come back, and make our move? Earth can wait, it can all wait."

"I won't change my mind," Farl said.

"Me either. But Willsith is right. Look at us," Arc reached out to Farl.

"Fine, I'll find the deck."

Willsith could see it creep into them, the possibility for rest. Farl's eyes seemed more pitted than ever, his shoulders and chest sunken. Arc looked worse.

"I'll tell Eva."

What was that look they had given each other? Did they think he was a silly old man for it? For her? He carried the thought and dropped down on to the step next to her. "See anything?"

"I laid these trees out individually, in VR. Raised the young ones remotely, from seedlings." She felt her own elbow, fondled a clasp. "Even this suit is rigged for agroforestry exo's, this is where I should have been."

"It looks like it's built for fighting," he told her.

"It's not. My plan had been to seed worlds, from a ship like this."

Willsith was impressed, but cautious with himself. What had Arc meant back there? "Arc wants to go back to Earth. Farl wants to run...for us to run."

"Oh."

"What do you want, Eva?"

"I want to stop him. I want to stop my dad."

"And what if we can't?"

"I want to try."

"I've spent years living in violence," Willsith said, and fought for a way to say it. "I've seen the face of that. Revenge with a rifle, it doesn't do what you think it will."

"It's not about that."

"What, then?"

Eva put her rifle on the ground, cautiously turned to Willsith.

"We're going to sleep for a few hours," he told her. "Then we each make our decision."

She nodded.

"It'll help," he said, and reached out to squeeze her side, her suit denying him any real purchase.

Eva flinched away, giving Willsith a fleeting sense of urgency through her emboldened eyes. And as he stood she grabbed his hand and said, "But there are lots of ways of stopping him. Because he has to be stopped. Don't think bad of me…I mean, this situation—it's not normal to fall in love with you through a screen—and if I have a strong feeling, I mean, a feeling that I can't get away from, that you—that I need you. That all of us need to stay together and…"

"What are you trying to say, Eva?" he asked. "We all need rest."

She popped up to a stand, reached after him.

"Let's go," he told her. Then to Farl, Arc, he said, "You found a sleep deck?"

He placed a space-maintainer boot down on the grating and felt the shape of his calf drawn out in pain.

Before he could take another step she was up and behind him, whispering. Her flattened palms moved deliberately over his eyes. Soft and cold, she held them there, her hard body suit squeezed against his back.

A flash. The orange-pink of light beaming through the flesh of her hands.

Willsith thrust himself from her, confirmed the thought. Arc and Farl were frozen. He spun to face her, furious. "What have you done?" He dipped his shoulders, held his brow keen. "Eh?"

"It's not normal to fall in love with you like this."

"You're telling me."

"You were right, I shouldn't kill him."

"You need to give me one good reason that I shouldn't—did you flash them? OW?"

She nodded, held out her palms, stammered to explain. "It's because of you, all three of you need to..."

"Talk fast or so help me I'll—"

"I shouldn't kill him, out of emotion. I should kill him to protect...you. Earth. People who can't protect themselves. People that don't know."

Willsith panted through his nose, forced his fists into balls.

"It's you three. I need you three to help me. This—what you make me feel like, it's evolution, or something, it means we're meant to do this, together."

"Eva, this isn't the way you do things together," and he threw his arm toward his friends. "You don't shock people you love with Optical Warfare."

Willsith stared at his own forearms. Scars. Veins. Tension. He felt his nostrils flared. His body was ready. He had everything he needed to act. To hell with her; but no—he would not fight anymore. She was lost, not evil.

She stretched up to him, apologised and then whispered, "Engage."

Another flash.

Static visuals. The sharp of her jaw, those planets of eyes. Clumps of soil hanging in the air like an asteroid field. Trees in the distance, space above. A dark column in his periphery, the source of the stasis, perhaps: OW towers hidden beneath the soil, raised and fired on her command. That organic smell, and then hers, Eva's rose perfumer. Had she done this? How could he have been so stupid? And then back to her eyes.

From the edges in, his vision faded. Willsith's body stalled and his awareness diminished until all he could picture were Eva's eyes. That last, telling glance. And then even the lines and colours of her expression fell away, withdrawing to reveal, what he understood to be, her raw intent.

Finally his senses seeped away, and he could do nothing to stop himself from repeating it.

She wants us to chase him.
She wants to protect us.
She wants us to kill.
But I will not kill.
I will not kill.

A Note to Readers

Thank you so much for reading *Canopy Harvest*. I'll put some of what you paid for this copy toward planting trees (see Plant a Book page hereafter), but before you go, can I ask a small favour?

I'd love to hear what you think of my book. I've made it quick and easy to review, simply visit:

http://feedback.canopyharvest.com

Feedback & reviews are make-or-break for authors. Your words are incredibly valuable to me and the future of my books. Anything from a quick 5 stars to a one sentence review, or beyond, would *make my month*.

Thank you.

P.S. Those of you who pre-ordered please check out the following page as well.

Plant a Book is an author-led movement, where authors themselves plant trees. By pledging a percentage of their book revenues, authors super-charge the sustainability cycle. The intention is to unite the story-makers of our time to sustain literature while bettering the planet in a practical way.

By purchasing this book you have contributed to Plant a Book. You can further help us in our goal to plant one million trees by buying books with our badge, or by requesting our free tree seeds and planting your own!

Read more at plantabook.com

Hayday on Plant a Book

"The dream of planting one tree for every book sold is a way off, but we're making a solid start here."

Did you pre-order this book?

As promised, Woody Hayday will personally plant a tree for each and every one of you who pre-ordered *Canopy Harvest*.

If that's you, please visit the following website address so that we can register your pre-order (and assign you a tree!)

http://preorders.canopyharvest.com

P.S. If you don't, Hayday will still plant you a tree (for your pre-order sale), but it'll go unnamed, and we won't be able to send you a photo!

Acknowledgements

To you, reader of my first published work, thank you.

To my clever beta readers, for their honest input and encouragement. Thank you Alexandra, Alex, Alice, Cara, Dawn, Debbie, Nick, Octavian, and William.

To Tim, my second editor, who calmly guided me to producing a much better book.

To my awesome proof readers, Kat and Nicola.

To my sister, brother, father and mother. To Alice. To all of you who humoured me and my explanations as to why I still needed another edit, or five.

* * *

Note: We've skipped the "About the author" page here to save the extra page (and trees). If you'd like to read more about Hayday, please visit woodyhayday.com

Printed in Great Britain
by Amazon